SHADOW
FALL

SHADOW FALL

ISBN print: 978-0-9970104-9-7
ISBN ebook: 978-0-9970104-8-0

Library of Congress Control Number: 2016945100

Cover design by Kimberley Marsot
http://www.kimg-design.com/

Blaze Publishing, LLC
64 Melvin Drive
Fredericksburg, VA 22406
Visit us at www.blazepub.com

First Edition: November 2016

To Angela, my consummate reader and better half.

PROLOGUE

The asteroid that will destroy the earth is named Pandora. Some Royalist high up in the Emperor's court thought they were being clever, stealing the name from the stories our ancestors once only whispered about the gods.

My mother repeated Pandora's myth so many times I have it memorized: *Zeus, the mightiest of mighty, formed Pandora out of clay. Cunning and beautiful, she was mankind's destiny—and eventually their downfall.*

Dig past the irony, and you'll find admiration. She always liked powerful, destructive things, my mother. Which explains why she never really cared much for me. A Bronze. Born to a Gold mother and a Bronze father.

Born to be Chosen and ordinary.

Born to slave in the factories and marry a prince.

Born to love the light and languish in the dark.

I've always known my world would end. I've known the exact day, the exact hour, the exact minute. But no one has ever explained to me why.

The Royalists say that the gods, angered by the Everlasting War and bombings, have decided to punish us.

Those on the other side, the Fienian Rebels, claim that the Emperor somehow harnessed the technology he keeps from us to conjure the asteroid. After all, it is the asteroid that allowed the Royalists and their promise of salvation to gain control of the last remaining Fienian Rebel cities.

They don't mention salvation anymore, though. No one does.

Darkness begets beautiful, wondrous things—my mother's words. *And Cronus, the Titan son of Gaia and Uranus, was forced to slay his father, the blood from his wicked deed covering his mother, who spun and spun, each droplet birthing giants and nymphs into the world.*

My mother assured me the asteroid was a gift from the gods that would change my life for the better. I was a bead of blood, borne from tragedy, destined to change our dying world.

I was *Chosen*.

For someone who prided herself on always being right, my mother sure picked an inconvenient time to be so wrong.

CHAPTER ONE

I am more earth than person now. More dirt than flesh, rock than bone, mud than blood. In the tunnels, in the *darkness*, I have become something less than human.

I have to get out of here!

I carve another useless handful of dirt from my tomb. It's a wasted effort. There's no way I can claw myself out of the pit beneath Rhine Prison. Even if my hands *are* forged from the strong metalworking bones of my ancestors. Hands meant to hammer steel into blades and work precious gold into the sigils of the High Colored Houses.

But I have to do *something*. Anything to take my mind off what's happening above.

Is she here yet? Does Max see her too? Is he afraid? The breath catches in my chest. *Is he even alive?*

Rage bubbles inside me. I fall to my knees, try to scream out the pain, fists throbbing as they hammer the tunnel wall. Max is all I have. If I admit the truth—that there is no way my brother has survived out there alone—I will have nothing left to fight for.

My chest shudders with silent, tearless sobs. The night that wrecked my life comes in mangled bits and pieces. My father's blood, oily-black, unspooling down the stairs. The Centurions charging, their boot steps like a thousand thunderclaps rattling my spine as they splattered shiny red stars onto the white wall. The terrified expression on Max's face as I ripped him from my bed and we fled the only home we had ever known.

But you left me, Max's childish voice accuses.

My ravaged lips split wide. "You were hungry . . . so hungry . . ."

We were starving. I knew there were Centurions around the market that day. But I couldn't bear one more night curled together for warmth as my little brother moaned for food, the sharp, protruding points of his spine pricking my sternum.

A horrible beggar and worse thief, they caught me before I could even claim a bite of the pilfered loaf warming my pocket. We had only haunted the streets for a month. Even so, I must have looked so different from the Chosen girl with the Gold mother that the Centurions assumed I was just another Bronze girl hiding from her factory duties, or perhaps shirking conscription.

Some days I wish they had recognized me. I would be dead, gloriously, numbingly dead, not eking out this miserable joke of an existence. Not dining on rats. Not tormented by ghosts and always, *always* afraid.

"Help me," I wail, fighting out of my memory. "Please! I can't do this anymore!"

I'm losing it. For the fifth time this morning.

Or is it night?

Deep inside the earth, there are no mornings. No evenings. No seasons or baby brothers, and no asteroids named after the gods. Only time. Time to dig and pretend I'm actually accomplishing something. Time to cry and feel sorry for myself. Time to scratch at the lice wriggling through my nest of hair.

Time to go full on crazy.

I call it the Doom. That feeling that takes hold, tangles my insides, nibbles my ribs, and carves any remaining hope from my heart.

A noise shatters the stillness, and my breath catches. Frozen, I listen for a few seconds, but all I hear is the terrified pounding of my heart. *Don't be a wimp, Graystone,* I scold myself, thinking like the voices the sound was a figment of my imagination.

Now another sound creeps from the tunnels, almost like muffled whispering—but definitely *real*.

Sometimes, when I hear them searching for me, I pretend that I am Persephone, imprisoned in the Underworld, and the monsters that seek me are only Hades and his minions. They do not want to hurt me; they want to make me their immortal queen.

The monsters' whispers wriggle along the walls. They have finally found me, and they will not place a crown upon my head.

Now my digging has more purpose behind it. I claw and tear pockets of rock-pitted earth from the wall. Dirt patters quietly against my bare feet. I have a just-woken-up-falling feeling, as if I've opened my eyes and tumbled into a nightmare. A *worse* one, if that's even possible. I am a Bronze inside a pit full of monsters.

A Bronze with a secret.

The sound of something scurrying by my feet makes me jump, but it's only Bramble. The machine-like sound of his metal legs scraping together gives me a tiny bit of comfort.

Shaped like a spider, Bramble has six jointed legs, a spherical body, and pinhole sensors affixed to the top of his head that glow red. I found the prison sensor beneath a heap of rags, one of his antennae nearly broken. I straightened his sensor and cleaned the dirt from his joints, expecting he would go back to counting Pit Leeches, but instead he followed me into the tunnels. Soon after, he brought Duchess to me. A slightly newer-model sensor, she was harder to fix.

"They found us, B," I whisper.

Bramble lets loose an angry barrage of chirps.

"Where's your sister?"

Duchess is the opposite of Bramble. Headstrong and independent, she's most likely exploring the tunnels.

Before Bramble can respond, taunts invade the stillness.

"Hey, Digger Girl, there's nowhere left to hide." The first voice, clearly Rafe's, lodges in the pit of my stomach. Which means his cutthroat companion, Ripper, will be right behind him. She got the name because she likes to cut things. No, not things. People.

"Digger, Digger, in the dark," Ripper coos. "Digger, Digger, ain't too smart. Got her a hole that she fell into. Got her a grave that she'll die in too."

I nudge Bramble away with my foot. "Hide!"

A soft golden mist slithers along the floor. As my hands then wrists then legs come into view, I grow dizzy with emotion. It's the first real light I have seen in years.

Two shadows sprout from the floor. One waifish and still, the other hulking and twitchy. They smell of smoke and rot. The headlamp banded to Rafe's forehead bobs side-to-side, illuminating my home for the last seven years, a six-by-six-foot hole in the earth.

"Got your filthy little nest here, Digger Girl?" Ripper says, tossing something—a half-eaten rat carcass—at Rafe's boot. "Watch out, Rafe, she like to bite. A savage, she is."

A dull smile livens the slackened flesh of Rafe's face. He gnashes the air, his few remaining teeth clanking together. "Well, I bite back."

"I'll do more than bite," I hiss, pulling out the wooden shard I use to kill rats. I thrust it out low and center and hope they don't notice how it trembles in my hand.

The last time I saw Ripper, she was leading me to the catacombs, where the creatures that infest the pit wait every few days for their sacrifice.

Somehow I got away. Now, though, there is nowhere to run. I will have to fight, and I'm not sure I can do that.

I hate my fear. The way my body goes all rubbery and weak.

Calm down. Form a plan. They will both rush me, so I decide to go after Ripper first. Rafe specializes in blunt force trauma. In close quarters, Ripper and her blade will do the quickest damage.

Ripper darts forward, silver flashing. I grunt. Tingly fire zips up my side. Ripper's nearly toothless mouth is yawned, her chest wobbling with excited, hungry breaths.

She must have stabbed me, but my body masks the pain with adrenaline. It needs me to keep going. To fight back.

Fight back, Maia Graystone!

This time Ripper lunges with the knife aimed dead center at my stomach. I twist, catching her by the arm and trying to throw her off balance. Impossibly she squirms from my grasp, all muscle and bone, and springs for me again at lightning speed. Her knife jabs methodically at my belly.

Stab.

Stab.

Kicking and clawing, I recoil backward into a sweaty wall of hard muscle. A hot, rancid breath warms my neck.

Rafe.

My body goes numb. The Doom is setting in. Both my shoulders are viced between Rafe's cement grip. Pain cords through my chest as he squeezes, bones cracking.

I blink. Ripper's knife twirls inches from my face; slippery light twinkles along its bloody length. "Hold her good, Rafe."

Rafe grunts behind me. "She all carved up, they not gonna pay."

I barely have time to wonder who would be desperate enough to pay these two homicidal savages to retrieve me when Ripper's knife slips under my nose. Her eyes are gleaming. "Just the nose. She don't need it."

"Ripper, I take her without you just as easy as with you." The pressure eases from my shoulders. Behind me, a hollow object— probably Rafe's favorite metal pipe—clanks against flesh as he passes it between his meaty palms.

Whatever they are being paid to collect me, it's enough for them to turn on each other. Impossibly my situation has just gotten worse. Because only someone outside, someone Royal, can offer something like that.

Which means the Emperor has finally found me.

My muscles quiver. It won't take long for one to snuff the other. But all I need are a few seconds to disappear into the earthen maze just beyond that hole. I prepare to run.

At least I'm good at *that*.

But my fragile hope evaporates as Ripper's knife-blade whispers back into her shirtsleeve. "No worry, yah, Rafey-boy?"

Before I can protest, Rafe strings a corded rope around my neck, looping it over my arms and legs and back to him so that the slightest pressure causes me to choke.

I know the rope system Rafe has set up is a mistake the second we enter the hole. The tunnels are a snaking maze of vertical and lateral burrows, laced with dead ends and circular passageways. Most are a tight fit for me, meaning that Rafe must be barely squeezing through. Because of the rope connecting us, I am forced to rest my manacled hands on the backs of his legs, making it hard for him to move and impossible for me to keep enough slack in the rope to breathe. The faster he tries to move, the more entangled I become.

Like an animal caught in a trap, Rafe goes berserk. He lunges forward, grunting wildly, breaking off large chunks of earth that pile on top of us. The rope bites under my jaw and rips my head forward. My lungs scream for air. *Air!*

Just as the blackness swallows my eyesight, the walls release me. As if on springs, my arms shoot up and I slip four fingers beneath the rope constricting my neck. A trickle of air burns its way down my throat and into my lungs, clearing a pinpoint of vision. Rafe careens forward, and we crumple into a sweaty pile. My head, pressed into his sweat-soaked chest, rocks up and down with his panicky breathing.

My eyes follow Rafe's headlamp as it hops around the small cavity, briefly revealing another passageway near the roof, and my mouth goes dry. If Rafe forces me to follow him into that hole, we are all dead.

Ripper, who has slipped into the shaft, is quietly studying Rafe. "Lemme lead, Rafe."

"Can't . . ." Rafe's strangled breath cuts out. His white egg eyes twinkle with panic as his gaze rolls between her and the hole. "Can't breathe."

The Doom. It's found him too.

Ripper slides carefully to his right, where the shadows are the wettest, the darkest.

I know Rafe is about to lunge because his entire body coils. Although I'm pretty sure my neck will snap the second he springs, I squat anyway, readying my legs to jump with him. I have a plan in place on the off chance I survive.

Get the knife. Cut the rope. Go for Rafe first, under the ribs. Try for the kidneys or liver. Then free your legs. Get the knife . . .

There's a sharp puncturing noise, like ripping fabric. Rafe gives a groaning sigh and melts to the floor, forcing me to my knees.

Ripper resolves from the shadows. Wiping her bloody blade on her thigh, she bends down, retrieves the headlamp, and slashes the rope from Rafe's body.

A gunmetal flash draws my eye. Duchess is pressed hesitantly against an outcropping rock protruding from the wall. Rafe's metal pipe peeks from the pincer grip of her collecting arm. I shake my head and mouth no, but she inches determinably closer, her lights dimmed to tiny glowing stars.

Always the gutsy one, my Duchess.

Ripper is distracted. I overcome my fear and allow myself a sliver of hope. This may be my only chance to escape. "You were friends," I say to Ripper. "And you killed him." While I try to keep her talking, I am slowly leaning for the pipe. Duchess sinks low and scuttles a few inches closer. She is shaking. I spread my fingers in anticipation.

"You know nothing, Digger Girl." Ripper fixes her dead gaze on me; behind her heavy lids, her all-pupil eyes shine liquid black.

Cold metal brushes my fingertips. They vice shut—but there's nothing there.

The pipe thuds softly to the ground.

Something changes in Ripper's expression. Her head swivels down to the pipe, back up to me. "Digger Girl, she found herself a weapon, found herself a little hope."

I'm kneeling. I can pick it up—if I want to. Duchess is urging the pipe forward with her leg.

"Now watcha gonna do with that?"

"Nothing." My hand curls into a rock. We both know that even if I pick it up, it will be useless inside my inept fingers.

The kick happens so fast I barely have time to flinch. A spray of dirt pelts my face, followed by a dull thud against the wall behind me. Duchess, dazed on her back, emits a string of pitiful chirps as Ripper bends down and digs her knife into the fissure on Duchess's belly. There's a final release of high-pitched beeps, similar to a scream. Then Ripper twists the knife and drags it down Duchess's insides, and Duchess goes quiet.

My breath escapes in a quiet hiss. I force my watery eyes off Duchess. *Do not cry.*

Ripper is inches from my face, her own face strangely emotionless and slack. "Hope don't belong to us leeches. Hope for the Outside. Hope for fools and corpses."

She's right, and I hate her for it. I try and swallow as a wave of emotion crams my mouth with bile.

I hate Ripper. I hate this place. And more than anything, I hate myself for being so afraid. "What would you know of the outside? You've never seen how blue the sky can get. Tasted freshly picked peaches, still warm from the sun. And the stars, so many it would take you a lifetime to count. They twinkle as if alive, tiny bits of white fire—"

Ripper clamps her hand over my mouth. "You thinks you's better than me, Digger Girl?"

"Yes."

This is obviously the last thing in the world I should have said.

She blinks, her eyes wild in a way I can't predict. Slowly, the animalistic look sinks down inside her. "Shut your mouth, or I carve out your pretty little tongue."

Ripper jerks me to my feet, sadistically tweaking the rope so that I'm choking and wheezing as she clambers into the hole. I twist my head to try and glance at Duchess one last time, but the rope bites into my neck and I stumble forward, gasping for breath.

Given my current way with words, this might actually keep me alive.

CHAPTER TWO

The stench of human waste hits me like a wall. A cacophony of wails and moans echo off the high ceilings of the pit. Squinting through the darkness, I make out the ten-story walls, tears from the underground streams seeping through the earth and making glistening rivers down the sides. It goes on for miles. Or maybe without sunlight everything seems larger.

Someone shrieks. Farther off, howls reach a fever pitch and then abruptly cut off. Except there are no animals here. No guards, either, or cages to keep us from tearing each other apart. Only a boarded up hole in the ceiling called the drop that connects us to the upper levels of the prison where the regular prisoners reside.

They call us Pit Leeches because we live off the prison above, forced to eat their scraps. Funny how I ended up here for that very same reason: searching for scraps. Not that I'd call the fuzzy, glistening lumps that rain down every seven days food. Half the time the maggots and beetles infesting it are more edible.

The sound of Ripper's headlight flicking off grabs my attention. Judging by her tense demeanor, we are going to travel straight through the catacombs—a mazelike collection of dark caves hollowed out in the walls.

Small fires burn inside the holes, their weak light scattering hundreds of shadows. Ripper's head swivels left to right, eyes sharp and hungry as we near the first cells. This is the most dangerous part of the pit.

Fear purls through me. "This is stupid."

"Shut your mouth, Digger Girl, or we both be a tasty little snack." Even she isn't guaranteed safety in the catacombs, a fact she has to be acutely aware of now that Rafe is gone.

It takes all my effort to keep the rope slack enough to breathe. I am also careful to keep my movements slow and smooth. Here, the classification system is simple.

Predator or prey.

And the predators are always watching, always working to determine which category you fall under.

Flickering pools of firelight dot our path as we continue. Inside the bottom cells, bodies with protruding ribcages and jutting spines hunch around simpering fires. They clutch sticks impaled with stringy chunks of gray meat. I try not to think about what they're eating—*who* they're eating—or how that was almost my fate, years ago. Their eyes gleam eerily in the firelight as they trail us.

Despite my revulsion, the sickly-sweet smell of charred flesh makes my mouth ache. I try not to gag on my hunger as we pass a cell crowded with creatures. Gaunt shadows skitter along the walls. There's a scuffle as two small boys attack a skeletal, wild-eyed man. He shrinks to the ground, moaning. A tidal wave of frantic limbs swallows him.

The crowd spits free a wispy cadaver; the girl is pale and slight, a tattered yellow dress hanging off sharp bones. She snatches the meat the man dropped. Our eyes meet just as the fatty chunk worms down her scrawny throat.

She has to be cunning and resourceful to have made it this far. But her feral expression can't mask her fear. And if I can see it, so can they.

I give her a week, tops.

We are nearing the last cells when I pause, just for an instant. Ripper is moving fast now. Her momentum jerks the rope, and I stumble.

A hundred skeletal faces hone in on me at once. I have screwed up. Have declared myself prey. And all the predators have noticed.

"Walk faster, Digger Girl," Ripper orders.

I notice the glint of a dull knife inside her palm. The hairs on my neck shoot straight up as my peripheral vision picks up shadows.

The walls seem to jolt up and down as we run. I wonder how long our composure will last. I wonder if Ripper regrets snuffing Rafe.

I wonder if this is how I will die.

The air cools. The catacombs and their sweltering fires are behind us. I shiver, and not just because of the cold.

The shadows have thickened. I can hear them. Shuffling. Growling and biting at each other as they trail behind us. Soon, the only thing I can hear is my breath wheezing rhythmically inside my head.

Bones litter the floor beneath the drop. They have been cracked, gnawed, and gouged clean. A spotlight bursts on. The shadows that have been trailing us cry out and scatter—though not far enough for comfort.

Ripper shields her face with a hand. "I got the Digger Girl."

Half a minute passes before the metal lid grates open; dirt and rocks sprinkle the ground. I blink as the spotlight catches my face. The light goes away, and there's the sound of something heavy being lowered. Ripper's headlamp skips over a bucket, barely large enough for one person.

When the bucket thuds to the floor, Ripper doesn't seem to know what to do. She twists around to the shadows, which are slowly circling us again to form a tight, inescapable ring.

"The bucket's too small," Ripper shouts at the faceless hole. She pulls me close; I am surprised to feel that she is trembling.

"Put the girl in first," a man calls. "We will send another bucket down for you."

"The deal was we both go." I feel the cold edge of Ripper's blade catch under my Adam's apple. "We go together or . . . or I spill her blood right here."

Now I understand Ripper's payment: a trip upstairs. Once again, alarm bells go off. Very few people could have clearance to make such a deal.

But a powerful Gold would.

There's a pause. "You have one minute to relinquish the girl. After that minute is up, the deal is off and the bucket goes away."

Ripper licks her lips and eyes the growing mass around us. A few shadows dart forward, and she slashes the air with her knife, sending them surging back.

The knife bites into my skin, and I think she is going to fulfill her promise from earlier, but then the rope falls from my neck and I'm shoved toward the bucket.

Hard wood scrapes against my bare feet as I clamber inside. The bucket sways as it lifts, the chains jangling. I sink to my knees, my hands knotted knuckle-white around the bucket lip.

Suddenly the bucket rocks hard, as if someone has grabbed onto it and is dangling. It heaves violently to the side. I'm flipping, my arms and legs spinning uselessly, my mouth open in a silent, airless scream.

The ground slaps the scream from my chest. I fight to my knees, Ripper spewing a stream of curses beside me as the prisoners close in.

The spotlight once again peels back the darkness, but this time it has little effect on the frenzied crowd.

The fear makes me want to die now and get it over with. But I can't die. Max needs me.

A hard shoulder spins me around. Cold dirt presses into my cheek. The top of my head burns—someone is dragging me backward by my hair. I think I cry out. My heels dig into the ground, and I twist and buck.

Bony fingers clamp onto my bare foot, and a mouth framed in jagged teeth prepares to take a chunk out of my calf.

A small shadow wriggles almost comically up the creature's arm and clamps onto his face. *Bramble!* The creature shrieks in blind fury, whipping his head side to side.

Bramble loses his grip and falls to the ground.

Wiggling from the creature's grasp, I kick blindly, my heel smashing into its cheek with a sick *crack.*

Suddenly the pressure from my hair is released. Someone slips an arm under my armpit and leg, and I go weightless before collapsing headfirst into the bucket.

I scramble to my knees and make eye contact with him, the man who helped me. Not a man, an older boy, although it's impossible to tell exactly how old. Shaggy hair haloes razor-sharp cheekbones and windy white scars. One particularly nasty scar creases his eye socket, where his left eye must have once been. The other eye is wild and intoxicating, a startlingly bruised shade of blue.

On the outside he could have been striking, maybe even handsome. But in here, beauty is the first thing they take from you.

A hard smile splits his face open. "Hold on, Digger Girl."

"Thank you," I start to say, but then I pause. He looks so familiar . . .

Now I remember. He was with Ripper the day they captured me and took me to the catacombs. In fact, he helped tie my wrists. He had both eyes then, and he was younger, softer, less savage looking.

He's just like them! I recoil from the boy as I remember how he ignored my pleas for help.

"You're . . . You're just like them," I say.

The boy scowls.

The bucket jerks upward, and I scowl right back. *Yeah, I remember you, Pit Boy.*

I exhale with relief as Bramble scrabbles over the side. He ducks under my shirt and curls into a ball, his body cold against my stomach.

At the top, two screws, our nickname for the guards, yank me to my feet. Cold steel shackles *clack* loosely around my wrists. For the first time in years, I imagine what I must look like.

What I must *smell* like.

"Walk, Pit Leech," the first screw orders. The tone of his voice implies that if I give him trouble, he will push me back in and enjoy it immensely. His eyes are watery and glazed, and he reeks of tar, the cheap drug rampant among the Low Colors. It's rumored the Royalists secretly supply it to keep us weak and sedated.

"What about the girl?" I gesture to Ripper. We both look down at her, a tiny white flicker in a sea of filthy, churning bodies—a lonely, dying star. She is still swinging her knife. Still waiting for the bucket.

The last thing I hear before the lid grinds closed, sealing off the pit, is a high-pitched scream.

One that I imagine Ripper would make.

Grinning, the screw spits onto the ground, brown tar-laced saliva splashing droplets onto my legs. "What *girl*? All I see are Pit Leeches."

CHAPTER THREE

This part of the prison is nice. Clean and orderly and quiet. Another world, really. Old halogen lights buzz from the ceilings and walls and chase away the shadows. Electricity isn't regulation, but nothing here is. We pass a room where well-groomed prisoners in crisp, orange uniforms form a neat line as they await rations.

My brain immediately categorizes them as prey before I remember that we're not in the pit, where something as small as giving up your back will kill you.

There's a whining shudder and the lights flicker, die. Immediately, the torches along the walls spark to life. The screws and prisoners hardly react, so the power must fail often.

The prisoners here are Bronzes from the nearest Diamond Cities. To stay above ground, they must be in good standing with their local magistrate, be current on tithes to the Emperor, and prove they are a decent producer in the factories.

Needless to say, the pit is just a bit overcrowded.

The last time I was in these halls, I was scared to death. They were leading me to the drop. I remember the way my hands shook. The way my breath caught in my chest. I didn't know what to expect; I just knew that I couldn't make the fear go away.

I was nine.

The bucket was the same one I used going back up. Except when I huddled in it then, so small it nearly swallowed me, it was wet with the warm piss of the girl who went right before. She had screamed the entire way down.

At the bottom, her screams had abruptly cut off.

I resolved not to make a sound.

As soon as the bucket hit the ground I ran, sprinting blindly, my heart exploding inside my chest. Hands reached from the darkness, but I twisted from their grasp. I ran toward the light. Naively I thought it could protect me. That I would be safe there.

My young brain couldn't yet understand that there are some places where you are never safe.

I spent the first night in the catacombs, learning to be a ghost, to slink in shadow and breathe quietly and use the balls of my feet. I learned that firelight glints off the eyes and mud can be used to mask your skin. I learned that sometimes light is bad, not good. I learned that it takes less than a day to strip away your humanity, to peel it right off like an extra skin.

The feel of daylight on my face calls me from my memories. We are in a sparsely furnished office with a flimsy rolling chair and desk, two holographic bookshelves, and a floor-to-ceiling window looking down on the prison yard. The screw unshackles me and retreats. Just like that, I am alone.

The first thing I do is scour the desk for food, but there is nothing. I pace, searching for anything even slightly edible. I'm prostrate on the floor looking for crumbs when the clouds must part and it happens.

Sunlight.

I stumble to the window. As much as I want to drink it all in, my eyes cannot take the bright light and I squeeze them shut. I dig my cheek into the warm glass, fingers splayed on either side of my head.

Bramble lets out a curious chirp. He's never seen the outside. I feel him lift my shirt, give a soft coo at what he must be seeing, and then his weight leaves me. "Look, Bramble. There's nothing else like it."

I brave a stare. The light leaves fuzzy yellow rings around my vision. Past the yard are thick green spruce trees. Beyond that, the sea, a shimmering blue-green ribbon smudged with darkness.

"Cypher." My breath clouds the glass. I trace a hand over the dark ridge as I picture the old Diamond City, a skyline brimming with metal and glass factories that glitter in the sun. From the bay, when the sun first peaks the waves and catches in the meshwork of buildings, the entire city seems to catch fire.

After the Everlasting War, Cypher was one of only a handful of surviving glass and metal cities. Diamond cities, they call them, because the Gold owned factories we are forced to slave away in shine like jewels in the sunlight.

Looking at Cypher now, I wonder if the three-story home I grew up in is still there, just as Max and I left it. I choke back tears at the thought of my brother. What must he have thought when I didn't come back? That I abandoned him? How long did he wait for me under that bridge clutching his ancient, bedraggled cat, Cleo, his blue eyes blinking away tears?

"I'll be back," I think I called.

I can still hear Cleo's squalls as Max clung to him like a life preserver, lower lip quivering. I know it took all his courage not to chase after me.

I see now that I must have known, somehow. I must have known it would be the last time I saw my brother. I must have. Because it took every single ounce of energy I had to force myself to leave him.

The door clicks shut, startling me. At once my body prepares itself to fight. I whip around. My first instinct is to find a weapon. The only thing available is a gold quill pen, and I jerk it up like a dagger.

The woman is tall and angular, wearing black riding boots and a chartreuse-green duster coat. A gray top hat slants across her shoulder length, whitish-silver powdered wig.

She is handsome, in a masculine sort of way. Full forehead. Strong patrician nose. Dark ashy eyebrows that arch sharply over eyes hidden behind smoky, metal-rimmed glasses. White silk gloves slink up her sleeves.

She has Royalist written all over her.

My eyes fixate on the head of the Emperor's golden phoenix peeking from her collar. The brand on her neck tells me she's a Gold. Sweat breaks out over my palms as I search for the Sigil that will tell me which Gold House she hails from, but she wears nothing that hints at her lineage.

"All hail the Emperor!" she snaps, slapping a bony hand over her heart. It's been years since I've heard those words. I'm supposed to respond in kind, a public declaration of my allegiance to the Emperor, but the idea revolts me.

"Food." I fall to my knees, still, inexorably, holding my useless weapon. My voice is a pathetic croak. "Whatever you have. *Please.*"

Disgust twists the woman's face. "For Emperor's sake, stand up, Bronze."

I manage to obey. Two men in identical black velvet tailcoats flank the woman. *Centurions.* When they spot the pen in my hand, they both reach for the pearl-handled revolvers neatly tucked into their waistbands.

Their brands, a smooth raised Bronze phoenix, emboss the flesh above their stiff, white collars.

As the woman shifts, the rest of her brand comes into view, and my eyes land on the red scorpion gripped inside the phoenix's claws. Only a member of the Emperor's War Cabinet would wear that brand—the symbol for death to all Fienians—or be allowed the color red.

The color was outlawed years ago, after the death of the Emperor's first wife and newborn daughter at the hands of Fienians. Red stands for rebellion, for uprising.

To some, red stands for freedom.

Biting my cheek, I refocus on the woman. She holds up a hand, and the Centurions relax. But their fingers twitch around their pistols. Conscripted at the age of six from Bronze families, the Microplants embedded inside their skulls and years' worth of training mean the two Centurions are blindly loyal to the Emperor—an assertion they will gladly prove if I give them cause.

A short, unremarkable woman wearing dingy gray scrubs pushes a squeaky cart into the room, escorted by the Centurions' wary gaze. A Silver phoenix flashes below her jaw to indicate her station.

After the Everlasting War, the first Emperor separated the empire into Colors. Those on the losing side of the Everlasting War received Bronze Colors. The few not working in the factories were shipped north to Gold estates to work as servants. Silvers have it better: cushy state jobs, decent hours, and a livable amount of vouchers.

Scalpels, syringes, an assortment of needles, and a clear test tube clank against the Silver's cart as she steers it into the corner. Her wide-eyed gaze bounces off the others. I'm guessing this is the first time she has encountered a high-ranking Gold.

"Dear, I am Archduchess Victoria Crowder," the woman in charge says, her voice deep and soft and commanding all at the same time. Her face is slick and tight, like the bloated flesh of a corpse.

I swallow the unsettling feeling wriggling up my chest and lift the pen an inch. "I don't care who you are; tell your Dandies to stop fondling their weapons, and we can talk."

The corners of her lips flicker, the way a cat's whiskers might twitch at a trapped mouse. She crosses to the window, arms folded behind her back. "How long has it been?"

"I'm . . . I'm sorry?" It's harder than I remember, conversation. At least one with a human being.

"The sky. The outside. How long since you have seen it?"

I lower my pen a bit. "You went to all that trouble to get me here to ask me that?"

"Trouble?" Behind her glasses I can feel her eyes assessing the bloodstain on my side. "Indeed?"

I clear my throat. "A boy died. And the girl you promised a trip upstairs, she's probably dead too."

"My, my. That is grievous." Her words are coated with smug indifference. "Did you kill them?"

"Does it matter?"

"Not particularly." From the window reflection I catch her lips stretch into a yawn. "Pandora is about to kill millions. The untimely deaths of a few Bronzes are hardly significant."

"How . . ." I clear my throat and try again. "How soon?" Inside the earth, days became weeks became entire years. Staring into darkness. Listening to the rats cannibalize each other. Dreaming about the taste of food, the smell of food, the feel of it sliding over my tongue and between my teeth. Morning became evening and each day a lifetime.

And then my last match burned away and night became eternal.

"Two weeks, five days until D-Day," she says in her bored voice. Very carefully she removes her smoky glasses and slips them into her breast pocket, as if whatever is beyond that window deserves clear viewing. "Exactly 552 hours."

Deliverance Day. The day the Golds and all their servants watch from their space station in the stars as Pandora wreaks havoc on our planet and those remaining.

Deliverance from fear. From death. From us.

Deliverance. The word makes me want to vomit.

She turns to me.

I jerk my pen up. "Close enough."

Victoria gives a small, disappointed sigh. "For Emperor's sake, dear, put that thing down." She nods at the Centurions. "You're making those two trigger-happy mongoloids twitchy."

A lie: those two have been twitchy from birth. "Water," I demand. "Food. Bread. Whatever you have."

"Deal."

I know it's another lie, but I'm too desperate to care. Sensing my weakness, the Archduchess plucks the pen from my grasp. "Good girl." Her voice oozes control. I shudder as her cruel gaze lazily floats from my forehead to my feet and back up to my face.

Then I notice the wavering image in the corner, and any hope I have for food dies. The Emperor's hologram studies me, his eyes shiny, mouth twisted into a grin. A jagged gold crown inlaid with phoenix-shaped rubies sits atop his head. Even though I know it's a hologram—the pencil-sized Interceptor on the floor confirms this—the details of him are so real I imagine that if he moved, the black fur hem of his robe would scrape the dust from the tile.

"Pathetic creature, isn't she?" the Emperor remarks.

"Yes, my Emperor," the Archduchess agrees in a reverent tone. "If only her traitorous father could see the worm she is now."

My lips part an inch, and a startled breath escapes. I have hidden from the Emperor for so long that I had convinced myself he would never find me. Now that he has, it's hard to control my fear of him.

He runs a finger over his lips. "Hmm, it is unfortunate that Graystone died before we could properly draw and quarter him. That kind of death would have sent a louder message to the worms."

"But how wise you were," the Archduchess says, "to mount his head on a pike over the wall, afterward."

"Yes." The Emperor rakes his sharp gaze over me. "You are sure this is his daughter?"

"We'll know soon enough." The Archduchess twines a tangled orange strand of my hair between her long fingers and tugs, turning my head and exposing my neck. "She removed the Chosen brand. Smart girl. If they knew that she had been Chosen, they would have ripped her limb from limb years ago." She releases my head. "Lucky for us, she's still relatively intact."

The Chosen brand, given to me at birth—along with five thousand other Gold children—is a phoenix, similar to the others. But instead of a color, an orange flame shivered over my flesh. Getting it at birth wasn't painful, so I'm told, but taking it off with the jagged lip of a glass bottle hurt like hell.

My mouth is bone-dry, and I have to force the words out. "You have the wrong person."

It's true. The naïve little girl named after the star from my mother's favorite constellation shriveled up and died somewhere in the dark of the tunnels.

Victoria cuts her eyes at the Silver girl. "That dreary little thing there is going to collect your blood. Care to amend your statement?"

I roll up the tattered sleeves of my uniform and expose my dirty arm. "Meat, and I will willingly give it to you. Or bread . . . Whatever you have. I'll take anything." I hate my weakness, my hunger. "Please."

"Shut up, filthy maggot, and listen. They call you Digger Girl because you hide in the tunnels. The girl who disappeared, they say. The girl who somehow survives against all odds." Victoria's strange pupils enlarge with excitement. "The girl who can manipulate the sensors."

I shake my head, but it's a futile gesture. The evidence of my lie is in this very room. Hiding. Hopefully for my sake and his, well enough not to be found.

"You see, Maia, Emperor Laevus has tasked me with finding you and your brother, and for seven years, seven *godforsaken* years, I have scoured every rotting Diamond City, every filthy maggot prison for you." Her lips twist into a jagged sneer as she whispers near my ear. "Because of you, the Emperor and his sniveling court are up there now, enjoying what is rightfully mine, while I languish here with you worms."

"I'm sorry that you wasted—"

Her finger presses hard against my lips. "Shh, maggot. You are just like the other maggots. Blind, greedy, ungrateful. Do you know they are rioting now? Emperor Laevus offered them a chance at life"—her voice grows hateful—"but they want more. It's always more with you worms. Begging for this, whining for that. Dull maggot faces imploring us to save them, save their worm-brained children. More! More! *More!*"

She stops suddenly, blinking as she struggles to slip her mask of composure back on. "Maia, I am going to restrain you, carefully peel off your flesh like the skin of an orange, part your tendons and muscles from the bone, and sift through you, every part of you. Your bones will be snapped, your marrow collected, your organs plucked out and examined, all while you are conscious." Red capillaries tangle across her cheeks as her excitement grows. "I can't kill you, because if I do, the thing inside you, the thing your father stole from us, it may die too. But that doesn't mean I won't find it."

She gathers the Silver girl with a wave, and I think I might faint, especially when the needle slips into my forearm. Even though every part of me is screaming, I watch calmly as the syringe gorges on my blood.

"Where is your brother, Maia?" the Archduchess whispers.

I have been staring out the window to avoid her gaze, but now I look straight at the Emperor. "I'll die before you ever find him."

For a fraction of a second, something dark spoils his expression. I have the feeling of looking at a still lake and seeing something black and slimy scuttle just below the surface.

The Archduchess slaps my cheek, forcing me to look at her. "How dare you speak to the Emperor that way, maggot!"

Tears of pain spring to my eyes. "Please, I'm not—"

"You have one minute to admit you are Maia and tell me where the key and your brother are." An alarm sounds outside. Victoria glances at the golden timepiece hanging from her jacket pocket and then nods at the window. "Go peek while you think over the offer."

This time I don't press my face against the glass. Something is wrong. A chill runs through me as I watch the filmy black curtain shroud the land. "She's already here."

"Pandora eclipses the sun from late afternoon to near sundown. They are calling the dark hours Shadow Fall."

Pandora's shadow. From here, she is about the size of a large grape, which explains why I missed her earlier. Dark brown, pitted black in certain spots, she has completely blotted out the sun.

I was four when my father first told me. I can still picture his slim fingers—fingers made for figuring complex mathematical equations and flitting over piano keys—as they steadied the telescope's eyepiece so I could peer into it.

Inside that small circle of glass, Pandora looked different, perhaps beautiful. But that's because she was so far off. A chunk of rock millions of miles away.

Now, she's here. And she's not beautiful anymore.

Somewhere up there, I know, far away from the asteroid and our doomed planet, is the space station Hyperion. That's where the Emperor must be communicating from right now, alongside his court of Golds and his precious Chosen.

I cover Pandora with my thumb, as if somehow that can stop her. "Have the Shadow Trials started yet?"

The Emperor chuckles, and for some reason the sound makes my skin crawl. "She is an insolent thing, isn't she?"

The Archduchess lifts her gloved hand to strike me again, but the Emperor shakes his head. "In a few minutes, you may have all the fun you'd like with her. But for now, let the worm witness our coming destruction."

I peer again into the darkness. It's like a murky pond, where you can just make out the bottom if you look hard enough. "Why do they clear the yard?"

I fight the urge to slap a hand over my mouth as the question hangs dangerously in the air. *Smart, Graystone.* Keep asking questions and maybe they'll kill you now instead of dragging it out.

"Because in the shadow murk," Victoria says, "you worms do horrible things to each other." She glances at her timepiece, and a hideous smile stretches her face. "Minute's up."

Before I can move, the two Centurions pin me, one on each arm, against the wall. The hard edge of a frame gouges into my left shoulder. I smell the sharp tang of the polish used on their weapons and the subtle talc of their wigs.

Victoria's immaculate left glove rustles as she slips it off. With her ungloved hand, she removes a long hatpin adorned with the Emperor's golden phoenix from her hat. Her thin, hooked nose nearly touches mine.

But there's something off about her eyes. Strange white marks pock her pale-gray irises, her pupils jagged and torn. "Where did he hide it, maggot?"

My heart hammers inside my chest. "What?"

"The key. Is it here?" She taps my nose with the sharp end of the hatpin. "Here?" The needle pricks my lips. "I know you hold the key and your brother holds the map. What I don't know is where."

"You're crazy," I say, flinching as she scrapes the hatpin along my jawbone and cheek until it hovers over my right eye. And she could be. Crazy. With her feverish stare, her gaping smile, the subtle tic of her left cheek.

But we both know what she says is true. My father hid something in my brother and me. I'm not exactly sure what—they killed him before I could find out—but whatever it is, the Emperor must want it badly enough to send the Archduchess scouring the country for it.

"My guess is here." The needle jabs at my eyelashes, making me blink. "With the eyes you must be delicate. Use pliers and they may burst. The same for a scalpel. But an ordinary soup spoon pops them out in seconds and leaves them perfectly intact."

The Emperor's face is flushed, his breathing shallow and rapid. *He enjoys watching her hurt me.* When she releases me, a dissatisfied grunt escapes his lips.

"Take her." The Archduchess waves to the Centurions. "Careful, idiots, she's crawling with vermin."

"Victoria," the Emperor says, "take care of our problem; I know you won't let me down again, *whatever* it takes."

Beaming, the Archduchess bows. "I'm your loyal servant until the end, my Emperor."

The two Centurions heft me easily toward the door. I manage to kick one in the thigh, but I might as well be punting a tree trunk. In response he flips me into a headlock, my windpipe sandwiched between his forearm and bicep, and squeezes.

Black dots circle my vision; my eyes feel as if they'll burst out of my sockets.

Won't the Archduchess be happy about that? I think, a bit madly.

The room begins to spin, but one face stays in focus. Victoria appraises me with a demented smile. Her right hand crosses over her heart. "All Hail the Emperor, little worm."

Absurdly, I feel myself smile. In the chaos, Bramble has managed to sneak out. I watch him scuttle down the hall, growing smaller inside the tiny dot of vision I have left.

Run. That's it, B. Run!

I somehow manage to snatch this one small comfort, drawing it in and savoring it like the breath my body pleads for as the dark closes in.

Safe. He's safe . . .

Chapter Four

I am curled in a ball on a cold, hard floor. A massive headache bear hugs my brain, my side stiff and throbbing. I'm hoping the injury is only a flesh wound but can't be sure unless I look. Given my recent luck, it's probably best I don't.

The scent of old urine mixed with the coppery smell of blood tickles my throat. Mine or the previous occupant's, it's impossible to say.

How long was I out? I wonder, just as a rodent the size of a large cat zips across the small triangle of light streaming in and begins to lap at a dark puddle on the floor. *My blood.*

In the pit, the only things worse than the darkness are the creatures that hide inside it. I kick at the rat.

It hisses, gnashes the air with finger-length incisors, and brazenly continues its red feast.

See, Maia, even the rats aren't afraid of you.

My vision begins to swirl. I lean over my knees, blinking away oily mist. A deep ache bores up my side. Looking down, I discover the upper half of my uniform is soaked. *Not a flesh wound.*

I am bleeding out.

My wobbly thoughts echo off memories. Fleeing with Max the night they killed my father. Max's tiny, pitiful cries as we huddled together in the escape elevator concealed inside my father's lab. The cold nights and brutal days hiding in the streets so the Centurions wouldn't find us. Starving.

I want to laugh. I want to cry. Perhaps it is a mercy to die this way. I will go to sleep. *Sleep . . .*

The sound of the rat's claws scraping the stone as it flees brings me back. Something is wrong. Just outside my cell, keys jangle softly. The door lock releases with a sharp click and an inrush of fresh air.

The test results. They already know.

It's a different screw this time. In fact, he's the same screw that led me to the pit my first day here, although I can't tell if he recognizes me through his dead twitcher gaze, the half-stare all tar-heads eventually get from the nanos mucking through their brain. Next comes the twitching as the nanos invade his nervous system.

I kick out at him and nearly collapse with the effort. Ignoring my pathetic struggle, the screw manacles my hands in front of my waist, clipping the long chain that holds the shackles to his belt.

We don't say a word to each other as he drags me down the narrow hallway separating the cells.

I feel helpless, defeated. *Just like old times.*

I'm more than a little surprised when he leads me through a door to the outside. I gaze up at the stars. It's nighttime and a big pearly moon guides our path. The cool wind pierces my tattered clothing and nestles in my bones.

I must keep pausing because the screw keeps yanking my chain. The blood loss is starting to get to me. My vision spins every time I take a step, and my legs feel cold and heavy.

I try to wiggle my toes, but nothing happens. *Not good, Graystone.*

Soon it's as if my brain has turned the volume down. I can't hear our footsteps, can hardly hear the keys jangle as the screw unlocks the two unmanned gates we pass. I peer through heavy eyelids at the concrete buildings ahead, rumored to be for the rare, wealthy Bronze. I fight the growing urge to lay down right here on the grass and sleep.

The screw yanks on my shackles. "Move it, Pit Leech!"

I stumble toward the enclosure leaking smoke from its chimney. "Where"—my gaze skips across the weathered wooden door in front of us—"are we?"

"Shut up." The screw fumbles with my restraints.

My arms spring free and I flex my sore wrists as he gives two quick raps on the door, opens it with a key, and then pushes me inside the dark room. The door slams shut behind me.

"I'm sorry about the light," a man says from the darkness. "The blackouts last for days now." There is something off about his voice, an electronic, warbling timbre.

The remnants of a fire smolder behind the man. I am silent as I wait for my eyes to adjust.

Two chairs come into view. A table. The small, barred window against the back wall is open, and the candle on the table flickers in the breeze, dancing light off the form of a man slumped in a chair, his hooded face cloaked in shadow. Judging by the shiny gold timepiece hanging from his pocket, the luxurious black fur lining the cloak, and the subtle air of superiority in his voice, he is a Royalist. Even the wealthiest of Bronzes wouldn't own such luxuries.

The man clears his throat, and I startle from my thoughts. For some reason I have the feeling he's glad for the darkness. I search the shadows for his Color but come up empty.

"Sit, please," the man commands. "We are short on time." His speech comes off as refined despite its unnatural quality.

I hesitate. An oblong, convex silver capsule the length of a tall man protrudes from the wall. It's an Uploader, what we Bronzes call a Casket. Made from a mixture of titanium, steel, and silver, it was undoubtedly manufactured in Cypher, at one of the hundreds of metalwork factories lining the bay. "I'll stand," I say, gesturing toward the Casket with my head. "Why do you have that? Lags are prohibited from uploading."

"Who said I was a prisoner?"

"Then what are you doing here?"

"Oh, you know. Little bit of this, little bit of that."

His smugness leaves a sour taste in my mouth. I cross my arms.

"You're Fienian, then?"

"Do I look like a Fienian Rebel?"

Not in the slightest. Shaking off another dizzy spell, I flick my gaze to the Casket. "Will you do it? Upload when the time comes?"

He shrugs. "The cold does horrible things to my skin."

"You mean being turned into a hunk of ice and living inside the mind of a Chosen isn't your idea of a good time?"

"Oh, I've met the Chosen. Most are boring clods whose minds would be a ruthless form of torture." Tapping his fingers on the table, he nods toward the chair closest to me.

I stay rooted to the ground. If I have to walk, I'll undoubtedly keel over.

He sighs. "I will make this simple. Are you Maia Graystone, daughter of the traitorous Bronze, Philip Graystone?"

For the second time tonight my heart skips a beat. "He wasn't a traitor!"

"The bomb he built to kill the Emperor says otherwise." His words are slathered in arrogant boredom. "Not that I blame him, of course."

"That's a lie!" I don't care what the Royalists accuse my father of, or the fact that I know he was building *something*; I'll never believe he could knowingly build a bomb.

"Spoken like a loyal daughter."

"I never said I was her—"

"Shame. I was going to help you escape. But if you are not Maia . . ."

"What's the point?" I cross my arms. "Or haven't you looked at the sky lately?"

"You haven't heard the rest of my offer, Everly."

"Everly?" I repeat, trying to keep the confusion from my voice. "But you just—"

"Your new name: Everly. It rather rolls off the tongue, wouldn't you agree?" His shroud suddenly shifts, revealing part of his forearm. The skin is stretched and waxy. "Everly, how would you like to compete in the Shadow Trials?"

His question thrusts me into a world I have been trying the last seven years to forget. "But the Shadow Trials will be held in Royalist country, on Emerald Island, and the contestants are exiled courtiers from once prominent Gold Houses—"

"Yes, yes," he interrupts. "Let's not dally with the obvious."

"This is a joke, right?"

"A joke? I imagine the thousands of northern lords and ladies waiting to be chosen don't think so. It's not a joke, Everly. A simple yes and you get a second chance at life."

I somehow manage to cross the floor and pool into the chair. I am acutely aware of the blood swimming down my side. "Who are you?"

"There can be only four champions at the Shadow Trials. The right question is how will you be one of them? Or have you forgotten what the winners—?"

"A seat." My head is spinning, but I can't be sure if it's from the blood loss or the offer. "The winners receive a seat on the space station."

"Right. A seat alongside the Emperor and his beloved Chosen on Hyperion, the castle in the stars. And the best part is you are not required to do anything for me until you win."

"You mean *if*," I say, enunciating carefully. "If I win."

"Naturally."

I shift. "What's your end in this?"

There's a pause. "Do you recall what transpires after the Shadow Trials?"

It's been years since I heard any Royalist news, and I rack my brain. "There's a . . . a ball. The Immortalis Dominium." I shake my head at the crop of memories that come rushing back. "The last feast for the Chosen."

"And the Shadow Trial champions, those lucky four, will be invited to dine with the *magnificent* Emperor Rand Laevus." Grunting, he flips back his hood to reveal his face.

Or what's left of it.

I give a startled gasp. His ears, nose, and lips are gone. The entirety of his exposed flesh is shiny and pitted, pulled taut, missing in some places, melted in others.

Strapped to his throat gleams a shiny, metallic electro-larynx. "Behold, Emperor Rand Laevus's masterpiece. Don't bother concealing your disgust. I react the exact same way every morning when I gaze into the mirror."

I avert my eyes. "The Emperor did that to you?"

"Now you understand, don't you?"

"Retribution." Any hope I harbored bleeds out of me. "You want retribution."

"Well, to be clear, I want you to plunge a knife into Emperor Laevus's twisted black heart. Although a blunt instrument across his skull would make me almost as giddy."

He stifles a groan as he twists his mangled body into a more comfortable position. I notice his fingers have been burned to bony nubs. "Fire would be the poetic end," he continues, "but not particularly pragmatic, given the circumstances."

"Pragmatic? We're talking about assassinating the Emperor, head of the Royalists, second firstborn descendent of Emperor Marcus Laevus from the most powerful House in history." I rise unsteadily as a wave of dizziness crashes over me. "You're . . . You're insane!"

I make it two steps toward the door before I see him. He must have been here all along, slunk against the wall deepest in shadow. There is something inherently predatory about him, and my senses scream as our bodies nearly collide. It's only when he shifts to catch the light that I recognize he's missing an eye.

Pit Boy.

"Is he here to scare me into saying yes?" I snap, glaring at the one-eyed boy who is still appraising me quietly. His intense, detached gaze seems to bore straight through me.

"That lovely specimen is Riser," the burned man says. "Your partner."

I snort, holding my ribs as pain lances down my side. "Impressive.

You are delusional *and* insane."

The blood from my wound, masked by the dimness, has soaked my pants leg and is now dripping quietly onto the floor. Riser cocks his head, just enough I know he has noticed. I can't help but feel he is constantly assessing me, tallying my strengths and weakness, searching for chinks in my armor.

"We could debate the veracity of my mind all night," the burned man says. "Except by now the Emperor's favorite genetically mangled attack dog has discovered her new toy is missing. Trust me; you don't want her to find you again."

Her strange eyes pop inside my mind, and my body shudders. "I didn't know there were any Malignants still alive."

"Emperor Laevus kept the ones he found useful, and I imagine the Archduchess is extremely useful."

Malignants were the first subjects genetically tampered with. That was before we understood nanotechnology and tissue engineering. Before the glitches in the procedures were fixed. The rare Malignant that survived conception, like the Archduchess, looked human, but they weren't—not completely. They were something else. Something damaged.

Something *wrong*.

I turn to face him. "Why me?"

"Because, contrary to appearances, you are Chosen, that abundantly fortunate, genetically flawless subgroup that represents us all. You were around enough Golds to know how they talk, how they think. Given the right aesthetic enhancements, you can blend into their world."

It feels like lifetimes ago that I was called Chosen. Well, I don't feel Chosen, at least not for anything worth choosing. My blood looks the same as the others'. My insides, I imagine, if I were cut open like the Archduchess seemed so eager to do, would look entirely the same as well.

But I'm not the same, and sometimes I forget that.

"Exactly," I say. "And Riser . . . or whatever his name is"—I nod at the one-eyed boy—"can't. The Bronze candidates for the trials are picked from fallen Gold Houses, and they've spent at least one summer at court. They will never believe he was once . . ." A wave of dizziness washes over me, and I clench the chair's seat. "Once . . ."

"Shamelessly privileged, impeccably bred?" the burned man finishes, eying me carefully. "Please, have a little faith. The Shadow Trials begin in less than a week. By then, with the right tinkering, Riser will resemble every other well-heeled contestant." He gives what would have been a winning smile, if not for his grotesquely disfigured face. "Emperor Laevus isn't the only artist to create masterpieces."

"He's not a canvas!" I snap. "He's a killer." I still remember the day they caught me in the pit, the way Pit Boy's ragged fingernails jabbed my wrists as he tied them together. Snot and tears pouring down my face, I begged him to help me.

Shut up, Pit Boy had said. *Look, just be quiet, okay? Everything will be all right.*

I force myself out of that dark memory and focus back on what the burned man is saying, but not before shooting Pit Boy a death stare.

"Precisely the point," the burned man continues. "You see, for the right sum I can fix his scars, his horrible teeth. I can make him speak eloquently and open doors for ladies and perform the most exquisite bows. I can even endow him with a new eye. But what I *cannot* do is give him your knowledge of their world. The little nuances that even the best Reconstructor in the world cannot implant. If you want that seat, it has to be a team effort."

"What if we don't kill anyone?" Again I cut my eyes at Riser, who is watching our interaction with mild interest, like a sated snake watching two mice play. "What's to stop us from splitting once we win our spots?"

"Besides your word?" The burned man lifts what must have once been an eyebrow, the stretched skin of his face twisting almost comically. "Considering what the Emperor did to your father, Everly, I thought you would jump at the chance to kill him."

For the span of a breath I am nine again, watching my father fall seemingly in slow motion, bright red blood weeping down his forehead, his once vibrant green eyes flat and faded . . .

I gasp and refocus on my current surroundings. Riser's eyes sharpen with cold curiosity, but I keep my face impassive. *The snake is suddenly interested.* "I don't want revenge," I finally say. "I just want . . ."

Max.

To be alive.

To be safe.

But I don't dare say this, because now that I'm out of the tunnels and some of my madness has faded, I realize there's no way he's still alive.

"Pity." The burned man frowns. "Then perhaps one more spot on Hyperion will motivate you. To whomever actually spills Emperor Laevus's blood."

"Why would I need more tickets?" My heart hammers. Very few people would have access to another spot on Hyperion. The cost alone would require more wages than a Bronze could earn in a lifetime at the factories.

"Why, Everly, surely you weren't thinking of abandoning Max, *again*?"

It's as if the air has been stripped from my chest. "Max is . . ." I try the words, but I've never stated them out loud before, and they lodge in my throat. Blinking away hot tears, I try again. "My brother is dead."

I quickly rub at the tears; I cannot show how much this hurts me.

"Well, that's a disappointment. The Maximus I met told me all about himself. How his parents named him after the god of the skies, Jupiter Optimus Maximus. How his big sister would yell at him for messing with the nice new telescope she got for her birthday, but she always gave him the last bite of toffee. How she was Chosen but he was left to enter the factories when he was six, to slave away his childhood until forced to upload." He leans in. "How you left him one day and never even looked back."

"Where?" My voice sounds hollow, desperate. "Where is Max?"

Before he can answer, a screeching alarm pierces the air.

CHAPTER FIVE

The screw bursts through the door. Without so much as a blink, Riser slips behind him, knife twinkling at the screw's throat.

"Nicolai, get this Pit Leech off me," the screw growls to the burned man, obviously named Nicolai, who gestures Riser away.

When Riser doesn't budge, Nicolai says, "First lesson outside the pit, Riser. Don't kill the man that's going to help you escape."

Riser's fist tightens on the dagger, but he melts back into the shadows, a disappointed frown tugging his lips.

"Decision time, Everly." Nicolai's voice is brusque with impatience. "Although, if you say no, I will instruct our civilized friend over there"— he nods to Riser— "to *assist* you to the extraction point."

The dizziness comes in waves now. Crashing over me until I am on the verge of drowning and then letting me up for tiny gulps of air. Black bits float across my eyes. I am dangerously close to passing out.

I want to say I am not Everly. I am Maia Graystone. I want to say I am not strong enough to do this. I want to say that it's my mother, not Emperor Laevus, who should be punished. I want to say if the brutish one-eyed boy dares touch me, he'll find himself missing the other eye.

Instead, I lift my chin and whisper, "I'll do it."

For Max.

"Good." Looking relieved, Nicolai nods to a black bag on the floor. "Now, take that and go. It may already be too late."

I watch in disbelief as Nicolai and the table disappear. *A hologram!*

I scan the dark floor for the Interceptor that relayed his image, but the screw grabs my arm and yanks me out the door.

As soon as the chilly outside air hits me, I catch a second wind. Sirens shriek, and spotlights roam the grounds, dark shapes slinking along the fence line. Dogs bark in the distance.

We stick together, scurrying low along the shadowed path in between the houses. My lungs burn with cool, fresh air for the first time in years, and I wonder if I am still inside my dark little tomb, dreaming.

The woods rise up like a dark wall. We claw our way through the trees, branches tearing at our face and arms. The sky twinkles through the treetops, the stars so bright, so wonderful that I get lost in them for a moment.

Someone is shaking me by my collar, and I open my eyes to see the world doing lopsided pirouettes. I anchor myself to Riser's one blue eye. Despite our predicament, he is calm, scanning the trees as he drags me along, my toes digging into the ground with each clumsy step.

I greedily inhale the smells of earth and grass and sea. The sensation is overwhelming, like gulping giant swallows of ice-cold water after being stranded for years in the blistering desert without a drop . . .

The screw is cursing under his breath at me. I must have been drifting off again. I get the feeling he is regretting his deal with Nicolai.

That makes two of us.

The dark ceiling of branches parts to reveal the diamond-encrusted sky. We fan out in the open, a few feet apart, fighting our way through knee-high grass. I can hear the ocean . . . smell it . . . taste it on my tongue . . .

Another jerk rips me from my reverie. *Keep going, Graystone. One foot, now the other—*

A black chasm opens beneath my feet. My hands flap in a desperate attempt at balance. Rocks clatter down the cliff's face and disappear into the frothy waves sixty feet below as my stomach lurches. Just before I tumble over, hands grip my shoulders and rip me backward.

Riser. His chest is warm against my shivering flesh.

Fighting the urge to sink into his heat, I let out a nervous laugh. "Is this a bad time to mention I'm terrified of heights?"

Riser glowers at me.

The screw paces along the cliff's edge, his gaze skimming the woods as the shouts grow louder. "Nicolai isn't paying me enough for this."

Riser taps me on the shoulder and points. Nestled inside the obsidian swells bobs a small, white boat. "We have to swim to it," he says, his voice as emotionless as a piece of wood. "Can you make it?"

"Of course she can't!" the screw snaps. "Look at her. Nicolai didn't say nothing about her being injured." He runs a hand through his close-cropped hair. "They're gonna catch you two Pit Leeches." His hand falls to his stun baton, the slender black metal stick on his hip. "And you're gonna have a lot to say."

Riser cocks his head, watching the screw in a way that chills my blood.

Let's just give up. I think I say this, but maybe I am thinking this. Give up. Go to sleep. Find warmth . . .

Burning in my cheeks. Riser is lightly slapping my face; I must be drifting off again. Pain cuts through the fog inside my head. A peal of laughter works its way out my lips as I realize I can't feel my legs.

"We have to jump," Riser states again. "The water will be freezing. Can you make it?"

What will you do if I say no, Pit Boy? Snuff me so I can't tell them Nicolai's plans?

I think of Max. All those times I had to swim out past the buoys and drag him to shore after he floated out too far. Max was like that. A dreamer, head buried in the clouds.

No, not was. Is. Max is still alive, so get your shit together, Graystone.

I nod to Riser, telling myself I am swimming out to save Max one more time.

A tiny flash wriggles across my periphery. The screw's stun baton spits sparks, a jagged blue line buzzing from its two points. "Over here!"

the screw yells, his gaze rolling to the woods as he pokes the baton at Riser. "I—I found them!"

In the span of a second, Riser sidesteps his reach, snakes behind him, and shoves.

The screw careens over the cliff, his arms windmilling comically. Two seconds later, there's a *thud* against the rocks below. Blue sparks jump from the baton where it hums in the grass.

He didn't even blink.

Our eyes meet. I begin to tremble as Riser appraises me, much like he did the screw.

Am I an asset or a liability?

I nod, never breaking eye contact. With a grim smile, he clamps a strong hand on the back of my neck, guiding me to the very edge. I notice a small gap between the rocks. Riser points to it, says, "Follow me if you want to live," and steps off the cliff.

The blackness swallows him. Counting in my head, I get to eight before the ocean spits him back out.

My turn. Fear invades every cell in my body. I close my eyes. Take a deep breath. "For you, Max."

My plunge isn't nearly as graceful as Riser's; I somehow go horizontal right before slapping the water. Then white-hot pain slams into my body, followed by numbness.

I am underwater. Tumbling. *Sinking.*

Something has wrapped itself around me. Our bodies struggle with the sea and each other. My head breaks the surface, and there's a sweet release as my lungs fill with air. Cool wind stings my face. Waves tug and claw at my dead limbs, jerking me in multiple directions as saltwater burns my throat.

The thrust of hard wood against my back knocks air and seawater from my lungs. My eyes scrape open. The water sloshing against the boat's sides is oily with blood.

My blood.

You probably need that, Graystone.

There's a scrabbling-scraping sound against the side of the boat. Something scurries over the side, clinging to Riser's oar to keep from getting wet. *Bramble!* Riser tries to dislodge the sensor, but I moan for him to stop.

"Please, let him be." Wasted from this small effort, I curl onto my side.

Riser allows Bramble to scamper to higher ground. Bramble tweets angrily at him, shaking a leg in protest, circles twice, then folds into a metal ball.

Our little boat skims the water, ricocheting from wave to wave, spinning and weaving. Each wave snaps my head and hollows my stomach. To steady myself, I look up and find the cliff we just jumped from. Something catches my eye. Despite my daze, it takes only a second for me to recognize the ghostly wig blowing in the wind, cape whipping behind her like a shape-shifting demon.

The Archduchess.

Her cruel eyes follow me as we surrender to the sea. I think a small, brutal smile quivers across her lips, but I could be wrong. I could be.

Riser drops an oar at my feet. "Row."

I glare at him. His drenched gray lag uniform clings to his body, revealing starved, ropy muscles that strain with every thrust of his oar.

An ice-cold wave smashes into the boat. We teeter sideways. I watch the sea snatch the oar from my dead fingers.

A lunatic smile finds my face. "Oops."

Riser shoots me a ruinous glare. His first real emotion. *So Pit Boy is human, after all. A murderous, bloodthirsty one, but I'll take it.*

There's a gentle period of gray nothing. I come to shivering so violently that my jaws clack together and my head rhythmically taps the boat's side. I can see Pit Boy cutting his eyes at me every so often. Finally, he pulls something from the black bag Nicolai gave him and tosses a coarse blanket at my face.

"If you can hear me," Pit Boy says, "wrap yourself in that."

"H-How . . . g-gentlemanly . . . of . . . you," I croak through clacking teeth.

"If you can't do that simple task, there's no point covering you."

"I'm . . . not dying, Pit Boy. Not . . . N-Not here with . . . with you." Somehow I manage to drape the heavy blanket over my legs and left hip. I find a cool blue star in the sky, the Dog Star. Focus on it.

Do not close your eyes, Maia Graystone. Focus. Prove him wrong.

Somewhere inside, I know my mind is wandering because the blood that's supposed to be nourishing my brain is floating in the water around me instead.

I am dying.

My gaze keeps tearing from the sky, to the sharp, melancholy form of Riser. *Like a rabbit, unable to take its eyes off the wolf.* The muscles in his neck strain as he rows even harder.

My eyes close. Just for a second.

"We will be there soon."

I come to with Riser adjusting the blanket to cover my upper body. "Cypher?"

He nods without looking at me; his gaze, I notice, is constantly flickering to the sky, the sea.

"Do you even know what that *is*, Pit Boy?"

"Yes, Digger Girl. The place we need to be."

I start to wonder what Pit Boy knows of the outside. "Do you know about the Everlasting War?"

He looks out to the sea. "The outside was never important."

"My tutor said the factory workers and miners in the south revolted against the wealthy factory Barons in the north."

"Factory?"

I blink at the sky, remembering the Bronzes who passed my window after their shift, shoulders hunched and heads too tired to do anything but stare at their feet. "We make things for the Golds. Baubles, silks, and linens, you know. Stuff." I cut my eyes at him. "But the workers didn't want to make their stuff anymore, and they used the technology available then against the Barons."

"What happened?"

My throat scratches into a rasping chuckle. "The entire world nearly died."

I've seen archived videos of pre-Reformation Act life. Bombs exploding in marketplaces and festivals, cratering entire cities. Hospitals packed with mangled bodies, the hallways smeared with blood. Schools reduced to ash. I shudder, trying to imagine a world with so many bombs, so much uncertainty and death.

Technology is dangerous. The few remaining Fienian Rebels have proved that over and over. Most Bronzes I know agree with the Reformation Act, even if they despise the Emperor.

I wrestle with the water-soaked blanket and manage to shift onto my side. I know Cypher is waiting for me, rising from the waves in all its towering glory, its million solar-powered lights like stars in the sky. A sharp ache fills my chest. It's all I have ever wanted. To see Cypher again.

And now I'm going to die minutes from its shore.

"Will you dump my body in the ocean?" I whisper. I have stopped shivering. *Surely a bad sign.* "It has to be where the water is that impossible shade of blue . . . kind of like your eyes . . . I mean eye."

Riser regards me quietly as I am overcome with hysterical, silent, choking laughter.

But I'm not all crazy. I can't let the Archduchess find my body. She'll dismantle it piece-by-piece, tweezing through organs and bone until she finds what my father so carefully hid.

Another peal of lunatic laughter bursts out of me. "And don't eat me, either, Pit Boy."

Pit Boy pins me with a deadpan stare. Muscles grind in his jaw. Slowly, a jagged smile tears his lips. "Don't worry; you're not my type."

I swallow down more crazy chuckles. A bunch of comedians, we are. Unless, of course, he's being serious.

It's hard to tell.

Riser resumes rowing, his oars depositing cool drops of water onto my face. The sky is smoky gray and laced with thin, stringy clouds. Behind us, near Rhine Island, where the clouds are still bunched like dirty blankets, traceries of bluish light laser the sky. They are searching for us.

We need to hurry.

"I'm not a Pit Leech." At first I think Riser is speaking to me, but he's gazing at the horizon. I get the feeling he's talking to the guard he killed. "I'm not a Pit Leech," he says again. His voice trembles with rage as he murmurs, "Neither was she."

She? For the first time, I wonder if there's someone Riser had to leave behind. Except he said *was*.

So someone he lost.

More silence. His eye keeps flicking to the ocean. "If you were born in the pit," I muse aloud, "how did you learn to swim?"

Riser doesn't take his gaze off the water. "Nicolai gave me a memory."

"With a handheld Uploader?"

No response. Of course he has no idea what that is. He's probably more concerned that the memories are temporary, lasting no more than an hour.

Which means that if the boat capsizes, he drowns.

The wind comes in petulant bursts. It rifles my hair and twirls our boat, bringing with it an oily, burned smell laced with traces of rot and chemicals that sting my nose. A smoky curtain blackens the sky.

Objects begin thumping our boat. Bramble lets out a string of surprised chirps and shifts nervously as the pungent, eye-watering stench saturates the air.

Grunting, I struggle to my elbows and lean over the side. The water as far as the horizon glistens with dead, rotting fish, bits of trash bobbing among the bloated silver bodies.

I follow Riser's gaze to the city. For a second, I can't tell what I'm seeing; the smoke is too thick, mixed with tendrils of white, curling fog.

But then it parts, and I make a horrible wailing sound.

The beautiful shimmering city of my childhood is a charred, mangled landscape, flooded with rancid seawater and clogged with dead fish and decomposing dogs and other putrid, unidentified things. Seagulls, their feathery bodies stained gray from the smoke, swoop and dive through the jagged skeleton of the broken metalwork factories like flies swarming a corpse. The enormous golden body of the pier bridge has snapped and fallen into the ocean.

And the giants fall one by one, to fill the cup of Rot and Ruin. A city laid waste by the feats of man, never to rise again.

Stolen words from my mother's poems. They eddy inside my head like the filth outside our boat. That's my mom for you. I'm dying and there she is, reminding me that she's always right. That she's a super genius who also happens to have lyrical talent.

"Go to hell, Mother," I rasp as my body gives out. Just quits. And I collapse headfirst into the poisonous water of dead things and memories.

CHAPTER SIX

A jagged scream tears through my chest, scaring away my nightmare. Light diffuses softly across the room. Dust motes whirl with my every breath. My neck aches and burns. I stretch my entire body out, curling my toes inside the cool sheets of my old bed. Soft, supple flesh has replaced the wound on my side. Reconstructed. Meaning Fienian Rebels are close; only the Fienians would dare touch the banned nanotech.

Looking around, I see my teal lamp on the nightstand where I left it. The golden stars my mother helped me paint when I was seven whorl across the ceiling—one of the few good memories I have of us together.

"Lights," I rasp. The room fills with cool white light. "Brighter." The light surges, worming through my half-closed eyelids until I command it to a soft glow.

I know I am dreaming because this is the room I grew up in. There's even the crooked crack in the corner and yellow handprints from when Max and I stole my mother's paints and marked the walls.

Except I can't be dreaming. Because when I try to stand, the line attached to my arm dislodges, blood splattering my fresh yellow sheets. The tiny oozing hole in my skin causes *real* pain. The other end of the line dangles from a machine that churns with thick, black-red liquid. It begins to *beep* in alarm as I cross the floor to the large bay window.

Someone has taken all the silk pillows that used to line the window seat. Old ashes smudge the floor where my telescope used to be, along with broken glass and rusty tar-needles. A smoky breeze lazily curls through the starburst hole in the glass, the smell hinting at chaos and death.

Cypher stretches out below me, hauntingly beautiful in its decay, smoldering and brittle and ruined. What the flooding didn't destroy, the fires burned. But I was wrong: Cypher isn't completely lost. Parts of it remain, little enclaves of life in an otherwise dead city, like maggots stirring a corpse to make it seem alive.

Hovels infest the winding streets and bridges, and desperate voices quiver through the rubble. A drone buzzes somewhere close by.

Below my window, I see that my childhood park has been destroyed by fire. Now it's a makeshift market with tents and sluggish rivers of people. No one looks up. I do, though, and discover that today She is about the size of a walnut. Her edges burn orange, her center black, giving her the appearance of an eye.

My heart sinks as I realize my favorite trees have been burned too. They were centuries old and tall enough to scrape my bedroom window during the spring storms. Max and I used to watch them in the evenings, making up stories about nymphs and fairies that lived in their gnarled branches.

One day my mother scolded us for playing near them. She explained that during one of the Fienian uprisings before I was born, our part of the city was Fienian controlled, and they hung the captured Centurions from their boughs. Sometimes entire regiments swung from those beautiful, ancient trees.

There was even a Fienian song about them:
Dandy Apples, Dandy Apples, smell like roses in the fall.
When they're swingin' and they're screamin',
Ain't they the dandiest sight of all?
So maybe it is a good thing about the trees, after all.

I am intoxicated with light. Drunk on its warmth, its fragility, the way it splashes across the walls and smears the floorboards. It is not enough to have a windowfull of it; I must turn on every light in my room.

But the light also forces me to acknowledge how much I have changed. Gathering a breath for courage, I brave the dressing mirror in the corner. The girl inside the steel frame is a wraith draped in papery skin that looks about to rip over her sharp bones. Her skull droops beneath the matted, muddy orange carcass of hair, and two enormous, sunken eyes bulge from shadowy eye-sockets.

She tries to smile, but her cracked lips can't seem to remember how. Most of her teeth are in various states of rot.

Her freckles, though, the perfect coppery pinpricks formed to mimic her parents' favorite constellations, are still there, peeking beneath the muck. Which in a way is ironic, since that was the thing she most hated about herself.

For some dumb reason tears burn the back of my throat. I'm a monster: a slimy thing that yearns to slither back under her rock and hide.

Even though I haven't seen my mother in years, I can imagine what she'd say. *Do you think pity will save you, Maia?* And she's right; one of the first lessons I learned in the pit was that pity is a useless emotion. So I tear myself away from the hideous creature in the glass, swallow back my tears, and begin to assess my surroundings. There is one way to determine if this is a Simulation or real. Something Nicolai wouldn't know about. Crossing the floor, I slide open my nightstand drawer and carefully remove the fake bottom.

The tiny ornate frame of Prince Caspian Laevus sits right where I left it, its glass smudged with my fingerprints and dust. I peer down at the champagne-colored eyes and tousled flaxen hair in the photograph.

Countless nights I stared at that perfect face, trying to decide what he was like as questions swirled inside my head.

Would he like me? Hate my freckles and bright-orange hair? Was he staring at my picture, thousands of miles away, thinking about me too?

I didn't quite understand, then, the significance of being matched to the Crown Prince. Me, a Bronze. I sent him a poem once. We were supposed to write something about ourselves, but I couldn't think of anything worthwhile to say, so I scribbled a hasty twelve-line poem about the stars instead. Two weeks later, a smooth blue envelope with the House Laevus seal—a Sphinx—arrived at my house, carried thousands of miles by Royal messenger.

Now, my hands tremble as I set the frame face down and fish out the blue envelope. The crude charcoal sketch still rests inside, obviously drawn from the picture he had of me, my lips teetering on the mysterious smile I get from my father. He hadn't changed my nose to better fit my face, which I liked. And every freckle is accounted for. But there is only half my face against a charcoal black background. And meticulously engraved where the other half of my face should be are perfectly rendered constellations to match my freckles.

My throat burns. What did they tell you, Prince? That I was dead? A traitor's daughter? That there had been a mistake with our matching? My lips tremble as I imagine his relief at not having to marry the ugly Bronze girl from a Diamond City.

Gouging at my watery eyes with my knuckles, I move on to the large book at the bottom. The old leather tome is heavy, and my knurled fingers have trouble turning the pages, but I don't really need to. I know every inch of these pages. My mother's slanted, scribbled inscription. The beautiful illustrations gilded in gold.

It's a book of stories about the gods. My mother gave it to me on my seventh birthday, right before she left for good. I can't even imagine how much it cost her on the black market; as far as I knew, all the old Pre-Reformation Act books had been destroyed, and only Golds were wealthy enough to own sanctioned texts—not that my little book is even close to sanctioned.

The book falls open to the page I used to read the most. My eyes flit past Aphrodite to the two doves resting on her shoulders. Those same two doves make up the Sigil for House Lockhart, the Gold House my mother hails from.

My body sags. There's no denying Nicolai brought me to my childhood home. An incredibly smart or incredibly stupid decision.

I can't decide which.

Considering the Archduchess and her Centurions are searching for you two cities over, a voice buzzes in my head, *I would go with incredibly smart.*

The left side of my brain tingles as if a miniscule pulsing electrode is imbedded inside my skull. *Microplant.* Even without the robotic timbre of the electro-larynx, I recognize Nicolai's arrogant, refined tone.

The one and only, the voice confirms. Its smugness dissipates any doubts I had left.

I find the mirror and part my hair just above the left temple, rubbing away the grime to expose a fresh, faint-red line no longer than an inch above the old Microplant scar. Nicolai has imbedded a new Microplant into my brain that allows us to communicate.

Correct again, Nicolai says. *It was a risk, given your condition, but entirely worth it. Now I know just how broken you are.*

I'm not broken. But saying it doesn't make me believe it.

Your nightmares say otherwise.

You're sick. You probably get off on this. To drive home my point, I imagine me violently punching what's left of his face.

I can't hear him laughing, but I can *feel* it.

Why did you bring me here? I mentally shout, shaking my head in an effort to dislodge the itching/crawling feeling his presence creates inside my brain.

The Archduchess, my dear, is cunning, but she lacks creativity. She knows this is the last place you would go—but she fails to understand that reasoning makes her predictable. By the time she searches here, we will be gone.

I get the feeling there's more behind his reasoning. That he wants me to remember what happened here the night my father died. But all I can think about is the Archduchess tracking me down. *Promise me she won't find me, Nicolai. Please.*

Sorry, I don't do promises. But the plan is sound.

"No, it's stupid," I say aloud, testing if the Microplant can pick up spoken voice as well.

Time will tell, Everly. There's a long pause. *Rest up. Tonight is your big transformation.*

Can't wait. Hopefully my sarcasm translates.

I stare into the mirror, ignoring the pitiful creature staring back.

"Connect me," says the creature.

My heart pounds as I wait for the interface beneath the mirror's surface to respond, connecting me to Royalist sanctioned news. Instead, fuzzy black-and-white dots snow across the glass. It turns black, and the words *No Connection* pulse across the surface. That's when I notice the continuous newsfeed running across the bottom.

Do not gather in groups larger than ten. Do not go out during Shadow Fall or after dark.

More edicts scroll across, but I look away. There is no more news. No way to learn what is happening in the world. Not that we ever got anything other than what the Emperor wanted to spoon-feed us. I know because my mother headed the propaganda division.

The bathroom is exactly as Max and I left it. Sunbeams gush from the skylight above. A red toothbrush peeks from a cup on the counter. Wind-up action figures line the counter in full-scale assault, and Ms. Jane, my favorite doll, slumps in the corner, a key-shaped dial protruding from her back.

My mother was a devout Royalist from the esteemed Gold House

Lockhart, controller of the west coast shipping lines. Their massive steamships ferried the Royalists' precious goods from the Diamond City factories to the north.

My mother made sure that most of our toys were Reformation Act approved, lacking any form of technology. Most prewar items had been systematically destroyed in the Great Purge anyway, right after the Reformation Act came to pass.

I never broke the rules. I wanted to make my mother proud. *See, Mother*, I wanted to say. *I can be good.*

Max, on the other hand, traded his rations for any pre-Reformation Act toy he could get his grubby little hands on. *The imp!* And somehow he never got in trouble. They felt sorry for him. Soon he would have to enter the factories.

My father knew from experience how Max would suffer. My father worked the forges until age twelve, when his uncommon brilliance earned him a coveted serving position on a Gold estate and eventually a Gold education. When Max asked what it would be like down there, my father's eyes went all distant and he changed the subject.

So Max got away with being Max while I had to be perfect, had to fight for every smile, every fleeting look of praise my mother afforded me. Sometimes being Chosen wasn't all it was cracked up to be.

I lean against the counter, close my eyes for a moment. If not for the red and black Fienian graffiti scrawled across the faded ocean-blue walls, I can almost pretend I am eight again, perched on the counter, Max yelling behind the door for me to hurry up, steam from the hot bath filming the mirror as I trace the constellations in the condensation.

Now the words *Death to The Chosen* and *Royalists Blow* drip down the mirror instead. The Fienian symbol, a scorpion wrapped around a dying phoenix, covers the ceiling.

I open my book to the last chapter titled *Bestiary Mythology*, turning the pages until the same enormous red scorpion appears. A drop of poison glistens from its tail barb. I scan the caption below: *In his hubris, Orion swore to kill all the beasts of this world, but Gaia, goddess of the earth, sent the Scorpion to protect them, and it felled Orion with one mighty blow.*

The graffiti reminds me that everything's different now. Even me. *Especially* me.

"I hate this place," I say to the monstrous girl in the mirror. Her face twists into a scowl.

Apparently she agrees.

I put away my forbidden book. Like so many countless mornings before, I head downstairs. At the landing, my gaze stops on the wine-colored stain warping the wood and then follows the fingers of old blood down the steps.

The breath inside my chest seems to disappear.

Breathe. It's the girl from the mirror, the one who ate rats and carved sticks meant to impale people and counted rocks to keep from going insane.

She counts to three. Whispers the same words she chanted to me in the darkness.

Inhale. Exhale. Survive.

The kitchen is small but comfortable, designed especially to make use of the minimal space. A slant of golden light sparkles and stretches across the shiny cupboards. I want to touch it. No, I want to paint it, to possess it somehow. Make it last forever.

My gaze falls to the corner. *Max, Dad?* Their names die in my chest as Riser's one eye locks onto mine. He's scrubbed clean. Razor-edged jaw shaved smooth. Dark, wavy, shoulder-length hair shiny and freshly washed, pulled neatly back. Smartly tailored gray trousers and a charcoal vest hang off the sharp angles of his body.

I frown. This is a dangerous lie, like dressing a crocodile in sheepskin.

After what feels like a brief assessment—Riser's eye roams from my feet to my head, systematically cataloguing my body—Riser turns back to watch the man hunched over the range. The one who I thought might be my dad.

Of course he is nothing like my father. Barrel-chested, short, with sandy-gray hair shaved at the sides and twined into a long braid. Stripes mark his eyebrows, and stubble shadows his blunt, square jaw. He wears a partially undone, worn leather vest, with coarse gray hair peeking through. Two crude, black noose tattoos adorn each burley shoulder.

Mercs. Nicolai hired Mercenaries. Disgraced ex-Centurions with no master except currency.

The Merc turns and flashes a greasy smile, revealing more than a few non-sanctioned gold teeth. Brown tar-stains muddy the rest. "Lady." He tips his ill-fitted brown bowler hat, and the neat half-inch scar above his eyebrow where he removed his Centurion Microplant flashes, erasing any doubts I had left about his shadowy profession. "Name's Brogue."

I cross my arms, scanning his pockets for pilfered silverware or anything else a Merc might find worthy of stealing. "Where's Bramble?"

Brogue lifts a hoary eyebrow in question.

"The machine that was with me."

"Ah! The sensor." He nods toward the basement. "A bit waterlogged at the moment, but nothing I can't fix."

I jut out my chin. "I want him back."

"Okay. But first some grub, yeah?"

The smell from the food hits me like a train. My stomach tightens, and my gaze fastens to the scrambled eggs slowly forming in the pan. Their vivid yellow color and rubbery texture tells me they are synthetic, but that does nothing to dampen my hunger.

Brogue scrapes the mixture with a spatula and folds the lumpy blob over, sprinkling in a few bits of something brown. His movements are smooth and exact, not jittery like most twitchers. But the telltale almond aroma of tar clings to his skin like cologne.

When Brogue turns around to dole out the eggs onto the two green plates on the counter, both Riser and I flank his back, guarding the food.

Old habits die hard.

Brogue ducks beneath us and manages to toss a bit onto the first plate before Riser snags it and wolfs the eggs down, steaming hot.

Chuckling, Brogue holds up a fork. "Ever seen one of these, boy?"

Riser stares through him. I'm pretty sure handing Riser a pronged utensil is a bad idea.

Brogue shrugs and sets the fork down. "Well, at least chew before you swallow. There's enough for everyone."

I can't seem to help myself. The eggs barely hit my plate before they are burning their way down my throat.

Sighing, Brogue slaps the rest of the eggs onto my and Riser's plates. I inhale the food so fast I can't even taste it. A tiny glob falls onto the floor, and Riser and I both drop, scuffling for the morsel

Riser wins. He clamps his fluffy yellow prize between his dirty thumb and forefinger and holds it up.

One deep-blue eye assesses me over his fingertips. I can't read his expression. It's as if his face is a shield guarding the contents inside.

The idea that I cannot break through his walls and access his intentions is maddening.

Sighing, he offers the bite to me. *Is there a slight curve to his lips? Maybe.*

My fingers itch to take it. My tongue waters in anticipation. And yet I hate him for his unexpectedly kind gesture. He thinks he can trick me into letting my guard down, but he doesn't know that I remember him.

"Take it," Riser orders. His eyebrows furrow together as an impatient breath hisses from his parted lips. Obviously this is new to him. Sharing. And the vulnerability that comes with it.

"No," I growl, clenching my fist to keep from giving in. I make my face flat and unreadable. He cannot see my desperation.

"You need it more than me. *Take it.*"

It is an order. Refuse and I am establishing my position while questioning his. Tension thickens the air until it feels as if electricity skips across my skin.

I study his one eye, thinking how my mother would have loved trying to capture it on canvas. The blue so deep and rich the shadows turn it inky-black. She collected broken things, my mother. She found them interesting, a challenge.

But I'm pretty sure Riser is too broken, even for her.

"I'd rather starve." I leave him there still holding his offering.

Brogue turns away when I pass, but not before I spot the pity in his eyes. Now that my stomach is full, I am mad at myself for acting so desperate before.

It won't happen again.

"What happened to the city?" I ask, pausing by the window.

Brogue follows my gaze. "Your sector didn't upload when they was supposed to, and the Emperor stripped their rations. Then the bitch in the sky sent tsunamis to batter the coast, destroying the factories. She warmed the waters till the fish died. Made the crops stop growing too. So they rioted." He rubs a thick finger over his jaw. "But the drones stopped that madness quick as a Fienian uprising, they did."

My concentration is broken by a change of some sort. Something that I can't quite pinpoint but my senses pick up. A dark shadow spills from the window, creeps across the kitchen, unspooling to fill the corners.

Shadow Fall. Brogue crosses to the door and creaks it open, then disappears. I follow.

The door barely cracks before Brogue is pushing me back. "Sorry, girl. We're in lockdown during Shadow Fall. Arm the alarm, and don't let anyone in until you see the sun again. Even us."

There are two more Mercs posted on the doorstep. A young woman around my age, red hair French-braided to her lower back, and a baby-faced young man. Although they don't turn to acknowledge me, the pit has taught me that their tense shoulders and fidgety hands mean they are afraid. *Scared Mercs. That's a new one.*

The door shuts in my face.

Seconds after I set the alarm, there's a droning sigh and the power shuts off. The alarm beeps, goes silent.

"The sun," I mutter. Solar energy is useless without it, although there should be enough stored to keep working for a few more hours.

The shadow murk drapes my bedroom in darkness. I stand in the middle of the dim room, trying to hold my food down as my weak stomach tries to force it back up. Noises draw me to the window. Loud banging like metal pipes being slammed against brick reverberates the walls. Glass shatters somewhere close. Shouts erupt, followed by the sound of scuffling.

The floorboard creaks behind me. Already on edge, I whip around to see Riser, shadows layering his face and body. He looks completely at home in the shadow murk.

"What are you doing?" I say, taking a step back. "Get out!"

I say this on instinct just like I have to Max a million times before. Immediately I know that Riser will see this as a challenge.

"If I don't?" The pitch-black eyebrow over his good eye arches. His voice is soft, curious. *Another test.*

"Then I will *make* you."

"All the blood you lost yesterday . . ." His head cocks sideways, a half-smile on his face. "I'd hate to take more."

"Would you? Because I'm beginning to wonder."

We face off in a staring contest. Finally, I throw up my hands. "Fine! Stay. But this isn't the pit. You have to knock before you come into someone's room."

"This is where you lived before?" He somehow inches closer without appearing to move.

"Yes. This is my house—or was."

Looking around, he pauses on the stars glowing above my bed. In the dim light, it's hard to read the fleeting emotions that soften his face and make him momentarily seem to forget about me.

"It's nothing," I say. "A stupid paint that fluoresces in the dark."

"Why paint them?" Riser frowns at the idea. "You can see them from your window."

I stare up, remembering the silky feel of the iridescent paint as it glided over the ceiling. The glimmery drops that freckled my mom's skin and hair. Her rare, carefree laughter as I tried to wipe the spilled paint from my cheek, smudging it. "Because I was a kid, okay?" My voice cracks with anger. "A dumb kid who didn't understand anything."

I can't look at the fake stars anymore. Can't sit in the fake room that belonged to the dead girl for one second longer. But I don't know where else to go. I feel like I'm in prison all over again, except this time the walls are invisible.

Tiptoeing around the broken glass, I carefully pop the windowsill and lift. It catches halfway, but the gap is wide enough I can slide out headfirst and crabwalk along the eaves. It takes only a few seconds for Riser to follow; he doesn't make a sound as he slinks across the tile, perching a few feet from me.

The solar tiles crunch beneath my bare feet. Remnants of the old world when everything ran on the sun, they must be at least fifty years old. That explains the shortage of power.

An eerie shade of green haunts the skyline, flickering orange here and there where the city burns. The faraway shriek of drones stirs the air. Crowning the horizon is the enormous wall that separates our Diamond City from the Royalist cities beyond. A few dark spires peek from the other side.

Hanging from the divider are corpses, the dark cloaks of the Royalist guards flapping in the breeze. Most of the Royalist cities this far south will have been evacuated by now. The Silvers to the mountains, the Golds to Hyperion.

And we're left here in the shadow of Pandora.

I find Her nestled between the clouds, seeping red fire. A shiver wriggles down my spine. If I look close enough, I can almost see the dusty haze encircling Her: the debris field. Even if the Royal astronomers are right and Pandora doesn't hit directly, the chunks of rock shadowing Her will take out entire cities, smashing into oceans and kicking up deadly clouds of dust that will enshroud the world.

I look down. Shadow Fall has cleared the market, but tent fires still smolder, hanging metal pots *clang* in the wind, and feral dogs sniff out what the occupants so abruptly left behind.

"It wasn't always like this," I say to Riser, who's watching the feral dogs like he wants to spring from the rooftop and join them. For some reason it's important he knows beautiful things exist outside the pit.

While Riser studies the ruined city, I study him. Wind ruffles his dark, wavy hair back, revealing soot-colored eyebrows and eyelashes and knife-edged cheekbones that trap deep shadows. In this strange light, the scars crisscrossing his face are silvery-white. Except for the gash over his eye, the scars are fine and delicate, marking nearly every inch of his exposed flesh.

"Brogue's a twitcher just like the screws," Riser remarks from the corner of his mouth. He probably knows I've been studying him, just like he knows about Brogue. Pit Boy misses *nothing*.

"Just figured that out?" I immediately regret my childish tone, but I can't stand him thinking he knows more than me.

Riser slowly turns to face me, his expression unreadable. "I'm not the enemy, Everly."

I feel something inside me soften. Riser would make a strong ally. And I don't hate him, not exactly. In fact, right now he's about the closest thing to a friend I've had in years. But I can't forget that he was one of them.

No, *is* one of them. He helped capture me and tie me up. Who knows the horrors I would have suffered if I hadn't broken free and escaped?

No, Pit Boy can't be trusted.

"Together," Riser urges, "you'd have a better chance at saving Max."

I grind my jaw. It's like he's slowly peeling away at me. "Please, don't say his name."

"What happened to him?"

"He was hungry." My voice catches. "I had to. I had to leave to get food. I told him I was coming back, but then the Centurions caught me stealing at the market and . . ." The pity in his eyes makes me realize how foolish I am for letting Pit Boy see my weakness, something he'll undoubtedly use against me. Hands clenched in my lap, I swallow the tears burning my throat. "Forget it. If I wanted to discuss my feelings, the last person I'd do it with is some one-eyed freak who's just as likely to kill me in my sleep as care."

"You're wrong." One side of his mouth quirks. "I prefer to snuff people when they're awake."

Is he making a joke? I cross my arms. "Okay, let me make this clear. I find you deplorable, a reminder of the pit and everything it stands for. So cut the caring act. We're partners because we have to be, but we're not friends."

Part of me is sorry for saying it, but the other part is relieved. Now he's clear that I know who he really is so he can stop pretending otherwise.

The muscle in his jaw flickers as he looks away. Perhaps he's glad to be resolved of the normal civilities expected between two people. After all, neither of us excels at it.

I suddenly realize what's been bothering me about him. Although just as ruthless, he's different than Ripper and Rafe. "Why don't you talk like the others?"

His shoulders tense. "I was born to a prisoner in the upper levels of Rhine."

"What happened?"

He has been staring at the sky, but now his head swivels my direction. "Discussing our feelings now, are we, Digger Girl?"

"No," I say, rolling my eyes. "Just thinking out loud."

He resumes gazing at the asteroid. Almost as if he's staring Her down, showing Her he's not afraid.

I nod to my right. "Do you see the red Xs on the houses over there?"

Riser follows my gaze.

"It means there are Sleepers inside, people already uploaded to Caskets."

A small furrow splits his forehead. "Caskets?"

"Cryo-machines that can keep bodies in a hibernating state for years while your mind experiences everything your Avatar does. Once inside them, you connect the same way we are to Nicolai, through a Microplant, only you get to choose from a pool of Avatars." I struggle to explain the Chosen. "Special people with special privileges, created to carry on the human race."

"Why would you want do that?"

I let out a breath. "Look up. See that thing in the sky? She's going to pass right by us, and she's going to do a lot of damage. It will take years for the earth to be habitable again.

"The Emperor and his court of Golds and Chosen will be safe in their palace in the sky. The Silvers get Caskets located deep inside the earth so they'll be protected. But the rest of us have to upload above ground and take our chances."

"And people have actually started . . . uploading?"

"The Royalists sold it like this once-in-a-lifetime experience. Taste the Chosen's food." My voice deepens to mimic the announcer from the propaganda videos. "Wear their sumptuous clothing and experience all the fineries court life has to offer. And don't forget the courtly intrigues." I let out an angry sigh. "The populace watched the Chosen grow up. They're beloved figures from famous Houses. Our *saviors*."

Riser tears his gaze from the sky. "And if we're frozen in our Caskets, we can't cause trouble."

"Exactly. And when they come back down from Hyperion here we'll be, preserved and ready to work their factories again." Bitterness taints my voice. "Except, as you can see, not everyone wants to go to sleep. Even with the rations dried up and the water shut off, they refuse. That's what the Shadow Trials are for. To entice the rebellious populace to comply."

"And the ones that still refuse to upload?"

"I don't know." It's a lie, of course. I do know. But I wish I didn't.

Riser goes dead still, his head cocked slightly, my first indication that something is wrong. That's when I notice that the dogs have scattered.

To the right in the woods behind the curving row of residences, small shadows trickle from the trees. Young kids it looks like, ranging from seven-years-old to fourteen, a group too large to count, carrying sharpened-sticks and pipes.

They converge on a building seemingly at random, kicking and clawing at the door. A boy no older than nine whacks the head off a garden statue. They whoop as it tumbles down the path.

They smash a window. One, then two, and finally the entire group snakes through the broken glass. After a minute, a solitary scream erupts and then dies. Two more screams shred the air. These take much longer to subside.

They are killing the Sleepers. I imagine the family resting inside their row of Caskets. They believed the Royalists when they promised to protect them. To give them a better life.

I turn my head and cover my ears as more shadows dart from the trees and scurry through the streets, grateful for Brogue and the other Mercs guarding our door.

All at once, the shadows scatter as a shrill whistle stabs the air, followed by the sound of faint buzzing.

At first, in the hazy shadow murk, the drones look like large birds. But the way they dart and zigzag gives them away. Bramble and Duchess are crude versions of the drones watching us, except the sensors in the pit were used mainly for gathering information.

These drones aren't here to gather anything. They're here to enforce the edicts.

My breath catches as they rotate in place ten feet in front of us. A red laser serrates the darkness, and I blink against its angry light. More bizarre noises as the machines seem to communicate and my heart threatens to explode. *The Archduchess. What if the drones recognize me? What if she can see me right now? I can't let her find me. I can't—*

My breath releases as they zip to the street so fast I can't see them move. I catch sight of them gliding low through the alleyways. A few seconds later, an explosion rocks the buildings, followed by the sound of childish screams of pain. More explosions. More screams.

And then no more screams.

Feeling relieved and strangely empty, I stand up to go inside.

Riser, who's watching it all with detached curiosity, rises with me. "They came too late to protect the Sleepers."

I hear myself laugh, but it is a hollow, sick sound. "They don't care about protecting us. Only making sure we cannot group together. Because that would be dangerous for *them.*"

Riser peers down into churning smoke. "Just like the pit, then. Only more scenic."

I've decided Riser needs to work on his humor.

CHAPTER SEVEN

A gazillion and one days. That's how long it's been since I've had a bath. After putting my request in to Brogue, the small tub in my old bathroom is miraculously shimmering with water. It's even warm as if it's been heated over a fire. Brogue insisted I use the noxious delousing powder under the cabinet first—I happily complied—so I'm covered in a fine layer of white poison dust.

The uniform peels from my body and makes a slopping noise on the floor. Shadow Fall is over, and muted light slips through the skylight and refracts in the tiny waves my finger stirs up.

My legs wobble as I step into the now lukewarm water. I sink to the bottom. Tiny bubbles escape my nose as I watch all the ugly remnants from the last seven years leave my body.

Lungs burning, I rise and come face-to-face with Pit Boy.

I glare at him. "You really have to work on the knocking thing."

Despite the fact that I'm indecent, his attention never falls from my face. I almost wish it would, just to give me a break from the intensity of his focus.

"I only get a few more hours to be the 'one-eyed freak' from the pit. Might as well take advantage." He doesn't dare crack a smile, so it's hard to tell if he's joking or serious.

"Don't worry. In my heart, that's exactly who you'll always be."

His words remind me that soon we'll be reconstructed using forbidden nanotech. But it won't just be our flesh they'll reengineer. It will be our brains, too.

I don't foresee my rewiring being too complicated, but Riser needs to upload almost twenty years of false memories. That will be tricky and time-consuming.

And time is the one thing we don't have.

Riser flicks his gaze to the mirror. He lifts a hand, touches the patch of mottled flesh where his eye should be.

"How did it happen?" I ask.

"Careful, my lady." His gaze settles on my face. "You're beginning to sound like you care."

I roll my eyes. "And I thought *I* was lacking in conversational skills."

He focuses his attention on the graffiti sprayed across the mirror.

"It's written language," I blurt, even though all I want to do is end the conversation so Pit Boy can leave. His presence unnerves me more than the other Pit Leeches ever could. "It's how we communicate."

"I know what it is." He examines his jagged thumbnail. "I just . . . can't read it."

"It's just stuff about the Chosen. You know, insults." The populace is finicky. As much as they love watching the Chosen with their petty intrigues and court life, they would be just as happy to see their heads on a pike.

"Chosen?"

Time to explain what you are, Everly, Nicolai's voice grates inside my head. Riser's eyes flutter just enough that I know he's heard Nicolai's voice too.

You do it, I think, watching Riser's reaction. But his face remains emotionless; either he's a good actor or only Nicolai can hear my response.

"The Royalist astronomers discovered the asteroid twenty-one years ago," I begin. "It's actually a slow moving planet called an earth-crosser, meaning its orbit and ours intersect every twenty-thousand years. Usually it's too far away to affect us, but this time it will pass close enough to wreak havoc and make the earth uninhabitable for years." I stir the water with my big toe. "Before I was born, the

Emperor decided that creating a population of genetically superior humans would be a great idea, you know, just in case the Caskets don't work or the asteroid does more damage than predicted."

Riser's hyper-focused gaze bores through me. "You're one of them?"

"Yes." I run my hand through the filthy water. "But my father's a Bronze, so even though my mother comes from a Gold House, the Emperor only allowed them one Chosen instead of the customary twins. So it's just me . . . not Max."

"What makes being Chosen so special?"

"I don't know . . ." I bite my lip, trying to remember everything my parents told me. "My genes are perfect, I guess."

For some reason, talking about my body makes me remember that I am naked in a room with a boy. As if reading my mind, Riser slowly lets his gaze fall, his expression both curious and unapologetic as he takes me *all* in, his thoughts cryptic.

"What are you staring at?" I blurt, smashing my breasts beneath my hands. Not like there's much there *to* cover. "Haven't you seen a naked girl before?"

A smile twitches his lips. "Not one that's *genetically flawless.*"

"It doesn't work that way! You can't just look at us and tell. We look like everyone else—"

"No." Riser shakes his head, a dark swath of hair covering his damaged eye. "You don't. Whatever you are."

"You must be happy . . . about our reconstruction, I mean," I mumble, trying desperately to change the subject. "They'll fix your eye . . . and . . . and all those horrible scars."

I freeze as he slides off the counter, unable to look away as he hooks one finger beneath his shirt and lifts.

Scars ravage his anemic body in varying shades of red and silver and white. Some deep and pitted like the craters of a far-away planet, others smooth and neat. One particular nasty scar carves down his shoulder, tunneling across his chest and stomach. A fresh red wound nestles just below his throat.

He carefully touches the long ugly one. "I'm not ashamed for surviving."

"How could you want to keep them?"

He abruptly kneels beside the bath, his eyes holding mine, and parts the water with his hand. My breath catches as his elbow brushes the inside of my knee.

"Don't," I gasp, but he seems to be looking through me at something I can't see. I want to kick him; I want to scream.

His breathing is shallow and rough as his hand emerges cupping the soap. His fingers are long and deft, perfect half-moons adorning his otherwise ruined fingernails. Every muscle beneath his damaged flesh seems to spring and strain, trapping shadows.

His breath cools my wet cheeks. "Let me."

But he's not really asking. Rubbing the soap into a rich lather, his fingers slide gently through my tangled nest of hair, separating the gore of seven years from my scalp.

Our eyes meet. I'm startled by the agony in Pit Boy's one haunted eye.

Somehow I find my voice. "Why are you doing this?"

"Oh . . . I'm . . . I don't . . . Sorry." As if breaking out of a trance, Riser jerks his hand away and stands. Water bleeds from his fingertips. "The, uh, guards forced my mom to do manual labor until she couldn't stand up." His hands clump into fists. "Eventually, she broke, so I helped take care of her. Feed her the little bit of food they gave us. Sometimes wash her hair."

Nicolai's words taunt me. "And you think I'm broken too?"

"No." But he's frowning.

Somewhere deep down, the girl from the pit understands that this interaction, whatever it is, is meant to break me. Break open the barriers between us, the ones that one day may save my life.

Riser takes a faded-yellow towel from the counter and dries his hands. "I remember when you first came to the pit." Even in motion there is stillness to him. "We called you Digger Girl because you hid in the tunnels."

I pause my feeble attempts at smoothing my hair. "Neat. I bet that came in handy when you talked about me. Like, hey, there's Digger Girl; let's sneak up on her while she sleeps and gut her."

He shrugs, any intimacy from his strange gesture earlier gone. "I didn't make the rules."

"But you chose to play by them."

"No. There is no choice but survival, Everly."

"Well I *chose* something different."

"You hid," he amends.

I straighten, sending water sloshing over the tub. "There are ways other than violence to respond to conflict."

"No, Digger Girl, there aren't." He goes silent for a moment. "I had a friend in the pit—or as close to one as you can have there. Karl wasn't like the others. He had these rats that he fed and they followed him everywhere, begging on their hind legs and doing little tricks. Pretty soon there were hundreds of them. Too many to feed." Our eyes meet, but my stare keeps gravitating toward his disfigurement. If he notices, he doesn't say anything. "One morning I found Karl—or at least what was left of him. The rats had gotten to him while he slept."

I swallow down my horror. "Oh . . . I'm sorry."

"I'm not." His expression hardens. "Karl taught me two important lessons. First, caring for someone other than yourself makes you weak." For some reason he looks away from me as he says this. "Second, only the savage survive. The rats knew that, but he didn't."

I stare at Riser. And maybe it's the water, but I suddenly remember that I still don't know how I survived after falling out of the boat. "Yesterday in the water, did you jump in to save me? Even though you couldn't swim?"

He rises to leave. "The water was waist deep. I simply fished you out. I'm a lot of things, Digger Girl, but a hero isn't one of them."

I'm sitting on my bed, staring into the darkness, when Biotech arrives. A small candle flickers on the dresser. The last hour of sunlight has left me with enough solar power I can use my lamp if I want to, but I have this desperate need to conserve it.

Downstairs I can hear the two Biotechs talking with Brogue. Teenagers—a girl and a boy. The girl is agitated, her voice high and jumpy as she persistently fends off Brogue's offers of food. Smart, considering I checked the pantry earlier and there was nothing near edible.

Nicolai must be paying them a hefty sum because the penalty for reconstructing someone is severe. The Reconstructor machines, I'm guessing, are downstairs in the basement. They would need close proximity to a generator and to be easily hid if we are searched.

I need to get up and find something to eat. But the feeling that in the next hour I will be made into someone else paralyzes me. Undoubtedly my freckles and nose and bright orange hair will be altered—most parents followed regulations and chose the most aesthetically pleasing attributes for their children. My divergent looks will make me stand out when I desperately need to blend in.

But it's more than that. Once the reconstruction is complete, the girl who looks like her father and loves the stars will be gone for good. And as much as I long to forget her, I also long to salvage a small bit of her. Her crooked teeth or her dry humor. Just a bit, like a child keeping a patch of fabric from a once precious teddy bear.

They will be coming to fetch me soon. I hop off my bed, intending to go downstairs, but my attention's drawn to Max's partially open door. Blue and red strobe lights pulse from the room, along with the sound of Max's favorite electric violin remixes. It's as if Riser has turned on every single anti-Reformation Act toy Max owned.

I nudge open the door. The music is so loud it reverberates inside my chest. *Who does Riser think he is, listening to Max's music, playing with his stuff?*

Riser has taken the navy comforter and matching blue sheets off Max's bed and made a twisted nest on the floor. Max's highly prized strobe cube pulses, disjointing my movement. The airplane model I secretly got Max for his fourth birthday—blatantly anti-Reformation—*whirs* in the air, diving and ducking, its propeller creating a slight wind.

It takes a moment to spot Riser; he's crouched, his entire body rigid like a cat about to pounce on a mouse, fixated on something beneath him—Cleo's food dispenser. He's too engrossed in whatever he's doing to notice me.

In the pit, this small act of carelessness would have already gotten him killed. But I don't want to kill him. At least, not *yet.* I want to study him without his highly perceptive gaze. To ferret out his weaknesses so when the time comes I can use it against him.

His wavy hair has already escaped its ribbon and fallen to the side, eclipsing part of his face. His lips, at least half of them, are pressed together in a thin line of concentration. I watch as he cautiously waves a finger at the bottom of the dispenser and it whirs, spitting out a dollop of cat food.

Riser flinches at the noise. By now the small brown balls form a spreading mountain on the floor. Pinching one mud-colored bit, Riser examines it, sniffs it, and then places it on his tongue.

Gross. Although just days ago I would have killed for that tiny morsel.

Riser straightens, pocketing some for later, and acknowledges my presence with an infernal look. Maybe he knew I was here all along and *chose* to ignore me. This infuriates me.

Next time you won't hear me arrive, Pit Boy.

"Max." Riser points to the picture of Max on the nightstand.

I concede with a look meant to freeze Riser's soul. "Stop touching his stuff."

"This thing." Impervious to my glare, he nudges the cat food dispenser with his foot, his normally detached voice filled with awe. "It gives you food. Want some?"

"All yours, Pit Boy."

Grinding the cat food beneath his teeth, he shrugs.

"Someone brought me food when I was in the tunnel. Scraps from the drop." I bite my lip. "Why would they do that? Help me?"

Blue lights pulse across his cheeks and paint shadows in his eyeless socket. A knot twinges in his jaw. "They wouldn't. That would be weak and stupid."

Before I can respond, his interest flickers to the strobe cube whirling across the floor. He picks it up and presses a green square. An image projects onto the wall. It's the park by my house. Max tromps through a carpet of orange and yellow leaves, his shaggy blond hair nearly to his shoulders—meaning my mother was already gone.

"There's Max being *Max*," an annoyed girl complains through the speakers. It takes a second to realize it's my voice.

Max is sword fighting an imaginary foe, jumping and stabbing the air.

"Gabriel!" Max calls. He holds the plastic sword out in unspoken challenge.

I feel a surge of raw emotion as a man enters from the right. Although he wears the traditional Centurion garb—black tailcoat and brown leather riding boots—the golden phoenix emblem on his shoulder indicates he's higher ranking.

Whipping out an imaginary sword, Gabriel engages Max in a duel that ends with Max stabbing his gut and the man making an elaborate fall to his death. The clip stops just as Max pounces on the Centurion and they go tumbling through the leaves.

"Turn it off," I order, even though it's now only a blank white projection splashed across the wall.

Riser sets the cube back on the bed, and the device powers down.

You were supposed to protect us, Gabriel.

Of all the betrayals, even my mother's, our bodyguard's may have been the worst of all. By then, the Fienian Rebels had already begun targeting Chosen children, so they gave us Gold Cloaks to keep us safe.

Gabriel was with Max and me always. Gabriel held my hand on the way to the park and didn't tell my parents the time I spent part of our rations on toffee for Max. When the boy across the street started teasing me, Gabriel taught me how to throw a right hook.

I trusted him with my life—right up until the moment he helped the Centurions kill my father.

"Maia, are you okay?" Riser asks, and I'm thrust back into the now. He reaches a hand out almost as if to comfort me, but then his gaze flits behind me.

I turn to see Brogue coming up the stairs. He pauses on the landing just as the airplane dive-bombs his head. Clearly not a man to duck, it smacks his forehead with a dull thump.

He eyes the injured airplane wobbling at his feet. His focus dances from me to Riser to the cat food scattered across the floor. The sardonic grin Brogue flashes hints that he thinks we are both more than a smidgen mad.

"Biotech's here, little ducklings," he says in a gruff, gravelly voice. "Time to become swans."

CHAPTER EIGHT

The only way to the basement is by elevator, another pre-Reformation Act invention. I've been down there exactly once: the night my father was killed.

I find the four bricks in the wall behind the stairs and push them. *First. Third. Fourth. Second.* The bricks yawn open, and lights flicker in the small steel rectangle hidden behind the wall. The elevator is a tight squeeze for two, which means all five of us are crammed elbow to elbow. Someone's breath—Riser's, by the cat food aroma—warms the back of my neck.

The Biotech and his assistant are plastered against the far wall. Slight and waifish, they sport crimson-streaked hair, smudged eyeliner, and countless red tattoos. Matching silver spike implants spiral over their cheeks, eyebrows, necks, and down their forearms and fingers.

It's obvious they are close, maybe even siblings. And it's just as obvious they are Fienian Rebels. Only a Rebel would dress this way and use the forbidden color red, the color of House Croft.

Confirming my suspicions, the girl turns her half-shaved head, exposing her neck and giving me a clear view of the red Fienian scorpion tattooed around her state-issued Bronze phoenix, its tail barb sunk deep into the bird's breast.

Really, Nicolai, I think accusingly. *I thought Mercs were bad, but Fienians?*

There's no answer, of course. Because Nicolai can't possibly have a plausible explanation to have terrorists involved in our already overwrought plan.

They look extremely uncomfortable, especially the girl, who keeps glaring at Brogue with her wide pupils reconstructed into the shape of birds.

Brogue lobs the girl a sloppy wink, and she flattens herself to the wall, wrinkling her nose like he's spoiled milk. She appears seconds away from impaling him on one of her spikes.

Fienians and Mercs, together. And they haven't killed each other . . . yet. It has to be some kind of record.

The laboratory is nothing like I remember. Curtains separate austere white furniture and lab stations. An island of desks cluttered with metal gadgets and gears, microscopes, and other scraps is where I imagine my father worked most of the time. Poring over his slides and samples, scribbling maniacally inside his notebooks. Tinkering with the spare parts he was able to glean through the Fienian ran black market.

Brogue retreats to the corner, kicks his scuffed black boots up on a thin desk that looks as if it might crack under his weight, and loosens the brass buttons of his vest. The rest of us file around a circular white table.

Introductions are made. When the names Cage and Flame roll off the male Biotech's studded tongue, I groan.

What's the joke? *How do you catch a Fienian Rebel in a crowd? Call out a one-syllable word. Hardy har.* They're all renamed after they convert. River, Fog, Blue, Chain. I once saw an alert for a Fienian Rebel named Post.

How do you get a Fienian out of a tree? Cut the rope.

What's blue and red and rolls down the street? A Fienian's head.

Why are all Fienians fast runners? All the slow ones are hanging.

Cage opens a metal briefcase and hands each of us an electropen and a white slip of electropaper to sign.

I scribble my name without reading the contract.

Riser fists his pen and frowns.

"Well, aren't you a dandy?" Flame places her fingers over Riser's, impervious to how he stiffens, and guides his hand to the paper. "Like this," she says, peeking at him through wispy red eyebrows fringed with spikes.

Winding up the other side of her neck are a flock of black ravens, hundreds of them, each one just a tad bit different. The last bird, a graceful bright-blue specimen, curves her jaw.

Momentarily, the savageness behind Riser's eye seems to soften and his lips transform into a pleasant half-grin. "*Thank you.*"

His storm-blue gaze lands on me, and my toes tighten involuntarily.

"Yep." Flame guides his hand over the row of spikes winding down her arm; each one looks sharp enough to draw blood. "There are ways to get close to me without the pain. Unless you like that kind of thing."

Reclaiming his hand, Riser studies her the same way he did the cat food dispenser—as if she's something to either love or kill at the first hint of danger.

"Gag me," I mutter under my breath.

"Louder, Gold bitch," Flame spits behind a tight smile. She thinks that because of the nice things around us I am like my mother.

"I was pretty clear, Fienian scum."

Flashing me the Fienian sign—pinky finger and pointer finger splayed—she pokes her impaled tongue between her fingers and wriggles it lewdly at me.

"Charming. Blown up any innocent children lately?"

"Choked on any silver spoons?" Her scalding look says she can help me out in the matter.

"Put the claws back in, kittens," Cage says, fixing Flame with a don't-mix-with-the-natives look. "Business first." Cage smiles, each one of his teeth glittering with a delicate diamond no larger than a grain of sand.

How'd the Fienian pay his tithes? With a tooth, of course.

"You do voluntarily consent to these procedures we are about to perform," Cage says, "knowing they are binding and irreversible and understanding the risks stated in the contract you just signed, including potentially severe hallucinations, catatonia, deformity, coma, and loss of life?"

I cough. "Well, when you put it that way . . ."

Cage does not look amused.

I exhale. "Yes."

"Yes," Riser repeats, looking about as interested as a slug.

"Excellent." Cage procures two vials from the briefcase and hands them to us. A bubbly green liquid swirls ominously inside. "To prepare your blood for the transformation." The studs rimming his lips flash as he grins. "Bottoms up."

The concoction fizzes all the way to my stomach and leaves a metallic aftertaste. The veins beneath my skin jerk taut. In the span of a breath, a warm tingling sensation bores through the top of my spine and screams all the way to my toes.

I touch the blue tangle of veins crisscrossing the back of my left hand; they're cold and hard as if my blood has frozen into slush.

Right after Riser downs his, a static sound echoes across the room. We all turn to the glass wall where a bright rectangular screen wavers and then solidifies.

Riser is transfixed. Flame looks like she might throw something at it. "Royalist propaganda," she explains, rolling her eyes at the rift screen. Every room of the house has one, but only the rifts in rooms with people will activate. They're in all the public places. Factories, markets, even the parks. "They are about to tell us not to panic. It will all be fine. The Chosen are our saviors, blah, blah, blah. Now go to sleep like good little subjects."

"Turn it off," I say. No one moves.

"Not possible," Brogue says, telling me what I already know. He has quietly joined us. "The Royalists play these clips morning and evening. We are required by law to watch them."

"Well, that's not entirely true." A proud smile transforms Flame's face. All technology is under strict Royalist control. On occasion, the Fienian Rebels managed to insert their own rebellious messages.

I know what I'll see, but the images still send shockwaves through my core. Beautiful young boys and girls, dressed in Gold, smiling for the camera with their families. One porcelain-cheeked girl, wearing a supple green frock garnished with gold lace, gazes seriously into the screen as she says how privileged she feels to represent mankind. Her mother weeps proudly beside her.

A boy wearing a blue velvet top hat and stiff silver doublet with ornate gold buttons says he will do his very best to remember everyone left behind.

Lies, I think bitterly.

The screen cuts to fair-haired children playing in the grass while their parents look on. A calm, serene voice fills the room. "Mankind's greatest hope, its very survival, rests on Project Hyperion. Five thousand of the empire's brightest children, engineered to perfection, have been chosen to carry on our legacy until the earth is once again safe."

"Lies!" Flame hisses.

Well we agree on that, at least.

Cage shushes her with a stern look.

Darkness fills the screen, followed by the images of Diamond Cities thronged with well-fed Bronzes. They smile gratefully and wave to the sky. I wonder how long ago this was filmed. Surely there are no cities left that look like the one pictured.

"Be calm, be productive," the woman's voice continues. "Live your end days with dignity and humanity. In four days' time, the finalists for the Shadow Trials will arrive on the Island. One hundred Bronzes chosen by you. So have your Headboxes ready to upload. And remember, if you correctly upload to one of the four winning finalists, your Color will automatically be upgraded to Gold."

It's then I read the warnings ominously slinking across the bottom of the screen: *Stay inside during Shadow Fall and past sunset. Do not incite panic or riots. Do not join gatherings of more than ten. You have five days to voluntarily upload. Anyone caught breaking the aforementioned rules or not uploaded after the five-day period will be summarily terminated.*

Well, I think darkly, *the drones are about to get busy.*

The screen cuts away to a woman. If not quite beautiful by modern standards, she is interesting looking, with a practical, shoulder-length silver wig and sharp hazel eyes too big for her long, thin face. Two Gold Doves, the symbols of Aphrodite, fasten her blue cloak. *The House Lockhart Sigil.* Her presence fills the screen in a way I could never hope to do.

I'm supposed to hate my mother. I *do* hate her. And yet the first thing I feel as she begins to talk, her voice confident and warm, is a jolt of longing. Of course, this only makes me hate her even more.

"Do not worry, Citizens," she is saying. "Emperor Laevus and I have done everything possible to make your upload a wonderful experience."

Her hands are tangled together in her lap, her fingers twitching nervously. *That's not like her.* I study her for signs that something is wrong, but other than her wringing hands, she is a study in composure and charm.

"After you choose your Avatar, you will be immersed in a world of refinement, beauty, and luxury. A world of order, where everyone not only knows their place but is content." Her smile is captivating, and I want to believe her. "Please join us so that you may live on forever."

The screen cuts away to a family sitting on a worn brown couch. The parents hold the hands of their three children: two young boys and a teenaged girl. Bronze brands flash on their necks. The parents smile as they strap the Headboxes to their children's heads and place them inside their Caskets. The glass lids seal shut over them. Cold fog immediately crystallizes the glass.

The parents embrace and look at the screen. "We were afraid, at first," the mother says, "but we knew that our children deserved a chance to become Golds."

The husband nods and kisses his wife's cheek. "I mean, what kind of parents would we be if we didn't give them that?"

The last shot is the entire family resting in their Caskets, frosted by the ice fog. Blissful smiles adorn their white faces beneath the Headboxes.

The video ends with the Chosen Anthem, a chorus of young voices—hundreds of the highest-ranking Chosen—rising and falling in breathtaking harmony. "We are the few, we are the many; we lift our voices and sing for all the world to hear."

It's supposed to be uplifting, but there's a strange, unearthly sound to all those artificially perfect voices joined together. "Close your eyes and rest your head, Citizens, let us show you how beautiful it will be."

Even though no one's staring at me, my gaze finds my nails, and I'm thrust into the past. I was grateful when they finally sent me to Emerald Island. After all, I was a Bronze invited to join the Emperor and his court of high-ranking Golds at the most exclusive strip of land in the world, a playground for the Emperor's favored. I felt *Chosen* for the first time since I had discovered the truth about my origin.

Then I met the other Chosen, and my excitement withered. They were tall, beautiful, exotic. They were *perfect*. But I clung to the hope that my differences weren't noticeable when a willowy, blond girl named Delphine Bloodwood took me downstairs to meet her friends on the ferry ride to the Island.

She was a Countess, she explained in a bored voice, her father the Minster of Defense. They commented on my *frizzy orange mane*, and then, as if on a whim, Delphine ordered her friends to hold me down while she used the emerald-inlaid dagger she carried to shear my hair to the scalp, while she sang, "Little worm, little worm, why do you squirm?" in her perfect voice, and her friends finished, "Oh the birds will tear your eyes out, you poor little worm!"

I found my mother on the Island and begged her to send me away.

Instead she took me to the Emperor, who smiled when I told him what the other Chosen had done. He examined me with his sharp, blanched eyes, as if sifting through me, and I felt my world shrink to almost nothing. "I see," he finally said. "If the toe is gangrenous, you cleave it from the foot." After that, I waited for my mother to come for me.

But I would never see my mother again.

CHAPTER NINE

The memory of my mother fades, and my eyes refocus on my surroundings. The video is over. I'm leaned over the table, my hands curled into trembling, white-knuckled fists.

Everyone is staring at me.

But for some reason it's Riser's face I'm drawn to. One sharp smudge of an eyebrow is lifted above his searching eye, and he gives me a soft, slow nod. *I understand, Digger Girl,* he seems to be saying. *My soul is haunted too.*

"If I have to hear that song one more time, I'll die," Flame says, breaking my focus away from Pit Boy.

No one moves.

Flame twirls a neon-red cord of hair. "What? Bad choice of words? *Die. Die. Die.* We're all going to." She flicks her gaze to Riser. "Shame, too."

"Well," says Cage, clearing his throat, "I'll take that drivel any day over the Matches."

"Matches?" Riser asks, running a hand through his hair. He seems a bit lost. I imagine all the novel things his brain is trying to assimilate right now. What a world this must seem compared to the savagely simple one he knew.

What a crazy, beautiful, strange, tragic, jacked up world.

"Yeah, you know," Flame says, "the programming they blasted for a week nonstop? You'd have to be living under a rock to not see it. They ran bios on every Chosen and then let us vote for who we wanted to be matched together. They announce the results tomorrow."

"Together?" Riser shifts in his chair. "For what?"

Flame laughs. "Are you for real?" Lowering her eyelids, she rests a spiky hand on his forearm, oblivious to the way his hand clenches. "When a mommy and daddy love each other very much—"

"Stop it!" I interrupt. "He's not an idiot. The Chosen they matched will get married when they turn eighteen." Riser's uncomprehending stare makes me elaborate. "It's a contract, sort of, like the one we just signed, where you promise to be with that person forever."

My mother's brilliant idea. Just another way to distract the masses. Keep them interested in something other than the giant fiery rock in the sky.

Riser's dark eyebrows meet in a scowl. "Why do you need a contract?"

"I don't know." I mesh my fingers together. It didn't stop my mother from leaving. Or my father from letting her. "Look, it doesn't matter. It was all for show. A way to keep you from thinking about what's coming."

"It wasn't for show," Flame says, jutting out her chin. "I voted. It used up three of my saved water rations and took all day—"

"The marriages were predetermined before conception." Everyone stops to look at me, and I cringe at how cynical my voice sounds. "We were matched based on genetic harmonization and temperament compatibility. Every effort was taken to ensure a strong bond; nothing was left to chance."

"*We?*" Flame raises her eyebrows, which aren't so much eyebrows but tiny glistening spikes tipped teal with gems. "You're one of . . . *them*. But you don't look like one. Where's your twin?"

"Was," I amend carefully. "I *was* one of them. Sort of." Although we both know there really is no way to undo what I am. "I'm a Bronze, I didn't come from court, I don't look like they do, and I have a little brother, not a twin."

"Wicked. A Chosen Bronze." Flame's eyes gleam. "Which Chosen were you supposed to marry?"

Riser, who has been a statue of disinterest until now, suddenly looks up.

My lips pucker as if I've tasted something bitter. "What does it matter now? He's matched to someone else."

Flame makes a gagging noise. "Wow, Princess, the Royalist noose would be more fun than you right now."

"A Fienian that participates in Royalist-sanctioned matches?" I raise a disapproving eyebrow. "A bit hypocritical, don't you think?"

"Well, I only bomb the ones I don't like."

"Play time's over, sister," Cage says, easing the tension. "Before we begin, our mutual employer would like a word."

That's when I notice the thin white strip in the center of the table. The Interceptor crackles, clicks, emits a quick flash of blue, and projects a life-sized, four-dimensional face, mostly eclipsed by a cowl, just above it. Even though the hood casts deep shadows over the face, it's obviously Nicolai.

"Hello, children," he purrs. "I thought since our last meeting was a bit rushed we could iron out some details."

"Like what?" I ask, crossing my arms as Riser runs his hand through the hologram, disrupting it momentarily.

There's a pause.

"Cage, Flame," Nicolai says in a dismissive tone.

They rise in unison, mirror reflections of one another, and clear the room.

"Now then," Nicolai says. "First things first. You are both entered as finalists into the Shadow Trials, along with ninety-eight other desperate ex-courtiers, as Lady Everly March and Lord Riser Thornbrook." Static interrupts the picture. "These are your court identities, replete with your Houses and the fancy titles and estates they stripped from you. Soon, if you manage to survive the reconstruction, you will have fully realized memories to go with them."

"Sounds promising," I remark, drumming my fingers on the table.

Nicolai shoots me an annoyed look and continues. "In three days' time, you'll be escorted to the north, where you'll be remanded to the custody of the Royalists for travel to the Island."

"How can you be sure we've been chosen as finalists?" There must be thousands of other exiled courtiers vying for our spots.

Nicolai chuckles darkly. "You know better than most that everything Emperor Laevus does comes at a price."

"The selections are . . . are paid for?"

"I daresay they are." His mangled lips stretch into a smile. "The Emperor does have an evil empire to fund, after all." The projection crackles, static rippling across his form before solidifying once again. "As soon as you step foot on Emerald Island, you will be given another Microplant. The moment you accept it, you are open to populace upload."

"And what if someone working for the Royalists decides to piggyback onto our upload along with the Sleepers? They can see everything as well. Our thoughts. Our memories—our *true* ones."

"Anything that could jeopardize your mission or safety has already been encrypted," Nicolai explains. "The first night will be the Culling. It will look like an elaborate feast, but don't be fooled. Every interaction you have, every innocent gesture or eye contact will be watched and speculated on until evening's end, when the fifty finalists with the highest Avatar count will proceed to the next round."

For the first time since the projection began, Nicolai glances at Riser, who's still warily eyeing the projection as if it's a threat. "That's also the night the twenty-five highest ranking Chosen will decide on which two finalists to mentor. It's absolutely crucial that you are paired with Lord Thornbrook."

"No—"

"This is not a debate," Nicolai interrupts. "There's never been a more dangerous time to enter court. The Emperor's paranoia has spread through the halls like poison, and they're turning on each other."

Great. I sigh. "Okay, just how do we get paired together?"

"First we worry about your Avatar ranking. Sleepers don't have to choose their Avatar until the Culling, so they'll be watching, looking for who's the most interesting. Give them something that will make them forget about the giant rock above their heads just waiting to eliminate half the populace." Beneath the shadows I swear I see him wink. "Perhaps sparks of love will fly between Lord Thornbrook and Lady March?"

Suddenly uncomfortable, I plaster my eyes to the table. "The viewers will see through it."

"The Sleepers," Nicolai says, "will see exactly what they want to see. Just don't overdo it. I need you memorable but not exciting enough to interest the mentors."

"You have that rigged, too, don't you?"

Nicolai gives a bored shrug. "Don't like surprises."

"Me neither. So maybe you can you tell us which mentor to look out for."

"Sorry, Lady March. You are just going to have to trust me."

I glare at the wavering hologram. "But I don't. *Trust you.*"

"Then I recommend you start," Nicolai says, motioning dismissively with his hand. "Now, after your reconstructions, we will spend several days testing you. Let's hope it's enough."

I get the feeling he's not exactly optimistic about this, which makes two of us. "So, that's it?"

"Not quite. Brogue will be there on official capacity, so if something goes wrong, find him. Then there's the matter of your escorts. You are each allowed one on the Island to assist you. I have chosen the Biotechs, Cage and Flame. But there's a catch."

My heart leaps into my throat. I can't imagine what it could be. Riser's body snaps to with interest.

Nicolai clears his throat and delivers the worst possible news. "If one of your attendants manages to kill Emperor Laevus before you do, the extra tickets go to them, not you."

My mouth opens to protest just as the projection dissipates.

Nicolai must have some way to communicate with Cage and Flame because they instantly appear, arms loaded with gowns and medical bags that *jangle*. While they busy themselves in the back room, I pace.

I find myself standing outside of a door by the elevator. The padlock has been broken, and the hinges *creak* as I open it. A mountain of banned tech toys fills the dark space. My father built them for Max, tinkering late into the night. I can still hear my father humming, see his slender fingers as they worked the tiny gears, an eye loupe covering one eye.

My mother hated them, of course. And eventually they all found their way here.

Something stirs in the mound of metal on the floor. There's a muffled buzzing, and a small metallic sphere spits from the dead parts, spilling dust into the air.

The sphere buzzes around my head a couple times, too fast to follow, then hovers playfully in front of my face. Inside its reflective surface, my nose looks huge, my eyes enormous.

It zips away and then pauses in front of Riser. He stiffens and his hands begin to move upward, slowly, as if he is trying to catch a fly. The sphere darts out of reach, and Riser spins around, stalking it.

I laugh, ignoring the death glare Riser tosses me.

"It's toying with you," I explain.

The sphere buzzes above Riser's head, and he pounces on my father's workstation, causing a glass beaker to fall to the floor and shatter.

Brogue comes sprinting out of the other room. "What in the Fienian hell is going on here?"

Riser lunges after the device, but it evades him, and he lands softly on his toes. He's ignoring Brogue, which I gather from Brogue's incredulous look is adding insult to injury.

I'm laughing too hard to speak.

The sphere has stopped midair. The buzzing is now a quiet whirring as the silver globe's surface ripples, the bottom elongates into a chin, and a nose pokes out from the mercurial surface. Air escapes though Riser's teeth. His look reminds me of Max's boyish wonderment after visiting the Hall of Shadows, the Royalist museum that houses nearly every anti-Reformation, prewar invention.

"Is that . . . ?" Riser's mouth falls open, and he reaches out.

"You," I say. "It's mimicking your face."

"Is that . . . ?" the face says. It even tilts to the side, just like Riser did.

Riser frowns, sticks out his tongue.

The sphere-face frowns, sticks out its silver tongue. And then the device creates another eye where Riser's missing eye should be.

Something passes across Riser's face, transforming the sphere's expression to mimic it. Before the face can fully change, Riser knocks it across the room with his fist, and the ball slams into the wall and drops to the floor.

Flame emerges from the doorway. "Who's ready to become aweso—?"

Riser stalks past her into the room before she can even finish speaking.

Heart hammering, I follow them. The Reconstructor machines, two oblong steel capsules similar to the Caskets, lie long ways, one on each side of the wall. Red triangles of light pulse across a square screen in each Reconstructor's center, making strange geometric patterns. A faded-blue curtain that smells of mildew separates them.

Riser and I are given yellow gowns to change into. I dress quickly, trying not to stare at the slender shape wavering on the other side of the curtain. In the corner of my room is a screen with a bunch of numbers and lines. Cage hooks me up to the machine to gather my vital signs and then exits.

After a few minutes Flame enters, garbed in hot-pink gloves, a black apron with glow-in-the-dark skulls and a mask that has the words *shut up* plastered over her mouth.

I eye her now that we are competitors. She expertly ignores me.

Everything inside me is screaming not to do this. But Flame taps the red triangles until they burn orange and yellow and flicker wildly. Then the lid pops open with a *hiss*. As I clamber inside, my gown flips up, and I scramble to cover my left side.

"Don't bother," Flame instructs, glancing away from the screen. The mask muffles her voice. "I've seen every inch of you. Who do you think placed that bootleg Microplant inside your skull?"

"Right," I say, adjusting my gown anyway. After Nicolai's revelation, I can't shake my mistrust. This machine will tamper with my mind. Who's to say Flame won't do something awful to me to give herself an advantage?

Her glittering eyebrows lift in exasperation. "Ready now, Princess?"

My fingers brush the fresh scar on my side. "You healed my wound, too?"

"Well, it wasn't that disgusting oaf, Brogue."

I hesitate. "Can you leave a part of me? Something small . . . It doesn't matter what."

Her fingers pause over the screen. "Our employer won't like it."

"Gee, if he won't like it, I guess you can't do it."

Flame scowls. Without another word, she stabs the screen with her finger, and the lid seals shut.

The inside of the Reconstructor is a shiny metallic material that glows faintly, emitting a low hum. As soon as I lie down, a cold ache spreads through my back and makes me gasp. Neon-green tendrils snake around my body. Tiny shocks emit from their fingerlike touch.

Before I can shift into a more comfortable position, the apparatus just above my face, which resembles black goggles, drops down, pinning my head and blinding me. Straps of some sort paralyze my wrists. A soft pinching feeling, like a fine needle entering my flesh, gathers in my neck, just below the jaw, and becomes a dull, throbbing pressure as the nanites they inject me with spread.

They move slowly. Numbing every cell, every molecule of my being, until I am drifting, disembodied.

Speakers crackle to life. Flame's voice, a garbled whisper murmured from the end of a long tunnel, mixes with the steady thump of my heart. "Don't fight it. Concentrate on your breathing. Think of something nice, something safe. The machine will help you."

I'm floating in an ocean of black. Thoughts collide into one another and break apart. I'm buoyed toward a pinprick of light no bigger than a diamond; with every slow, shallow breath I take, another jewel appears.

Soon, they are innumerable, a winking tapestry of lights engraved in the darkness, spanning an eternity.

Not diamonds, I think I hear myself whisper. *Stars.*

Goodbye, monster girl.

And then I soar away.

CHAPTER TEN

The first thing I'm aware of are noises. Constant, low humming. Gentle whirring. A slow click-click sound. Far-away voices and high-pitched beeps, muffled as if underwater.

But the noises are intensifying. The beeps becoming shrieks, the voices screams.

My memory floods back. I spring straight up, slam my forehead into the top of the Reconstructor. The lid creaks open above my palm.

After the dimness of the Reconstructor, the room is painfully bright. Shadows scamper behind the curtain. Cage's harried voice barks commands over the shrill cacophony of alarms.

The first step I take is wobbly but not bad. The second sends me to my knees. Using the counter for support, I stagger up and fight my way to the curtain. I don't feel any different. I wonder if perhaps I've woken up before the reconstruction completed.

The scene on the other side is chaotic. Riser's Reconstructor lid hangs open, the screen a wild jumble of red shapes whirling helter-skelter. Sweat beads on Cage's forehead as he works over the machine. Veins bulge in his neck and forehead, and he's blinking fast and muttering. Behind him, her face taut with emotion, stands Flame. Her desperate look tells me all I need to know about Riser's condition.

Although my mind's a bit fuzzy, I must have walked closer because now I can see Riser. His gown tangles around his lower half, exposing most of his pale upper body, which is curled in on itself like a pitiful, dying creature. His thrashing legs make a rhythmic *thumping* against the machine.

His scars, the ones he showed me only hours earlier, are now an angry reddish-purple. Spidery blue-black veins river his flesh, converging around his eyes, nose, and mouth.

"He's dying," I say. There's no emotion in my voice. It's like my feelings are locked away somewhere. I can access them if needed—or not, depending on their value to my cause.

Maybe I am different, after all.

Cage looks up from Riser's body, startled.

"You're supposed to be resting." Cage's voice cracks.

How long have they been working on Riser? Too long, from the way their shoulders slump.

We all freeze as a guttural cry erupts from Riser. It's horrible, the most wretched, pleading sound I've ever heard. Flame slaps a hand over her mouth, her eyes burning with tears. "He can't find it. The safe place. He can't—"

"That's enough." Cage's tone is defeated. "Close it. Let him go in peace."

"Wait." My hand's on the lid, inches from one of Riser's balled fists. I let one of my fingers brush his knuckles. A ragged sigh escapes his bluish-gray lips. "He's cold."

Again, no emotion one way or the other, just a mental note that he's vital to my mission. I climb in beside him. I was wrong: He's not just cold; he's frozen, his body stiff as marble.

I shiver from the cold as I enfold my limbs around his skeletal torso, his sharp-edged spine jutting painfully into my sternum. My fingers strum across the deep chasms between each rib, and I realize now just how emaciated he really is.

He begins to breathe hard and fast, his ribs rising and falling; the wild, erratic beating of his heart feels like a desperate animal trying to escape its cage. "Don't," he moans. "Don't hurt her."

I can't tell if it's helping, but the Biotechs must think so because they close the lid. His body softens and warms. His breathing stabilizes, his heartbeat now strong and regular under my fingertips. And maybe it's the slow hum of the machine, or the steady lull of his breathing, but I find myself drifting off . . .

This time I awaken in my room. I'm warm, deliciously so, buried beneath a mountain of covers. Bramble rests on the other pillow with a note from Brogue: *I thought he might cheer you up.* It's still dark, the silly painted stars shining down on me, and for a moment I swear I can feel their warmth on my skin. That reminds me that my skin is no longer *my* skin.

I realize I forgot to ask what I would look like afterward. Now, it takes all my nerve to lift out of bed, my sleek new abdominal muscles tightening with each step as I pad to the mirror.

Sensing motion, the mirror luminesces, imparting a faint golden glow. The girl from the day before is gone. In her place stands Everly March, a healthy, porcelain-skinned creature who looks as if she's just come back from summering somewhere bright and airy.

She's willowy, tall and fair, with perky breasts, high cheekbones on a heart-shaped face, a thick shock of dark red hair cascading past her shoulders—the perfect shade to compliment her skin—and an exquisitely-shaped nose. She wears green, a color that used to make me look sickly, like it was made for her. A Bronze phoenix curves her supple neck.

She is everything I wasn't.

She is everything I was *supposed* to be.

I'm pretty sure I hate her.

I lift a hand, massage my face, just to make sure it's still me. I raise my arms, now long and toned, and turn side to side. I stand inches from the mirror and make silly faces.

My hair, a rich, impossible red that somehow looks both natural and glamorous, captures the light, and the effect is indescribable. Except for my eyes, which are still the same hazel color, and a smattering of stubborn freckles that Flame must have kept, there's no trace of Maia Graystone left.

I am Nicolai's creation now, a creation with one singular objective: Revenge.

Breakfast comes early. I sit at the table with Bramble chirping in my lap and examine my new clothes. Gray-cropped riding pants; rich chestnut-colored leather riding boots; and a stiff, high-collared pale-green tunic that itches my neck. I pick at the cumbersome bra my new body demands. My mother once said a woman's form could be used as a weapon against men, but, so far, having cleavage is more irritating than lethal.

My bulky assets are forgotten as Brogue graces my plate with the mysterious egg-like concoction from before. I scarf it down. Flame and Brogue, who are sitting at as far apart as possible, quietly study me.

Brogue looks at me sideways and frowns. "Wasn't her hair supposed to be blond?"

"Yeah," Flame says, "but I like her better like this."

"And how does Nicolai feel about that?"

Flame pokes at the rubbery yellow mound in front of her. "Don't know. Don't care."

I shovel another forkful of mystery into my mouth. I am ignoring them both. My stomach growls, and I tap the fork against my empty plate, causing Bramble to stir in my lap.

Brogue grins. "More?"

I nod, and he heaps more sticky yellow clumps in front of me.

"The transformation made her hungry," Flame says, in case he thought it was because I actually *liked* his food. She's sparkly in a rose-gold jumpsuit cinched together by a red leather belt and thin red cloak that matches her lipstick and hair.

Brogue winks at me. "Well, there's more where that came from."

"No," Flame says. "We need to test her."

Brogue and I share a conspiratorial look. I bite my lip. For the first time since I got here, I feel a connection to someone. It feels good. Really good. To have a friend, even if it is a Merc.

Brogue lifts the pan to deposit even more food on my plate. "She's been through hell. Let the girl e—"

"No." Flame's hand darts out and bats the pan from Brogue's hand.

Brogue's face goes still. The hand that held the pan is still open. He hasn't moved a muscle, his eyes nailed to Flame, who doesn't seem to notice or care. The vein in his temple throbs.

Flame stands and dumps the pan into the trash. "We have to test her. Make sure there are no kinks." She turns back around and challenges Brogue with an intense stare. "Now go prepare for the physical tests."

Frowning—I'm guessing he's not used to taking orders from people, especially a spritely, tart-tongued, red-haired Fienian Rebel—Brogue rises, his chair squealing across the tile, and stalks off.

"Kinks?" I say, reluctantly pushing away my plate. "What kind—?"

"Name?" Flame barks.

"Everly March." My brain fires without hesitation.

"House March's sigil?"

"The golden Lyre."

"Parents' names?"

"Lady Olivia and Lord Statham March, previously Baroness and Baron of Brandywine Estates—before our Color was stripped."

"Which one did you love more?"

I pause. "My father." I see him, or what he is supposed to look like. Medium-blond hair, soft-gray eyes, a youngish face, cigar delicately perched between his beautiful white teeth. My chest threatens to burst with his love and my love for him . . . this stranger—my *father*.

"How and when did they die?"

"Fire. Two months ago." My throat clenches, and for a second I taste ash and soot. It clings to my mouth, coats my throat, burns my lungs until I feel like I'm suffocating.

A crushing headache splits my skull. Something . . . on the tip of my tongue, a memory. A horrible memory. Thousands of phantasmal needles prickle my skin. I look down to see flames melting my flesh, peeling it off my bones.

I scream.

"Everly!" Flame shouts, as Bramble hops from my lap and scuttles across the floor.

My new name brings me back. I take a deep breath, hold the air in until my head swims and the memory is gone. "What was that?"

"A phantom memory." She fidgets, entwining her thumbs as she stares at the table. "The traumatic memories are the hardest to filter. Sometimes the extractor picks up a few. They should fade."

"But that means . . ." My mouth hangs open. I thought Nicolai had created me. But what I just experienced was real. The fear. The pain.

The horror.

"Is there . . . *Was* there a real Everly March?"

Flame tweaks the spikes on her eyebrows. "We are off track."

My heart drops. "How did she die? The fire? She burned to death with her parents? Was it an accident?" My chair scrapes as I stand. "Nicolai!" My hands flutter to my cheeks. I'm wearing another girl's face. A *dead* girl's face. "*Nicolai!*"

Flame crosses her arms and kicks her leg onto the table, her face cross, as if she's being forced to endure a child's tantrum. "Let me know when you're done."

My leg itches to kick the table. Better yet, Flame's chair, send her flying to the floor. That might make her smug look disappear, though I seriously doubt it.

I smother my rage—something that would have been impossible before my reconstruction—and fight words through my dead girl's smile. "Done."

She narrows her eyes. "Sure?"

"Positive." My breath hisses through clenched teeth as I sit.

She continues as if nothing's happened. "Siblings?"

"No."

"Virgin?"

"Yes."

Flame lobs questions at me like weapons, and I fire back. My mouth responds, and as soon as it does, the memories are there, fleeting but salient technicolored pictures that, put together in sequence, almost make a life.

Flame mercilessly continues trying to stump me. "Favorite color? Favorite season?"

"Green. Summer."

"First kiss?"

"Lord Bradley, a Gold from House Royce and my best friend's brother, beneath the apple tree, the crooked one—"

Her voice changes intensity, becoming suddenly empathetic. "What is the pit?"

"It's . . ." For a split second my heart skips a beat, but then it steadies. My mind goes blank. "I don't know."

"Who is Maia Graystone?"

Me! my brain screams. An image of the frizzy-haired, freckled girl pops into my head. *Me*! Still, I open my mouth to say it, to *scream* it, but it's like my tongue is twisted into knots.

"What is your opinion of Emperor Laevus?" Flame leans slightly forward, just enough that I decide my response is important.

"He is our savior, the one man we should all be grateful to. Without him and his tireless dedication, humankind would perish." It's scary how convincing my voice is.

She doesn't blink as her gaze burns into mine. "What will you do when you meet him?"

I know my answer before I say it, and my blood runs cold. "Ram a knife into his skull. The best entries are at the base of the skull and the eye sockets. But a sharp knife will penetrate the temples just as easily, and a long blade can slip beneath the jaw and reach the brain."

"Good." The tension melts from Flame's face. I wonder what would have happened had I answered wrong. "The reconstruction seems successful. We will know soon enough."

"And Riser?" It's the first time since I awoke that I've allowed myself to think about him. I cringe at the awkward memory of my body folded over his. If I was still Maia, I would turn bright red and splotchy and it would take several minutes for me to recover. But with a cold shrug, the emotion fades.

I smile; I am going to like being Everly March very much.

Flame's face rearranges into an unreadable mask. "That does not concern you." She clears her throat. "It's likely his reconstruction was irrevocably corrupted. We won't know how much until he wakes up."

"If he wakes up, you mean?"

For the first time since we sat down, she blinks.

After breakfast I take a longer test, where I answer what seems like a zillion questions about Everly March.

On the surface she's exactly what everyone expects. Demure. Compliant. Well educated. She loves horses and silken gowns and expensive gold jewelry. She can play Symphony No. 9 in D minor and sing in high octave. She was devastated by the loss of her parents.

It seems we have something in common, after all.

But past the shiny façade she is something more. Cold, calculated. Whip-smart. Singularly determined. Everly March would have been someone Ripper and Rafe would have steered clear of.

I pass the test with flying colors. Before I can go, Flame inundates me with warnings for the first forty-eight hours post reconstruction.

No sleeping—I could slip into an irrevocable coma. Expect painful memories from my past to pop up—fighting them only makes them worse—and an enhanced emotional state. Drink twice the normal amount of water. Expect an insatiable appetite, crushing headaches, hallucinations, and moments of delirium. Itching is normal, but tingling in the lips or fingers should be reported immediately, along with strange smells and problems with my vision. I get the feeling if this happens, I'm screwed.

Flame ticks off my rough post-reconstruction itinerary. More tests, including Sims, and not the kind you can buy black market. The real kind. The fry-your-brain-if-you're-not-careful kind.

I shrug her off, nearly skipping to the elevator. I expect Brogue to be in the basement, but my heart drops when I see him warming up in the room at the end of the hall. Just one look at the thick white padding covering the walls of my mother's old training room and my knees go weak.

I hesitate; bad memories cling to this place. Memories I would rather not dredge up.

But Brogue is smiling at me. Beckoning me to join him. And Brogue isn't my mother. He wouldn't hurt me. So I return his smile and enter.

Brogue's feet sledgehammer the ground as he charges me. My smile dies. His face is deathly calm. I'm too dumfounded to do anything—

Last second before he crashes into me, my body reacts seemingly of its own accord. I sidestep, stick out a foot, and ram my palm into the small of his back.

I think his head is going to slam into the wall, but he rolls sideways to offset his momentum, his shoulder taking the brunt of the force.

My mother's voice finds me. *Faster! Raise your foil. Aim it at my heart.*

Grunting, Brogue runs at me again, thick arms flailing at my head like he means to cleave it from my neck. This time I duck beneath his arms, snake behind him, cinch my arms around his muscly, perspiration-soaked back, and stomp my foot into the soft part of his knee.

He crumples to the ground, and I straddle his barrel chest, digging my knees into his ribs. My raised fists cast shadows across his flushed face.

Brogue grunts under my weight, the taunting grin he's been wearing replaced by a grudging look of respect. "So, the little alley-cat and her sidekick know their stuff."

It takes a moment to catch my breath, my new abdominal muscles quivering gloriously beneath my shirt. "This was a test?"

"Something like that."

I back off him, arms in a defensive position in case he comes at me again. I feel utterly betrayed. "You could have warned me."

Springing to his feet, Brogue rolls up his right sleeve. The Mercenary hangman's noose inks down his shoulder, along with the Merc motto, a string of words written in Latin. "Parati ad omnia," he reads. "Know what that means, girl?"

"Don't mess with me?" I half-joke.

"Be ready for everything."

"Well, I don't even know if I can do that again—"

Before I can finish my sentence, Brogue has his arm raised and is swinging a round wooden stick at my head. He must have been hiding it. I cry out as I duck, and the stick just clips my hair.

"I thought we were done!" I hiss, sucking air.

Oblivious to my panic, my body springs sideways, pivoting and sweeping out a leg. My foot catches Brogue's boot, tripping him.

He recovers easily. With a roguish grin, he winks, taps the words on his shoulder, and swings the stick at my face like he's trying to crack a watermelon.

I drop just in time. The stick hits the wall instead and ricochets off the padding, the edge striking just below my right eye. I feel blood begin to ribbon down my cheek.

I see my mother standing over me, slender in her white fencing uniform, visor down so that I cannot see her eyes. One arm is folded behind her back. *Are you going to cry over a little blood? Get up!*

It becomes a dangerous dance. Our labored breathing the chorus, our grunts and pounding hearts the tempo. Brogue swings and stabs and slices with the stick, and I evade him. Sometimes I move with ease, as if our movements are choreographed. But mostly I thrash and flail and buck like a wounded animal trying to throw off a much larger predator.

I learn that I know things. Where to kick the thigh to shock the femoral artery and cause unconsciousness. How to hook my legs around a man to hold him while I use the blade of my forearm to strangle his carotid artery. How to shape my hand into a rough spear that can easily slip past the chin and strike the throat.

Sweat drips from our bodies and puddles on the mat. Every muscle coils, every neuron fires, every tendon tightens. The potent, tangy smell of adrenaline and perspiration fill the room.

My body is no longer mine to claim but an efficient, well-oiled machine controlled by a different, more powerful master.

Survival.

Finally, I collapse in a hot, boneless heap. Brogue smashes his boot into my chest, crushing me to the floor. The air flees my lungs. My cheek aches where the splintered end of his stick gouges, twisting mercilessly. "Girl," Brogue says in a voice as rough as sandpaper, "you make a pretty corpse."

The tip of my mother's foil presses into the soft area of my throat. She lifts her visor so that I can see the disappointment in her eyes. Weak, she is saying. Weak and slow. I am crying. I am seven.

It's almost as if I can hear something inside me break. Without thinking, I hook his boot with my right arm and twist, rolling end over end like a log. Rather than let me dislocate his knee, Brogue rolls with me, falling as he does. Once more I am straddling him, my knees smashing each of his sinewy biceps so that his arms are pinioned.

I am no longer tired; I am enraged.

Blinking away my mother's face, I lean down, close enough that his warm, tar-laced breath ripples over my face. "My name is Everly. Everly March. Not Digger Girl. Not maggot or worm or Pit Leech. And certainly not *girl*." I make sure and jam my knees into his muscle and bone as I push to a stand. His eyes bulge with pain. "And from now on it's Lady March to you, Merc."

It's the first lesson since becoming Lady March. We are not friends. None of these people will ever be my friends.

CHAPTER ELEVEN

Brogue rises a bit slower this time. He's tiring, but so am I. We've been doing this for hours, and every bit of my flesh screams in agony; I've lost count of the times I've hit the mat.

The Merc's eyes have a hard glint to them. "Give up yet?"

I'm too winded to reply, so I simply shake my head, even though Maia's begging me to stop. But I can't.

I *can't.*

The stick *clanks* to the floor. Twirling ominously in his left hand is a short, fat blade, the sharp edge twinkling. A wave of fear and adrenaline surges through my body. My eyes rivet to the shiny steel. Nothing else exists. The walls seem to shrink, disappear.

"But you might really kill me," I say, lifting my hands, now numb with fear.

I try to will away my horror like my other emotions, but it clings to me. Apparently even Lady March is not immune to fear.

My mother stood right there. Welts from where the foil lashed my tender flesh crisscrossed my arms. I was begging her to stop. Please, Mother. It hurts. You're scaring me.

But that seemed only to make her angrier, and I fell beneath a barrage of whips, her foil slicing the air with each enraged stroke.

Now I have made the same mistake, asking Brogue for mercy. He takes a quick, confident step toward me, his eyes shining ruthlessly. "One small misstep on the Island, you *really* die." Another step.

"Accidentally reveal your true identity, you die then, too." His boot slides a foot closer. "Fail to win the Shadow Trials, well . . . you get the picture." For his size, he has a feline grace, shifting through spaces with a quiet ease that lulls me into thinking he's farther away than he really is. That he is my friend.

His last step puts him a mere foot from me. "Death is all around you, Lady March. It's the silent, phantasmal specter, breathing oh-so-quietly down your neck." His tarry breath is hot against my cheeks. "It'll find its way in, eventually—"

The knife flashes as it drives toward my neck. There's a moment right before it enters my flesh that I can actually feel the blade burning through my neck and lodging in my spine. But last second, I move and instead it carves a fiery but superficial trail from my collarbone to my jaw.

"You stabbed me!" I scream. Panic frays my voice as the space between my breasts pools with blood.

Suddenly I'm dead sure he's intent on killing me.

Brogue wipes his blade on his shirtsleeve. "I grazed you. Next time, move faster."

"Next time?"

He's coming again, stalking me. "Better yet." A wicked smile curves his jaw. "Catch it."

He grasps the knife blade between thumb and forefinger, aims it at my face like a dart, and snaps his wrist.

I fall to the ground. I'm sure the knife has impaled me. There's no way I could have avoided it; he's too close, his aim too sure.

My eyes, which must have closed, snap open. Pinned between my flat palms, glinting mere centimeters from my nose, is the knife blade.

The blade slides through my fingers and buries itself in the padded floor. I know I'm supposed to use the weapon on him, but the thought makes me ill.

I force my body to a wobbly crouch. "I'm done," I say, pressing my fingers to my neck to staunch the dripping blood. "This is torture."

This is survival, Everly, Nicolai's excited voice says into my head. *Now pick up the knife and stab him with it.*

"No." My body is shaking. "I said I would kill Emperor Laevus, and I will. But I refuse to hurt anyone else."

Your reconstructed neuron pathways need to be solidified, Nicolai says. *To do that, we need two things: traumatic, stress-inducing situations and repetition. We don't want Everly March to lose her memories and skillset prematurely.*

"You should have told me you were giving me a dead girl's memories!"

It wasn't pertinent.

I pinch the bridge of my nose and close my eyes. "It was. Pertinent. To me."

"The girl needs a break," Brogue interrupts. His voice is gruff and uncaring, same as always. But there's something about it that tells me different.

My mother's voice whispers, *Pick it up. Use it. He is weak.*

I pick up the knife. It's surprisingly light, the steel handle cold and smooth in my palm. It feels good to hold it. Empowering.

A quiet rage comes over me. I smile at Brogue like we're friends again, like all's forgiven, flick my wrist, and watch the knife arrow toward his head.

He grunts in surprise, ducks. The knife buries into the wall behind him with a thud. It warbles back and forth a moment and then goes still.

If he hadn't been distracted by his emotion, he would have seen that coming. I've found the chink in his armor.

Brogue touches the thin red line across his cheek where the knife grazed and regards the blood darkening his fingertips with wide eyes. "I told you," I say, smiling, "not to call me girl."

Except for cobwebs and a few cans of synthetic green beans, the pantry is empty. I scan the barren shelves, my stomach rumbling, as

Bramble pokes and whirs at the few crumbs dusting the floor. That's where the bread and pasta used to go. The flour and spices just below. The salt-bread crackers and Max's coveted sweet raisin cakes to my left. Whole racks of dried plums, apples, and saffron-infused lamb strips near the back.

We were luckier than most Bronzes, with my mother's Gold rations and my father's place in the Royalist College across the wall. I see that now, even if I didn't then.

I select the least rusty can. It's heavy as I lug it to the kitchen counter, Bramble skittering by my feet. The cut on my neck protests beneath a strip of gauze and tape.

I peel back the lid, grayish green droplets spraying the new blouse I changed into. Hopefully Nicolai has a surplus, given my current rate.

I'm lifting the can when the rift screen above the kitchen table zaps to life. *Oh goody.* Given my mood I would rather not watch, but the rift screen will follow me wherever I go, so I might as well get it over with.

Dramatic music fills the kitchen, the screen skipping over pairs of Chosen. *The Match results.* I swallow and focus on depositing the contents of the can into the bowl and not my blouse. *They can't force me to listen.*

But a knot forms in my belly at the thought of court. Even now, with my perfect hair and pleasing features, I still feel the sting of their taunts.

I poke and prod the musty smelling slop with a wooden spoon. A black oily ooze bobs to the surface, and Bramble chirps suspiciously at it. *Not a good sign.* Hunger parts my mouth. The spoon hovers at my lips. But I literally cannot fight the congealed bite into my mouth.

"You've got to be kidding me!" I yell to the matched faces on the rift screen.

They smile down at me. Beautiful. Healthy. Even though they cannot really see me, I feel their scorn.

I fight the urge to chuck the bowl at their stupid Chosen faces, knowing that tampering with a rift screen carries a stiff penalty.

Instead, I watch with grim satisfaction as the bowl sails through the air and then explodes in a gooey starburst of green against the wall.

I regret my childish action immediately; I'm still hungry.

I see that Flame needs to tweak your impulsive streak, Nicolai's voice grates in my head.

Let her try, I snap back.

And make you more amenable—

"I would be more amenable if I wasn't being starved!"

Lady March would not touch that excuse for food if she were dying of starvation. Nor would she suffer petulant outbursts.

I deflate. "So . . . I can't eat?"

Not can't. Won't. At least, not that muck.

Applause from the Matches shatters Nicolai's connection. I roll my eyes at the gorgeous, elaborately draped couple accepting white roses from the crowd. They drip with rubies that catch the sun.

Probably the children of high-ranking generals. They touch hands shyly. Tears well inside the girl's wide blue eyes. After D-Day, after most of us have been killed, all the matched will have elaborate weddings on Hyperion. When your job is carrying on the human race, you get started early.

For a strange, disconnected moment, the girl looks directly into the rift, and it's as if I can see every Sleeper that has uploaded into her. Their sad, screaming gaze burns through the screen.

Soon they'll be inside me too.

Sliding out the knife I pocketed from practice earlier, I notice the way its handle perfectly fills the basin of my palm. My thumb closes over the cold steel, and a primitive, euphoric feeling rushes over me.

In this moment, I could do anything. I have no control, no moral boundaries I cannot cross. I wonder if this is what it's like to lose it.

"So, let me get this straight." My voice begins to crack as if I'm a rotten fruit about to split wide open. "I can't eat certain foods, but I can ram this dagger into someone's heart?"

Exactly, Nicolai purrs into my head.

"Stop it," I beg. "Please. Whatever you did to me, undo it."

A long expanse of quiet fills my skull. I can only assume Nicolai is giving me time to collect myself.

Impossible, he says at last. *You are Lady March. From now on everything you do must reflect that.*

"But I'm hungry," I whisper.

Then figure something out.

There's a strange release inside my head as he leaves, and then I find myself slumping to the cold tile. Bramble pokes cautiously at my shoulder as I focus in and out on the dust coating the floor, watching the tiny spheres dance with my shallow breathing. I feel light, hollow, as if I can float away on the smallest breeze.

What have you done, Graystone?

"Not Graystone," my new, perfect lips whisper. "Lady. Everly. March." Every word is a struggle, but once they're spoken, some of the panic evaporates. "You're still you, just better. Stronger."

Dusting off my cheek, I rise and say, "You are Lady Everly March, and if you're going to survive, you must think like Lady March."

Hysterical episode averted, I pocket the knife and spend a few minutes searching the kitchen cupboards, although I know anything near edible has already been picked from this place. Time to leave the house.

My stomach tightens. The thought both scares and elates me. Shadow Fall isn't for another hour. There will be sunlight and fresh air and sky. I remember the throng of people in the makeshift marketplace. I convince myself it will be safe in the daytime. That my knife and newfound skills will protect me.

I scour the house for things to barter with. It doesn't take long to fill a sheet full of items. A can opener, batteries, a water distiller, a half-used bar of basil and thyme soap, some cutlery from the kitchen, a dusty jar of what looks to be blackberry jam, Max's windup flashlight.

Right before I leave, I peer up. Caspian's face smiles at me from the rift screen above the door. He's older, of course. His face leaned out, his eyes more somber than I remember. He's standing on a platform, his black fur cape wobbling around his legs as he impatiently taps his foot.

An enormous golden crown sits sideways on his head. Cheers burst from the crowd as he gives a stiff nod, his white-gloved hands balled into fists at his side. He scans the crowd with vague indifference.

In a word, he looks *bored*.

"Are you reeeady?" the announcer drawls with grating enthusiasm. "This is it, royal watchers, the Match results we have all been waiting for. Prince Caspian Laevus, the Royal Prince Sovereign and future Emperor, third firstborn descendant of the beloved Emperor Marcus Laevus, the very reason half the crowd is near swooning—right, ladies?" There is the sound of squealing and excited laughter, overlapping with the dull buzz of applause.

The camera pans to the massive crowd, nearly a mile deep, all dressed in white for the Matches. They are on Hyperion, deep in space, but you would never know. Not with the golden castle rising behind them and walls made to look like perfectly blue sky. "And the lucky Chosen lady, our future Empress, is none other than . . . the universally beloved Gold from House Bloodwood, daughter of the esteemed and honorable General Bloodwood, Countess Delphine Bloodwood!"

Screams and applause roar through my eardrums. For the tiniest of seconds my brain tingles with something. An emotion.

But then as I open the door, the sun warm on my face, the feeling evanesces like a foul odor carried away on a breeze until I can no longer remember the actual smell—just that I did not enjoy it.

The young male Merc posted against the column jumps to attention. "My lady," he says, jutting his shoulder into my path. "Shadow Fall is coming."

I meet his panicked eyes, prepared to fight, if necessary. "Then you best stay sharp."

A tense moment. A standoff, really. We are eye-to-eye. I notice a fine layer of blond hairs just above his upper lip. And his chest is barrel-shaped, indicative of the breathing disease. Most likely a miner from Gaul, the next Diamond City over. Not your usual Merc.

They're growing desperate.

I know I've won when he edges back. Brogue would have stopped me. Or, at least, he would have *tried*.

I make it to the broken wrought iron gate by the street when he calls out, "Between the fifth and sixth intercostal, my lady."

"Excuse me?"

"Your knife. It's how you stop a man's heart . . . In case you get into trouble."

I pick up my pace. The sun is already high in the sky.

Too high.

I am running away. I know myself, or used to know myself enough to understand that. Running from the house that's not my house, from the people who aren't my friends, from the food I can't eat and the dead girl inside my mirror.

The rift screen above the market is active. I watch as the woman on the huge screen steps into her Casket and demonstrates how to upload, all the while a serene voice floats through the speakers. "Subjects of Cypher, your city has been ordered to upload. Failure to comply will be considered an offense against the Emperor, punishable by death."

The Bronzes swarming the tents ignore it. Instead, their dirty faces and glassy eyes peer up at *Her*, sifting through the smoke-churned sky. They are more afraid of Shadow Fall than they are the Emperor and his drones.

Fighting through a wall of elbows and shoulders, I clutch my sack to my chest and lose myself for a moment, ignoring the pockets of chaos around me.

Two boys my age beat a limp pile of rags on the ground with clubs.

Thunk. Thunk. A foot twitches beneath it.

Look away. Run.

A young girl offers herself to the man to my left. To me.

Look away.

I nearly trip over two women fighting in the dirt where the beautiful rose garden used to be, before the fires reduced them to ash. The larger woman on top has the smaller woman's long brown hair twirled around her fist and is grinding her face into the ground. Jeers rise from a ring of men circling them.

Look away. Keep going.

An elbow glances off my ribs and rips me from my daze. I'm under the makeshift row of tents. The smell of burnt meat mixes with acrid sweat and rotting garbage. Just where I need to be.

I choose a stall near the back. The meat hanging from the racks doesn't resemble Max's cat, at least, and the frail, stooped woman standing at the counter appears clean.

A small part of me admits I've targeted her because she looks nice. *Weak.* I should feel pity for her, but I feel nothing.

Well, except hunger.

The woman's faded eyes peer behind large glasses at the goods I set out. Her gaze flits greedily to the silverware, a pearl-engraved knife and fork, two delicate silver spoons. A toothless smile splits her face.

Something crawls just below my skin.

I meet the old woman's eyes. She's no longer the weak, smiling grandmother. An image flashes inside her glasses, and I go cold.

I turn just in time to meet them: three men, each one bigger than the last; each one clutching a nail-studded baton. They have sadistic smiles and dead eyes.

In the pit, I know which category they would fall into.

Predator.

And that puts me squarely with the prey.

CHAPTER TWELVE

Bait. The woman was bait. I don't have to turn around to know the woman has fled. Just like I don't have to look up to see the fiery ring in the sky is fading.

This was a huge mistake. *Huge*. Of epic, I'm-screwed proportions.

"So, you're the three idiots I have to barter with," I say, proud that my voice doesn't shake at all. My hand, though, trembles uncontrollably as it snakes into the bag and clutches Max's flashlight.

I pray to the gods the gears are still working.

My fearless voice makes my tormentors halt a few steps from me. Their putrid stench cuts through the foulness of the spoiled meat swaying just above my head.

A quick glance tells me the crowd has disappeared with the fading light. I am alone.

"She's got a smart mouth on her," the largest man says. He has burnt-orange hair, lanky limbs, and large hands, and he looks to the middle man—obviously the leader—as he talks.

A rictus grin splits the leader's face. "Drake, Mathias, why don't you show her what we do to the smart ones?"

This is not going as planned. If this were the pit, I would already be running mindlessly, my mind flooded with the Doom.

I briefly wonder what Lady Everly March would do. Before I can think further, my body reacts and I drop and roll. Sharp rocks from the crumbling cobblestone sidewalk scrape my cheeks and elbows.

Sky, ground, sky. Over and over I roll, beneath two stalls, under a table. I finally wedge against a wooden chair.

I spring to my feet. Shadow murk chokes the air so I can hardly make out my hand in front of me. My ragged breath aligns with my footsteps. I trip over a stall. Knock into an iron rack overflowing with dried herbs.

Before I know it, thick gray trees surround me. A path opens up. My father and I used to stroll this part of the forest, collecting rocks and leaves.

Other things use these woods now. I remember the sound of the window breaking at the house across the street, the screams as the children funneled inside.

Not children. Not anymore.

The footpath disappears. Tree limbs scratch my face as I fight my way through dense foliage, kicking and punching my own path. But I am too loud, and soon the forest fills with the sounds of snapping branches and heavy breathing—not my own.

That's good because I have a desperate, lunatic plan. And it requires that my attackers and I make as much noise as possible.

I enter a clearing just as a shadow breaks off from one of the trees. Then another. Now there are three. Their height and stench tell me they are the cretins from the market.

I retrieve Max's flashlight from my pocket, twist the gears, spreading my hands out as I back up. A faint elliptical of light bounces across the faces of my tormentors. The wind lashes strips of my hair across my eyes. I vaguely notice that my shirt is ripped at the bust, exposing part of my white bra, which seems to glow in the darkness.

Another shirt, ruined. A hysterical laugh bubbles up my chest.

No, don't panic. Panic is for the weak. Panic is for prey, and you are not prey.

They circle me until I cannot back up anymore. After my escape earlier, they are being extra careful. I get the feeling they are drawing this out. Enjoying it.

"Shouldn't have run, my lady," the leader says in a soft, menacing voice. Because of my appearance and dress, he probably assumes I am a High Color. "We was just going to have a little fun. But now . . ."

My heart clenches. The redheaded cretin is lazily stroking the half-a-dozen sharp nails sticking out of his club. He spits at my feet and laughs, a jumpy, high-pitched sound. The others join in.

I scan the trees. *Where are they?* The woods are quiet. All at once I'm flooded with doubt about my plan. I've made a mistake. A small, unforgivable mistake that will cost me everything.

Curl into a ball. Hide. Disappear.

No! I'm no longer Maia Graystone, the girl who hides in the tunnels. The girl who eats rats and cries in the darkness and is scared, always scared.

I'm Everly March—the girl who'll fight back.

Hefting the flashlight into my left hand, I slide out the knife I have hidden inside my sleeve. It dances inside my fingers. Now I wish I'd found something larger. At least then they wouldn't be laughing at me like I just told a joke.

But the leader isn't laughing. His eyes linger on the blade. He thought I would not fight. His dark eyes catch my gaze, hold. I can tell by the cruel twist of his lips he does not like surprises.

Watch out for him.

"Looky here," Mathias says as they close in. "Little Royalist bitch has claws."

"Won't be so funny when it's sticking out your gut, will it?" I taunt him with a smile. Apparently Everly March has an impulsive streak. If I make it out of here, I'll have to work on that.

The big one rushes me. I whip to face him.

Mistake. It's a feint, I realize, as Drake lunges at my exposed back.

I instinctively cringe, pivoting as I do. But other than a quiet *whoosh* of air and rustle of leaves, nothing happens. There's a sharp grunt and the sound of something being dragged quickly into the trees. Slippery shadows flick and dart in my periphery.

Drake is gone. The quiet stretches out then is shattered by a high-pitched scream.

And now there are two. So my plan is sound, after all.

My two former tormentors huddle close, their backs pressed together as they circle slowly.

A small shadow darts across the open space and hits the leader in the thigh. Childish laughter echoes through the trees. The leader touches his leg and holds his hand up. His face is blank with shock. Aiming the light at his palm, I see it drips with shiny red blood.

I fall into a quiet, loping jog. My flashlight bobs uselessly, so I put it away and concentrate on my knife and making sense of the darkness. Blurry bodies flash around me. A branch thwacks me in the cheek, but I'm too numb to feel it.

Part of me screams to go back. Find refuge with the others. I was better off with my tormentors, because three will always be better than one.

But I'm staking my life on the lesson I learned in the pit: When fighting over prey, the predators have to snuff each other first.

A small grayish sliver of light cuts through the pitch black. I'm out of the trees and running. Sprinting wildly. Now I can't stop. I think I hear shouts and screams from the woods, but I can't be sure. I have won. Have outsmarted the predators—and I didn't even have to use my knife.

The marketplace is empty. I cut through two stalls selling medicinal herbs and brace my hands on my knees. Now that my adrenaline has worn off, my body is shaking, and I'm reminded that I still desperately need something to eat.

I should go back to the home-that's-not-my-home. Judging by the shadow murk, Shadow Fall still has another half-hour to reign.

Go home, idiot. It's just food.

Except it isn't. It's walking back inside that house empty-handed and having to beg someone else for food. It's admitting that I am still the weak, scared Pit Leech living off others' scraps.

The flashlight whirs as I wind it, and the half-moon of light bursts into a brilliant star.

It takes five more stalls to find something suitable. Apples, an entire bucket full. They are bruised and overripe, but they smell of heaven. I find eggs, too, although most have been cracked. There are even a few potatoes and a leaking, half-empty sack of flower. Everything goes into a frayed green quilt someone was using as shade, which I tie together to make a sack.

I am as quiet as possible. Last minute I find some perfectly ripe strawberries scattered on the ground. Their fragrant smell moistens my mouth. Dusting them off, I remember how much Max loves strawberries and smile.

"Should have kept running, my lady."

A thin flap of flesh hangs from the leader's cheek, like perfectly sliced deli meat. One hand is trying to press it back into place. Two of his fingers are missing, but he doesn't seem to notice.

I feint right and twist to my left, ducking as I do. He catches me with an elbow to the cheek. Bright red stars. The ground smashes my face. I roll, kicking blindly. My heel smacks something meaty. He snares my leg and hooks his arm around my ankle, my foot now wedged inside his armpit. I cry out as his forearm slices into my Achilles tendon.

He's grunting like an animal, his eyes bulging with rage. For a moment we just stare at each other. He's making it intimate. Personal. He won't just be satisfied hearing me scream. He has to feel my breath on his face, my fingernails scraping his chest as I die.

It's now or never. If I don't use violence, he'll kill me.

I miss the knife until it's right above me. It glints softly. Then it drives straight down into my abdomen.

I turn on my side and use my thigh as a shield. The knife glances off my muscle. He raises the weapon again, and we play a cat-and-mouse game where I move my knee in line with his knife.

Kill him, Everly, Nicolai orders. *Kill him!*

In the pit, I often dreamt the monsters were trying to hurt me, but when I raised my weapon, it was something useless. A shoe. A butterfly. Once it was even a banana.

That's how I feel now, brandishing the tiny dagger from the padded room. The handle is slippery and light inside my blood-slicked palm, the blade no bigger than my pointer finger.

Just before I drive it up, in that long, stretched-out second, I see my mother's face looking down. *That's my girl*, she whispers.

Then her eyes become huge white saucers of surprise as the blade slips into her chest and sinks to the hilt. The grip on my ankle relaxes. My mother slumps, her head resting on my shoulder as her weight pins me to the cool earth. The warmth of her body seeps through my clothes and into my bones. Hot blood trickles down my neck and drips by my head.

I know it cannot be my mother lying over me. But I saw her. I saw *her*. *Reconstructed hallucination*. I gulp greedy breaths and tell myself what I need to hear. I'm not covered in blood. I'll close my eyes, count myself to sleep, and when I wake up, I'll be in my bed. This will be a nightmare. And I'll be me again.

Except I can't remember who that is anymore.

Everly, Nicolai says. *You are Everly March. Accept it.*

A choice. Be Everly March. Turn off my emotions. Finish my mission. Or be the girl I cannot remember. The girl afraid of her own shadow. The girl who would never take another's life.

The girl who will let Max die.

I rise. The body slips away like an apron, and blood rivers down my arms and legs. It's no longer warm.

A shadow stirs, and a flame comes to life. The lantern's soft glow centers on a man's white tunic and charcoal vest. A fashionable blue ribbon secures his shoulder-length raven-black hair.

But despite his gentlemanly trappings, his visage cuts to the bone, as if every part of him has been chiseled. Jagged widow's peak. Arched, dagger-ish eyebrows. Razor-edged cheekbones I could slice an apple on. One eye is stark blue, the other a clear, riveting green. Both are framed in charcoaled lashes so thick it appears he's wearing eyeliner. And both drink the new me in with unrepentant curiosity.

I suppose his features should be familiar, but it's his countenance—the way he holds his head at a slight angle and rakes me with his gaze—that I recognize.

Riser doesn't look corrupted. But I'm not sure what a corrupted person looks like. Certainly not *that*. Nicolai has given him a cruel, overwhelming sort of beauty that's meant to unsettle, to burrow deep under the skin and wriggle around a bit.

The other Chosen are aesthetically pleasing by design. Their good looks a harmonization of complimentary, symmetrical features meant to convey perfect health and impeccable breeding.

I think of Caspian. If his physical traits are a calming salve, Riser's are a crude weapon. But it doesn't matter how much Nicolai improved Riser's features because Nicolai could never completely erase the wild, predatory look that haunts Riser's face and makes him appear seconds away from ripping something apart.

For some reason, I feel relieved that he's okay and frown at the unwelcome feeling. My reconstruction must have softened my feelings toward Riser somehow.

The sun reappears, glistening off the pools of blood wetting the grass. I retrieve the strawberries, tie the blanket around them, and heft my loot over my shoulder. I'm surprised at how easy it is to ignore the body.

I hold up the bag. "Hungry?"

Riser's mismatched eyes cut to the corpse, my bloodied shirt, my face. A frown twitches his lips. His teeth, I notice, unlike the rest of his face, are not quite perfect. Slightly crooked. A small chip in the left canine. Not enough to draw attention, but enough to notice.

"You are bleeding," he points out.

"Obviously."

He hesitates before taking a tentative step closer. "I cannot shake this feeling I should . . . I don't know, help you, somehow."

He shifts under my stare. Hard as I try, I can't ignore the pity I feel watching him struggle with his newfound emotions.

But I quickly come to my senses. I am a monster now, just like him. A beautiful, vengeful monster. And in this game of monsters Nicolai has constructed, becoming something else, something that *feels*, means I lose.

I die.

I toss him the bag. "Ready, Pit Boy?"

Riser's intense stare never leaves my eyes as his hand snaps out to grab the food. I ignore the storm cloud of emotions brewing in his face. "On your command, my lady."

Bending down, he carefully retrieves my knife from the body, wiping the blood on his white handkerchief before handing it to me.

Between the fifth and the sixth intercostal.

A horrible, dark feeling comes over me as I realize instead of guilt I feel a sick sense of pride.

Chapter Thirteen

I know I'm having a waking memory. Even though I'm sitting on my bed, I can see my mother hunched over her desk as if she's right in front of me. Her hair is snared in a limp knot, a blue silk robe swallowing her slight figure. She's speaking to a hologram. I struggle to focus on my current surroundings, but my bed transforms into the scraped wood floor of my mother's office. They're discussing the low upload predictions. "Fienians are spreading rumors the upload is really a mass extermination," my mother is saying. "People are scared."

"Let the worms be scared!" Emperor Laevus hisses. There's a loud boom as his fist smashes into something hard, and I grip my bedcovers, trying to blink the vivid images away. "Most are going to die, anyway, and for the life of me I can't figure out why I'm trying to make it easier on them."

My mother hesitates. "Perhaps we should consider brokering a truce with the Fienians."

"How dare you speak of a truce with those worms to me! You remember what they did to Eleanor? My newborn daughter, Grace, barely past her name day?"

"She was my friend, Rand, of course I—"

"And she was my wife!" The Emperor leans forward, scratching his neck with his finger. "Why are you speaking of peace? Has there been talk of sympathy for the Fienians? What are the bloodsucking parasites at court saying?"

"No, my Emperor—"

"Perhaps it is time to cull the court again."

At first I wanted out of my hallucination, but now, curious, I focus on my mother as she holds up her hands in a soothing gesture. "When the Shadow Trials begin, Emperor, the populace will rally behind the Bronze finalists because they can relate better to them, and the uploads will improve. You'll see."

"No worms can ever enter Hyperion." He shakes his head to himself. "The finalists must be well bred and of noble blood, accustomed to court and our ways."

"Of course, there are thousands of disgraced Golds from once prominent Houses who would jump at the chance to—"

"We must be careful that no worms slip through, Lillian. Once the finalists enter the Island, they must be mentored beneath Chosen so that we can monitor them. Now"—he steeples his hands together—"let's discuss that droll little Bronze you insisted on marrying."

The memory is beginning to fade, my mother's desk melting into the walls of my bedroom, and I fight to see what happens next. My mother grows very still. There's a sense of menace I don't understand, and the idea someone could make the strongest woman I know practically cower forms a cold pit in my stomach.

"I've learned he's been asking around about certain banned tech." The Emperor's sharp eyes glitter dangerously. "Do I need to have Victoria speak with him?"

"No! You will not have that—"

A knock on the door jolts me back into reality. Before I can recover from being thrust into the past, Brogue enters wearing a stained yellow apron with bright-purple tulips and smelling of something delicious. Bramble chirps at his presence and scampers to the edge of the bed to greet him. After a pause, Brogue crosses the floor and then sits on the bed next to me.

He clears his throat. Two-day old bristle shadows his jaw, and his eyes are tarred—shiny and loose. As he struggles with where to place his hand, I wonder how far gone he is. It's hard to tell with tar. Twitchers can look fine one second and completely unspool the next.

"Flame bartered for meat," he says, stroking Bramble's smooth back. "That and what you nabbed, we got ourselves a fine meal."

"Not hungry," I lie, glaring up at the stars. Considering my arms have begun to itch like crazy, and my brain has decided to replay my memories with an invisible projector, my threshold for Mercs in silly aprons is rather low. I grunt as I dig my fingernails over my flesh in an attempt to curb the worms-under-my-skin feeling.

Brogue clears his throat. *Again*. Clearly talking to girls isn't his specialty. "Got Simulations tonight. Need your strength."

I scratch my neck. "I'll survive."

"Quiet out there." The bed lifts as he stands. Crossing to the window, he raps the glass with his knuckles and frowns.

"Curfew."

"Not for another hour."

My stomach rumbles. "What'd she barter with, anyway? Not her charm, that's for sure."

"The little firebrand?" There's a gruff chuckle. "Now that I got no idea about. Don't think I care to, either."

"Squirrel?"

"Meat, Lady March. Ain't gotta know what kind."

I roll to face him, grinning. "How do you know if a Fienian's close?"

Brogue's eyes sparkle. "All the cats and dogs go missing."

"So you don't mind that she's a Fienian Rebel?"

"None of my bloody business."

I cross my arms. "The Marquis Ezra Croft, he none of your business either?"

As soon as I mention the dead Fienian Rebel leader, Brogue's entire body tenses. "Not anymore."

Anymore? "But it was . . . once?"

He sighs. "Another lifetime ago. I was there for the bombing of

Dominus during the truce agreement. The Emperor was a fool to think Fienians and Royalists could make peace and a bigger fool to trust Ezra, but he was just a pup then, a foolhardy Emperor who had to prove his father wrong. He even broadcast the truce agreement, as if he was some kind of hero."

Emperor Rand III played the video of the event on the rift screens every morning for ten years afterward so the populace would never forget the Fienians' atrocities. I can still picture the tiny furrow that would crease my mother's forehead as we stirred our steaming oatmeal and watched the Emperor's wife and child blown to bits.

I remember the first time I realized the girl in the front row of the ceremony was my mother. Barely twenty, she wore the long white wig popular then, a royal blue cloak cascading gloriously around her, hiding her scandalous pregnancy with me. She stood with several from House Lockhart and the other prominent Gold Houses at the time. Silvers packed the stadium in front of Laevus Square, Bronzes overflowing the streets to watch.

Emperor Rand Laevus's family stood off to the side, protected by Gold Cloaks, the guards assigned to protect the Royal family. The lustrous cloaks they're named for sparkled around the Royals like a ring of beautiful, deadly flames. Prince Caspian and his twin, Princess Ophelia, barely one, each held a guard's hand while their mother, Empress Eleanor, cradled the newborn Princess Grace.

Ezra's red cloak rippled across the podium as he exited, a bright spot in a sea of blue and black and silver and gold, and then red blood painted the rift screen, and a deafening shriek roared through the speakers. That's what I remember.

Then the silence.

Then the screams.

The bomb was a Fienian specialty, a nano-shredder, meaning when the Empress strode across the podium to speak, holding her infant daughter, the millions of nano-shrapnel implanted beneath the scaffolding basically turned them to dust. But the nanos weren't through. They still had thousands of bodies to find, flesh to pierce, blood to splatter, bone to pulverize.

Surrounded by the Gold Cloaks, Prince Caspian and Princess Ophelia remained untouched, as did the Emperor. But my mother still wears the large, pale-pink scar across her collarbone and neck from that day.

Now, with those unsettling thoughts weighing on my mind, I frown at Brogue. "Well, you might trust the Fienians, but I never will."

"And yet, here you are."

"That's unfair."

"War is unfair. The asteroid shadowing us is unfair. Life is unfair. Maybe it's time, my lady, you stopped believing your life is going to *be* fair."

What he says is true, yet I can't help but dislike him for it. "Well, if it were, I wouldn't be stuck with Mercs and Fienian Rebels, would I?"

Brogue stiffens. "You should eat."

His voice is clipped, formal, and hints at the demise of our friendship. It also smacks of an order.

We face off in a staring contest that I win. He makes it all the way to the door before he turns around. "You know, what Nicolai does or who he employs, it ain't my business." One hoary eyebrow arches over a wink. "Above my pay grade."

"But that's the benefit of being a twitcher, right?" I prop up on my elbows. "You get to just dance along to the Puppeteer's strings without a single emotion to get in the way."

Brogue narrows his eyes. "Clever girl. But if you were really sharp, you'd know I don't dance for no one, Lady March, least of all a man like Nicolai."

"Then why are you here?" It comes out more accusation than question. I can't shake the feeling there's more to his story. And I need to ferret it out if I'm to stay ahead of Nicolai's game.

"To keep you safe."

"Funny." My voice sounds cold even to me. "Could have used you earlier. Or was that the Puppeteer's plan all along. The ultimate test?"

"Hear you did just fine without me."

My fingers flutter to my collar. "Fine isn't the word I'd choose." I pause. "You meant *us*. To keep *us* safe."

"Right. What I said."

"No. You said to keep *me* safe."

"We twitchers say the screwiest things." Winking, he brings three fingers together over his brow in the Centurion's salute.

"Then it must be the tar made you forget a lady of my stature gets a bow, Merc."

The artery in his neck jumps. With a tight jaw, Brogue performs a sweeping, elegant bow I would never have imagined him capable of and then slips out the door.

Thing is, I've seen that particular curtsy—chin tucked, knee an exact inch from the floor, hand circling three times—before. It's the elite Centurion bow, typically used for members of the court and Royalty.

So Nicolai is employing a Merc who was once a Gold Cloak in the Royal Guard. I smile, knowing I am one step closer to understanding Nicolai's game.

CHAPTER FOURTEEN

"Maggot." The voice stirs me from sleep. The Archduchess stands over my bed, her face in shadow, the end of her hatpin a hair's breadth above my cornea. I try to blink, but two Centurions hold my eyelids open. My arms are tied to the bed.

I thrash, but it does no good. "No, please—"

"Did you really think you could hide from me, Maggot?"

The hatpin plunges down . . .

The curfew sirens blast me from my nightmare. I'm lying in a pool of sweat, my arms red from scratching in my sleep. *Blasted itching!* Wiping my eyes, I try to erase the image of the Archduchess. But her shadowy face haunts me.

She's going to find me. I can feel it.

I peel off the bed and wet my lips with a glass of tepid, suspiciously metallic-tasting water. It settles uneasily at the bottom of my empty stomach. *Remember who you are now. You're Everly, not weak Maia. And Everly isn't afraid of anyone.*

The crew is gathered in the foyer. All eyes find me as I descend the stairs.

"Have a good nap, Princess?" Flame asks, her voice deceptively sugar-sweet.

She's trying to embarrass me. My feet whisper down the stairs and across the faded-yellow wool rug. Everyone goes quiet. I stop when Flame and I are toe to toe. Flame blinks, and I smile. She's about to learn Lady March doesn't tolerate teasing. "Why don't you ask Brogue how much I enjoy nicknames?"

Flame grins. "Aww, Princess, loosen your corset a bit—"

"You created me. You know exactly what I'm capable of." I watch with deep satisfaction as Flame's grin dies a slow death. "You might be able to get your hand on your dagger, but thanks to you and your outlawed tech, mine will already be at your throat, or your belly, or the numerous other places I now know to snuff someone."

Silence. Flame has finally lost her voice.

I'm beginning to like being Lady March, I think, as I follow the others down the hall. Riser slows. I try to increase my pace to pass him, but his hand cups the inside of my right arm. His fingers are surprisingly warm and strong. "My lady, for you." A bright-green apple rests on his open palm. It matches his one green eye. "From dinner."

I stare at the apple. Imagine the sweet, fragrant juice, the crunch as my teeth pierce its shiny skin. My stomach burns with need. I fight off the unexpected feeling of gratitude bubbling up inside me, chalking it up to my reconstruction.

"Thanks, but no thanks." I reclaim my arm; he steps in front of me. For a moment I look around, because this dapper, generous man with wide shoulders cannot be Riser. But the blue eye, the one colored like a bruise and haunted with unspoken horrors, tells me otherwise.

"Take it. I know you're hungry."

I bristle at his order. Using my newfound skills—thank you, Flame—I pivot, smash my shoulder into his chest, and wriggle past him. There's just a hint of leather and soap.

Cage sticks his head out of the office and wags a stern, come-hither eyebrow at me.

I hold up a wait-finger and whip around. A normal person would crash into me, but Riser isn't normal, not by half, and his body gracefully halts an inch from mine. "You might think things are different now," I blurt, "but I know underneath that shiny façade, you're the same murderous creature from the pit."

"Maybe." His mismatched eyes hold me in place with their intensity, his teeth grinding as he searches for his words. "But . . . I want to say . . . *thank you*."

I raise an eyebrow.

"What you did during my reconstruction."

All the air leaves me as I remember how I cradled his pitiful, dying body in my arms.

"I know what I am, Everly," he continues softly. "But I won't hurt *you*. What can I do to prove that?"

"Die." And I mean it. Thanks to my mother, I already had trust issues. But now, as Lady March, I know trust is weakness. "That's the only way I will ever trust you."

The ghost of a smile flits across his lips. "Fair enough."

Fair enough? Who responds that way, a psychopath? Irritated and still itching, I stomp into my mother's office where they have the Caskets rigged for Sims.

"Have a good talk?" Cage asks as I slip by him.

"I think we came to an understanding."

My mother's office is small, and the Caskets take up most of it. Flame has rewired them to act as Simulators, but my stomach flutters anyway at the thought of climbing in. The only part of the room that's still the same is the bookshelf on the far wall.

As if reading my mind, Riser inspects the book nearest him. His tunic rustles as he reaches for the worn tome, but his fingers slice through the mirage.

I dig my nails into my forearms and groan. "It's not real, Pit Boy." My voice comes out more annoyed than I plan; the itching has made me grumpy.

Flame cuts her gaze at me before interjecting, "The Royalists destroyed all the real books years ago, Riser. Remember?"

"Right." Riser's sharp Adam's apple bobs as he swallows. "I . . . I know that."

Cage and Flame share a cryptic look. As I climb into the Simulator, I wonder just how much of Riser's reconstruction actually worked. By now he should be as familiar with this world as if he grew up in it.

My back arches against the cold metal, and I stretch out inside the smooth shell. It smells like burnt plastic and metal. Riser disappears into his Casket to my right, and I rest my head and try to concentrate on Flame's instructions.

"This will be the final test," Flame says. "We will be checking your new skills—problem solving, adaptability, resourcefulness, cunning, calm under duress—as well as rooting out traces of old habits that could get in the way of the mission. You'll both be working separately, but a guide will talk each of you through the Sim." Her gaze lands on me this time. I'm guessing she's my guide and she's not particularly thrilled about it. "Afterwards, we'll fix what we can."

Brogue crosses his meaty arms. "I've seen level 5 Sims run before, minx. They need two weeks post-reconstruction and an entire day of prep. You know the risks of going in too soon."

Flame throws up her arms in annoyance. "Thirty-six hours from now, these two need to report to Royalist Headquarters, so we go now or not at all."

My mouth goes dry. In less than two days, I enter the court I despise. As much as I want to say I'm not afraid, I'm terrified.

"We clear?" Flame says, glancing at me. My blank expression confirms her suspicion I wasn't listening. "If you see anything strange or out of place," she repeats, "like something that shouldn't be there or even just a sideways feeling, it means there is a glitch in the program and you need to pull the red lever near the ceiling."

For some reason I raise my hand. "And if I don't?"

Flame's expression leaves no room for argument. "Do."

Cage's head appears upside down over me, his minty breath

puffing over my cheeks. "And, darling, try your very hardest not to die suddenly."

"Draw it out," Flame adds. "A bullet to the gut gives us enough time to extract you from the Sim before you expire, but if we don't manage to pull you before death—"

"Headaches," Cage interjects, "concussion, coma, irreparable brain damage. The usual."

I blow out an anxious breath. "Noted."

I've seen the cage-like apparatus they strap onto your head from the propaganda films, so I'm expecting the cold, hard weight against my temples. I wasn't, however, expecting the panic having your head immobilized induces.

Just before the visor rolls down over my vision, I see Brogue, his head cocked sideways, a sleek silver flask held to his lips. He nods toward me as if I'm a prizefighter he's betting on, takes a long pull from the bottle, and salutes with his free hand.

Suddenly the apparatus makes a sharp hissing noise and clamps like a vice. My eyes bulge and flutter with the unexpected pain. Nothing. A gray, formless nothing. Sound is muffled, as if I am underwater.

Can you hear me? Flame's voice swims lazily through the water.

Yes. I think I speak it, except my mouth hasn't moved.

Good. Just so you know—Riser is going to win, and then everyone will see you for the weak coward you are.

Wait . . .

Vibrations. My Casket is moving. No, it's something else. The sound of something powering up, gathering steam. There's a powerful release of air followed by a shrill whistle. I am swaying back and forth. *Chugugugugugug.*

I'm on a train!

Other sounds fill my ears: passengers conversing, chinaware and delicate silver rattling, operatic music, the shriek of wheel breaks.

The landscape outside the window is blinding white. Muted-blue sky flows through the snowy canvas like a swollen river. Occasionally a puff of snow breaks off from the top of the train and gives the illusion of clouds.

A stiff daffodil-yellow dress with dark fur trimmings and blue soutache embroidery rustles around me and screams Royalist. An exquisite emerald-green fox muff warms my hands. I fight a teasing breath from the corset pythoning my ribs and try to sit, but the adjustable bustle interferes.

Really? I think, twisting to alleviate the corset bone stabbing my side. *Nicolai couldn't find anything more comfortable?*

Beauty has a price, Princess, Flame's voice purrs.

I think about what she said just before the Sim. So Riser and I are working against each other. *Well, it doesn't matter what you dress me in; there's no way in Fienian hell I'm letting that one-eyed freak win.*

If you say so. Her voice sounds bored. I'm wasting valuable time—I doubt Riser is conversing right now about his outfit.

I approach the first table. A sharp-dressed man and woman laugh at something, the woman's pinky circling the gold-gilded teacup's edge as steam curls through her fingers. The enormous diamond-encrusted Gold ring dangling from her knuckle threatens to fall in.

What should I say?

"What's your Color?" the woman demands.

Flame's amused voice interjects. *Lady March isn't a church mouse, Princess.*

Right. And she wouldn't plead either. She would take control of the situation. After all, before her family fell from grace, they were high-ranking Golds.

"None of your concern," I stammer, glad for the muff hiding my fidgeting hands.

The solemn face of a tall gentleman in a dark suit blocks my way. Behind him stand two twitchy Centurions. "Well, young lady, it certainly is my concern. Ticket, please."

Crap. I search both my pockets, but they're empty. That means no ticket. A whisper of panic trills through me as I hide my sweaty hands back in the muff.

Be cool. There has to be a point to this. Think.

"She obviously doesn't belong here," the woman quips. "Arrest her."

"Ticket." The conductor's jaw tightens. "I won't ask again."

I swallow. If I am arrested, the Sim is over and Riser has won. *You will not let Pit Boy win. Think. What is out of place? What doesn't make sense?*

Suddenly, calm comes over me as my brain works the mystery out. Slipping one hand out of the muff, I flip my wrist, offering up the golden ticket that has been here the entire time.

The man glances at the ticket, glances at me, and gives an irritated nod toward the back. "This car is for Golds, my lady."

"Sorry," I say. "I must have gotten myself turned around."

I scan the walls as if trying to gather my bearings to leave. *What do I do now?* I feel helpless, inept, and completely out of place.

A little help, Flame?

Just give up. She barks a high-pitched laugh at my expense. *I bet you're good at that.*

If Flame intends to make me feel defeated, her words have the opposite effect. They remind me of the darkness. The fear. They remind me how naïve and ignorant I was. They remind me I can never be that girl again.

I spot a dapper looking man by the window. Shoulders back and chin held high, I glide purposefully toward him. "Excuse me," I say, resting one hand atop his right shoulder. I angle my head so my neck is exposed. Just as planned, his deep-set brown eyes trace a quick route from my pulse-point to my breasts, which are squeezed uncomfortably high on my neckline. "You look like the kind of man who knows what to do next."

Flattery and seduction. Two readily accessible weapons apparently

Lady March excels at. My mother would be proud. "Why," he says, "Lady March, I was beginning to think you would never ask." His eyes settle over my breasts again as he hands me the note. "Read this quickly but carefully. You haven't much time."

Retreating to the corner, my eyes flicker over the elegant script scrawled across the white paper: *Find the man in the middle train car with the Gold rose on his lapel and kill him.*

Just like that, I know I've lost. There is no way I can beat Riser when it comes to this kind of challenge. He's probably already halfway there by now.

But Fienian hell, I have to try.

CHAPTER FIFTEEN

The train curves around a gray mountain, allowing an unobstructed view of its length through the frosted window. I stop counting at twenty. Twenty plus cars, at least ten standing between me and the man I have to kill. Even then, I have no weapon.

The next train car is larger and louder than the first. Silken dresses, in every shade of black imaginable, rustle and spin over a parquet floor meant for dancing.

Dark, beautiful men slip through the shimmery sea of women like slippery black eels. One such man takes my hand and pulls me into the foray. Bowing, he holds his hands palm up, left higher than right. My hands meet his and we are moving in step with the others, acting out a dance I have never done before but should know. There's pressure at my waist as he turns me. The mirrored ceiling spins into a whirlpool. My count is off, and my elbow collides with a woman's shoulder.

Everyone looks at me at once. I find the count again with my feet— shuffle, shuffle, step—using my breath to find the rhythm, but another misstep has me stumbling over my partner's patent leather shoes.

The dancers don't look at me this time, but something has changed. They're spinning faster, arms and legs moving in an almost violent display. The music hammers inside my chest. The air's so thick I can hardly catch my breath. My partner seems to have slipped away.

An opening appears between two women, and I take it, darting through. A mass of bodies blocks my escape, and someone shoves me back. Although they are not looking at me, the crowd is slowly closing in.

A flash! I twist just in time to miss the knife aimed at my neck, and kick at the mob, making just enough room to slip through the tangle of flesh.

A woman breaks off from the group, a whip clenched inside her white glove. The air snaps as her whip comes down across my thigh. I cry out. With a calm smile, she brings the whip down again, the tip strafing my cheek. There's a white-hot sting and then my cheek goes numb.

I flinch, but the next blow never comes. The tip of the whip, a black horsetail, has wrapped around my hand. I yank it free and run.

The next car is quiet and nearly empty. Sun pours in from the large windows, filling the space with bright, relentless light. A man stands behind a table in the middle of the room. Drawing near, I see weapons are laid out on it.

"Lady March," the man says in a nasally voice. He eyes his pewter timepiece. "You are unacceptably late." A black top hat crowns wispy white hair and watery, pale-blue eyes. As he talks, his fingers pinch the ends of his white handlebar mustache.

"My apologies," I say. I can't draw my eyes away from the table. Lined in a neat row are a small pearl-handled knife, a garrote, a wooden club, a silver crossbow and three sleek arrows, a large silver pistol, and a vial of poison, clearly marked by the skull and crossbones.

I quickly weigh my options. The weapon needs to be small enough I can hide it on my person, which eliminates the pistol, club, and crossbow. And the poison has too many unknown factors. So I'm left with the garrote and the knife.

I reach to examine the garrote, but the man stops me. "There is a price for everything, Lady March."

"Of course," I say in a surprisingly calm voice, considering I have no idea how I will pay. I find both pockets of my dress empty, *again*. My muff . . . but I lost that in the last car. I have nothing to barter with. Perhaps I was supposed to pickpocket someone while dancing, but that option is lost to me now.

Ooh, not good, Flame remarks in my head.

One bushy white eyebrow rises. "Problem?"

"No." I shake my head for emphasis, setting a few of my tresses—curled and teased into a romantic nest crowning my skull—free. "No problem. I'm just"—looking around, I spy a crystal decanter; the sunlight turns the dark red liquid a tumescent plum and skips inside the three cordial glasses beside it—"thirsty."

The man hasn't taken his eyes off me. The way his stare keeps flitting to my pockets tells me he suspects I am up to something, but he wants to believe me. His greed blinds him.

I reach into my cleavage as if there is actually something in there. "I will pay you twice the asking price."

His gaze lands on my chest, and an expectant flush reddens his cheeks. "A toast, then."

As he pours our glasses, I think about my next move. My heart beats so loudly I think he'll surely realize that I don't actually plan to pay. But he hands me the cool, light glass, raises his, and smiles. "To your unfailing generosity and my unfailing health."

And then I understand. He was expecting me to try and use one of the weapons to kill him and take what I wanted. Well, I'm changing things a bit.

Our glasses meet in a loud *chink*. There's the sound of shattering glass, and the liquid in my cup bleeds from the jagged edge where it has broken, staining the fur lining of my sleeve. "Oh, goodness," I say, trying to look embarrassed. "That was my fault."

The man's glass still wavers in the air. A beam of sunlight pierces its contents and dances over his impenetrable expression. "Of course," the man says, his words slow and careful. "How clumsy of you."

The last remaining glass swells with the dark liquid. He hesitates before handing the drink to me.

"Bottoms up?" I say, my words slurred with impatience.

The liquid hits my lips first. Blackberry rum, by the taste of it—a Royalist favorite. The man, who still seems troubled by something, lifts his glass, slowly, his mouth parting. I stop breathing as I watch the red liquid swim up the glass. Kiss his lips . . .

He slams the drink down with a crash, spitting. Purplish-red rum explodes onto the table and rivers down his chin. I can't tell if he swallowed anything or not.

"You cheated!" he accuses. One finger touches the red stain under his chin where the poisoned liquid still dribbles. His gaze rests on the bottle marked with an X. I didn't have time to put it back exactly where it went, and it sits on the edge of the table now. A smile stretches his lips. "Clever girl."

My hands go numb. *Fienian hell, he didn't swallow it.*

Then his jaw slackens, his eyes dull, and he melts to the floor, the mannequin-grin still plastered across his face. A flimsy red ribbon trickles from his nose.

"I'm sorry," I say, dropping the garrote and the knife into each pocket—all that will fit. But I'm not. As hard as I try, I am not sorry.

Not one bit.

There's a clawing sense of urgency now as I slip into the next train car. I stop dead in my tracks. Children, a carload of boys and girls clothed in clean white linen. Relief washes over me as I realize I won't have to use violence at least, whatever this car holds in store for me.

Various children's toys—wooden trains, blocks, a spinning top— litter the floor. I step over them as I walk. The children scamper around me as if I'm invisible. The floor shakes with the stomping of their bare feet. My skirt hem sweeps in front of me, knocking over a spinning top. It rolls across the floor and bangs against the side of the car. A dull, nagging sense of unease tickles the nape of my neck.

This is too easy.

I'm nearly to the door when a breeze whispers against my cheek. A free strand of my hair, coppery-red in this pure light, tickles my bottom lip. The window to my right gapes wide open. A child is clinging to the outside. Little fingers clench the windowsill, his head pressed down, acting as a lever to keep him from falling as his brown hair waves in the wind.

One of his hands slips and he cries out, just barely holding on, his fingers smudging the glass. The other children ignore him.

I have to make a decision. Save the boy or finish my mission and win. I am surprised by how little I feel for him, despite knowing I am his only hope. Actually, I resent him for being weak. For not helping himself.

My feet move. The wind tugs mercilessly at my hair and waters my eyes. I see the boy's face as he peers up at me. I don't know why I'm here—I meant to go the other way. But part of me is relieved I'm not a complete monster. I'm still redeemable.

I help him over the side. That's when I notice the golden whistle dangling from his neck. He smiles up at me, brown eyes sparkling with gratitude, takes the whistle between his lips, and blows.

The children stop playing. "What are you doing?" I shout over the hum of the train. "Stop!" I yell as he brings the whistle once again to his lips. Through the door leading back to the dance car, I see the faraway form of a Centurion. His head turns in question as another loud shriek from the whistle pierces my eardrums.

"You're not Lady Everly March." The boy's face has twisted into a hateful grimace, and his lips curl around the whistle for a third blow. The Centurion will find me if he does.

"Please," I beg. "Don't."

I thought I wasn't a monster. But my hands, beautifully slim, graceful, aristocratic hands meant for dancing across a piano or pouring tea, cup each tiny shoulder, his child's bones sharp and fragile beneath my palms, and give a small push.

I stare at the void where he clung. My hands are still held up, perfectly still, remorseless. A snow flurry dances through the window and lands on one manicured fingertip, disappears.

I dig through my pockets, searching for the weapons as I make my way to the next car. I feel distant, removed from myself. My reflection catches in the windowpane of the door right before I open it. The sunlight illuminates my right half, leaving the left side dark. For the briefest of moments, I see the girl I used to be resolve from the darkness. Her innocent, plain face smiles at me, my reflection perfectly opposite halves.

Old and new.

Weak and strong.

I'm sorry, I think, as she melts away just like the snowflake, and I open the door to the next train car. *There's no place for you anymore.*

Except that I'm wrong. My mother waits for me, dressed in a gold jumpsuit, her foil raised in guard position, ready to lunge. The entire train car is an exact replica of the padded room. A golden foil rests at my feet.

"Mom!" I know she's not real. I know she's not. But all I want to do is fling myself into her arms and cry. "Mom—"

"On your guard!" she snaps, her coiled body trembling with anticipation, just like all the other times.

And then I realize they put her in here to mess with me. Somehow—probably during my reconstruction—they know about those torturous sessions.

This isn't a reunion; it's a duel. One that I have to fight and win if I want to beat Pit Boy— which I do, *desperately.*

I lean down, grip the pommel, hefting the foil from one hand to the other to test its weight. Satisfied, I salute and drop low, stretching my arm until the foil is aimed directly at her heart. My left arm curves back and over my head like the tail of a scorpion. I make eye contact with my mother. "Ready."

My mother lunges forward like a cobra. I counter and retreat. The tip of her foil stabs just inches from my heart. Before I can recover, she is lunging again. A scream rises inside me, and I slam into the back of the train car, circling to my right. She follows, hardly moving, a steel spring. She's getting closer. I trip, nearly miss getting ran through. As she recovers guard position, her eyes lock onto mine. "You're weak, Maia. Weak and slow and—"

She springs forward, her foil whistling through the air toward my throat. The tip glances off my neck. Warm blood seeps onto the hem of my bodice.

"Weak and slow and easily distracted," she continues, her feet silent as they gain ground without seeming to move. "Are you giving up, Maia?"

She attacks again, and I drop low for a stop-thrust, barely missing her chest. "That's not my name!"

"No? I had a daughter like you once. She was weak, scared. *Helpless.*"

"And then you abandoned her!" I lunge, and she parries without so much as a grunt. "You left your children to die!" I lunge again, but she snakes her foil low, and it pierces my shoulder.

I howl with pain and fall back before she can thrust again.

Her lips press together in derision. "Weak, weak Maia. You're no daughter of mine."

Blood drips to the padded white floor. I can't beat her. The anger and disappointment I feel is so real it nearly chokes me. My mother is right. Even reconstructed, I'm not good enough. I'll never be good enough.

I can end this now, Flame offers. *No reason to suffer if you've already lost.*

Oh, what I would have given for someone to have ended it back then. Outright losing on purpose would have only enraged my mother, so I learned to make it look like I was losing on accident, finding more and more inventive ways to lose.

If anything, those sessions taught me to be cunning and resourceful.

My mother resumes the guard position in preparation for the finishing blow. But my eyes are glued to the faint outline of the door. "I wasn't what you wanted, Mother," I say, working to keep my voice from cracking, "but I was clever."

She scoffs, her body coiled to spring. "And how does being clever win a fight?"

"It doesn't. It gets me out of one."

I leap for the door as she strikes. My hand slams the door handle, it cracks open, and I wedge my body through. Slumping down the door, I suck air for a moment, going over my plan. The idea is so simple I wonder how I missed it. I don't have to fight my way to the middle train car. In fact, if I have any chance of winning at all, I need to go back to the pilot car, which is closer. I squint at the door in front of me, grimacing at the thought of crossing through the cars I have already passed.

Unless I'm being clever and I cross *over* them.

Hysterical laughter seeps from my throat.

Princess, you've gone crazy, Flame accuses. Coming from her the term might be a compliment.

You want crazy, Fienian? Watch this.

The ladder leading to the roof is slick with ice. At the top, a blast of wind pelts snow against my cheeks and rips the last of my trapped hair free, whipping it across my vision. The sun has peeked below the mountain.

I force a tiny step, trying not to look at the ground thousands of feet below. The unfinished bridge looms ahead, closer than I hoped.

My boots slip and slide across the thin icy slush covering the roof. My stomach plunges each time as my brain unhelpfully provides scenes of me plummeting to my death. I make it to the end of the car and have successfully navigated my jump to the next train car when I hear it. Or, rather, *feel* it.

Someone is behind me.

I know it's Riser before I even turn around. For some reason, I'm not surprised. All the fears I had about him suddenly come true as I glance at the pistol hanging loosely in his left hand. My chest lightens, and a strange hollowness fills me.

I had assumed all along Riser's orders were the same as mine. And they were similar. He was ordered to kill *someone*.

Me.

"Lady March." Riser is wearing an irreverent grin, his hair blowing in the wind. His coal-black doublet and crimson cloak makes a striking contrast against his pale skin. Not one trace of doubt or remorse graces his admittedly handsome countenance.

He runs two fingers over his chin, as if he finds my predicament curious. Only the gap between train cars separates us—not that his pistol particularly minds. I fight the brief tinge of pleasure his presence brings, knowing it is only my reconstruction.

Seriously, how could I be happy to see someone who's about to kill me?

"Pit Boy," I yell in greeting over the wind, suddenly wishing I'd chosen the crossbow. An arrow sticking out of the hollow of his throat would make me giddy right now. "You've won, so follow your orders like a good boy and shoot me."

His brow furrows. "Is that what you want?"

I pause. Something's off. He should have shot me by now. Maybe he's toying with me? Does he want to rub in his victory? Give me a tiny glimmer of hope so he can snatch it from my hands?

"We received the same orders, Lady March. The man with the Gold rose? I met him. Nice fella." He lifts a defiant eyebrow. "But I'm not following their orders."

Our eyes lock. He's leaned so far over the gap even the tiniest bump would send him over. Although I'm sure I would like that, the thought makes my palms sweat. Whatever he's trying to do, he seems conflicted. As if one part of him wants to jump across the divide and push me into the abyss and the other part is fighting him.

"Then whose orders are you following?"

He sighs, as if he can't believe what he's about to say. "Yours."

My hand slaps the scream back into my mouth as he plummets

over the side, his cape streaming behind him. I watch his body flip end over end until it becomes a dark pebble against the snow.

There's a shriek of surprise inside my head as Flame reacts. "Quick! Pull him!"

Her voice snaps me out of shock. The bridge looms ahead, too close. *Run, idiot,* my brain screams.

And then I do.

CHAPTER SIXTEEN

Tiny, piercing pinpricks. They stab at my exposed face and fingers. My lips feel hard and cold and hurt to move, and the blood on the neck of my blouse has turned into an icy crust. I relax my frozen body into the lounger at the back of the empty engine car, trying to work enough warmth into my fingers so I can grip the garrote. Luckily, the heat from the engine furnace has made this room insufferably hot and my fingers become bendable again.

I'm not sure what I'm expecting when I open the pilot door. I know there will be a conductor. I know to change the train's course, I will have to kill him.

But I'm not expecting the conductor to be my father. "Hello, Maiabug," he says.

I blink and rub my eyes. For a second, he wavers. The tiniest of glitches. So small I assume I have made it up.

Something's not right, Flame says. *Look up, above the door.*

I do as commanded.

See the red lever? Pull it!

I want to, but I can't. My father is smiling at me, his gentle eyes warm and bright. I know it's not real, but I don't care. He's talking to me. It's a conversation we had right before he died. I struggle to hear the words.

Pull the lever, Flame orders. Her voice is unusually calm, which actually scares me more than if it was panicked.

"It's okay," my dad is saying. He reaches out to comfort me. Just like when I was nine, I pull away, angry at him because my mother isn't here to blame. "We all want to cling to who we were. But you're not a child, anymore, Maiabug, and it's time for you to grow up."

"If I do," I say, "I'll become someone else."

My father's face distorts so that his eyes droop a bit. The leather conductor's chair he sits in becomes his favorite green club chair, and part of the train's windshield warbles and transforms into the lit fireplace behind him.

His normally rich voice becomes mechanical sounding. "We all have to change." The garrote, which has somehow made it into my hands, quivers. His big melty eyes glance at the garrote. He smiles. "But no matter how much you change, you will always be my beautiful little girl."

The windshield wavers, and just like a screen changing channels, the image flips back to the landscape outside the train. The bridge rises up to the right. If I don't switch tracks now, I'll miss my chance.

Last time I tell you, Princess, Flame says. *Pull it.*

The lever, Everly. Nicolai's voice joins Flame's.

Instead, I turn to my father. "You know what I have to do, Daddy."

He nods, a small frown darkening his face. "Survive."

The garrote slips easily around his neck. I avert my head and twist, counting to sixty. His body slumps at forty-seven. Somehow my fingers find the right button on the dashboard to switch the tracks. There's screeching. The train rocks to the right, shuddering as it navigates the sharp turn.

I look up, but the red lever at the top is gone. I call to Flame for instructions, but she no longer responds.

Ignoring the body in the chair, I find the door, crack it. The wind rips it from my hands.

Bridge, sky, bridge, sky.

I wait. Time dribbles by. And then I look down, and instead of train tracks I see air.

There's a hideous metal-on-metal noise, as if the train is screaming, and the floor vanishes from my feet. Total silence, as if I'm inside a vacuum. I am suspended in the air. Weightless. A curious falling feeling fills my middle. Steaming black coffee trickles from the black mug floating by my head. For a single, haunting moment, I am frozen.

My father stands amidst the paused wreckage. But not the glitched version—the flesh and blood one. The kiss-you-before-bed one. The burn-your-toast one.

The dead one.

Every last detail of him is real. The white hairs that make his auburn hair appear blond in the sunlight. The two deep-set lines that crinkle his forehead. His wire-framed spectacles, lens cracked in the corner, peek from his pocket. Glass shards, frozen in time, sparkle around his head. And I understand that somehow, somehow, he has left this last piece of himself for me inside the Sim.

"The key," he says, his deep-set eyes imploring. "You must keep the key safe. Do whatever it takes."

"Daddy, wait," I beg in a strangled voice.

"We don't have much time. Listen, don't trust anyone. You need to find your journ—"

Just like that, he's gone. As if we were paused and someone has pushed play, everything erupts at once. Glass shards embed inside the exposed flesh of my head and hands. Something smashes my mouth, and I feel my front teeth grind to bits. The air shrieks with horrible death noises—a cacophony of horrifying screams.

One of them, I know, is the man with the Gold rose.

It takes all the energy I have left to hold onto the open door, drag myself over the side, the wind painting my face with my blood.

Survive. My father's voice pierces the chaos. I straighten up, my dress billowing out in a whipping plume of yellow.

I will, Daddy, I promise, *whatever it takes.* Then I spread my arms and fly.

A god-awful noise awakens me. It takes less than a second to realize I'm screaming, or rather, gurgling animalistic half-shrieks and flailing madly. Brogue bear-hugs me to a stand.

I go limp, but my mind is wild with rage. "What the Fienian hell was that?" Flame is the closest, so I focus my wrath on her. "Did you put my parents in the Sim to mess with my mind?"

"Believe me, Princess," Flame spits, "that ship sailed a *long* time ago."

I look to Cage. "I want to go back in."

Brogue squeezes my shoulders. "Easy, Lady March—"

"No!" I bat his hands away. "He was trying to tell me something, and Flame extracted me before I could hear it!"

"No," Flame says carefully. I must look on the verge of violence because she's backed against Riser's Casket, keeping at least four feet between us. "That was the glitch. It makes you see and hear things that aren't there." There's a pause. "And I didn't pull you. You were too far gone."

"O-kay," I say, "then who did?"

Everyone is staring at me. I realize something has gone wrong and they don't want to tell me.

"You did." It's Nicolai. Or rather his hooded hologram. The following silence tells me pulling yourself out is not a normal part of the Sim.

"But how?"

"Good question, considering it's impossible."

The way the others are looking at me makes me uncomfortable. I clear my throat. "So, what next?"

Brogue crosses his arms. "I don't think you're ready—"

"She's right," Flame interrupts. "We need to move on."

They argue for a few minutes, but Flame gets her way. The first thing we do is correct the flaws pointed out from the last Sim, an exercise that takes only a few minutes and feels like I'm dreaming.

Next, the weapons training Sim. These are pretty straightforward level two Sims. I learn my speed makes me good with the dagger, short-sword, and hand-to-hand sparring, but my marksmanship with the pistol and crossbow is atrocious. Riser excels at every form of weaponry, something he's only too happy to point out as he beats me every time.

Brogue finally goads Flame into conceding us a break. Fifteen minutes, then we'll fix the glaring deficiencies in my marksmanship and Riser can choke on that gloating grin he's wearing.

My body must need the break more than I think because I find myself in my room. It's well past midnight. Outside my open window a black city engraved against a velvet-blue sky crackles with stars. Crawling through the small space, I skirt across the roof and peer over the edge, probably closer than I should, shivering in the windy night air. One question burns at me.

What kind of monster kills their father?

"Going to jump?" Riser's voice startles me back to myself. I pivot just in time, clinging to the crumbling shingles with my entire body as a gust of wind sends a loose tile clattering over the side.

My cheeks burn as he watches me clamber to a steadier position posted against the eave. "Do you care about anything?" I demand, angry he startled me. "I mean, besides yourself."

"I care about you trusting me."

His response is not what I expected, which explains why I can't think of a single reply. Again there is that unwanted twinge of affection. The smallest purl of longing.

Reconstructed feelings, I remind myself. *Not. Real.*

"Even with everything they did to me, there are still so many things about your world I don't understand." He blinks, the moonlight etching flimsy shadows under his bottom lashes. "But I know if we don't trust one another, this won't work."

"That's why you did it? On the train?"

He leans in close, warmth radiating from where his breath spills against my neck. "Die and you'd trust me. Your words. So I did."

"I was doing fine on my own."

"Taking out the entire train. Smart." Part of his mouth curls in a soft smile. "Still, I let you win."

He says it simply. He's telling me what he gave up for me, how much my trust is worth.

"How'd you get to our mark so fast?"

Something flickers inside his normally detached eyes. If I didn't know better, I would say it is remorse. "I found the note immediately, and then I killed everyone in the first train car, and I didn't stop killing until I reached the man with the Gold rose."

He averts his gaze. At least I know Flame has managed to interject a bit of humanity into his black soul. I think of all those children and shudder. It's strange, though. I understand testing my ability to kill, but Riser didn't have any problems in that department. So what were they testing him on?

"Why go to all that trouble if you were just going to let me win, anyway?"

"I had no intentions of letting you win. Just"—he frowns—"when I reached the man with the rose, he handed me this small mirror, and it had a vision of you on top of the train, like I was watching you through a lens." He pulls at the bronze button of his collar, as if struggling to breathe. "Then I was with you. I should have killed you, but for some reason I couldn't."

And all at once I know what they were testing. His loyalty to me. Or maybe just his ability to ally with another human being, or to trust, or perhaps it's specific to me, like protecting me. I'm not sure. Obviously from Flame's reaction, they weren't expecting him to take it that far, though.

The one thing I do know is now I have an extra weapon in my arsenal to use against Riser. And I will use it, fighting the affection they reconstructed into me with everything I have until we've killed the Emperor and can go our separate ways. Unless Riser turns on me before then. The thought fills me with a heavy sense of dread, and I promise myself that I'll do whatever it takes to win the extra seat on Hyperion and save Max.

A star streaks across the sky. It trails away and my eyes adjust, picking out a dark form in its wake. Pandora makes me think of the Archduchess—they're alike, after all—and a strange feeling tickles the back of my neck. The Emperor scares me because I know what he is. But the Archduchess frightens me more, exactly because I *don't* know what she is, or how far she'll go to find me.

"You're thinking about the woman from the prison, aren't you?" Riser's voice is soft, confiding. "You have the same terrified look you had then when Nicolai mentioned her the first time."

"She did. Terrify me," I say, unnerved by how easily Riser can read me when I find it impossible to decipher him. "She still does. And she won't stop until she finds me." Worried my hands will begin to shake, I fold them in my lap. Even Everly March is scared of the Archduchess, apparently.

"What does she want?"

We sit in silence for a minute as I mull over his question, wondering how much to tell him. "My father gave me something, a key, I think. I don't know what it unlocks, but the Emperor sent her to retrieve it."

I know Riser's emotions for me are reconstructed. So I discount the way his body maneuvers to form a protective barrier around me. "Does it have to do with the thing your father was working on?"

"I'm not sure what you mean," I lie, choking down my surprise.

"Here." The book Riser offers me is bound in leather, M.G. embossed on the cover. "Consider it another token of my trust."

I cradle my journal protectively in my lap. "You read this?"

"Not all of it." My face must mirror my horror because he elaborates.

"I didn't plan to, I didn't even think I could read . . . but then, I don't know"—he cracks a devilish smile—"it was just so *riveting*."

My mouth hangs open. Stripped naked. That's how I feel right now. No one was ever supposed to see those pages. "Well, you had—you had no right to read it!"

Something flutters in the wind at my feet—a photo. It must have fallen from the book. I retrieve the faded picture, twisting it to catch the meager moonlight. My throat constricts, and I lay the image face down in my lap.

"Who are they?" Riser asks, his voice less sarcastic than usual. Maybe he's trying to make up for invading my privacy? Despite myself, some of my anger fades.

I flip the photo and brave another look. The emotion I thought I felt dissipates into apathy. "It was before I was born, when they were at the University."

"Who?"

"The two on the right standing up are Maia's . . . my parents." My father looks sharp in a crisp white tunic and brown doublet. My mother, the strict Royalist even then, shows off a stunning high-necked silver gown—to hide her scar—and chin-length silver wig that makes her hazel eyes appear a vibrant green. "It was the evening of the conference put on by the Emperor to discuss their plans for the asteroid." To their left stands a tall, pale, delicate Gold girl no more than eighteen, hugely pregnant, who looks as if the slightest breeze will topple her.

As if anchoring herself, the young girl's slim fingers curve around the shoulder of the young man sitting in the redwood chair in front of them. His face holds the arrogant look of youth and privilege, his left leg slung over his right, white-gloved hand holding up the near-empty crystal tumbler in a subtle demand for more. War medals adorn his gold military jacket, and a deep-purple cloak embroidered with the Royalist phoenix coats the chair like blood.

I've seen the picture before; otherwise I wouldn't recognize the young man who seems to be the focus of the picture.

"You must know who that is." I gesture to the man with the medals.

"Of course." Riser rubs a finger across his bottom lip. I wonder if the habit belongs to the old or the new Riser.

"The Emperor and his wife, Eleanor." I point to the young girl, Caspian's mother. "They were my mother's childhood friends." My fingernails gouge into my palm. "This picture was taken on the one year anniversary of Pandora's discovery." Not two years later, Eleanor and her newborn daughter were killed in the bombing.

Riser studies the picture with his miss-nothing eyes. "They seem happy for the occasion."

Don't they? I clear the bitterness from my throat, slipping the picture randomly inside the book pages. "They had just announced Project Hyperion. They were going to save the world."

I don't like the way my voice catches. Or the way Riser is looking at me, like I am about to cry. Maybe I am—or would be—if Lady March were capable of tears. I thrust the book at him and shake my head. "Take it. Burn it. Whatever. I don't want it."

Riser refuses. "Keep it. You may change your mind, later."

"What do you know?"

"I know," Riser says softly, "if I had a picture of my mother, I would want to keep it."

His voice has gone cold, his face slackened to camouflage the emotions he must be feeling. But he can't hide the deep-set pain flickering inside his mismatched eyes.

Fighting off the sudden, overwhelming urge to touch him, comfort him somehow, I say, "What happened to her?"

He blinks, swallows hard, as if he can somehow swallow down her memory, and presses his lips into a thin white line. "The *pit* happened to her."

The angry tone of his voice tells me I have crossed a line. He's already pulling away from me. I struggle with something to say that will bring him back. "You said this was a token of trust." I hold up my journal. "What did you mean?"

Slowly, the haunted look fades from his eyes as he focuses on my journal. "Because I could have given it to Nicolai."

Creep! Anger warms my face as I realize Riser has been digging through my family's private things at Nicolai's behest. "What else does the Puppeteer have you searching for?"

Riser shrugs, looking less embarrassed than he should for this deep invasion of privacy. "He mentioned a key. One that can help him unlock the thing your father hid."

That again! As always, at the mention of the machine my father was building, the thing he hid from all of us, the thing that got him labeled a traitor and killed, my brain begins to whir with questions.

Why would my father build a bomb? Was he working for the Fienians? But no, there is no way the father I knew—the man who used part of his own rations to feed the stray cats behind our house and insisted on tucking me in every single night, no matter how tired he was—could have built a bomb. At least, not to hurt people.

But is there any other kind?

Forcing myself out of my memory, I pick at Lady March's perfect fingernails. "What else did you find?"

"Nothing."

Surprisingly, I believe he's telling me the truth. *How much does Nicolai know?* I wonder. And how did he learn of the key? Now that I think about it, it's probably why I was chosen in the first place, and probably why we have Microplants—so Nicolai can discover the key's location through my thoughts. The only reason he hasn't discovered the key so far is because I'm careful when I feel Nicolai mucking around inside my mind. But that could change, so I must be careful.

I stare at the dark outline of the city for a minute. Then I stand, careful to keep my feet steady, and with an angry, clumsy throw, watch my journal disappear. There's soft fluttering as old pages and photos separate from the book, bursting in the wind.

I turn to Riser, now also standing. "Tell Nicolai the key is safe as long as Max and I are."

We both freeze as a noise interrupts the quiet. Shuffling, or maybe whispering down below. Before I can say a word, Riser slinks past me along the tiles, lowering himself until he can peek over the roof. That's when I realize how still the night is. Brogue had commented on the quiet earlier, and I blew him off.

And only one thing can make a Diamond City go silent.

Centurions. Ignoring the hollow feeling in the pit of my stomach, I join Riser. The street is empty. The wind tosses an empty bucket across the cobblestones and into the grass. Somewhere far away a door opens and quickly shuts.

Riser nods toward the row of houses just below us on the left. It takes a second for my eyes to wade through the shadows.

I was right about the Centurions: There are twelve of them. And I was right about the Archduchess finding me, too. She stands apart from her men, silver wig braided beneath her hat. Gold-handled pistols glint from each hip. She has a page from my journal clutched inside her hand, examining it. Slowly, her dark lips peel from her teeth in a horrid little smile.

She looks up at the roof.

At me.

A hideous buzzing noise cleaves the quiet, as if we have awakened a hive of furious bees. Two spinning shadows dart toward us.

Drones.

CHAPTER SEVENTEEN

I don't recall moving, but I am suddenly inside my room. The stars spin around my head. My body, obviously taking over, clears the stairs in two leaps. Where to go? I am at the front door before I realize my folly. Of course they will have someone posted here as well.

Trapped. I am trapped!

I bolt for the office, Riser on my heels. Unlike me, his breathing is even and he appears quite composed, so I let him tell the others. They don't seem surprised, which gives me hope they were expecting this and have a plan. Brogue gathers the other Mercs, who somehow have procured two black leather backpacks with what I assume are supplies. I almost kiss him when he snatches Bramble from the stairs and tosses him into one of the packs.

My hopeful feeling dies as I listen to Brogue's plan. Something about fighting our way past the Centurions at the front door. My mind stops listening after that because I know the plan won't work. The Archduchess would not leave our escape to chance.

It needs to be something she's not expecting.

I explain my plan, trying hard to sound rational and in control, but it takes a few minutes to convince them to follow me. We take the elevator in silence, the emergency backup generator making the ride a bit choppy, Brogue and the others cutting their eyes at me. If I'm wrong, we'll be trapped, at the mercy of the Archduchess. And there's no question how that will end.

I sprint from the elevator before the doors completely open. From somewhere above comes the sound of shattering, something heavy hitting the floor. Everyone is looking to me, waiting for me to prove myself.

"It's here . . . I uh . . . ?" My gaze skips from wall to wall as I try to remember. I used the escape lift once before. It is hidden, of course, somewhere behind these bricks. I just have to remember which ones.

Except either Nicolai or I have scrubbed that memory from my brain. The last time I used it was right after they killed my father, so it was probably me who made myself forget.

"Please, take your sweet time, Princess," Flame purrs as the lights blink and shudder. They're using Fienian blue-bombs to gain control of the power. "It's not like we're in a hurry."

Brogue puts an encouraging hand on my shoulder. "A few more of those blue buggers and they can override the elevator's systems."

The answer comes to me in a flash of memory. I'm still not sure, not entirely, until my fingers slip through the mirage meant to look like the rest of the brick wall and feel the cold metal door. The mirage dissipates. I hold my breath. If they discovered this the last time, after Max and I escaped, it will have been rendered inoperable.

Or worse—mined.

Only one way to find out. I lift the heavy metal lid and crawl inside. It's barely big enough to sit in, which means we will have to go up one at a time.

"Does it work?" Brogue asks, his voice gravelly with impatience.

"I don't know." I scan the single button on the wall. It emits a faint red glow.

Flame's spiky hair nearly jabs me as she leans inside the small space, tapping the backpack. "In case we get split up, there's a locator in here that will tell you where to go. You have to be at Royalist Headquarters by tomorrow morning or you forfeit the Shadow Trials."

"And listen for Nicolai," Cage adds. "Once you're far enough away they can't trace his communications, he'll make contact again with further instructions."

"Okay," I say. My fingertip hovers over the button. "Let's do this."

"Lady March." It's Riser. Behind him I see Brogue and the other two Mercs, weapons trained on the dinging elevator door. He tosses something at me; I grab it on reflex. A knife inside a black sheath. By the crude appearance of the blade, it's handmade, and not a stranger to violence. "Doesn't look like much, but it'll do the job."

I eye the space above the elevator, where the in-use arrow glows. "What about you?"

"I'll fare just fine, but thanks for your concern." I reach to push the button, but he stops me. "One more thing. If I'm not there after a sixty count, don't wait."

"Don't worry," I say. "I won't."

And then I push the button.

Nothing. Nothing happens. My heart slams into my throat just as the elevator door on the far wall whooshes open and the room erupts in pistol fire.

Ratatatatatatatat!

I clap my hands over my ears and close my eyes. Open them. One blue and one green eye, both eerily calm, are inches from mine. Riser grins. "Second time's a charm."

Darkness. The feeling of moving upward, slowly, laboriously. Flame yells, voice muffled, "Get some, you rotten-faced Dandies!"

The gunshots and yelling grow farther and farther away until all I hear are the muted pops, like firecrackers outside a window. Occasionally the power flickers, and I stop moving. But the little red button always lights up again.

Fading stars and cool air. I am on a roof. For the moment, I am safe. The air cracks with sharp reverberations, reminding me that the others are not.

I begin counting immediately. *One, two, three, four, five . . .*

The blast that shatters my count is so loud, even though I'm sure

I scream, I can't hear it. I'm on my knees—I must have fallen—the building shuddering beneath me. A flock of starlings erupt over my head, screeching their annoyance. The drones' buzzing quickly drowns them out.

I scramble to the exit. The elevator has already been sent back, so it's really just a gaping hole. Smoke and dust and tiny debris cough from the shaft and blow my hair back. The air is hot from the explosion and smells of charred things.

Not things. *People.* My people. I stare into the exit for a second, blind from the dust, and try very hard not to scream, again.

My backpack is heavy. I busy myself with cataloguing its contents so I don't have to think about what to do next. Synthetic beef powder packets. A lighter. Two thin blanket rolls. The locator. Water purifying drops. I know exactly what to do with the glass vial full of thick foundation, rubbing it quickly into my cheeks to cover my freckles.

At the very bottom I find Bramble, curled in a terrified ball. He chirps at me, and I hug him to my chest. My eyes sting with tears, and I wipe them away while giving myself a silly pep talk.

"You're alone now; get used to it."

"Sorry to disappoint, Digger Girl."

I know the voice, but I still don't believe. Not until I turn around. Riser emerges from the hole where he has obviously risen from the dead.

I bite my cheek to restrain myself from hugging him. "How?"

He shifts his backpack to a more comfortable spot on his shoulder, and then wipes his sleeve over the soot covering his face. His shirt is torn and speckled with blood. "The escape elevator never made it back, so we looked inside and discovered a ladder."

Of course. My father wouldn't have trusted the power source. "Are you hurt?"

Riser looks down at the blood on his shirt. "Flame's blood. Brogue and Cage volunteered to carry her up."

The relief I feel at knowing the blood isn't Riser's unnerves me. I shift on my feet. "The two Mercs?"

"Not so lucky." He nods toward the edge of the building. "Shall we?"

I replace Bramble, the smell of petroleum thick as we cross the tarred roof to where the fire escape ladder should be—except now only a faint black outline on the brick remains.

"Perfect," I say, eying the three-story drop between here and the next building.

Riser hops onto the ledge, all coordination and grace, and proceeds to taunt me with a charming smile and the offer of a sooty hand.

Brushing it aside, I join him, focusing on anything but the ground and my legs knocking together. Cement pieces chipped loose by my heels clatter over the edge. "Why is it whenever I'm around you," I say, "I find myself having to jump off impossibly high things?"

He glances sideways at me in a way both endearing and reckless. "Afraid, Lady March?"

The drones' buzzing is much louder now. With their heat sensors, the lifting darkness means nothing. Dropping my backpack, I lean away from the ledge and peer at the ground. Maia would be afraid. My mouth dries, my breath becoming strangled, as if I am sucking through a straw. The sound of my blood charging through my arteries fills my skull.

But I'm not afraid. I'm *euphoric*. My mind clear for the first time in years.

"See you on the other side, Pit Boy."

I don't recall actually pushing off the ledge, but I am suspended in the air. Then the ground is coming at me. Cradling my head in my arms, I duck, roll, deflecting some of the fall. The impact screams into my shoulder and ripples through my body.

I lie here for a dizzy moment, watching the fingers of pale-orange dawn streak the sky as I catalog the damage. Achy shoulder. My head hurts, but my vision is sound and I can wiggle my fingers and toes.

I stand in time to see the two backpacks span the chasm, followed by Riser. He lands hard and quiet, rolling to break his fall the same way I did. But unlike me he pops immediately back to his feet.

We make eye contact. Something passes between us.

He smiles.

I smile.

We both lunge at the same time. I am a few feet in front and make it to the next roof a half-second before he does. We roll in tandem, land on our feet, and explode into another sprint. Winging my elbow out, I manage to force him back so I take the lead.

Run, jump, land. Repeat. At this ferocious pace even the slightest miscalculation will most likely end in death. But the spike of adrenaline, the hollow-chest feeling and blankness right before I jump, makes me almost forget.

This time when the ledge comes up, I don't even look down before pushing off. I'm midair when I spot the Centurions below, but I manage to land softly on the gravel roof. Fear springs me to my feet.

Riser has just hit the roof when I hear the crack. We both do. Riser reacts first. I see his hand reaching out for me. There's the sound of glass shattering, the sensation of falling, and Riser's form grows small, disappears.

A second later—or maybe longer, because I might have been knocked unconscious—I open my eyes. My brain screams behind my eyes as I look around. Shiny steel cabinets and kitchen table. I blink, focus on the shattered skylight above. Riser's face pops over the broken glass just as voices call from outside.

Riser holds a finger to his lips and mouths, Dandies.

I nod, flinching with the pain as I struggle to stand. Glass shards burrow into the flesh of my palms and knees.

"Don't move," Riser whispers.

"Sure." I rub my head. The pain has lessened, and my vision is clearing. I realize immediately what needs to happen. "Go," I say, plucking a glass shard from my left palm. If the tables were turned, I would already be gone.

He doesn't answer. I look up to see him hanging by his fingertips. He swings his legs like a pendulum and lets go. He was aiming for the kitchen counter, but his shoes glance off the slick surface, and he crashes to the ground beside me.

He rises wearing an implacable grin. "That went much smoother in my head."

"Idiot." We limp our way to the living room, our boots crunching glass. The voices are on the porch now.

Slants of dawn pierce the windows and trap in the cylindrical grooves of Riser's revolver. He holds it down low against his leg. His arms are loose, his shoulders back and head held high, as if he's the most comfortable when there's the threat of violence. The knife Riser gave me is still in my pocket, so I pull the blade out and try to mimic his confidence.

The door handle rattles, but luckily it is locked. I am backing up, trying to decide if I will just stab wildly or go for one at a time, when I feel something hard press into my leg. There's no time to explain, so I jump into the Casket and hope that Riser gets the idea. I slip on the Headbox, lie back, and pull the curved-glass lid shut. I keep my hands plastered to my sides for fear of hitting the button that will sync with my Microplant and start the upload.

The Casket has sensed my presence, and there's a loud hiss as cold fog envelops me. My teeth chatter in the stillness. The intravenous pump that will force lifesaving nutrients into my bloodstream and allow me to survive being frozen powers on.

Before I can peek to see if Riser followed, pieces of the door splinter against the glass as an explosion rocks my Casket.

CHAPTER EIGHTEEN

I can't see what's happening from my Casket, but I can hear them coming for me. Footsteps. Crude laughter. Muffled, though, as if from the end of a tunnel. The footsteps fade as the Centurions search the house before coming back to us.

The lid lifts with a creak. Warm, glorious air cascades over me, easing the stabbing cold.

Sour, almondy tar breath thaws my cheeks where the Headbox ends. I feel the top of my blouse lifting, cool air prickling my chest and stomach. "Found a nice-looking one," Tar-Breath says. "Sleeper girls are the best kind. Quiet and willing."

"Leave her," says the other Centurion. "Unless you want the Emperor's Mad Dog to wear your balls as a charm."

"I'm not afraid of that malignant bitch. The Emperor will put her out of her misery soon enough." They're talking about the Archduchess. Something—a rough finger?—caresses the side of my head. "Besides, this one won't tell on me, will you?"

Panic wells inside me, but I swallow it down. I think of the others. Immobile. Unprotected. Unaware of what's happening to their bodies. My mouth waters, a nauseous feeling worming up my throat. In this moment, I don't care about our cover or staying safe. All I want to do is kill him.

Before I can do something stupid, I feel the air move over my chest as Tar-Breath stands straight, and then both Centurions go deathly silent. Sharp clacking noises rattle the floor, followed by the sound of glass crunching near my Casket. As soon as the strong talcum odor hits me, my body goes rigid.

One of the Centurions moves, knocking my Headbox slightly askew so I can peek beneath. The Archduchess stands four feet from me, cut off from the waist up. The Centurions are pressed against the wall.

"My apologies, Archduchess," Tar-Breath stutters. "Didn't mean no-no-no disrespect."

The Archduchess's skirt hem rustles over the floor as she walks toward them. Now I can see the back of her hat, her braided silver mane, but not her face. She turns to Tar-Breath's friend. "Check the status of the building and report back to me."

It takes a moment for the man to realize he is being spared. "Yes, Archduchess, right away."

Tar-Breath begins pleading with the Archduchess. "What I said before—"

Two puncturing noises, followed by bizarre sounds, like a dog baying, hiss through the room and cut off Tar-Breath's apology.

She is barking.

Barking.

"Now that's a mad dog for you," the Archduchess says in a horrid voice that tells me she's grinning ear-to-ear.

Tar-Breath stumbles back, arms flailing. He misses the porch step and falls on his rear, scuttling backward like a crab to get away.

A red rose blooms over his chest, spurting blood with every beat of his heart. Tar-Breath grabs his chest, his eyes white marbles of shock. He makes it two more feet before his body crumples out of sight.

Victoria pulls a red silk handkerchief from her coat pocket and meticulously wipes the bloody end of the hatpin. The side of her face I can now see is stretched into a dead grin.

Then the lunatic is coming toward me. I squeeze my eyes shut and struggle to relax my adrenaline-spiked body. As a Sleeper, I should be in a deep state of metabolic depression: slow breathing, lethargic heart rate. And my body should feel hard.

Basically, I should be frozen.

My heart races as I hear her lean over me, her perfume burning its way up my nose and into my brain. "Pretty thing." Her voice sounds like paper bags ripping. "Poor, pretty, cold thing."

I can *feel* her strange blend of hatred and curiosity, like a child watching a bug beneath a magnifying glass right before the sun incinerates the poor creature. If she looks closely, she will see the blood oozing from my palms.

Something cold and sharp drags over my clavicle. I know it's the hatpin. I imagine the needle burrowing through flesh and bone to my heart. My body yearns to shiver; it takes everything I have not to scream.

"Pardon . . . Archduchess," a man says from the door, voice hesitant. "We, uh, found a young female body inside the blast. Far as we can tell, she fits the description."

There's a pause. Then she adjusts my blouse so I am covered again and says, "Back to dreaming, little maggot."

My body has decided I am safest curled into a tiny ball on the floor beneath the kitchen table. I don't remember leaving the Casket. I should have stayed put—Centurions can still be heard shouting orders outside—but at least now, with my limbs trussed around my body, the shaking is controlled.

Nicolai killed the two Mercs. I know this with absolute certainty, and it scares me almost as much as the Archduchess does. He planned for us to be discovered, planned the explosion, and made certain the Archduchess would think I was dead. I don't know how, but he did.

I am caught in an impossible situation between a madwoman, a deranged puppeteer, and a psychopathic freak turned dashing partner. What else does Nicolai have planned for us? What other secrets does he keep squirreled away for special occasions?

"You need to get up." Riser is peering under the table at me.

"No."

"Are you scared?"

I snort. "Isn't that obvious?"

Shame burns my cheeks. Why am I so afraid? Why can't I stop being Maia, scared little Digger Girl? The reconstructed part of me hates my weakness. *Get up, and choose to be Everly. Maia will only make you small and powerless.* But my body refuses.

Shuffling. Chairs squeaking across the floor. Riser is coming in after me. Cold, half-frozen fingers pry apart my arms.

"I won't let the Archduchess hurt you," he says, as if it's the simplest statement in the world.

"Don't make promises you can't keep." Not can't keep. *Won't* keep. That's what I mean. Because if there is anyone who can protect me from the Archduchess, it's Riser.

In fact, I'm not certain who scares me more: the lunatic or Pit Boy.

Riser lies down beside me, his cheek kissing the dirty floor. "I know what I am. But with you"—puzzlement tinges his voice—"with you, I'm different."

"Welcome to the world of feelings and humanity. Maybe when I'm done getting over the gazillion times I've almost died the last couple days, I'll plan a parade in your honor."

"Look." He is holding my gaze with his eyes, willing me to believe him. "This is new to me, too. I didn't ask for it. All I know is I can't let anything happen to you."

I study his face, ignoring the comfort I find in the sharp planes of his cheeks and jaw. How can I possibly trust him? He could be lying to gain the upper hand, to force my trust and make me weak. "But you still have some scars, which means . . ."

"My reconstruction wasn't complete." His fingers trace the brow bone above his new green eye. I like it better than the blue eye, I think. "The physical transformation will probably hold, but the rest—"

"Won't last." And we have no idea how long until the old kill-now-ask-questions-later Riser rears his psychotic head.

Taking my hand, he pulls me from my little enclave. "I need this to be clear, Everly." I shiver at the sound of my new name from his lips. "I'm not a good person. I've done horrible things, and I don't regret them. But I promise"—he guides my hand toward his chest, the hard muscle pressing into my fingertips; his heart thumps heavy and slow beneath my fingers—"I will keep you safe."

Something deep inside me stirs.

Riser, I decide. *Riser scares me the most.* Because he possesses the one thing the Archduchess does not.

The ability to make me vulnerable.

To make me care.

CHAPTER NINETEEN

The rendezvous point is deep inside Riverton, the Royalist city just outside the wall. We slip through a crumbled spot beneath the empty guard tower. Even though we haven't spotted a Centurion or drone in hours, we stick to the tight alleyways between the shops. I hate what Nicolai did to the Mercs, but it has undoubtedly saved us.

The cobblestone streets are eerily quiet. Most of the town's occupants, almost all Silvers, were probably evacuated long ago to their underground shelters below the mountains.

The storefront rests atop an enormous hill, ensconced between a bakery and tailor shop. Just like all the other buildings, the windows are blacked out. From the alleyway behind the shop drifts the smell of something long dead. We slip inside the back door.

A thin layer of dust shrouds the shop. The front heaps with Reformation-approved antiquities, but on the other side of the door lurks another, very different room. Firelight from the half-melted candles on the walls illuminates books, hundreds of them. Stacked in corners. Spilling from the walls. *Real books*. I am so busy staring I almost step on Flame. She's curled fetal position on the floor, glittering with sweat and blood.

"Watch it, Princess!" she snarls through gritted teeth.

Brogue uses the distraction to pull the six-inch metal shrapnel from her hip. She moans, twisting her face into the floor as Cage pours alcohol over the gaping wound and sews her up.

Abruptly, all the tension leaves Flame's body, and she melts into Cage's long arms.

A weary sigh escapes Cage's lips. "She's passed out."

"Did she struggle the whole way?" I ask.

Cage looks up as if just now seeing me. "Why, only when she was awake."

Brogue hands me a chipped teacup full of tinted brown water, and I collapse onto a yellow lounger spotted with mold. The water tastes like piss, but I swallow it greedily. I can't recall the last time I actually slept.

My eyes flit over her form. Arms like twigs. Delicate, child-like hands curled into tiny doll-fists. Her shoes must have fallen off, and her dark purple painted toes flutter. Like dynamite, you would never guess something so tiny could be so dangerous. "Will she recover?"

Brogue flashes his gold-capped teeth. "I certainly hope so. I have a few words for the little tart when she wakes up."

That's when I notice the circular, bluish-black bite marks plaguing his arms and neck.

Flame yells something in her sleep and frowns.

"Feisty for such a small thing, isn't she?" I remark.

Brogue chuckles. "I've wrestled wild badgers tamer than her."

I snort between laughs. "And . . . did you . . . hear her cursing the Dandies?"

Cage lets out a high-pitched cackle as he tries to mimic her words. "*Get some . . . you . . . you . . .*"

"*Rotten-faced Dandies,*" I screech.

We all burst into laughter. I laugh so hard tears pour from my eyes. I am crying too. Snorting and crying and choking out all the anger and frustration and fear over the last week.

Flame rolls over, hair plastered to one side, a gob of saliva trailing down her chin. "What? What's so funny?"

There is a long pause. More hysterical cackling ensues. Brogue doubles over, slapping his leg, wheezing between barking guffaws, his face bright tomato-red. I practically fall off the lounger, giggling so hard I can't breathe. Even Riser has tears streaming down his face.

Cage hands Flame a blood-splotched towel. Not in the mood for coddling, she smacks it from his hand and bares her teeth. Of course this only makes us shriek louder.

Flame struggles to her feet and stumbles off, breaking a few things on her way. As soon as the door shuts behind her, the light mood dissipates.

Cage rises, swiping at the blood and drool streaking his trousers. "I'll go after her."

"No." Brogue has scrubbed any trace of humor from his voice. "Let me. You prepare them."

Riser and I take turns washing in the small half-bath behind the stairs. I do the best I can with the flimsy washcloth and bucket of rust-colored water Cage provided, finger-combing my hair and pinching my cheeks in front of the cracked mirror. Rubbing circles of foundation over my freckles, I watch my cheeks become luminescent porcelain.

Finally passable, I traipse up the tiny enclosed stairwell, my dirty boots rustling up clouds of dust. Flame is waiting for me in an upstairs apartment. Despite the triangular smear of blood across her forehead, she looks well enough now to inflict mortal violence, so I pause in the doorway while she rifles through a closet. My heart sinks when I realize the ivory plume of fabric bursting from her arms is meant for me.

With the ensemble laid out on the bed, I realize it's not as bad as I feared. It's a travel frock with silk trousers hidden beneath a detachable skirt and a modified corset that makes sitting and breathing easier.

I'm now officially a Royalist.

Once dressed, I sit on the bed so Flame can fix my hair. My gaze travels the smooth hills of white fabric cascading around me. Because most Bronzes worked the factories where white was impractical, it's a color associated with Silvers and above. I always imagined it would feel luxurious, but it doesn't. It feels wrong somehow. "It's rather creamy," I mutter, fingering part of the ruffle trim, "but at least it doesn't have bows."

"Quiet, Princess," Flame orders, a pick between her teeth, her comb wrenching pieces of my hair into whatever elaborate, braided concoction she has devised. I shut up and let her work on the off chance my silence will save my scalp.

Shoes next—a pair of sealskin boots a size too big.

After Flame deems me satisfactory, I kill time exploring the house. I am immediately drawn to the servant's stairwell hidden in the back. There is an arched window enclave niched in the wall. Old, cracking black paint covers the windowpane, spears of light seeping through. A book rests on a faded pink pillow. I climb inside, my too-big boots smearing the layer of dust that coats the wood.

I peek through a crack of paint. Riser stands perfectly still in the middle of an overgrown garden thick with tall scorpion-weeds, hands in his pockets, his face tilted up to catch the sun. A few pink peonies flash through the brown weeds.

I feel myself smile as a warm feeling pulses through me. I can't help it. He looks so silly, a sublime half-grin breaking through his usual masked expression.

Like the peonies breaking through the weeds. For the first time since I've known him, he looks unguarded.

Vulnerable.

Normal.

Again, something inside me stirs. I want to go to him. I want to . . . I don't know.

Did you really just compare Pit Boy to flowers? The voice is Lady March's. *These are planted emotions, Everly, meant to weaken you.*

All at once, the dark tide of shadow murk washes over Riser. My entire body tenses. Victoria's words whisper inside my ear: *In the shadow murk, you worms do horrible things to each other.*

Point taken. I search for a distraction. The book. I have only touched one other book before, so I pick it up carefully, blowing off years of dust. The cover is peeling, and the title has long since been worn away. Looking over the book's spine, I am surprised to see Cage is appraising me much the same.

And he doesn't look entirely pleased with what he sees.

I pluck at my gown. "It's the ivory. It doesn't go with my complexion."

Cage shakes his head. "No, it doesn't. But the right shade of rouge and lip cream will help."

He's off and back before I can blink, clutching an array of pigments and a lighted candle. Squinting against the meager light, he applies the pigments sparingly, even though he informs me the ladies of court now find it fashionable to paint their faces with every color conceivable. "Like peacocks," he murmurs, half his bottom lip caught inside his teeth as he works. "And this dress is glaringly out of fashion, but that can be attributed to your parents falling out of favor with the court."

"And here I was thinking this hideous dress was Flame's way of tormenting me."

The brush Cage is holding pauses over my upper lip. Something flickers inside his eyes. "Worn by the woman that piece was made for, it was stunning, I promise you."

"Oh." I pucker my lips for Cage's brush. "I didn't mean to offend you."

"You didn't." Done with my lips, Cage dots concealer over my stubborn freckles. His eyes flick to the dark windowpane. "Anything of interest out there?"

I clear my throat. "Not really . . . no."

"I bet he is still standing there, soaking up the shadows with that same intoxicated expression. Like a wee boy, that one."

"Oh, believe me," I say, batting my eyelashes as he swipes buttery-gold powder over my eyelids, "there is nothing innocent about *that* one."

"*Tsk*, I didn't say innocent." He dabs a circular sponge over my cheeks and forehead until my face shimmers. "But interesting? Absolutely. It's rare to find someone who is as comfortable in the light as they are in the dark."

"Yep, that's Pit Boy. Rare and interesting. How long until the interesting part wears off and the murderous one shows up?"

Cage lifts a perfectly arched eyebrow. "Oh, so he told you about his corrupted reconstruction, did he? Well, did he tell you *why* parts of it didn't take?"

I shake my head.

"We were waiting for you near the docks the morning your pitiful little boat drifted to shore, but when we searched the boat, there was only you, half-drowned and half-dead."

"Where was Riser?"

Cage's lips twitch. "We found him dead in the sand a few yards down where the waves dropped him. After such an event, our cobbled together Reconstructors had very little effect past the physical."

There's a strange burning lump in my throat. *Why did he lie to me?* Desperate to change the subject, I finger my hair. "Anything you can do about this?"

Cage frowns, tracing one of the tight red braids torturing my scalp. "I would say yes, if the color wasn't so perfect for you."

"But—"

He silences me with an open palm. "Yes, yes. I know. You are supposed to have fair, sun kissed hair."

"Exactly—"

"The court has no idea what you should look like because Lady March's parents fell from court when she was a mewling, hairless creature."

"You mean baby."

"*Creature.*" Cage clamps the makeup lid shut.

My new reflection greets me inside the cloudy windowpane.

"Better," I admit. I usually loathe makeup, but the dewy rose petal tint he has applied to my face and lips has somehow pulled everything together.

Cage gracefully hops from the alcove as if he's done it a million times before.

"Wait . . . can I ask you something?"

Turning on his heel, he raises a stern eyebrow. "Lady March, I am an attendant. You may—and *should*—do whatever you like."

Right. Must play the part. I hesitate. "Whose place did Riser take?"

Cage smiles cryptically. "There's only one Riser Thornbrook."

"I don't understand."

He shrugs, looking bored with the question. "*Pit Boy* is going as himself. Although I much prefer his official title of Dorian Riser Laevus, Royal Bastard Prince, half-brother to Prince Caspian Laevus." My mouth hangs open as Cage elaborates further. "His mother, known at Court as the Marquess Amandine Croft, was Emperor Laevus III's first love."

My mind is spinning. "So . . . Riser is . . . ?"

"His son."

"And the Emperor doesn't know?"

"Kitten, he would be in the ground if he did. When Rand Laevus and the Marquess fell in love, he was the Crown Prince and she a suspected Fienian Sympathizer, along with her brother, the Marquis of Coventry. But—"

"Wait." I suck in a breath. I'm still trying to wrap my mind around Riser being the son of the Emperor, and now he's the nephew of the dead Fienian Rebel leader, too? "So, his mother . . . Amandine, how did she . . . ?"

"End up in prison?" Cage chuckles dryly. "You don't think Emperor Laevus II would have let the Crown Prince become besotted by a suspected sympathizer, do you? And jeopardize his vision? No, no, he had her secretly incarcerated in Rhine prison as Violet Thornbrook, and poor Prince Rand assumed she had simply left him."

I feel a surge of pity for the Emperor. There's no worse feeling in the world than being abandoned. "He didn't know she was pregnant, then?"

Cage shakes his head. "No, and he eventually forgot about her. But her brother Ezra didn't. He searched for years. By the time he found her, she was already dead."

The pit happened to her. Riser's words echo inside my head, and I feel an unwelcome stab of empathy for him, too. "The bombing? That was to avenge Ezra's sister?"

"Ezra adored Amandine almost as much as he hated the Royalists. But after her death, he went from Fienian Sympathizer to the ruthless leader history loves to hate."

I want to hate Ezra for the people he murdered, but it's hard now, knowing why he did it. If Max had been falsely imprisoned and suffered the way Amandine did, wouldn't I do the same?

Stretching my arms, I yawn. "And how does Riser feel knowing the man he's supposed to assassinate is his father?"

Cage shrugs. "He got over it rather quickly."

Of course he did. "One more thing, if you don't mind."

Cage eyes me through narrowed blue slits. "You have heard the story about curiosity and the cat?"

"Right." I flash an apologetic smile. "It's just some moments I'm Lady March. I'm strong and confident and really, really sure of myself. And then"—my hands twist at my dress—"I'm my old cowardly self again. Maia Graystone. Afraid of everything."

"Your mind has to make a choice. Who do you want to be?"

"But I've already chosen—"

"No, you haven't. But there will come a time when you will have to. Trust me."

CHAPTER TWENTY

With Cage gone, I settle back and distractedly thumb through the old, dusty book by the window. I am surprised to see the slim silhouette of inky ravens darkening some of the pages. One here. Three there. An entire page full of them, sitting, flapping their wings as if about to take flight. Others hover near the top, seeming ready to fly off the page.

Flame and Riser laugh from the room above, and the book slips from my fingers, pain lancing my sternum. Why should it bother me they are friends? Or that everyone but me knew Riser came from nobility. And not just any noble family. The *only* noble family that matters.

And maybe, just maybe, I feel bad for the way I've been treating Riser.

Maybe.

Needing a distraction, I find Brogue downstairs in front of the crumbling stone fireplace, poking at some books. They catch fire all at once, the orange flame peeling away the bound leather covers and turning the pages to cinder. It seems a waste, but I don't mind once Brogue hands me the hot tea and warmed reconstituted beef patties on delicate gold-leafed china plates. Synthetic of course, not that I'm complaining.

And neither is Lady March, because she wolfs hers down without so much as a wrinkled nose.

Too soon, it is time to go. Riser jaunts down the stairs, an expensive ostrich-skinned travel bag slung over his shoulder and hair neatly pulled back. Admittedly, now that I know about his past, he looks different. Or maybe it's just the way he wears his white one-buttoned tunic, replete with peaked lapels and a midnight-blue vest—as if he was born to wear it.

Flame and Cage have changed into clothing fit for Bronzes. No longer are they pierced and colored and marked. On Cage's body hangs a dark morning coat over gray trousers. Flame, on the other hand, wears high-waisted men's trousers the color of smoke. They swish as she walks and highlight her slender waist. She twists unhappily at the poufy sleeves of her pale Delphine blouse, the high collar unsuccessfully covering the bird tattoos winding up her thin neck. A charcoal-gray sunhat dwarfs her head, the hair underneath tamed into short black tresses tipped red.

Geez, that'll go over well with the Censors.

Without the spikes and wild colors to distract me, I realize Flame is pretty. Really, really pretty, in a wild-eyed, pouty-lipped, porcelain skinned, spritely kind of way.

"Not so dangerous now, huh?" I tease, taking a small bit of pleasure in her obvious discomfort at the new look.

Without her contacts, her eyes are a pale gray. They cut sideways at me. She smiles the old Flame smile, retrieves something small and metallic from her high collar—a miniature, folding, triple-loading crossbow—and arms it with three sleek metal arrows plucked from the rim of her hat.

It is aimed inches from my nose, so close the tips of the arrows blur into one. "Don't forget, Princess," Flame purrs, "nothing is ever as it seems."

Riser uses two fingers to aim the crossbow at the floor. "I think she gets the point, Flame."

"And I think she needs more training on the subject." Flame's thick, dark eyebrows come together above a challenging glare.

"Actually," I say, "I would love to continue our lesson." I already know what I will do if the crossbow swings back up. How my left hand will swing wide, as if I am wiping a window, knocking the weapon from her hand, while my right palm smashes through her dimpled nose.

Riser wedges between us, fighting a smile. He leans forward and whispers something into her ear.

I fully expect her to challenge him, so I am surprised when she flashes a tentative grin, replaces her weapon, and adjusts her hat in a gesture totally girly and un-Flame-like. "Time to skedaddle."

Riser turns to me once she's gone. "Wow, Digger Girl, I think she really likes you."

"*Wow*," I parrot back. "Nicolai really botched your sense of humor, Pit Boy. And for the record, I don't need protecting."

A swath of raven-black hair has eclipsed part of Riser's forehead, and he swipes the locks out of his face, his lips teasing into a half-grin. "I know. I was protecting her from *you*."

Shadow Fall makes it seem like dusk. We cut through the alleyway and wait until Brogue, scouting from the corner, gives the okay to cross the street. I'm halfway across when I realize Flame has lagged behind. Turning around, I spy a soft-orange glow illuminating the dirty window I peered out earlier. There's a sharp pop as the glass explodes, and hungry flames leak out, spilling across the roof.

Flame makes it across the street just as a fireball consumes the house. She smells of kerosene and smoke and is clutching a tattered book to her breast. A feverish shine glimmers her eyes. We stand there a moment, watching, the heat caressing our faces. Cage reaches across and squeezes Flame's hand.

With the streets empty, we make good progress. Flame's fire lights our way. It's still burning by the time we catch the rail.

Most of the Silvers have already taken the winding railway to their Caskets below the mountains, so our car is empty. I sit alone, my eyes drifting to the growing fire. With no one to fight it, it greedily devours the sky, a starving monster set free from its cage.

Soon, the coach's rhythmic motion lulls me into a kind of stupor. It feels good to close my eyes.

In my nightmare, I am trapped between the fire and my mother. Her voice whispers through the crackling of the flames. "Do you see now how beautiful it is, Maia? Do you understand now?"

Everything in me screams to go to her, to find the hollow just above her clavicle where I used to lay my chin. But then Riser steps through the fire. He's wearing the rags from the pit and holding out his hand. "*Trust* me, Maia."

Looking back at my mother, I see she has changed into Everly March, with a sleek curtain of red hair and pale, dewy skin. She shakes her head at Riser, slowly. "Look at your Pit Boy now, Maia."

Riser holds up the ropes he used to tie me with.

"He wants to bind you, Maia, make you helpless, just like in the pit."

Before I can respond, Riser lunges at me.

I wake up to Riser gently shaking me. Still stuck in my dream, I cry out and shrink away.

"Whoa." He raises his hands. "It was just a bad dream."

"Promise?" I mutter, my heart still fluttering like a bird startled from its perch.

Riser's forehead furrows as he studies me. Not wanting to explain, I stare out the window. Shadow Fall's nearly over, which means we should be passing the string of Diamond Cities that trace the rivers and tributaries in the flatlands.

But all I see through the greenish shadow murk is Pandora's destruction. A flooded city, the tops of the factories barely breaking the surface of the water. Logging towns with forests burnt to stubs. Fields of crops that refused to grow. Factories that made the Royalists' favorite silks reduced to mounds of rubble.

The asteroid isn't satisfied pitting us against one another; *She* must destroy our homes too.

In the distance, a city burns, the black line of what must be escaping

Bronzes snaking around a hill. The fire reminds me of Flame, the way her eyes danced earlier as she watched the fire grow. "Why'd she do it? Burn it down?"

Flame sits with the others near the front. Riser studies her for a moment, the way a brother might look at an annoying little sister. "Exorcising demons."

"Seems a little extreme," I point out, annoyed by the affection in his tone.

Riser chuckles. "Perhaps Flame's demons need more encouragement than most."

Suddenly, a lightning bolt of understanding blasts my brain. The ravens in the book. The ravens winding across Flame's neck. They're the same! Which means . . .

"The rendezvous point was their home!" I blurt proudly. I remember all the beautiful books. Harboring or trading in banned items is a dangerous pursuit. Her parents couldn't have hidden their secret for long, not in a Royalist city.

A horrible thought comes to me. I hold up the skirt of my dress. "Whose clothes are we wearing?"

Riser blinks. "Why ask a question you don't want answered?"

My mouth goes dry. "Her parents are dead, aren't they? And these are their clothes?"

"They were Silvers, but that didn't stop them from taking two orphaned Bronzes like Flame and Cage off the streets and raising them like their own." His eyes glitter with anger. "When Flame was twelve, the Emperor executed them."

"The Emperor." My fingers knot together in my lap. "You mean your—"

"Father?" Riser's voice is knife-edged.

I nod.

"What? Are you wondering if I can kill him now that I know?"

"Yes, actually."

"I watched my mother torn to pieces because of him." He leans in, a tight, bitter smile curving his jaw. "So the answer to your question is: with relish."

Flame clears her throat, breaking the tension. "This looks fun." Her gaze finds Riser. "Care to join me, Prince?"

Riser chuckles, his dark mood evaporating. "Give me a second?"

She cuts her eyes at me. "Yup."

I watch Flame join the others at the front. "*Prince?*"

"A bit more distinguished than Pit Boy, don't you think?"

I laugh. "I don't know; Pit Boy was growing on me." There's a moment of awkward silence that stretches into a whole minute. I bite my lip. "So . . . you and the crabby arsonist are close?"

"*Crabby arsonist?*" He raises an amused eyebrow. "Not close. Comfortable. With each other." He shrugs, fiddling with the loose thread on his vest. "The *crabby arsonist* doesn't flinch when I'm around."

A bitter feeling rises in my throat. I swallow the emotion down. Peering out the window, I spend an inordinate amount of time studying smudges in the glass. To me, Riser seems complex beyond understanding: a coin you never know which side will land up. I could ask him a thousand questions and never understand him. Or feel completely comfortable around him.

"Well, Flame wasn't in the pit, was she?" I say, annoyed at how shrill my voice sounds. But she didn't have her arms tied so tightly behind her that her shoulders popped and her wrists bled. She didn't beg Riser to help her, only to be ignored.

"You're right." His hand rakes through his hair. "Which means you know me in a way no one else ever will. Maybe that's why I . . . I care what you think about me." He forces an empty laugh. "I mean, there has to be *something* about me that you find redeeming."

My breath catches as I study his face. Mismatched eyes study me back. The blue eye dark and unsettling, the green one warm and clear.

Who are you, Dorian Riser Laevus? Can I trust you?

Don't be stupid. I blink and look away. *Of course you can't trust the person who nearly killed you in the pit.*

The sound of paper being smoothed draws my attention back to Riser. He hands me the page without looking at me. "I found this on the roof. It's from your diary." He stands to leave. "I didn't read it, if you're wondering."

"Thank—" But he's gone before I can finish. *It's for the best anyway,* I tell myself, but my words ring hollow as I watch Riser and Flame laughing at something near the front.

The paper feels heavy in my hand. I decide not to read the words. They will only bring up memories of the past, and right now I need to focus. I dig in my satchel for matches to burn the page, and my fingers scrape cross Bramble.

I lift him up and plant a quick, motherly kiss on the cold metal of his back, then I switch him off. "Sorry, B, but they won't like you much where we're going."

Just like the letter, he belongs to my old life and the weak, cowardly girl who will get me killed.

I find the matches. There are two left. The letter is balled inside my hand, moistened with sweat. *Perhaps I should let it dry a bit,* I think, *since there are only two matches.* I set the paper on the seat next to me and lean my head against the window.

I will burn it. I will.

I finally succumb to sleep, and when I awake, the debris outside has been replaced by lush green mountains curving round and round. I must have slept through the night because it's near dawn, the dark curtain of night lifting slowly. As we top the mountain, Dominus spreads across the horizon, my mother's birthplace and the largest Royalist city.

Before they left for Hyperion, Golds lived here on majestic estates overlooking the sea, waited on by an army of Bronzes. Many of the Bronzes who served here have been granted entry to Hyperion.

Because what would the new world be without peasants to lord over?

One of those palatial, meandering estates along the cliffs once belonged to the accursed House Croft. After the bombing that killed the Empress, Ezra fled, so they raided the estate and imprisoned the entire House Croft—even though his family had publicly disowned Ezra years before.

In exchange for their release, Ezra gave himself up.

Impatient to announce their victory, the Emperor ordered the trade broadcast over the rift screens. Everyone saw Ezra Croft blow himself up, taking out a slew of unsuspecting Centurions. In retaliation, they hung his tattered red cloak from the square, along with every male from House Croft, ending the Croft line.

Or so the Emperor thought: He didn't know about Riser.

My gaze roves the now abandoned city as I try to imagine my mother here as a child. Pale marble spires and pillars and domes sprout from the white buildings, along with the long, slender aqueducts that bring water into the city and fill their famous hot baths. I think there's a street named after my mother's family—or maybe it's a park. *Lockhart.* I have half a notion to go find it so I can blow it up.

Careful, Everly. You're starting to sound like a Fienian.

The thought isn't as alarming as it should be.

More mountains, more abandoned Royalist towns. I must fall asleep again because when I come to I see flat verdant fields and impossibly thick swaths of blue sky, the occasional empty village.

Finally, a marble dome rises from the valley below. I blink sleepily at the Royalist Headquarters, about the size of a watermelon, surrounded on all sides by gray mountains and a barbed steel fence. It takes a moment to realize that the metallic spheres swarming above the headquarters are drones.

Just over the tallest snow-peaked mountain lies Emerald Island, really more of an inlet stretched across a shimmering green lake.

The windows abruptly darken. There is a falling-feeling in my middle as we descend the tunnel inside the mountain. The rest of the way will be underground.

It's time to destroy the letter. The match head erupts with a soft whoosh. I hold the flame to the corner of the paper, meaning to burn it, but as soon as my loopy, childish handwriting comes to light, I hesitate.

Alarm bells ring inside my head. The page is dated three days before my father's death, but I don't remember writing anything then.

I lean in close:

I, Maia Graystone, am writing this message for myself, with the full knowledge that as soon as it's completed, I will hide it away and forget I ever wrote it.

Father told me everything today. We decided, together, to store the map and the key inside Max and me. Afterward, I would record this message to you from Father and then forget everything.

Please don't be mad at him, Maia. I volunteered over his protests, and you know how stubborn we can be. I don't know where you are in your journey now, but I hope you're still the optimistic, funny, self-reliant girl I am now—of course you are!—and you are being nice to Max—I know it's hard. Just remember Father loves you and you are doing the right thing.

Oh, the most important part. Don't forget you are so incredibly brave!

Signed,

Your Younger, Amazing Self

My father's message, although delivered by my hand, has his elegant, meticulous penmanship:

My dearest Maia,

If you are reading this, then you are still alive and, I pray, healthy. By now I am most surely dead and Project Hyperion will be in its final stages. If this is true, then I hope it has not caused you much pain. I know I was not always the most attentive of fathers, but I promise you, everything I did was for you and your brother.

Project Hyperion began as a last-resort solution to the asteroid. In the case the damage done to the remaining population was catastrophic, the Chosen were to rebuild the human race. However, the Emperor promised to use a significant portion of his resources to research ways to protect the earth from the asteroid. As I discovered later, that promise was never kept.

Unable to accept the destruction of so many, I began to explore the possibilities using materials banned by the Reformation Act. Six years into development, I stumbled upon the breakthrough I needed. I worked in secret, calling my project the Mercurian. The Mercurian was developed to knock the asteroid off its course enough to minimize the damage and spare most of the population.

Unfortunately, by this time, the Emperor had also discovered the Mercurian. Blinded by his own warped ideology, he ordered it destroyed rather than use the technology he forbade. So I hid the Mercurian and ensured the only way to find it was through Max. You are the other failsafe, because in some ways, the Emperor was right: There are those who would use the Mercurian as a weapon.

Maia, this is very important. In the wrong hands, the Mercurian could do the one thing it was designed to prevent: destroy humanity.

I cannot tell you how long I wrestled with the decision to involve you and Max. I knew by doing so I would be putting you in mortal peril—but by then there was no one else I fully trusted. Although I weep for the life I will undoubtedly deprive you of, I know you are not like most children. You are strong, honorable and resourceful, and wise beyond your years.

You weren't meant to marry a Prince, Maia; you were meant to rule.

Please remember, Maiabug, to the moon, stars, and universe, that is how far my love for you reaches.

I hope this cryptic letter—by design—has allowed you some peace. I know I have already demanded more than any father should ask of his daughter, but there is one more thing I need from you. You must find your way to court. The Mercurian is hidden on the Island, in a place designed especially for you. There is still time to activate it and stop the asteroid. What others would use to destroy, you must use to save. But you cannot do this alone. You must ally with the people; you must wake them up. Billions of lives depend on you, darling—as hard as it is, I know you will not let me down.

All my love,

Father

I watch the page burn at my feet, a brilliant star whispering little red fireflies that drift silently to the ceiling.

I open my mouth to make sound, to cry, but all I conjure is the sour saliva that means I am about to puke.

Father wasn't a traitor. He was trying to save the populace. And now billions of people depend on *me*. Not just one annoyingly precocious little brother. *Billions.* For a second, the darkness seems to collapse over me. I am drowning, drowning in it. Then I wade through the murky haze of shadows and memories: my father, Max, the white gown I wore for the small procedure, the way my father smiled and hugged me afterward.

My brain struggles to process this new information. There is still hope. I look up, even though I cannot see through the ceiling of the rail and the mountain to the giant hunk of rock in the sky, hurtling toward us with quiet efficiency. I think of all the years, all the mothers, fathers, sons and daughters, who have looked upon their death crying for someone to save them, knowing no one would.

There is a way to stop Her wrath—and they have known about it the entire time.

It's like one of those nightmares when you are falling. You know at some point you will have to hit the ground, but at the last second, you realize it's only a dream and you wake up sobbing with relief.

Except I am not sobbing—not even close. And the relief I feel gives way to anger. Cold, hard, overwhelming rage that simmers beneath my sternum and ignites inside me a sense of purpose.

It's this same rage that drags the memory of my father's body to the surface. Eyes glazed and rolled to the ceiling. Blood pouring in thick, shiny rivers from his neck and side. His mouth open, gasping for breath—a fish out of water. Soft, gentle hands open as if still reaching for my door handle. He could have run, could have escaped, but he had come to save me instead. They executed him just as I opened my door.

"They killed him," I say aloud.

They killed him.

They killed him.

They *murdered* him.

My body rocks with the movement of the rail. The darkness is all encompassing, the loud purr of the rail echoing off the tight walls. In a few minutes, we will arrive at Headquarters, where Brogue will deliver us for travel to the Island. I am surprised at how calm I feel. How very, very determined. Somehow it feels as if I have been preparing for this very moment my entire life.

After all, it's not the first time I have been here. Scared and alone. Unsure whom to trust. Struggling for survival in a harsh, unforgiving environment.

Except this time will be different.

Because this time I am going to fight back.

PART II

The things that pleased us withered into dust.
And the things that haunt us sprouted from their remains.
Until the rotting harvest, watered in the blood of our children,
grew so tall it hid the sun—
And we forgot we ever loved the light.
~ Baroness Lillian Lockhart

CHAPTER TWENTY-ONE

Reformation Headquarters teems with people in androgynous white frocks, hundreds of them, each planted in front of a large screen with a number beside it. Although I don't see earphones, it is obvious each watcher can hear the screen in front of them.

As I watch, the number from the screen closest to me increases from 3,043,506 to 3,043,507. These must be the screens used to follow the Sleeper numbers attached to each Chosen. I try to imagine what it is like to have a million human beings piggybacked onto my mind. Seeing what I see. Feeling what I feel.

Being *me*.

As if reading my mind, Cage takes my elbow, whispering into my ear, "No worries, kitten, anything not for their sneaky little ears will be automatically wiped."

We're introduced to our guide, Lady Worsley, a short, priggish woman dressed in a black, corseted walking suit. Her severe bun stretches her eyebrows into sharp black peaks. Flame peeks from beneath the brim of her hat, surreptitiously scanning our surroundings. This is the hub of the Royalists' propaganda effort and the office for Minister of Defense, General Cornelius Bloodwood.

Making Flame the proverbial fox in the henhouse.

Flame's cunning gaze darts along the walls before settling on a large screen taking up the entire center wall. It's a map, peppered and streaked with tiny stars meant to represent Sleepers.

And there are still too many dark spots.

We pass through a collection of corridors and rooms to a waiting room of sorts. It takes me a minute to orient myself because the entire west wall is a deep green valley, shaded by tall, lush mountains. The ceiling, a big, beautiful upside down bowl of blue, erupts in birdsong. I can almost feel the breeze on my face.

It is a place meant to make you forget. They are good at that. *Minimizing fear means minimizing panic,* my mother once said. It also reminds me although this side of the mountain is a bastion of highly controlled technology outlawed from the rest of the empire, the Island on the other side follows the Reformation Act. After all, the court must set an example.

But the Shadow Trials? I highly doubt those will follow protocol. What fun would that be?

"Calming, isn't it?" The soft voice comes from a Bronze girl sitting against the opposite wall. Ashy-blond hair falls in sumptuous waves over a vibrant pale-blue gown, crowned with a stiff daffodil-yellow silk cape and embroidered with tulle trimmed with soft rosettes. Her face is oval-shaped and slightly plump, with a natural rosy tint to her lips and cheeks and rich brown eyes made for smiling.

"We once had a sitting room that made it appear you were in the clouds, but don't tell anyone." Beckoning me over, she offers a slender, boneless hand. "I'm Lady Merida Pope, and this"—she nudges the boy beside her—"is Lord Rhydian Pope, my cousin."

The boy looks remarkably like Merida, with a slimmer face and darker eyes, and he wears a similarly colored day suit. He nods coolly in my direction.

I squeeze her hand. "I'm Everly . . . Lady Everly March."

Merida's eyes flutter over my hair. "That color is aces on you. Is it reconstructed?"

"Of course not," I snap, perhaps a bit too quickly. "Aesthetic reconstruction is forbidden."

The girl laughs, her eyes sparkling. "Please, Lady March, join us."

I do as instructed.

"My father said the only crime in Royalist territory was being poor. Everything else was just a matter of price."

"Merida!" Rhydian scolds.

"What? It's true!" Merida protests. "Besides, every courtier I know had multiple reconstructions by the time they were old enough to attend the Emerald balls on the Island."

Rhydian's gaze darts behind me. That's when I notice the other finalist sitting near the back. I stare—perhaps longer than polite. She is not as I expected. Neat black pageboy hair. Midnight-black blazer and tapered men's trousers over a broomstick frame. The yellow-and-black-checkered tie that hangs from her neck matches her polished, steel-toed Oxfords. Startling red lips pull everything together.

Rhydian squeezes Merida's hand, gently. "Mer, such speech might have been tolerated at Coventry, but not here. Promise me you will not forget that."

Merida casts a dubious glance at the lone girl in the back. "Lady Teagan doesn't give two Fienian denaris for what I'm saying." One hand cupping her mouth, she whispers conspiratorially to me, "She's a Subversive. The House of Aster must have drained their entire mining fortune getting her here."

I do a double take. Except for the haircut and her clothes, she looks rather normal—not at all like the weak, genetically corrupt creature the Royalists make Subversives out to be.

I first heard the word when I was six, right after I kissed another girl on the lips, the same way I had seen my mother kiss my father. It was innocent, a childish whim, but that didn't stop the other children in the park from spitting that word at me as if it was the worst insult imaginable.

My mother explained the very unlucky few were born with a sickness, a disease, really, that made them unable to live harmoniously in society. Unable to have families. Raise children. Be productive.

Lady Teagan catches my gaze and smiles a slow, sharp grin. There is something refreshing about her, an unapologetic this-is-me-take-it-or-leave-it vibe.

I want to return the smile. Maybe introduce myself. Instead I press my lips together and look at the wall. I cannot afford to ally myself with someone who stands out, who doesn't know how to play the game.

Rhydian sighs, dragging my attention back to the conversation. "Just, promise, Mer, you will guard your speech?"

"Promise," Merida says, looking anything but contrite as she winks at me.

Merida is the opposite of Lady Teagan. Soft, playful, with a childish joy that is infectious. In my old life, we would have been immediate friends. We might have talked about boys and fashion, shared clothes and secrets.

Now, however, just like Lady Teagan, she is of little value and I resolve to keep my distance.

The taciturn Lady Worsley returns to retrieve our attendants and luggage, trailed by a furtive man with a dark, slippery mustache, thick sideburns, and a bowler hat.

"The Censor," Merida whispers as the man quietly assesses Rhydian's suit, a look of deep concentration on his face. The man digs around the pockets, searching for weapons. Whipping a slim wand from his pocket, he runs it quickly over Rhydian, checking for banned devices, I imagine.

Without a word, the Censor moves on to Merida and then me. He takes longer with my poor dress, but finally moves on to Riser, who crosses his arms and glares hostilely at the little man.

Teagan is last. The Censor stops just short of her, his round little eyes blinking, as if he has found something unexpected. A tiny frown upsets his otherwise indifferent expression. Teagan brazenly glances up at him, sending him scuttling away muttering under his breath.

I hand over the small satchel with my meager belongings to Brogue. Before he leaves, he leans into me. "Make no mistake, Lady March, your life is now in danger. The only thing more wicked than a courtier is a banished one. Good luck."

"What are we waiting here for?" I say, more to Rhydian than Merida, who is busy helping her attendant gather their large retinue of trunks.

Although Rhydian has a tranquil, composed face, his eyes are lost. It's a different kind of sad from Riser's haunted look. The kind that can't be reconstructed away. As if he's peddling furiously just above the surface and might drown any second. "They are going to plug us into the system."

Right. As soon as they do, we will be open to upload. My stomach churns at the thought. "Will it take long?"

"I don't think so," Merida says, now finished with her belongings. "They also check us for bootleg Microplants."

Riser and I share a glance. We are about to find out if Flame knows her stuff. The thought doesn't provide much in the way of comfort.

Merida gives Riser a wary once-over. "Do you know him?"

"Lord Riser Thornbrook," I say, frowning. "We met on the rail."

"From what estate does he hail?" Merida asks.

The Five Circles of Hell, I think darkly. "Sadly, I believe his family lost everything after their fall from court, even their lands."

"A rather savage creature, isn't he?"

Oh, you have no idea.

As if he knows we are discussing him, Riser directs his sharp gaze at us. Unused to such ill manners, both Merida and Rhydian smile uneasily and glance away. I glare at him.

He grins devilishly back.

Lady Teagan is first, followed shortly afterward by Lady Merida and then her cousin. We wait in silence. Ten minutes pass. Half an hour. I am about to stand when my name is called.

As soon as I step into the room I am immersed inside a rainforest. Giant rubbery green leaves rustle all around me. Diverse, overlapping sounds of birds, monkeys, and other animals make a soothing blanket of noise. The air is humid and smells of flowers and earth and rain. It's an amazing experience, really, considering the last surviving rainforest disappeared nearly a millennium ago.

I lay on a metal table, on my side. A woman instructs me to close my eyes. It's imperative I stay calm and still. There's the smell of alcohol, the cold feel of something being rubbed on my neck. A faint pinch, a dull pressure at the base of my skull, and it's done.

Next, I roll onto my back and the woman runs a small wand over me. It buzzes with a static sound, blue light pulsing from its tip. I blink as it hovers just over my eyes. There's a faint, alarming beep.

The woman's forehead wrinkles, and she leans forward. Obviously Flame messed up. My heartbeat, displayed on a screen, begins to rapid-fire. Just before the woman can take another swipe, the wand unexplainably dies.

"That's never happened before," she says. "But we don't have time to fix it." She flashes me a troubled smile and nods toward the back door. "You may feel a brief tingling with the first upload, but you'll get used to it."

I find Merida and Rhydian waiting in the next room, along with Teagan.

"Well, I guess you passed," Merida says, breaking into a congratulatory smile. She presses her fingers into the crook of my elbow. "I'm glad."

Rhydian is not so cordial. He knows what I know. We are not friends. Quite the contrary. But he's pleasant, at least, offering his congratulations with a tight-lipped smile and making polite but disinterested inquiries into my health and life. When it becomes clear by my guarded answers I'm not into pleasantries either, he seems relieved, retreating happily into a corner.

A different woman shows up with a clipboard. "Lady Teagan Aster III, please come with me."

Already expecting it, Lady Teagan has stepped forward, a whole foot taller than the woman.

"Let me guess," Teagan says, her voice more weary than ill-tempered, "my livery has offended thee?"

The woman presses her thin lips together, her face puckering as if she smells something rancid. "Subversive, your entire personage offends."

"Right," Teagan says. The way her face remains calm and detached tells me she's used to this type of treatment. As I watch them disappear into another room, I find myself inexorably rooting for her.

Riser enters just as Lady Worsley comes to collect us. Her wooden-heeled shoes clap against the tile floor. As she leads us away, Merida turns to me, lifts her ashy-blond eyebrows, and somehow perfectly mimics her warped face. The act is so juvenile and unexpected I burst out laughing. Merida laughs too, a small hand clapping over her mouth to hide it.

Riser turns just enough so his one blue eye is visible. A warning. Keep on task. Don't make friends. He's right, so I lose my smile and follow the rest of the way in silence.

We literally run to keep up with Stern-Face. Despite her short legs, she manages a very brisk pace, and before I can orient myself, we are climbing the steps to the roof door.

When we get to the roof, a pleasant wind rolls over me, tearing at my jacket and hair. The sun sits low and fat on the horizon.

As we walk to the craft, I peer across the valley. There's a small pass between the mountains, a thirty-foot-high barbed wire fence making it impenetrable. Writhing masses of people swell the pass like a river. The fence must be electrified because orange sparks burst from the fence whenever the crowd pushes too close. Other than a few sharp screams, their cries make a muffled din.

My eye catches on something darting down the road that leads to the gate—a wagon full of people.

Merida rifles through her patent leather satchel and hands me gold-plaited binoculars. "They say the Emperor sees rebels and Fienian Sympathizers in every corner. Each time they return from the space station, more courtiers are thrown to the wolves across the fence."

The people in my lens come into focus. By their dress, I'd say they're Silvers. Two Centurions march them, shackled, to the gate. It yawns open just enough for them to be forced through and then slams closed.

"Watch what will happen to those who don't make the Culling," Merida whispers.

I know what will happen, but I cannot look away. They disappear beneath the angry mob, their screams masked by the loud buzzing of the fence. Sparks burst wildly and then all goes quiet.

As I hand back the binoculars, I feel a renewed urgency to find the thing my father hid and win.

Whatever it takes.

CHAPTER TWENTY-TWO

The cloudcraft makes a light whirring noise. We pile in and find our safety belts. I have to admit, given my and Riser's history together in high spaces, I try very hard not to look at the ground as we clear the roof and arc over the valley. It doesn't help that the cloudcraft's walls and floor are completely clear, as if we are floating inside a bubble. The walls are really screens, projecting images. That doesn't make it any less daunting, though.

Surreal. That's the word dancing on the tip of my tongue. Looking out, seeing miles of green pasture, steely-gray mountains, open air and unbroken sky, it's like I am in another world. I can't remember the last time I saw anything but carnage and ugly.

Right before we arc over the mountains, my stomach hollows and there's this lighter than air feeling. I think for a second I might hurl, but then we stabilize.

The top of the mountain becomes empty space. Blue sky and rolling clouds. The massive lake that ensconces the Island unfurls beneath my fingertips, a silken fabric of greenish-blue, tossing little gems of sunlight off its surface. We drop low. *Lower.* My body tenses with the imagined impact. But at the last second we stabilize, barely missing the white gulls gliding low over the water.

Dense green woodland haloes the shore, fringed with the yellow-brown of the marshlands. Penumbria Forest. My body becomes heavy as we lift above the trees and glide for what seems like miles. The verdant, leafy rug disappears, and we cross a meadow, the cloudcraft's shadow startling a group of white-chested stag.

Nestled deep within the distant rolling hills, and carved from the mountainside, a bone-white monstrosity shimmers beneath the sun. *Laevus Court Palace.*

My eyes pick through everything. The Mercurian hides in one of those forests, one of those rooms of stone. Really, it could be anywhere. And how am I supposed to find it? Even if I knew *where* to look, the castle and grounds will be teeming with suspicious Centurions and courtiers. And how am I supposed to concentrate on finding it when all my focus needs to be on surviving the Culling and the trials?

A shadow spills over the craft. HighClare Tower sprouts to our right, taller than seems possible, its pale stones dark with moss, the enormous black flag that flaps from its crown bearing the Emperor's clawed phoenix.

Merida follows the tower with her eyes. "I was rather hoping they had torn it down," she says softly, to no one in particular. She turns to me. "Have you been to court before, Lady March?"

"Yes, when I was . . ." *Nine.* "A baby," I finish, clearing my throat. "But I don't remember anything about it, obviously."

Merida traces the top of the dwindling tower with her fingertip. "I was six and Rhydian was seven when we were banished. I watched my Uncle, Rhydian's father, hang from that spot right there, along with five others from House Pope."

Rhydian looks up for the first time since we entered the craft. "My father was a conspirator and Fienian Sympathizer, so he received a traitor's death."

No one says a word after that. There's a small bump as the craft settles in the middle of the cobblestone courtyard, next to the Deliverance Day Fountain, an impressive monument of marble, carved into the giant form of Emperor Laevus surrounded by one hundred creepy marble children.

When I was six, they began broadcasting the D-Day fountain's progress over the rift screens. It took over three years and countless Bronzes to build it. Every hour on the hour water spurts from the children's cupped hands, to count down the days until D-Day. Beneath it, basking in the fountain's spray, are flotillas bobbing with couples feeding the swans under frilly parasols.

There's a low hiss as the sides of the craft lift. Sundrenched air and the heady, sticky-sweet aroma of roses and warm grass fill the craft. My brain swims with the sounds of clattering hooves from a nearby carriage and swans trumpeting. My body, by now used to the gentle rocking of the craft, needs a second to adjust to the ground.

Merida and Rhydian exit first. I stare nervously out at the vibrant world that awaits. Is my mother here? Or is she above, passing her days on Hyperion? Of course she is. Relief eases the tension in my shoulders. I won't have to see her yet.

Real or imagined, I feel a slight touch against my pinky finger, as if Riser, for the briefest of moments, is practicing the all too human gesture of reassurance.

Riser leaps out and turns to offer me his hand. "My Lady."

His hand is warm and strong and surprisingly comforting, and he squeezes gently, perhaps lingering for a moment too long. But beneath the manners, his voice is cold. It's obvious our last conversation on the rail has changed our friendship.

I curtsy, dropping low to hide the twinge of regret I feel for hurting him. For some reason, the last few sentences from my mother's first sanctioned poem, written when she was my age, echoes inside my skull:

For I am flesh and I am bone. Forged in flames; set in stone.

For I am free.

Free to be a girl no longer.

"A girl no longer," I whisper. Then we are off across the plush lawn. A Lord and a Lady, playing our part.

The first upload happens just after I enter my apartment. Too late for the tour, we head straight to the Hawthorne Castle Apartments, the building reserved strictly for Shadow Trial finalists. It's an older building, wrapped in thick ivy and missing much of the finery of Laevus Court, but still impressive with its bold colonnades and gilded statuary. After all, visiting Gold Barons and their families used to stay here.

My apartment is on the second floor, just past the grand marble staircase. A thick rectangle of dust motes swirls in the light from the opened window looking out onto the Royal Gardens. The stables sit to the east, the pungent smell of horse manure and rotting hay drifting on the sedate breeze. The sun skims off the Palladium River in the distance.

Flame is here, hunkered over the apparatus she has managed to set up inside my wardrobe—for quick hiding, she explained. She's more surly than usual, due to the fact the encryption that will allow communication with Nicolai is taking longer than it should. I stopped counting her vulgar, expletive-filled outbursts at one hundred. Otherwise, we are doing an expert job of ignoring the other.

As my attendant, she is rather lacking. But as the techy mastermind keeping me off the Royalist grid and connected to Nicolai, I supposed she's earning her keep.

I'm near the window, enjoying the sun on my cheeks, when a tiny jolt goes off in the center of my brain. My lips and the tip of my nose buzz. The sensation is strange yet familiar, a word you say over and over again until it simply becomes an unrecognizable string of syllables. The pressure behind my eyes releases and I'm left with a dull, achy feeling, like a bruise inside my brain.

My first upload.

I smooth my hair, dress in the outfit Merida sent over—a backless, ivory-colored riding suit with poof sleeves and a high collar that would give the Censor a stroke—and curtsy for Flame. "How do I look,

Fienian?" Although better than the previous moldy costume, it is also bolder, corsetless, and flagrantly modern.

Flame glances up from her toy. "Like a Royalist strumpet."

"Perfect. How soon until we're back online with Nicolai?"

"We could make it now. That is, if you don't mind hanging by your neck from the Tower by Shadow Fall."

"No, thanks." Squinting, I take a closer look. "So, what *are* you doing, exactly?"

Without looking up, Flame says, "Piggybacking onto their system using a Trojan horse encryption. When I'm done, I'll be able to control their input and Nicolai will have a detection free mode of transmission. Any other moronic questions?"

"Nope. Fresh out."

Flame fixes me with an annoyed stare. "Don't you have somewhere to be?"

I throw up my hands. "Leaving."

"Wait." She procures a flat dirk from her sparse décolletage and hands the weapon to me. I roll the short handle between my palms. It is impossible to ignore the way my heart flutters at the dagger's cold heaviness.

"But they searched us," I point out stupidly.

She snorts, taking the weapon from me. "No, strumpet, they poked and prodded like prudish ninnies." She peels back the neckline of my bust and frowns. "What kind of suit doesn't have a dirk-pocket?" Before I can respond, she has slashed the seams from the hemline and slipped the flat blade inside. "Now you're *perfect.*"

"Thanks." I smile. "Try not to do anything terrorist-y while I'm gone."

The others are waiting for me in the saloon. By now there have been hundreds of uploads, their minds a low static hum inside my head. Getting used to it will take some time.

Merida has changed into a dusky, rose-colored suit that drapes in a way that makes every movement look like an elaborate dance. Daring and fun, it's pulled together with just a hint of coral lipstick. Appraising her outfit on me, she gives my hand a quick squeeze. "Like it was made for you. Have you, you know, felt *it* yet?"

"Yes," I say, shivering at the memory of the upload.

"It's like someone's wriggling around inside your head."

I don't point out they actually *are* inside our head. *Best to not think about it.*

Merida giggles. "But the weirdest part is thinking about who's inside you. I have four younger sisters, and they all plan to give me their uploads, so now I can't help wondering if every upload I feel is one of them mucking around."

Rhydian holds the door while Riser shepherds us out. It will take a little getting used to, being treated like a lady. Riser's fingers rest on my back, skimming lightly across my naked shoulder blade. "I like the dress, Lady March."

I turn, smile, ignoring the way my skin goosebumps beneath his fingertips. "Why, thank you, Lord Thornbrook."

I have to admit, we are playing our parts beautifully.

We take a carriage through the gardens on the way to Laevus Castle. I find the bumpy ride calming. Riser is lost, staring out the open door. If he's nervous or overwhelmed, then he's doing a good job hiding it.

Shadow Fall is due any second, so at first I think the shadow that slinks over our carriage is from the asteroid. But this shadow is fleeting, followed quickly by another. Peering out, I see the court's starcrafts in the sky, more like silver tear-drops, as they converge over Laevus Castle, too many to count, before lowering out of sight.

"The court's back from Hyperion," I say, all too aware of the fear their presence invokes. They've come especially for the Culling tonight.

The real Shadow Fall hits just as the carriage stops in front of the grand steps. Two Bronze attendants holding lighted torches help us out and up the stairs. Peacocks meander lazily under the portico, pecking at the legs of the silent Centurions posted along the wall. Each Centurion holds a torch and a pistol.

Once inside, I hardly have time to take in the grandeur because our attendants are rushing us. Even so, it takes seemingly forever to wind through the maze of corridors, stairwells, and around the servants lighting candles. Finally we are deposited in a sitting room strewn with silk cushions and a simpering fire and told to wait.

My first objective is to orient to my surroundings. As soon as I do, I can begin a proper search for the Mercurian. The futility of my situation is not lost on me. There are literally thousands of acres of land and countless rooms to search. Because of the risk of it being found, my father had to be vague in the letter. And I assume he was going to provide more guidance in the Simulation. Unfortunately, none of that helps me now.

This room, I think, feels somewhat familiar. From scraps of memory I build a rough map inside my head of where we are. Somewhere in the east wing, on the fourth floor. And if I'm right . . .

The observatory sits exactly where I remember it. A long hallway lined with portraits of the Royal Family leads there. Torches adorn the wall to my left, and with each flame I pass, my shadow stretches out to almost touch the winding wrought-iron stairs that lead up to the telescope domed in glass.

I pause just before the stairs and glance at the last painting. Inside the enormous, gold baroque frame, Prince Caspian sits erect on a white marble throne, heavy Gold crown slightly askew, his black robe nearly swallowing him. The artist managed to capture the ironic curve of his lips and the confident sparkle that warms his pale-champagne eyes.

"See something you like?" a male with a rich voice asks.

"Oh!" I whip around. "No . . . I mean . . . !" I glare at the trespasser. He has smooth, clean features. Elegant sandy-blond eyebrows. Full cheekbones and lips, strengthened by a long, straight nose. Light golden eyes and sun-burnished skin make the man's flaxen hair appear brighter.

And he wears an ironic smile.

The man nods to the portrait. "I'm—"

"Prince Caspian," I interject, forgetting every bit of grace I've been taught. "I know."

He lifts a royal eyebrow. "And you are . . . ?"

"Oh! Um . . . Everly. Lady Everly March." I offer a hand to shake before remembering the proper protocol for greeting someone above my station is a curtsy.

Damn it to Fienian hell! He's not just above my station. He's a Gold. *Royalty.* That requires a sweeping bow of some sort.

By the gods, girl, Nicolai groans inside my head. *I can hardly watch.*

Well, that was fast, I respond. *Flame said it would take a while to encrypt.*

There are a few kinks that need ironing out, but I assumed by the way things were going it was an emergency.

I snort. "You're the last person I need help from . . . oh." Realizing I am talking aloud, my mouth clamps shut.

"Excuse me?" Caspian's refined voice drips with amusement.

"I was talking . . . to myself."

There's a near imperceptible groan inside my head, and then I feel Nicolai leave.

Caspian studies me for a moment longer, as if I'm some strange creature that needs cataloguing. Then his lips curl back into his ironic smile and he laughs, taking my hand and squeezing it firmly. "A pleasure to make your acquaintance, Lady March."

"Sorry," I say, "I haven't been to court in a while. I'm a—"

"Finalist," Caspian finishes. "I *know.*"

It's hard not to stare at Caspian. He's exactly how I imagined. Warm, approachable, regal. A quick, easy smile. He's good looking, in a safe, pleasant sort of way, his broad shoulders straining against a buff leather jerkin cinched with gold taffeta ribbons only he could pull off. His Chosen brand, the same one I used to wear, rises from his high collar, the phoenix's wings shimmering as if afire.

The connection between us is immediate and impossible to ignore. He's staring at me as if he feels it too. We were matched, once, our DNA a perfect fit, so I imagine even with all of my reconstruction, parts of us still are. I clear my throat. "The others are probably looking for me."

He runs a hand through his thick, shoulder-length hair. My guess is courtly custom calls for it to be pulled back, but sometime during the day his ribbon fell out—probably during jousting or some other noble sport they have on Hyperion—and he hasn't yet noticed. "Yes, of course." He takes my hand, palm down, brings it to his lips. "A pleasure, Lady March."

I perform a small, wanting curtsy. "My Liege."

As I turn to go, there's a loud grating noise, and the telescope above shifts to another position. We both pause to stare.

Caspian bounds up the winding stairs. From below, I can just make out Caspian as he lovingly runs his palm over the telescope's long, sleek cylindrical body. "She's never done that before," he says, frowning. Part of his face disappears as he looks through the lens. When he's done, he wears a strange expression. "Would you care to see where it landed?"

Somehow it doesn't feel like a question. My boots pad softly on the stairs. The telescope seems larger than I remember, and impossibly beautiful, surrounded on all sides by clear glass. Torchlight runs down its golden length.

I peer through the lens at the sight I know by heart. "The Great Orion Nebula," I whisper. It sits within the sword of Orion. A blooming pinkish-red flower of hydrogen gas fills the lens, the bright white center a stellar nursery of baby stars. "The Pleiades Star Cluster sits just above it."

"So, you love Astronomy too?"

"I *used* to love it." My hands mesh awkwardly together. "Then I grew up."

"Well, I'm also an expert at giving up things I love." He chuckles darkly. "But I haven't had to part with this . . . yet." His hand scrapes through his hair. "I was actually on my way here when I found *you* . . . ?"

"Looking for this." I tap the telescope. "To calm my nerves."

My voice falters. Caspian has gone quiet, his eyes slowly, carefully searching my face, his mouth curled as if I'm something on the tip of his tongue, a word to be remembered. Does he recognize something in my demeanor? My face?

Frowning, Caspian turns to gaze out the dark window so only his profile is visible. "There was a girl I knew a long time ago, named after the brightest of the seven sisters. She wore both the Orion Constellation and the Pleiades on her face. Did you know, Lady March, mythology states Orion was half-mad with love for the seven sisters, so when he died Zeus placed them in the sky for him to eternally gaze upon?"

"No," I lie. We are venturing into dangerous territory, and I can almost feel my freckles burning like the stars we talk about.

"She wrote a poem for me once, this girl, about how horrible it was for Orion to have to look at something every day he could not truly have."

What he doesn't know is the meaning behind that childish poem. How my father was Orion and my mother the seven sisters, unable to be tethered to anything but her cause.

I study my nails. "What happened to this budding poetess?"

Even from my side view I can see I have made a mistake. Our tenuous rapport has vanished, his wide shoulders suddenly tight with tension. "A little advice, if I may, Lady March?"

"Of course."

"We never talk about courtiers no longer present."

"Right. I . . . I shouldn't have pried." I know if I don't exit now, it will only get more awkward, but I can't seem to move.

"Everly!" Merida peers from below. When her eyes shift to Caspian, she falls into a panicked, half hazard bow. "My Liege, apologies for interrupting—"

"No!" I quickly stammer, racing down the stairs. "I was just leaving."

Caspian calls out from the top of the stairs, but I bow, rather clumsily, and flee with Merida. Once back in the sitting room, we burst into schoolgirl giggles.

Mid-laugh, Riser takes my arm and herds me into the corner, forcing me to face him. "You shouldn't disappear like that."

"Excuse me?" I snap.

Easy, there, Nicolai says. He sounds more than mildly amused. *Remember the plan. I don't think wooing involves biting each other's heads off.*

Unfortunately for Nicolai, my words—or lack thereof—on the rail have already made wooing nearly impossible. I peel Riser's fingers from my arm. "Maybe you should stop trying to be my keeper."

The muscles in his jaw tense. "You could have been hurt."

The veiled concern in his voice settles deep in my core. For a moment, I want to tell him not to worry. That I hate the thought of him being upset. But I need to push him away, to keep distance between us. "Would you rather I stay here so we can work on the plan?" Pushing off my tiptoes, I close the space between us. "How about this? Does this make you happy?"

"This isn't about us. It's about the uploads. Making sure you make it past the Culling." His voice is low, soft as it rolls across my cheeks. I focus on his green eye. The one that means what he says.

The one I could fall for.

My chest tightens as invisible fingers strum each rib, all the way up to my throat. I realize my fingernails are carved into my palms. *No! They want this. My emotions are not real, not mine. Fight it, Everly! Don't let them control you.*

This isn't real.

I shrink back. "You think a stupid kiss will accomplish all that?"

He chuckles darkly. "Everly, the only thing I know is when the time comes," he leans down, "it will be anything but stupid."

Before I can say anything else to make him understand how that will *never* happen, the doors to the Great Hall grate open. Thankful for the interruption, I turn, fully expecting something extravagant. A feast, perhaps. Tables laden with food and wine. The perfect way to show off the Emperor's wealth and privilege.

What I see instead makes me go cold.

Riser's reaction startles me out of my surprised stupor. His hand jumps to his waist, where his dagger would usually be. Our eyes meet, and he orders something indecipherable over the shouts and scuffling sounds. Hands dig deep into my shoulders, and I am flung violently backward as Merida cries out.

"Stop!" I yell.

I see two—no three—men tussling with Riser.

And then a blindfold constricts my eyes, squeezing tight, and everything goes black.

Chapter Twenty-Three

The effect of having my vision stolen from me is debilitating. I pull air through my nose, out my mouth. Work to calm my mind. There's no doubt I'm standing on a table. My eyes are blindfolded. The feeling of panic permeates the room.

Nicolai, what's happening? Nicolai! But I know by the empty feeling inside my head he isn't there.

A lot of help you are.

The smell of candle wax and fear burns my throat. Judging by the other blindfolded finalists I glimpsed standing on tabletops, this is a hazing of some sorts. In that small second, with their faces covered, I didn't recognize any of the finalists. But most were Golds once, before the Emperor in his paranoia had them labeled Fienian Sympathizers and their families stripped to Bronze.

The room fills with jeers and laughs at our expense. It appears the kids at court haven't changed much since my last time here. The thought makes me queasy. I can almost hear their taunts. Feel their daggers raking the hair and flesh from my scalp.

The girl beside me yells in surprise. I find out why a second later as hands grab my left leg and twist it up until it's balancing on my other knee. Waving my arms, I find my balance and use my core to stabilize.

Tittering, as more finalists are forced to lift their legs. "Welcome to the Island," says a female with a high, lazy voice. "I'm Countess Delphine Bloodwood, and tonight after the Culling, my fellow Chosen and I will each be forced to pick two of you Bronze worms to mentor, so now's your chance to prove your worth."

I inhale a deep breath to keep from falling off the table. Countess Delphine? The cruel girl who shaved my head for entertainment? Who in their right mind would put a maniac like *that* in charge of the finalists?

Loud taunting makes me wobble, and I focus on keeping my balance. Something cold and heavy is placed into my hand. I hear and feel liquid sloshing inside it, so a cup. "Drink up," orders Delphine. "I want to see empty goblets in ten seconds."

I draw in furious gulps, the liquid burning a fiery trail to my belly. After I take a couple breaths of air, I realize it's blackberry rum, not acid—not that my esophagus seems to know the difference.

A wave of dizziness crashes over me. My leg wobbles, but I manage to stay on one foot.

"Again," Delphine commands. There's the sound of my glass being filled. I drain my cup. This time it doesn't burn so badly, and the flame in my belly becomes a soothing blanket of warmth that seeps into my limbs.

The girl beside me is having problems. I can hear her dry-heave between each shallow sip. Finally, though, she gets it down. Drawing in a ragged breath, she makes a grunting noise, followed by wet vomiting.

"Oh," says Delphine. "Oh, dear me. We can't have that." Footsteps *clop* our direction. "Your name?"

"Bri—Brinley Fox," says the girl. "I'm sorry. Let me try again."

"Well, Bri-Brinley," Delphine says, mocking Brinley's stutter, "I was hoping you would say that."

Clanging on the table. It sounds as if Brinley is being helped down. The sour smell of vomit burns my nose. After a moment, Brinley says, "I don't understand."

"Lick it up," Delphine says.

"What?"

Snickering echoes through the room. "Lick. It. Up."

After a pause comes the sound of lapping. My stomach tightens, and acrid bile tickles my throat.

The mentors are trying to humiliate us. Make sure we don't rise above our place. They are reminding us we are beneath them. That they—not us—were Chosen first, and we are an unwelcome afterthought.

Every time a leg hits a table, someone has to drink another cup. There is more puking. More lapping. More crying. People begin to fall from their tables, from drunkenness or fatigue it's hard to say.

Just as I become aware of the dull ache in my bladder, a boy begs to use the bathroom. Minutes later he must wet his pants because Delphine and a few of the others mercilessly berate him. Another round of vomiting. Another series of thuds as bodies tumble to the ground.

I'm thinking I might actually get by fine when something triggers the memory of Delphine and her friends snickering over me, and my leg wavers. I try to regain my balance, but it's too late; my foot has already touched.

My cup becomes heavy—but not as heavy as before. "Drink slowly," a male with a gentle voice instructs. One long gulp is all it takes, but I pretend to drink for another thirty seconds so it looks like my cup was full.

I blink as our blindfolds are discarded and we are allowed to stand on two legs. Not that that helps some of the others, who are already so drunk they can barely sit. Dark wet stains drench the front of more than one trouser. The hall smells of piss and vomit and rum. Many of the girls shake, shedding silent, streaky tears. My vision swims as my eyes follow the flickering golden light, tossed from the two massive chandeliers in the ceiling.

That's when I see the air seem to shiver, like invisible ripples billowing outward. I squint to make sure I'm not drunker than I thought, but the rest of the room must see it too because the hall goes quiet. Just as the air starts to solidify into a form, Delphine slaps a hand over her chest. "All hail the Emperor!"

The Chosen echo, "All hail the Emperor!"

And then a deathly quiet descends the room as the Emperor's hologram, a huge, larger than life figure spanning the ceiling, smiles down at us. "Hello, little maggots."

A girl beside me begins to cry, and a few of the other finalists look as if they're going to be ill again.

"So these are the traitors' children," the Emperor says in a booming voice. "A pathetic lot, wouldn't you agree, my Chosen?"

The Chosen stomp their feet and yell, "Yes, my Emperor," in unison.

"During the Culling tonight, it will be your job to discover the few deserving Bronzes to mentor beneath you and possibly enter Hyperion." A cruel grin twists the Emperor's face. "But right now, your job is to find the weakest worm and *squash* it."

Cheers erupt as the Chosen go wild, clapping and pounding fists on the tables while the finalists shake. I'm shaking too. But I remind myself the Emperor is only a hologram—for now, at least. He can't hurt me. And if I don't call attention to myself, there's no reason for him to notice me.

A sober-looking Riser stands near the back, surveying our tormentors. He makes small, smooth, maniacal movements that hint at murder. Giant blots of blood stain his vest.

It doesn't take long to find the owner of the blood. Unlike the other mentors, whose features are lithe and pleasing, the boy with the swollen nose is muscular and imposing, platinum-blond hair cropped over cruel blue eyes and a thick, square jaw. By the way he's sneering at Riser, the boy isn't too happy about their previous interaction.

A Bronze bloodying a Gold. Not the best start to the Shadow Trials.

I look around. It's impossible to tell which of the mentors spared my drink. I spy Caspian to my right. He's speaking softly to a girl who has fallen from her table into a pool of yellowish vomit. His eyes cut at me, and I look away. The last thing I need is to be noticed by someone like him.

The mentors are casually walking around us, talking and laughing as if we are chattel to be bid upon. Every once in a while, a mentor will take stock of a finalist, fingering their clothes or nudging them to see how drunk they are.

Above us, the Emperor stays quiet. But he watches. I can feel his gaze as it travels the finalists, looking for what, I don't know.

Our tormentors make up twenty-five of the highest-ranking Chosen, all descended from powerful Houses. *The Emperor must be proud,* I think as I study them. They are exactly as I remember. Each one different, a masterpiece of genetics and breeding, exquisitely made, their flawless features nearly impossible to look away from. They mill about, smooth and graceful, as if they float instead of walk. Each one carries a weapon of some sort on their person: The guys seem to favor short swords, the girls jeweled daggers.

One dark-eyed boy casts an indifferent glance at me, and I fight the urge to dig my pointed boot into his smirking lips. Instead, I stand stiff as a statue while he casually measures my ankles, tilting his head side to side as his eyes travel up.

Soon there are others I recognize. Delphine sits on an elaborately-carved redwood throne on an upraised stage, her deep-plum-colored dress overflowing the chair, whispering and laughing with a pack of sharp-eyed courtiers who pick at the dark cherries on the table next to her. She wears the casual arrogance of someone who's been told since birth they are better than everyone else. But it's her eyes—pale, fidgety, pupils swollen with cruel excitement—that scare me. Caspian's sovereign seat sits empty to Delphine's left.

"The Countess Delphine has never been able to resist a throne," a girl teases in a soft voice. I look down to the courtier who whispered it, a big-eyed, fair-haired girl, but she's already moved past. Prince Caspian glances up from his position on the floor and beams at her in a way I could only hope someone would look at me. Then she turns her head and glances curiously at me before dipping low to help Caspian with the sick finalists.

Princess Ophelia, it has to be. Did she notice me watching Delphine? But why would she say what she did? Unless the court is divided. After a while I see I'm right; there are two separate factions: those who follow Delphine and those who follow Caspian.

Hmm, won't that be an interesting marriage?

The Emperor watches it all like a god, his gaze implacable—except when he glances down at Caspian helping the finalists. Then The Emperor frowns, and an angry line etches his forehead.

But he perks up again when the brutish boy with the broken nose—undoubtedly Delphine's twin brother, Count Roman Bloodwood—leaps onto a table full of finalists and stomps loudly, whooping and hollering in their faces. "C'mon," he yells, his voice breathy with excitement and rum, "time to get to know you little worms."

Slowly the room fills with the chanting of the Chosen. "Truth or Risk!"

I know the game. My friends and I played it when I was young. Sit in a circle. Wait your turn and choose to answer a question or take a dare. Always stupid stuff. Who do you want to kiss? Run across the busy street. That sort of thing.

I have the sinking feeling this is not stupid, childish stuff we are about to do.

"Eeny, meeny, miny, moe," Delphine trills, strolling around the tables. "Catch a worm by the toe." She grabs a girl's leg and the girl cries out in alarm. "If it hollers, make it pay." Delphine smirks up at the girl. "Truth or risk?"

The girl chooses truth. Delphine seems disappointed. Sighing, she says in a bored voice, "What's the most deviant thing you've ever done?"

The girl's round eyes flit upward at the Emperor as she struggles for the safest answer.

Delphine points a remote at the wall, and a huge projector screen lowers. "Hold . . . that . . . thought." With one little click, the screen comes to life. My heart sinks as I realize it's the girl's memories being accessed somehow through the Microplant they gave us at headquarters.

Riser and I make eye contact. It's only a slight shake of the head, but I understand perfectly what he is saying. We cannot take the chance of them accessing something Flame has yet to encrypt.

Both of us will have to choose dare.

I miss the girl's memory, but it must not have been too inflammatory because Delphine quickly moves on. Slicing between the tables, she parts the crowd like a knife, seemingly choosing at random. Memories project onto the wall. Thoughts and actions and feeling that were supposed to be private.

A boy kicks his neighbor's dog to death for nipping his shoe. Two boys cheat on their final exams. Nearly everyone has had something reconstructed. Several girls had forbidden trysts with Centurions. Another is in love with her family's Bronze serving boy.

Despite the embarrassment to the finalists, I can tell Delphine is unsatisfied. She's become cagey, her bottom lip puffing out like a child not getting her way.

But then she comes upon two sibling finalists who introduce themselves as Lord Hugo and Lady Lucy Redgrave. With dark curly hair streaked silver and alabaster skin tinged gray, like dirty snow, they stand out from the others. Of course I remember them from the ferryboat. After holding me down so Delphine could practically scalp me, their faces are seared into my brain. They're the first Chosen pair I know of who were ousted from court, and I wonder exactly what happened.

My gut tells me it's an interesting story.

Hugo goes first. We all quiet as the screen shows him bash in the head of an older professor who gave him a poor grade. The man would have surely died had the rock Hugo used not have cracked. Lucy's memory seems different, at least at first. She's shown walking through the alleyway when a group of girls finds her. They torment her, pulling her mass of tight black curls and making jokes about her snowy complexion. After they tire of this game and go back inside the apartment building down the street, Lucy waits until nightfall, sneaks into their apartment, and sets fire to it while everyone sleeps.

At the end, both Hugo and Lucy display no emotion.

But Delphine is finally smiling.

CHAPTER TWENTY-FOUR

Delphine chooses Rhydian to go next. Smiling coyly at him, she says, "What's your darkest secret, worm?"

Merida, standing beside him at the table, gives his hand a quick, furtive squeeze.

Rhydian's ashy-blond eyebrows knit together, and he clenches his teeth in an effort to hide his thoughts. Delphine's little pointer is oblivious to his efforts as it clicks and the wall comes to life.

A dim, windowless room. No furniture. Someone is crying—Rhydian. He sounds young, maybe twelve or thirteen. A rope hangs from the rafters. No, not just a rope. A noose. A chair sits beneath it. The noose gets closer. The crying has stopped and there are only the sound of Rhydian's footsteps on the stone floor and a few sniffles. He steps onto the chair, his hands wrapping around the noose. His breathing becomes heavy.

One of the finalists cries out as Rhydian places his head into the noose, says one word, "Father," and kicks the chair away. Horrible gurgling noises. The room spins back and forth. There's a loud knock on the door and then a girl calling his name. It sounds like Merida, but I can't be sure. The voice gets more frantic. The choking noises become more guttural.

We are listening to him die.

Suddenly there's the sound of the rope snapping, and Rhydian falls to the floor. The view on the screen slips sideways. It moves up and down with his violent wheezing. Right before the screen goes dark, the door bursts open and we hear a gut-wrenching scream.

Rhydian is standing stock-still. He works to keep the emotions from his face, but something desperate flickers behind his eyes.

Slowly, with purpose, Delphine turns her back on Rhydian. The rest of the Chosen follow. After a pause, the finalists do the same. I hesitate, but not for long, before turning as well. I hear Merida whisper to Rhydian, "What do I do?"

But Rhydian, his face held together by a hard, trembling smirk, ignores her. Finally she turns as well. In Royalist society, suicide is one of the most heinous and cowardly acts one can commit.

It's only when Delphine moves on to someone else that I notice Riser didn't turn. Why would he choose not to follow the others after lecturing me on not standing out? Especially with the Emperor watching. The thought bothers me.

I'm so focused on being annoyed with Riser that I don't pay attention to the girl until I hear the quiet murmuring fill the Great Hall.

"Risk," the girl repeats again, looking up at the Emperor. A tentative smile lights up her eager-to-please-face. By the sound of her voice it's Brinley Fox.

Delphine claps her hands together. "Finally." As she helps Brinley down from the table, her gaze halts on a Gold phoenix brooch pinned to Brinley's dress. "You think you deserve to wear Gold, Bronze?"

Brinley shrugs. It's clear by the careful way she moves she is still drunk but trying to hide it. "My mother gave it to me for luck. It was from . . . from before."

This is someone worth allying with.

"Hmm, let's test your worthiness, shall we?" Delphine slips behind the girl and replaces her blindfold.

"Oh," Brinley says, giggling nervously. She stumbles as two Chosen take her by each elbow and lead her away.

I don't understand what they intend to do until it is too late. They appear on the upper level balcony. Just above them stretches a thin rafter.

It has to be sixty feet up, at least, and just as long. From down here I can't hear what the two Chosen whisper to Brinley before they leave, but she seems to sway in disbelief for a moment.

After a few minutes of feeling the length of the balcony railing, Brinley finds the wall to her left and braces one hand against it while climbing to an unsteady stand on the railing. My stomach churns as she reaches up, tentatively, searching for the rafter. Even on tiptoe the rafter is just out of reach. The room fills with shouts of encouragement.

"Jump!" someone yells.

She crouches down while I hold my breath. My palms are slick with sweat. I find myself rooting for her, my insides screaming.

Her small hands slap the rafter's edge with a loud *thunk*. The skirt of her bright-green dress ripples out, and then she's swinging her legs over. It takes her a moment to get her bearings enough to brave a low crouch. A collective cheer rises up from the finalists. Brinley Fox has surprised us all and allowed us to carve out a tiny sliver of dignity.

Holding her hands straight out like wings, she uses them for balance as she inches forward, her clunky heels scraping the wood. Murmurs of excitement fill the room. I can hardly breathe as I watch her, my neck aching from looking up.

The problem starts halfway through. Her balance is off and she teeters, windmilling her arms to right herself. It happens again. Then again. After the last time she sways, she rights herself and freezes solid; her entire body begins to shake.

Jeers rise up from some of the Chosen. Brinley wraps her arms around her chest, whispering to herself as one of her shoes falls with a loud bang.

After a couple of minutes, the taunts stop. Then I see why.

Riser has left his table and is standing beneath her. "Lady Brinley," he says, "don't listen to them; listen to me." His voice is conversational, soothing. "You are halfway there. The rafter is two feet across, so simply place one foot in front of the other, and you will be fine."

"No." She shakes her head. "I'm going to die."

"Say it," Riser orders. "One foot in front of the other."

Roman lumbers up to Riser, and I think there will be another fight. "Shove off, worm!"

But Roman stops just short of hitting Riser. I can't figure out why at first. Although Riser could get a few well-aimed blows in, without a weapon it wouldn't take long for Roman's sheer size and strength to overwhelm Riser.

But then I see Riser's look. It's simple and to the point: *You might kill me, but I'll make sure you suffer just as well.* Roman gives a baffled frown, and then he backs up an inch.

Riser holds up his hands and smiles so everyone watching thinks he has given in. Only he and Roman know the truth.

Careful, Pit Boy. That's a Gold you're provoking, and in front of the Emperor, no less.

As soon as Riser is back at his table, Brinley tries again. Her lips move in a continuous mantra. I know what she is saying.

One foot in front of the other.

The mood in the room lightens as she nears the end. The finalists all seem to hold their breath. Someone yells to tell her she's almost there. Her mouth breaks into a wide, relieved smile. She's going to make it.

And maybe she thinks she's already there, or maybe the words distracted her. Dust rains down on our upturned faces as her bare foot slips down the side of the rafter. She makes a strange squeaking noise. For a moment I think she's going to catch herself, but then her body topples sideways, and there's no way for her to recover.

It is surreal, watching her fall. Irrationally I think she'll be okay. There will be a net or some other type of safety device to catch her. Maybe she'll simply break a leg and they can mend it.

For the briefest of seconds, her beautiful green dress plumes out behind her like rich, silken wings. I think someone screams. Then

Brinley crashes on the table closest to the wall with a loud, sickening thump. Curled on her side, one bare foot sticking out, she could be sleeping.

I look away. She is not okay. Not sleeping. She cannot be fixed. My heart flutters sideways in my chest, and I feel close to vomiting.

The lesson is clear: Here, bravery kills you.

I hazard a look at Riser. From his deadly stillness, the way his hands clench and unclench, I gather he's either enraged or afraid. My bet's on the former.

And now both of us will have to endure the same.

Hugo stands near the table, coldly observing Brinley. It seems, now that I think about it, it was Hugo who yelled to her.

The body is taken away, and someone wipes down the table. No one talks as the Emperor laughs quietly from his invisible throne above.

They have broken us.

I know as soon as Delphine walks toward my table she will choose me. Her plump, heart-shaped lips are molded into a smirk. Since Brinley, no one else has chosen risk. So when I choose it, my words coming out clear and confident, her pale eyes flit over me again, her lips parted slightly. I get the feeling she doesn't particularly enjoy surprises.

Thing is, I should be afraid. Even with all of Nicolai's modifications, whatever Delphine has in store for me is undoubtedly dangerous. But now all I see is the cruel little girl who tormented and disfigured me. She thinks we are bugs that will sit compliantly while she tears off our wings for pleasure.

That is her mistake.

Holding my head high, I jump to the ground. My vision spins a bit and the beginnings of a headache nip at my temples, but otherwise I feel okay.

Delphine crosses her arms. A small frown trembles across her face. "And who might you be, Bronze?"

Now that I've had practice, my curtsies are improving, and I'm rather proud of the sweeping one I give now. "Lady Everly March."

My faux-confidence must throw Delphine off, because she hesitates. Apparently I'm spoiling her fun. Then her face lights up. "Do you like apples, Lady March?"

"Sure," I say, carefully.

"Perfect." Scanning the finalists, she finds what she's looking for in Merida. "And you, Lady . . . ?"

"Pope," Merida says in a soft, hesitant voice. Her face is pale, and her body seems to waver just standing, as if she might faint at any moment.

"Lady Pope, how do you feel about the crossbow?"

Merida emits a nervous laugh. "If I am being honest, Countess, the crossbow eludes me even on the best of days. My cousin, Rhydian, is much—"

"No." The giddy smile on Delphine's face chills my blood. "You will do just fine."

Except she won't, because she isn't fine. Partially dried vomit crusts the bodice of her dress and her hair. Bloodshot eyes roll loose inside her pale, drooping head. I had no doubt that whatever Delphine threw at me I would be successful. But Merida is soft. Merida is weak. Merida is *drunk*.

And now drunk, soft, weak Merida is going to kill me.

CHAPTER TWENTY-FIVE

The head table sits on a raised dais at the front of the hall. Shadow Fall is nearly done, and faint red and blue shafts pierce the stained lead glass, coloring my arms a bizarre bluish-red. Merida is standing on one end of the table, and I at the other, with twenty feet between us. Merida keeps fixing me with her big, wobbly, apologetic eyes, but I ignore her. I need her to focus, and pity won't do that.

But perhaps anger will.

Riser stands with the others on the four tables. I let myself glance at him once. He seemed about to leap off the table and go on a murderous spree, so I haven't made eye contact since. I am standing here, feeling my confidence erode, when Caspian comes to my side. He's taken something from one of the Chosen Delphine sent my way—an apple— and he leans close as he hands it to me.

"I'm sorry, Lady March," he says in a soft voice, "but you will have to place this in your mouth."

I twirl the apple inside my hand. It's perfect. Fragrant and shiny and reddish green, with hard, waxy skin. "Well, how else would I eat it?"

A flicker of emotion. It's fascination, I realize, as Caspian leans in close enough I can smell his salty, leather smell, as if he's just left a saddle. "You are not afraid?"

"Have you seen the state of my friend over there?" I cast a glance at Merida who's just nearly stumbled off the table and is being held steady. "I'm terrified. But displaying my fear won't make her aim any truer."

His fascination has morphed into begrudging respect. "As much as I hate to say this, we both know you are going to be injured. But I promise you, if you survive your wounds, I will have you treated by our physicians. You have my word."

It's a tempting proposition. But I'm playing the long game, and for that I need to stay in the trials. Simply surviving for a few more days is not an option. "You can do me something better. Pass a message along to Lady Merida."

Caspian pauses for a moment. This is shaky ground, and I may have overstepped my bounds. But then Caspian frowns and gives a quick nod.

"Tell her: Remember the day you found him. Remember how you felt, and use it."

Despite his puzzled expression, Caspian stays true to his word. After he is finished whispering into Merida's ear, I look for signs she understands. Nothing. Maybe I was wrong and it wasn't Merida who found Rhydian. Perhaps she's just too scared to feel anything else. Delphine has been watching our interaction, her eyes narrowed. A sour look poisons her face.

A Chosen boy is handing the crossbow to Merida when Delphine stops him. "Wait." She replaces the crossbow with a goblet brimming with deep-burgundy liquid and grins. "For your nerves."

Merida gulps it quickly. Probably her adrenaline has masked the taste.

When I see what Delphine has for Merida next, I know using Caspian must have pissed Delphine off. And pissing off the Countess Delphine has severe consequences, apparently.

Delphine ties the blindfold around Merida's eyes herself. Caspian purses his lips and looks away as I unhinge my jaw and wedge the apple between my teeth. My jaw aches. If I had any saliva left, it would be impossible to swallow. Delphine thrusts the crossbow into Merida's tentative, reaching hands. The hall goes deathly quiet all at once. The light twinkles off the slender golden arrow in the center of the crossbow as Merida's arm wavers under the weapon's heft. She nearly drops it, but then her hand clenches tight and the arrow tip stabilizes at my belly button.

Any hope I had left vanishes.

I can't make up my mind whether to close my eyes or leave them open. Closed, I decide, in case I flinch. What will happen if she misses altogether? Will she continue until some body part is impaled? I don't think my bladder or my heart can handle multiple tries.

My jaw is on fire. My heart beats so hard inside my chest that my body jolts to its rhythm. I focus on that. The raspy sound of air coursing through my nasal passages and throat. I'm amazed at the calmness that has descended. Every second, every breath, every heartbeat is elongated until they converge into a pattern.

And that's when I notice it. Merida's breathing. It's calm and even too . . .

Twang.

Everything stops, as if my body has hit pause. And then I draw in a ragged breath, the apple releases from my teeth, and I open my eyes to see it rolling lopsided down the steps, the golden arrow protruding from its center.

Merida slips off her blindfold. She nods at me, just slightly, but I think she means to thank me for what I had Caspian say. Clapping whispers through the hall. It grows to a loud thrum, finalists stamping their boots on the tables. I'm pretty sure I have ruined Nicolai's plan for me, but that cannot be helped.

The clapping abruptly dies as Delphine ascends the steps, the back of her gown swishing on the stone. Although her eyes, by now practiced at duplicity, look indifferent, her mouth puckers as if she has tasted something rotten.

My heart drops. A large, black, ivory-handled revolver sits in her hand. It must be heavy because when Delphine passes it to Merida she can barely hold it up.

"But, she passed," Merida protests, thinking it is for me.

"No, dear," Delphine says, each word dripping glorious smugness, "it's not for the lucky Lady March. It's for you."

I understand her intentions immediately, but it takes Merida a second. She sets the revolver down and shakes her head. "No, you didn't ask me. I get to choose."

Delphine addresses the finalists. "I need two Bronzes, please, to *help* Lady Pope adhere to the standard of bravery expected of a Gold." Hugo and Lucy quickly volunteer. Realizing they are going to force her, Merida tries to stand. There's a loud bang as Hugo slams her back into the chair while Lucy grabs ahold of her head and forces it back. Twisting and squirming, Merida kicks a leg out and pleads. "No! You didn't ask me! No!"

Somehow in the struggle part of Hugo's charcoal vest lifted, revealing what can only be a push dagger—a T-handled blade that anchors between the fingers of a fist, so each punch carries a lethal surprise. No true gentleman, I know, would carry one.

"This is my great grandfather's revolver," Delphine explains, "used during the Everlasting War. In fact,"—her gaze finds the Emperor—"it was this very weapon that my great grandfather used to save the life of Marcus Laevus, the first Emperor." She retrieves the revolver, examines it lovingly, and opens the chamber. A single golden bullet winks from one of the five holes. It makes an ominous ticking noise as she spins it. "Let's play a game of chance, shall we?"

Merida screams as Delphine cocks the hammer and presses the gun barrel against her temple. "House Pope. Hmm, let's see. How many traitors from your House did we execute?"

Merida's eyes are nearly all white with fear. She looks around the room, pleading for help.

"Five worms from House Pope were executed by the Crown," the

Emperor purrs, his voice reverberating through the large hall as it seals Merida's fate. There are five chambers, and Merida will be forced to pull the trigger five times. One of those times will kill her.

Delphine curls her finger around the trigger.

Watching Delphine, all I can think about is what she did to me. The immense pleasure she took in my humiliation. The sound of my voice, pleading for help the same way Merida is now.

Although I'm not conscious of making a decision, I'm off the table and halfway across the floor. Delphine turns my way, frowning slightly. A red rash of excitement laces her chest. "I said you were dismissed, worm."

I cross my arms over my chest. "I want to take her place."

A murmur stirs the crowd, and I feel the Emperor's stare on me. Delphine's eyes form icy-blue slits. "And why would you do that?"

"Because, you are going to play against me, and you are going to lose." She laughs, but there's no humor in her voice. I'm challenging her in front of the Emperor and Chosen. To save face she needs to find a way to still look in control without looking afraid. I have put her in a precarious position, one she won't thank me for later.

The revolver points to the floor, but her finger still wraps tightly around the trigger. "Be careful what you say from here, worm."

"If I stop first, I'm out. I leave, immediately." I force my dry mouth into a smile, playing to the crowd. I need them to be behind me. "And if I lose, well then you will be rid of me a bit more permanently."

A few laughs. Mainly, though, there is curious silence as finalists and Chosen watch to see what happens.

"And if I stop first?" Delphine pans to the audience with a skeptical look.

Squaring my shoulders, I look her straight in the eye. "Then Truth or Risk is over."

Delphine blinks, her smile slowly fading. She wasn't expecting this. She scans the crowd, her gaze finding the Emperor as if pleading with him to intervene, but he simply watches with a curious expression. The hint of a frown stirs her lips. The others are murmuring their approval, even the Chosen. After Brinley's death, some of the Chosen seemed hesitant. Obviously not all of them take pleasure watching us be tortured.

"Fine." She shrugs, forcing a smile while shooting me a look that makes it clear if we both survive she'll make me wish I hadn't. Delphine takes Merida's seat. I sit opposite, at the other head. Right before we begin, Roman jaunts up the stairs. He bows his head, and there's the sound of him and Delphine arguing.

"I have to!" I hear her snap.

I jump as Roman slams his fist on the table. They both glance at me and then he reluctantly retreats.

My list of enemies is growing longer by the second.

From here, Delphine's chin-length blond hair—cut to different lengths—and round, perfectly symmetrical face make her look both angelic and pure. Her striking sky-blue eyes show no hint of fear. I can see why she has gained such high status among the others. Without ceremony, she plants the barrel against her head and pulls the trigger.

Click. Not even a flinch.

As the Chosen boy hands it off to me, the raised phoenix emblem on the handle rough inside my palm, and I raise the barrel, I have a what-the-hell-have-I-done moment. It dissipates with the empty *click* of the gun, along with any other coherent thoughts I might have had. Hands trembling and numb, I hand the weapon back.

Caspian approaches the table. "Delphine, you don't have to do this." His eyes cut to me, then back to her. "I think we have all had enough for today."

In answer, Delphine looks him in the eye and pulls the trigger.

Click.

The revolver smells of oil and old gunpowder. The barrel is hard and cold against my temple. Caspian looks my way, shakes his head. The look he gives me is either respect or annoyance.

I'm going with the latter.

My entire body feels weightless. Every fiber of my being is focused on the sharp curve of the trigger nestled in the joint just below my finger pad.

The only thought I can keep inside my head is this will be the fourth shot, and there are five chambers. The chances are high I will die a fraction of a second after I pull the trigger.

But if I don't die, if I miraculously happen to be alive at the end of my turn, then I will have won. Because the next chamber will house the bullet. And Delphine looks like the kind of girl who would notice that kind of stuff.

Delphine wears a celebratory smirk. She thinks I am hesitating, that she has won. It's the same look she had as she mangled my head years ago. I cock the hammer, release a long breath, close my eyes, and squeeze the trigger, slowly, slowly, *slowly* . . .

Little worm, little worm, why do you squirm?

Click.

I feel all the nerve endings in my body fire as the vice around my lungs releases and I can breathe again. The revolver tumbles loudly to the table. I open my eyes, focus on Delphine. I want her to see my anger. To feel responsible for murdering Brinley. But mostly, I want Delphine to know there is nothing she can do that will scare me.

That I am not a worm who squirms anymore.

Caspian retrieves the revolver. His calmness tells me he counted too. He must know Delphine won't do it. Silence swells the air, filling every nook, every cranny as he walks it over to her. The silence has a weight to it. I find myself once again struggling to breathe. The revolver clanks on the table in front of Delphine, the noise splitting the silence like an ax splitting wood.

Delphine turns the weapon over inside her hands. Just like her, it is exquisitely made, impressive and arresting, without a single flaw, and I can't help but think both were created to be equally admired and feared. Delphine lifts the revolver to her head, using the muzzle to wipe away an errant strand of pale hair. Slippery folds of my jumpsuit slip through my sweaty fingers.

Cla-ack goes the hammer.

One by one, the hairs on the back of my neck lift. A weird, anxious feeling comes over me just as Delphine looks up from the table. Her eyes rivet to mine. Unblinking ice-blue marbles, they carry an unreachable blankness that makes me go cold all over. Confirming my fear is the big, rancorous smile stretching her face into something almost comically wicked.

She is going to shoot me.

CHAPTER TWENTY-SIX

Before she can aim the muzzle, Caspian plucks the weapon from her hand. "All right," he says in a voice created to give orders and galvanize huge masses, "enough. You have proven yourself courageous beyond measure, Countess Delphine."

Is there the hint of sarcasm in his voice for his betrothed? Surely not.

Not missing a beat, Delphine slides from the chair and does an elaborate curtsy for the Emperor. The Chosen roar with approval. Somehow, Caspian has allowed her to save face and appear to have gotten the upper hand. *Was she really going to shoot me?* It's hard to believe now, with her ebullient, almost girlish demeanor as she parades in front of the crowd.

And yet . . .

The growing din of voices quiets as Caspian holds up his hand to speak. "Lest we not forget the finalists for the bravery and honor they have shown here today as well."

His message is clear. The game is over. Delphine may appear to have won, but anyone with an observant eye will see otherwise.

There is an awkward pause as Delphine weighs her options. Roman lays his hand on his waistband, just beneath his morning coat, where his short sword hangs. An eager, expectant smile carves into his thick jaw. One tiny gesture from Delphine and he'll gladly unleash hell. Some of the other Chosen shift uncomfortably on their feet. All eyes are on the Emperor as they await his reaction.

So there are cracks in the court. I scan the others to see who might be allied with Caspian but come up short. It's obvious from this small interaction that the Emperor admires Delphine maybe more than he does his own son. Again I wonder what this means for Delphine and Caspian's betrothal. My small pittance of experience in these sorts of matters tells me the look Delphine is giving Caspian isn't borne of arduous affection.

Finally the Emperor frowns and nods to Caspian, as if declaring him the victor, and then his hologram unceremoniously disappears.

"Whatever," Delphine spits through pursed lips. "I'm doing the worms a favor by prepping them for the trials, but if they're ungrateful"— her eyes meet mine—"I have better things to do with my time."

Yeah, like plotting how best to murder me.

All of the tension my muscles have been carrying dissipates, and I sink into my bones. Thankful murmuring from the finalists fills the hall. I stand, dizzy with relief and hunger and alcohol and spent adrenaline. Part of me still assumes it's a trick, but I'm so desperate to leave I don't really care.

Before we go, there is a brief rundown of our itinerary. Back to the apartments to change. The Culling at sunset, where we eat a fancy dinner while the final uploads are counted. I just need to stay in the top half of the finalists. The thought is not comforting. It's impossible to tell where I am on the list. And I haven't felt a single upload since leaving the apartments. Probably because most of the prospective Sleepers are worried at the rate I'm going, I won't last very long.

Not that I disagree.

Pushing through the crowd, most of the finalists and Chosen steer clear of me. I wonder if I'm now a pariah, like Rhydian. It certainly doesn't help that Delphine's murderous gaze follows me as I leave.

I must really be tired because I don't feel the Centurions behind me until it's too late. With one latched on each arm, they easily pinch me from the crowd. As soon as I put up resistance, they simply lift me an inch off the tile floor so I'm suspended. Now that I'm over my surprise,

I could put up a real fight, and I'm fairly confident I could best my two new Neanderthals friends. But they have an endless supply of cretins more than happy to hurt me, while I have only one body. So I relax and wait to see where they take me.

We arrive inside a low-lit antechamber. Other than a few odd pieces of furniture and a cold hearth, it's bare. I'm hardly out of the oafs' clutches before a shadow slips in behind me. The knife inside the shadow's hand glints softly under the dull light. Except the shadow isn't here for me, I discover, as it maneuvers protectively between me and the guards.

Riser grins. "These two idiots giving you trouble, my lady?"

We both startle as another shadow rises from the corner. To my surprise it's Caspian. "Sir, reveal yourself at once!"

Riser chokes down a laugh. "Is he for real?"

Caspian's short sword whispers from its sheath on his waist, soft light spilling down the blade's length. "Is this real enough for you, Bronze?"

Riser's smile transforms into a dangerous smirk.

Oh, Fienian hell. I know that look.

"Wait!" I insert myself between Riser's wrath and Caspian's sword. "Lord Riser Thornbrook, meet Prince Caspian Laevus." They appraise each other carefully. After a few anxious heartbeats, Caspian's sword scrapes back into its sheath.

Riser, on the other hand, doesn't look ready to make nice. He throws an ill-tempered glance at me, the artery beneath his jaw throbbing. "I thought they were going to hurt you—"

"I brought her here to save her life," Caspian growls through perfect, clenched teeth.

Riser stiffens beside me. "Oh. Because from where I stood back in the other room, you seemed bent on the opposite."

Caspian emits an exasperated sigh. "Does this Bronze have to be here?"

"This *Bronze* isn't leaving without her." Riser's voice holds a dark, murderous undertone that makes me shiver. "But you're welcome to try and make me."

The last of my patience withers away. "Okay, both of you, shove off." I turn to Riser. "I think I've made it pretty clear I don't want your protection, Lord Thornbrook, but—"

"Oh you've been crystal clear on that, Lady March," Riser interrupts. "But I don't take orders from you."

"Give me the word, my lady," Caspian says, his voice coated in arrogance, "and I will have this interloper removed from the Island."

I turn on him. "What did you expect, forcibly detaining me?"

Caspian's mouth purses as if he has tasted something sour. I'm guessing people don't usually address him this way. Swallowing, he clears his throat. "My apologies, Lady March, if I startled you." To punctuate his apology, he presses my hand to his lips. "Truly."

My cheeks tingle in embarrassment, and I retrieve my hand. *Yes, idiot, you just spoke to Royalty like that.* "Apology accepted . . . my Liege."

Riser chuckles under his breath.

Caspian shoots Riser a look that could fell kingdoms. "My method may have been unseemly, but I have to use the utmost caution. If someone were to see us together, they might infer I am helping you, and that would be against the rules."

"And are you?" I ask. "Helping me?"

"I am *advising* you. You are treading dangerous waters, Lady March. I have no insight into why you did what you did—and it was unquestionably brave—but if you want to survive this competition, you'll need more than bravery."

"For instance?"

"Common sense, for starters." He shakes his head, his lips curling into an amused smile. "Only a fool would prick a lion's tail and not expect it to bite."

"Countess Delphine?"

"Yes, the Countess Delphine. Avoid her at all costs. Swallow your pride, duck your pretty head and be invisible—basically the opposite of what you did back there."

"Isn't she your fiancée?" I stupidly point out, thrown off by the word *pretty* and something about my head.

He flattens me with a look. Obviously my manners for court are rather lacking. "Lady March, I think everyone in the entire civilized world knows the answer to that question by now. Stating the obvious is wasting time."

He glances impatiently at Riser and then back to me, as if there's more he wants to say, but then he brushes his lips over my hand again and moves to take his leave. Instead of leaning back to allow Caspian room, Riser stays put, forcing Caspian to angle his shoulder like a battering ram to get by.

"Wow," I say once Caspian is gone, "Flame will be disappointed when she realizes the manners portion of your reconstruction was a complete and utter failure."

Riser shakes his head. "He doesn't deserve my respect."

"He is your half-brother, remember?"

Something cold presses into my hand. Holding it up to the torch flame, I see it's Brinley's golden phoenix, intricate and beautifully made, with two tiny glittering emeralds for eyes and a body embellished with tiny diamonds. A drop of blood smears its wings.

Riser closes my fingers around it. "*No*, he's not."

"He could make a strong ally."

"Ally?" He laughs skeptically. "With one of the Chosen? No, not just any Chosen. Emperor Laevus's son and the future Emperor. Brilliant plan, Lady March."

"He can't help what he is, Riser—"

"Funny, but you never afforded me those same excuses."

"But . . . you were . . ."

"A monster?" he finishes in a soft voice that tugs at my heart. "And you think he's not? He didn't have to put that apple in your mouth,

Everly. Didn't have to let them kill Brinley. But he *did*."

"I didn't make up the rules, remember?" My voice sounds harsh, even to me. "It's what you said about the pit. The only difference now is that I'm willing to fight, to do what it takes to survive. Are you?"

My breath catches as Riser closes the little bit of space between us. "Oh I'm willing to do a lot of things. But those things are ugly and dark and violent." He's close, *too* close. "Once you've crossed over my side of the line, Everly, you don't walk away, so make sure that's a price you're willing to pay."

I startle as his fingers hook under my elbow, glide down to my palm, and lift. The back of my hand tingles beneath his lips. His eyes roll up to meet mine. He grins, his breath warming my knuckles. "See, Lady Everly March. *Manners*."

I know I'm in trouble. It has been seven hours since I felt the last upload. Four hours being tortured by Delphine, only to incur more torture from Flame.

"Stand still!" Flame hisses.

"I *am*," I whine.

Such has been our conversation for the last thirty minutes. Flame's comb, more weapon than styling tool, gnashes through my scalp, ripping and stabbing, and my teeth grind with pain.

Finally I glance in the vanity mirror. Better than I expected. So much so, for a brief moment, I think it's someone else. My skin, pale and creamy. My eyes more green than brown and ringed by long, fluttery charcoal lashes. Whirling from the outer crease of my left eye down my cheek is a peacock feather made of sparkling jewels. The softest hint of crimson shimmers my lips. But it's my hair—twisted and braided and fishtailed into an elaborate work of art—that takes my breath away. A jeweled peacock hairpin holds it all in place.

My hands smooth down my sleeveless velvet emerald green gown.

It arrived at my door an hour ago, compliments of Merida, with a note simply stating: All Yours. Caped with a delicate ruby-rimmed hood and trimmed at the waist with two bands of multicolor jewels and Gold beads to match the peacock feathers, it's skirting the lines of Royalist-acceptable apparel, and way above my Color. But the best part is, although it masquerades as a dress, with loose plumes of fabric, it's really a jumpsuit.

"It's a bit . . ." I struggle for the right word.

"Flashy?" Flame says, but I can tell from the quirk in the side of her lips the dress is growing on her. She tweaks my hairpin. "No room in this flimsy fabric for a dirk, so this will work in a pinch."

I smile. "Any other hidden weapons I should be aware of?"

"No, but you can always strip your pantyhose and cord them around the neck—"

"Joking, Flame." I stand, appraising myself one more time. "But thanks for your concern. Gives me the warm fuzzies."

Flame frowns. "I'm concerned about the mission, not your person."

I slip my feet into the two-tone, Oxford-Style lizard boots that came with the gown. "So no hug then?"

I swear a smile almost cracks through her sour grimace. *Almost.*

A knock on the door announces my attendant. *So soon?* There's no possible way I could have enough uploads to even come close to where I need to be. Perhaps I should have followed the plan. Admittedly, I am attracted to Riser. And even if his lurking psychopath is in there, somewhere, surely I can pretend for one night that he's the striking, well-mannered courtier he's impersonating? It's probably too late now, anyway, but I decide to try.

What else do I have to lose?

CHAPTER TWENTY-SEVEN

"Be good," I say to Flame on my way out. I'm not sure what her plans are, but they undoubtedly are anything but. On impulse, I grab Brinley's gold phoenix and pin it to the bodice of my dress.

Flame grabs my wrist. "Be careful with that."

"Why?" I say, impatient to leave. "It's just a silly trinket."

"If by silly trinket you mean the secret symbol worn by Fienian Sympathizers, then yeah, you're right."

"Really?"

Flashing a rare smile, Flame reaches over and pinches her fingertips on either side of the wings. There's a clicking noise and a golden scorpion appears, wrapped around the phoenix, the single diamond on its tail barb flashing ominously.

"Poison." Flame's voice shivers in awe. "Pinch the wings twice in succession and that beautiful creature becomes a highly-effective weapon."

I carefully eye the brooch as Flame pinches the wings and the deadly scorpion slithers back into its hiding place. "Should I take it off?"

"I said be *careful*, Princess. Not a ninny."

I don't recognize Riser at the end of the hall until I am practically on top of him. The amused look he gives me states that he knew I was there long before. His eyes flick over me once but remain veiled. He bows, an indifferent nod really, and allows a guarded half-smile. "My lady."

After a quick curtsy, I hook my arm inside his and smile until my lips feel as if they will stick to my teeth. "Shall we, Lord Thornbrook?"

"It would be my pleasure." Through his confident tone I detect a hint of puzzlement. It is, after all, the nicest I have ever been to him. A small pang of regret hits me. It's made worse by the protective way he tucks my arm into his warm chest.

Stupid reconstructed emotions.

Riser picks up the game. "You look . . . ?" His piercing, mismatched eyes travel down my body. They take their time. Lighting fires wherever they linger. Finally they rest on my lips. "I don't know . . . What's the word?"

Mouth parted, I suck in a ragged breath and fight off the strange falling-feeling in my belly. "Beautiful?"

He scratches his chin, his eyes still drinking me in. "No. That's not it. Wait . . . I have it now." His face breaks into a wolfish smile. "Decent. Lady March, you look rather decent."

Fienian bum! "Decent?" But he's already halfway down the hall, his shoulders shaking with laughter. I catch up at the top of the stairs and restrain myself from kicking him to his death. Instead, I hook his arm again so he can't escape. I need to do something. Something that will garner at least a few uploads and wipe the smirk from his jaw.

Feeling completely desperate, I lift onto my toes. My hands rest on his warm, solid chest. I lean into him, and air hisses through his teeth as my lower lip brushes his earlobe.

He stiffens. I have never done anything like this before, and my heart beats wildly against my sternum. I fight the reconstructed pleasure I get from his familiar salty, earthen smell. "Maybe you should take another look, then."

The boulder lodged in my throat free-falls to my stomach as Riser shoves me away. "Don't," he says, his voice raspy, detached. "Not if it isn't real."

I chew my cheek, smarting at the rejection. "Real? Riser, I don't even know what that is anymore."

"I do."

I sigh. "C'mon, it's a game. Isn't it?"

"A game?" The muscles in his jaw knot as he looks away.

"Yes, Riser." Hesitantly my fingers slip down his knuckles and into his hand. "One that will keep us both alive."

There's a long pause. Finally his fingers curl around mine. "I want to know about the key. What does it unlock? Why does Nicolai want it so badly?"

"Suddenly you have a price?"

He smiles softly. "Did you think I was cheap?"

Not in the slightest. I try to pull my hand away, but his grip tightens. If I wasn't desperate for uploads, I would drive my knee into his crotch and enjoy every bit of it. But I am desperate. Enough to grit my teeth, swallow my pride, and say, "Fine. I'll tell you everything you want to know after the Culling."

"Now." His voice is final. "You will tell me now."

Outside, the air is magical. Pink and orange skies paint the lake, a cool breeze carrying the scents of crimson glories and plumeria. Ornate ivory carriages, wreathed in yellow tea roses and pulled by snowy-white horses, wait to take finalists to the Culling. Horses whinny impatiently and stamp their feet. Pandora is a peach-pit just above the mountain's peak.

Riser drops my hand as soon as the door closes to the carriage.

"It's safe to talk?" I ask, meaning the encryption.

"Cage assured me it was safe from our side," Riser says, "but they are still having problems communicating." He sits across from me, one long leg slung casually over the other. All confidence and poise. But I notice the way his hand—the one he used to escort me—clenches by his side.

I peer out the open window to my left. Tall, slender beechwoods line our path. The smells of stagnant water and sweaty horse mingle into a sort of intoxicating cologne. Through the gaps in the trees, I see we will soon be crossing the Palladian Bridge. Memories of my father recounting his many strolls over the expansive stone bridge, feeding the swans with my mother, pricks my brain like a thousand hungry fish nibbling the water's surface.

Riser is waiting.

I can't do this.

Pry myself open.

Spill my secrets.

Make myself *vulnerable.*

But I have no choice.

"I was nine-years-old," I say, still staring out the window. "I don't remember much—my father erased most of my memory of that day—but I do remember how I felt afterward." I toy with the beading of my embroidered belt. "He told me Max and I had been ill, that's why we couldn't remember much, but I knew it was something more." I turn to face Riser. He is leaning forward, elbows propped on his knees. "I could feel it, what he put inside me. It changed me, somehow, and I knew it was important, this thing. I found out later it was a key."

"And Max?" Riser asks. "What does he harbor?"

"The map."

Riser settles back slowly. I can see his mind racing to put it together. "A map to find it, and a key to unlock it." His expression has softened, and I realize he actually feels sorry for me. From the outside it looks cruel, a father implanting his own children with something that will put them in danger. "What is *it*, Everly? What was your father trying to hide?"

"It's called the Mercurian." We are crossing Palladian Bridge, and the carriage jiggles loudly. White petals snow from the bowed cherry trees that border the banks. "My father developed it to change the path of the asteroid, but apparently it's also a weapon—the kind that can wipe out entire populations with the push of a button. The kind the Emperor has outlawed."

Riser exhales slowly through clenched teeth. "You're telling me there is a way to save billions of people from dying?"

"Yes, but it didn't fit into Emperor Laevus's final solution, the formation of his perfect society."

Riser is sitting very still. The only thing that moves is the artery in his neck. If Riser had any qualms about killing Emperor Laevus before, he doesn't now. "Why do the Fienians want it?"

"Oh, I don't know, to blow things up?" I find myself laughing, more of a sarcastic grunt. "The Royalists. The mad Fienians. Schemers like Nicolai and Brogue and Flame. Everyone wants it because whoever controls this *thing* controls the future of the world."

"And to control it," Riser says carefully, "They must control you."

"Except, *that,*" I say, "Is proving easier said than done. How long until Nicolai decides to simply cut it out of me like the Archduchess?"

Riser leans forward, the muscles in his neck corded. "He wouldn't." He clears his throat. "I . . . wouldn't let him."

I shake my head. I can see now Riser really feels the emotions they gave him. Obviously it's the one thing Flame was successful at. Riser was programmed to keep me safe—for as long as I hold the key. "Don't you understand? We can't trust anything in this world, not our feelings, not each other . . . especially each other."

His hand reaches for mine, but I pull away. "These emotions aren't real, Riser!"

His eyes are glittery sharp as they pin me to me seat. "They are real to me, Everly. As real as my need to eat, to breathe. I cannot, will not let anything happen to you. I cannot help it."

I don't like the intimacy in his voice, the cramped space in this carriage, or the tingly warmth from where his knee presses into mine. "You said so yourself, Lord Thornbrook." I pull my knee away from his. "It's only a matter of time before your reconstructed emotions vanish."

I look out the window. We both don't want to think about what will happen then. The courtyard comes into view and the carriage begins to slow, my body jostling with each bump. "Has Nicolai mentioned my brother?"

"No."

It's impossible to ascertain if he's telling the truth. I begin smoothing out my dress as the carriage slows to a stop in front of the fountain. The breeze sprays tiny droplets against my cheeks. "Recent events tell me Nicolai hasn't yet figured out how to access Max's map. Which is why they need you to determine if I know where my father's device is."

"Do you?"

"No." Should I tell him about my father's message? Can I trust him? Part of me says yes; part of me screams no. But I have little choice. Without him, I'm almost guaranteed to fail. Exhaling sharply, I say, "But I may be able to find it."

Riser lifts an eyebrow in question.

The footman is dismounting. I have to hurry. "My father left a message for me in the Sim. I didn't have a chance to receive all of it, but I think he was trying to help me locate the Mercurian."

"And how does that help us now?"

"Because it's here," I say, watching the surprise flicker in his eyes. "And now I know all I have to do is find another way back into the system to find out where."

Riser shakes his head. "Won't work. This is the heart of Royalist territory. Simulations aren't allowed."

"Well," I say, rising, "then I guess it's good Emperor Laevus forgot that when he had my father build one here."

The door opens, a set of three iron steps unfolding to the ground, and the footman holds out his white-gloved hand. Before accepting, I turn to Riser and smile. "So, Lord Thornbrook, did I sufficiently quench your curiosity?"

Standing, Riser brazenly slides his hand around my waist. "Allow me."

I shiver as his breath rolls across the back of my neck and his warm fingertips press into my hip.

It's a simple act, but it's also an answer.

From this moment forward, we are fake courting—except suddenly it doesn't feel fake at all.

CHAPTER TWENTY-EIGHT

The tables are set up in the courtyard beneath a strand of cherry trees strung with pale, flickering lanterns. Against dusk's ethereal glow, the lanterns are unremarkable, but as soon as the sun falls, they will be a million twinkling stars. Somewhere in the distance a violin plays a haunting tune.

Riser and I are the last finalists to be seated. That makes eight of us at the table. Other than Merida and Rhydian, who sit directly in front of my seat, and Lady Teagan to my left, I don't recognize anyone. I feel, rather than see, Riser take his place to my right.

Something has changed. I find it hard to look at him. To breathe normally knowing he's near. I almost knock over my goblet of water trying to take a drink, and when I swallow it feels as if I will throw up.

Merida leans across the table. "That looks aces on you," she says, gesturing to my costume. "I didn't know if you'd dare wear it . . . but I hoped."

"I wasn't sure, either," I say. As I scan the other finalists and their staunch Royalist attire—corsets and petticoats and long, full skirts, all Color correct—I begin to wonder if I made the right choice. But then I shift and the airy fabric moves with me, not rigid and stuffy but light and free, and I understand it is a quiet form of rebellion.

The music and idle chatter dies. We all turn to the procession slowly coming down the courtyard steps, flanked by Gold Cloaks holding torches. As if on cue the last bit of twilight evanesces into watery darkness.

The Golds lead. Emperor Laevus, clad in a long, stately white wig tied back with a gold ribbon, heads the procession, carrying a large burning scepter that illuminates his chin, mouth, and cheeks but leaves his eyes hooded in darkness. And beside him, cloaked in shadow, is my mother. I know it by the way my body reacts as she draws near, even before the lanterns confirm it. The Gold phoenix medal pinned to her cloak, a mark of distinction, glints in the soft light.

So she's the Emperor's second, now. It only cost her a husband and her children.

All at once I know she will pass by me, inches, maybe even brush my chair, and if she does, I won't be able to stop my anger. Nothing else matters but the blind hatred I feel for her. My hand snakes over the table, snags a butter knife. *Blunt, but it'll do.*

Riser pins my hand to the table in a gesture that looks outwardly romantic. His thumb trails lightly over my knuckles. "Patience."

Someone at the table laughs at my ill manners, thinking I am merely hungry. I inhale a deep, choppy breath, my palm flattening in defeat over the cool knife.

"Remember," Riser says, his voice making it clear he disapproves of my rash impulse, "good things come to those who wait."

They are gone. Riser removes his hand, but not before quietly slipping the knife from my fingers. It returns to its place by the crystal butter dish adorned with perched phoenixes.

Riser knows who she is, of course. He read my journal. Which may account for the way he hovers near me, even as they take their place at the head table—just in case he has to forcibly stop me from doing something idiotic.

Some of the Chosen peel from the procession. They take seats at the finalist's tables, one at the head, one at the foot. Roman and Delphine, clad in their formal wigs, take their places at the table nearest the water. Lucy and Hugo Redgrave are there, along with other wealthy Bronze finalists I don't know.

In fact, most of the tables are grouped by wealth. Which is why I'm surprised as Caspian and his twin sister, Ophelia, join us. As far as I can tell, our table consists of the lowest esteemed finalists, those whose Houses were stripped of everything.

Caspian stands erect, arms clasped behind his back. Dressed in full military uniform, his chest sparkles with an assortment of metals—all of which I can't help but think he earned. A mottled gold crown sits atop his simple wig. My chest tightens.

Now this Caspian I can see as the Emperor someday.

We all clamber to our feet and quickly bow as Bronze attendants scurry to light the candles on the table.

The sound of silverware tapping against goblets vibrates the stillness. The other tables rise at the sound. I see why a moment later. Emperor Laevus stands erect at the head of the Chosen table, prepared to make a speech.

"Lords, ladies, courtiers, citizens, the historians will regard tonight as a defining moment in the empire," Emperor Laevus begins. "Every one of you present represents millions of souls, and it's those souls to whom I speak." He pauses to let that reality sink in. His words remind me I have still not felt a single upload since this afternoon.

"Your life is meaningful; it is sacred and beloved. And I vow to make your sacrifice mean something. Because of you, dear citizen, we have sifted through the ashes of our destruction and risen to the highest level, a flawless, perfectly designed society, free from the violent technologies that nearly destroyed us." He makes a dramatic, sweeping bow to thunderous applause. When the applause slows to a gentle hum, he quiets the crowd with a wave. "So thank you. *Thank you.*"

My mother, who has been sitting, rises slowly. I watch the court to see how they respond. Immediate silence. So she must still carry enormous weight. Wearing a cotton-white wig with tight ringlets, she waits with hands clasped together, her eyes picking out each individual finalist. Only my mother could command the silence like this. Our eyes meet, just for a second. Although her eyes hold no recognition, I feel as if my body will rent in half.

Done addressing us with her eyes, she speaks. "Finalists, I do not want to take up much of your time—we all know how precious that is." A few nervous laughs. "But I would like you to look around your table at the people, the food. Yes, this is a feast, but not the kind you are used to. With this food we are not celebrating life; we are rejoicing the end. The end of hunger. The end of warfare and disease. The end of an empire so plagued with rampant technologies we were systematically killing each other." She pauses to drive home her point. "And as you know, such a feat requires great sacrifice."

There is a sudden whooshing sound as flaming phoenixes descend from the sky and land on our table. They are holographic, of course. Made to seem even more real using our new Microplants. Mine, an angry, fidgety thing with white tipped wings, circles my aperitif plate, screeches, and then lifts into the air in unison with the others. Within seconds they are all frozen eight feet above us, wings spread wide. Every phoenix bears a number.

Everyone's except mine.

"Your Avatar ranking," my mother explains. "You may see all but your own."

The air stirs with shocked murmurs.

"You all came here in the hopes of a chance at life," my mother continues. "Unfortunately by the time dessert is served, only fifty of the highest ranked finalists will remain."

I scour the golden birds above our table. There are one hundred finalists. Merida is ranked forty-first, which means she currently has enough uploads to survive the Culling. Rhydian, fifty-first, is one ranking shy of staying as well.

"Tomorrow, those of you who remain will be tested further." Her voice has a hypnotic effect. I find myself wanting desperately to believe in what she says, even though I know every word is a bent truth. She is gifted that way. "Each test will embody a specific theme integral to our society. They are designed to peel away to your core so we may choose the very best among you." She picks up a glass and holds it in the air. A toast. "To the ones here today who do not make it, may your deaths serve a higher purpose and fortify the empire. All hail Emperor Laevus!"

"*All hail the Emperor!*" the Chosen chant, stamping the table with their goblets before drinking. We all do the same. Deafening chanting and stomping follow.

It seems my mother hasn't lost her silver tongue. It's what makes her so effective . . . and dangerous.

Caspian gracefully tucks into the head chair. As bad luck would have it, Riser is seated to his immediate left.

"Sit," Caspian commands the table. His voice is friendly, generous— but still a command.

We obey in unison, just in time for the first course, goose liver with goat's cheese and maize. An uncomfortable quiet descends. Merida forgets about the customary formal introduction and tries to eat. Realizing her mistake, she drops her fork in horror. It clangs against her plate.

Caspian's eyes crinkle as he laughs. "Please, relax. I simply would like to get to know everyone here."

Is it me or did he pointedly glance in my direction?

As the ceremonial introductions are made, I can't help but glance at the rankings above us. Teagan Aster—forty-seven. Two sisters, Alice and Marianna Graver of Wakefield—thirty-two and thirty-nine. Blaise Weston, the former Minister of Treasury's son—nineteen. Laurel Crawley—fifteen. All traitors' children. When Riser introduces himself, I see he is currently at forty-eight. My own ranking, however, is impossible to see.

As is customary for the highest-ranked Color at the table, Caspian teepees his hands, pressing them into his forehead. "May the gods honor our food and fellowship. I am Prince Caspian Laevus, and . . ."

Everyone turns to Lady Ophelia, who shifts in her chair, looking about as comfortable as a mouse at a table full of cats. Caspian makes up for her shyness with a quick introduction. "This is the enchantingly beautiful, Princess Ophelia."

Ophelia looks up from the table long enough to plant a timid smile on every finalist here. Clearing her throat, she smiles down into her lap and says, "Call me O, please."

I love her immediately. She is draped in a pale-gold, off-the-shoulder gown that expertly matches her sad, soulful eyes and catches the candles' light. She has foregone the formal wig, and her hair, a curtain of gold silk, hangs to her waist, white bird-boned shoulders jutting from its depths like glaciers, flowers running its entire length: orange irises and blush-pink azalea blooms, purple wisteria and soft red camellias. A string of dogwoods make a fragrant snowy crown.

In the daytime, she could be a goddess from the pages of my unsanctioned book. But in this phantasmal darkness, illuminated by an ethereal mixture of moonlight and firelight, she is a woodland nymph that will soon return to her enchanted forest and disappear.

Ophelia is watching me study her. "It's okay," she half-whispers. "I was studying you, too."

"Me?"

"You're the girl who challenged the Sulking Tigress."

"I'm sorry?"

Her voice takes on a playfully secretive tone. "It's our nickname for the Lady Delphine, Cas and mine. Fitting, don't you agree?"

I stiffen, not used to such candor in court. Perhaps it's a trick to loosen my tongue, get me talking? Smear a Gold. Isn't there a rule against that?

She gives an embarrassed little laugh, cutting her eyes in apology at Caspian. "It's silly . . . Anyway, it was a very brave thing to do."

"Thank you," I say, relaxing, "but I fear it was more stupid than brave."

"Well, if I had to choose, I would rather be brave and stupid than smart and cowardly. And you"—she turns to Riser—"you refused to denounce Lord Pope. Why?"

Across the table, Merida quickly looks away, her face mired in guilt. Rhydian stiffens.

The corners of Riser's mouth twitch. "I wish, Princess, I could also claim admirable intentions, but I just don't particularly enjoy being told what to do."

O glances at Caspian. "You sound a lot like someone else I know."

But Caspian is staring at Riser, his sharp eyes whittling away at him. "So, obstinate and foolish. Tack on ill mannered, if our meeting earlier is any indication. Do you perchance have any redeeming qualities, Lord Thornbrook?"

Obviously Caspian hasn't forgotten about their previous encounter.

Riser leans back into his chair, arms behind his head. Anyone else would be cowering in submission, and his calm demeanor puts me on edge—as does his insolent smile. "Well, Lord Caspian, not unless you count my striking good looks and unfailing charm."

"I do not." Caspian sits rigid, firelight playing across his refined cheekbones. "And as I am your sovereign and a Gold, you must address me as Prince Caspian. Or My Liege. Your preference."

Everyone at the table freezes. *Do it, Pit Boy!* Because for all of Riser's reconstruction, his newly polished appearance and mannerisms, the defiant expression twisting his face belongs to the boy from the pit.

His eyes flicker to me. My face begs him to do it. *Don't be an idiot, idiot!*

"My apologies, *Prince*," Riser says through clenched teeth, slowly tearing his gaze from me. "My courtly manners are rusty."

"And when were you here, exactly?" Caspian's face has gone completely serious. "Because I don't remember you."

I understand now Caspian will not let this go.

Riser lobs a dark grin my way, as if to say I tried it your way, now let's try mine, and I know things are about to spiral out of control.

Oh Fienian hell.

CHAPTER TWENTY-NINE

"I do," I blurt. "Remember him. I mean . . . Not from court—I was too young, obviously—but from . . . summering together at . . . my family's ocean villa." *That's something ex-courtiers do, right?*

Caspian turns to me, his head tilted in puzzlement. "Pardon me, but—"

"Greetings." A huge shadow has lumbered up to our table. The smell of brandy slaps me in the face.

O shrinks away from him. "Roman."

"Ahh, there you are, my little flower!" Roman, resting his massive frame on the table until it creaks, plucks an iris from her hair, ripping a cluster of golden strands with it. I notice with relief Caspian has directed all of his rage at Roman now in the form of a quiet, fury-soaked stare.

O's eyes plead with Roman to stop. "Roman . . . please—"

Roman plants a meaty palm on O's face, hard enough to make a slapping noise. Using his thumb and forefinger, he smashes her lips together until they look like she is forming words. "Nice to see you, too, my love," Roman says for her. His words are slurred and angry.

O feebly tries to brush his hand away while we all stare in horror, her crown of flowers breaking in the process and tumbling to the ground.

"Stop it!" My chair tumbles backward as I stand.

Grunting, Roman releases O, his eyes narrowed in my direction as he tries to focus. I imagine a lion that has just been distracted from his prey would look the same. When he recognizes me, his fat, wet lips wriggle into a sneer. "Well, aren't you the dew on a rose, stupid worm."

Both Riser and Caspian stand in unison, followed by Teagan. "You're jiggered, Roman," Caspian whispers. "And there are ladies present. I recommend you leave before you are forcibly made to do so."

But Roman's red, squinty eyes are fixed on Riser, fingers caressing the handle of his sword. Even sauced, Roman is smart enough to know where the real threat lies.

A taunting grin spreads across Riser's face as he appraises Roman.

The others, including Caspian, are bound by a sense of honor and civility. But Riser is beholden to none of these things. Perhaps sensing this somehow, Roman releases his weapon and leans down, clumsily forcing O's hand to his wet lips. "My flower, soon you'll be all mine."

Roman leaves, but the awkwardness remains. We all follow Teagan, who is the first to resume her place at the table, slipping a small wooden club back into her pocket as she does. Noticing my gaze, she answers with a subtle nod in my direction. Her eyes fall to my brooch. It isn't the first time, and I raise my eyebrows in question.

"Pardon me," Teagan says, in a voice that sounds as if it rarely apologizes. "But I have to say, your choice of adornment is aces. Especially once you press the wings."

I follow her eyes to the phoenix. How to respond? Is this some sort of rebellious handshake? Or perhaps a trick? I nod, carefully. "Thank you."

She winks, *carefully*. "Welcome, friend."

Peeking around Teagan, I see O quietly trying to salvage her hair. Caspian moves to help her, but she shakes her head. "No, Cas. I must learn to deal with him on my own." She smiles bravely, the flesh around her mouth red from Roman's violent grasp. "After all, once we are married, you will not be there to rescue me."

I shudder, imagining gentle, quiet-spoken O being married to that brute.

Caspian glares beneath lowered brows at the table. "Father will change his mind."

More broken flowers spill from O's hair as she shakes her head. "Break a promise to the General? Father would never dare dishonor House Bloodwood, not when they control . . ."

Apparently remembering they are not alone, she pauses.

General Bloodwood has leverage over Emperor Laevus. I file that away for later.

Attendants swap our untouched plates for the second course, a steaming-hot borscht soup with a basted egg and what looks like foie gras over poached herring. Hard, cracked bread is served on the side. Hungry as I am, I can't find my appetite.

"Thank you, Lady Everly." I look up to see O smiling at me. "If only I were as courageous as you."

"Yes, Lady Everly," Caspian says. "It seems your stupidity knows no bounds."

Riser is glaring at me as well. Well, they agree on something, at least. I lean across Riser. "You said to stay away from Countess Delphine," I whisper, crossing my arms. "You never said her goon brother."

Ignoring the others curiously watching us, Caspian says through gritted teeth, "I assumed that was *implied.*"

Rolling my eyes, I focus on my tepid soup, poking listlessly at the rich yellow yoke of my egg. I poke my way through the main course—roast wild boar with chestnuts—and the equally sumptuous second main course of steamed swordfish and risotto stuffed mushrooms. Why am I not getting any uploads? What in Fienian hell do I have to do to become interesting?

I glance at Riser, who isn't really eating either. Time to be interesting. "How is the boar, Lord Thornbrook?"

Riser glances up at me. Smiles. A slow, burning, toe-tingling smile that electrifies me. "It is wonderful, thank you, Lady Everly." His voice is syrupy-soft and hints at something more, a shared private joke. "And you. Is the boar roasted to your liking?" His voice takes on an even more intimate tone. "I remember from our days at *your villa* you prefer your meat rather *raw*."

From my periphery I see Caspian watching our exchange.

"Well, Lord Thornbrook," I say, forcing a smile, "things may have changed a bit since then."

"But I do hope you still swim in the buff, Lady March? It was always so entertaining."

Coughing, I manage a feeble laugh. "Always so humorous, Lord Thornbrook . . . if not lacking in decorum."

Riser takes his fork, impales a chunk of bloody meat, and holds it up to my lips. "I insist, *my lady.*"

He's toying with me! Choking down my anger, I dutifully open my mouth. Cold blood dribbles down my chin as he deposits the meat on my tongue. Caspian is frowning. Riser happily dabs a napkin at my moist chin.

Chew. Swallow. Hopefully the angry flush creeping up my neck can be passed off as an amorous blush. "Divine," I manage. "Thank you."

Not done torturing me, apparently, Riser parts his mouth and waits. Courting or not, I can't imagine anyone being this sappy. I stab a stuffed mushroom and angrily force it down his throat.

I'm pissed. Doesn't he know how low my ranking is?

Riser chokes his bite down, wiping bits from his face, and grins. "Always the clumsy one."

"What was my nickname for you?" I bat my eyes at Riser. "It's on the tip of my tongue."

Riser chuckles. "I don't know, *Digger*. There were just so many."

The uploads aren't coming. I understand that now, even if our courtship were more convincing. We all look up at once to see the attendants bearing the final course. They walk single file, the lids of the silver serving platters they carry rattling quietly.

It's too late. A heavy sense of foreboding weighs me down. I failed. I let down Max, my father. *Everyone.* Even Riser has just barely skated by.

In desperation, I lean into Riser and whisper, "Please, I beg you, save

Max—"

He presses his finger against my lips. "Everly," he says, "stop talking. I just want to enjoy this moment for a bit longer."

An attendant gracefully presents a small serving tray in front of me. I stare at it, hardly breathing. Only fifty of these platters hold a dessert. Mine will not be one of them. I know that just as I know Riser tricked me.

I'm sorry, Max.

Part of me wants to fight. For a delusional second I imagine battling my way to the head table. I wouldn't make it far enough to actually hurt my mother. But maybe just looking into her eyes, making her face what she has done. Maybe that would be enough.

The music has stopped playing. There is the sound of the lanterns jostling in the breeze, a horse neighing in the distance. I grasp the lid, hand sweaty and trembling, along with ninety-nine other finalists.

As the others begin to open theirs, I hesitate. *I can't. I can't do it.* Riser's hand suddenly rests on top of mine, warm and heavy and safe.

"What are you doing?" I whisper.

Riser stares at me for a moment. "Why do you continue to doubt yourself, when everyone else, the entire world, sees how amazing you are?"

The lid lifts. All at once I understand why he wasn't taking my silly attempts at courtship seriously. Resting on my plate is a simple strawberry tart, topped with an elaborate, rising phoenix made of spun sugar.

I am in. I have survived the Culling.

I glance up at my phoenix, which is now lighted with my number.

One. I am number one.

Now I understand why I couldn't feel my uploads. There was never a single upload.

The entire time it must have been one long continuous stream.

"But . . . You let me pretend . . ."

"You liked me?" His lips press together in a wistful grin. "I am sorry, but you've made it abundantly clear I'm contemptible, Lady March, and I couldn't pass up the opportunity to feel the opposite. If you like, consider it a parting gift."

I see it now. Riser's empty plate. Looking up I discover somewhere between the first course and now his ranking has fallen to fifty-one. Just below the cutoff. And I was too busy worrying about my status to notice.

I open my mouth to say what, I don't know. But he stands, folds his napkin on the table, bows courteously to the other finalists, and remands himself to the waiting Centurion.

I need to stay seated. Stay emotionless, calm. We knew this could happen.

"Wait!" I am up before I can stop myself. The Centurion leading Riser halts, and I nearly run into them both. It's Brogue, although I almost don't recognize him in his Centurion uniform, shaved and showered and halfway respectable. There's no recognition in his hard face. He has already manacled Riser's hands from the front. Hundreds of curious eyes bore into my flesh.

My first impulse is to slip Riser the hairpin to use later. In his hands it would be more than effective. But Brogue sees me reaching for it and subtly shakes his head.

Stupid, of course it is.

My second impulse is to say something comforting. *Even stupider.* I could beg him to run, but we both know he wouldn't make it far. Truth is I'm powerless to do anything helpful but watch as they take him to be thrown to the wolves waiting on the other side of the wall.

Riser locks eyes with me. He's begging me not to do anything stupid. *Too late for that.*

"Tell me what to do," I whisper.

He shakes his head, strands of his glossy hair falling over his face. "I lied to you, Everly. I saved you in the water, and I fed you in the pit. I thought my feelings for you were a weakness . . . but I realize now that was the one thing that made me strong."

A wild, desperate feeling comes over me. I know I should walk away. That part of these emotions are reconstructed. Just as I know if I do nothing about them, they will burst from my being. So I do something rash. Something I would never in a million years do otherwise.

I kiss him.

His lips are dry and hot. They part immediately. A surprised noise rises from somewhere deep in his chest. His constrained hands gather the front of my dress, pulling me into him. I'm startled by the softness, the curious sensation of his teeth grazing the sensitive part of my bottom lip, the alien feel of his tongue sliding over mine. Lady March had kissed a hundred boys by the time I stole her memories—but none have ever felt like this.

Riser is the first to pull away. I suck in a small hungry breath, the deep rooted reconstructed feelings inside me screaming to pull him close again. It's as if I have scratched an itch only to make it a thousand times worse.

Smiling softly at me, Riser lifts his hands, shackles jingling, and cups my chin, his two thumbs pressing on either side of my jaw. "I told you, Lady March, it would be anything but stupid."

And then they drag him away.

CHAPTER THIRTY

Five whole minutes. That's how long I have been standing here outside my room. I know as soon as I enter and tell Flame what happened to Riser, one of two things will happen. Flame will murder me or die trying. Although I prefer the latter, both are not ideal.

Footsteps. Lady Laurel and Lord Blaise are on their way to the midnight celebration being held in the courtyard to celebrate the Culling results. The finalists catch my eye and quickly look away. Now I'm not just some fallen Gold girl. I'm the fallen Gold girl with the most uploads.

The girl with a shiny new target on her back.

The room is in disarray. Wires and gadgets and miscellaneous strips of metal spill from the bed to the floor. They lead to Flame, sitting cross-legged, tweaking two sparking wires together. Without even seeing her face, I know she knows. Hoping we can just not discuss it, I go to the window to watch the displays. The sound of the cheering as the first face appears on the rift screen rattles the lead windowpane. The girl is smiling, her glossy red hair coiffed and plaited. It takes a few seconds to recognize my new face.

I close the window and turn around. "I tried, Flame—"

"No." Flame glances up. "Trying would have been following the plan from the beginning. Trying would have been slipping him a weapon so he had a chance—"

"I tried—"

"Stop saying that!" All five feet of Flame rises. Far as I can tell she is weaponless, but that means nothing. "Trying would have been stopping them! You *let* them take him." She rips the brooch from my dress. "You don't deserve to wear this!"

I slump onto the bed. Perhaps she's right, but I'm too tired to deal with that right now. My body aches, my mind aches, my heart aches. It's been days since I've slept well. The cheers continue outside, shaking dust from the stone walls. I toy with the torn fabric where the brooch was. "What can Brogue do?"

"Nothing." Flame's voice has lost its razor-edge. Like me, she sounds exhausted. "Sometime tomorrow Riser will be dumped outside the fence, and they'll tear him to pieces. But I'm sure your kiss will do him a lot of good."

My cheeks prickle with anger and embarrassment. "If you didn't want me to kiss him, then you shouldn't have reconstructed me to desire him." The word sticks in my throat. *Desire*. But I do. I have to admit that. Something inside me needs him, and even though it may not be real, it *feels* real.

Flame toys with a frayed wire. I wait for her to throw in a jab, but she's unusually quiet.

I begin gathering the debris off the bed. "Aren't you worried about someone coming in and seeing all this stuff?"

"Princess, right now we have bigger things to worry about."

"They discovered we're in the system?"

"Well, the wig-heads know someone's been playing with their toys; they just don't know who. Yet." She goes back to the wardrobe and disappears behind the high-tech apparatus she's been working on. "Get some sleep. Let the adults fix this."

"Sleep?" Crossing the floor to the wardrobe, I squeeze past Flame and rifle through leather corsets and horribly outdated petticoats until I find a short muslin nightgown. "You think I can sleep now after everything that's happened?"

Flame smiles up at me. "I could crack your skull. Lights out."

I'm fairly sure she's being serious.

I peel out of my clothes on the way to the bed. The nightgown is stiff and scratchy. I pause as I spy the partially opened bag by the wall, and a chill runs through me. Peeking from inside are two smooth, golden octahedra about the size of my fist, the shape similar to two pyramids put together. Ancient symbols cover them.

Nano-shredders.

Flame's gaze slowly travels from the bag to me. "Problem, Princess?"

"Why do you have those?"

She makes a pouty face. "Aww, is the Princess scared?"

Yes, I think. *She is.* Because I know those little, seemingly harmless objects have millions of nano-shredders writhing around inside them, whose only purpose is to seek out flesh like mine, the kind that's been modified and reconstructed. If it went off, the Chosen would be the first victims, followed by anyone who's been reconstructed. Basically half the Island would be shredded. Not that the shredders are picky. They'll maim anything within their path.

Why would Flame have this?

"The plan is to kill the Emperor," I remind her, my words sticky with fear, "not the entire court."

"Well, plans bore me, as do Dandies with a pulse and simpering Royalists."

I open my mouth to argue, but there's obviously no point. Instead, I lean over and close the bag, as if somehow I am now safer. "You don't like me much, do you?"

"Nope."

"Any particular reason?"

"Reasons. *Plural.*"

"Okay—"

Suddenly Flame is up and coming toward me. "I don't like you because you think you're better than everyone else." Another step. "I don't like you because you're like *them*." Now she's standing at the edge of the bed. "Currently, I despise you because Riser would still be here if you had just followed the plan from the beginning."

"The plan was flawed." Sitting up—I need to be able to ward off any blows—I lift my hands. "No one can pretend to be in love. Even with the help of a Reconstructor."

"Ironic, isn't that the pathetic act you were putting on when you thought you needed Riser's help?"

She's right. Riser's face flashes in my mind, and I shake my head, trying to dislodge him.

She stares at me for a second. I feel the breath I've been holding release as she crosses the floor and begins digging through her satchel. There's a fluttering noise as she tosses something at me. A book, I see, the cover filled with exquisite watercolor ravens, all black except one vibrant blue one—just like her tattoo. It's titled: *The Little Blue Raven.*

She nods to the book. "Open it."

I do as commanded, reading the dedication: For Charlotte, my beautiful, peculiar, wild creature.

The next page depicts a blue raven with lanky, slumped wings and a sad face. I begin reading the text, turning the pages in the dim light.

Me, you, and little raven blue,

We have places to fly and things to do.

Buttons to gather, yarn to twine, nests to build, friends to find.

Clouds to skate, branches to swing; wind to gather beneath our wings.

But one little raven is feeling blue,

And perhaps a bit lonely too.

Oh her buttons are stacked a hundred feet high, her beautiful yarn reaching the sky.

Her nest juts from the largest trees; her wings gather the wildest breeze.

But her friends, there aren't a single one.

To count her buttons, or chase the sun.

She is different, you see, than you and me.

Like the stars to the moon, and the fish to the sea.

It's a children's book. "My mother wrote that for me." Flame's small, angry laugh sounds like ripping fabric. "Fitting, for a freak unable to get along with the other kids."

No surprise there.

"Do you want to see what happens when a Silver gets caught with unsanctioned literature?"

I try to say no but there's a wild look to her eyes, and it's like she doesn't even see me. The memory switches on suddenly.

I gasp.

Bright light . . .

Clouds overhead . . .

Smells of sweat and dirty bodies and the greasy fried pigs' feet they sell on Sundays at the Riverton market. I'm standing on my tiptoes, peering over grimy hats and oily heads at the scaffolding in front of me.

"What is this?" I whisper, but I know. I know. Somehow, through our Microplant, Flame is uploading a stored synaptic memory.

"I'm twelve." Her voice has gone hard. "So I still think they'll have mercy on them."

Look away. But I can't. It's in my head, and I experience everything. My hand—Flame's hand—wrapped around Cage's as we fight elbows and shoulders. The excited jeers from the crowd that grow louder with every step the executioner takes toward Flame's parents. The ropes slink around their necks. Suddenly I call out, flailing wildly. Cage clamps his hand over my mouth . . . and I scream and scream out every bit of my heart.

The sound of Flame's adoptive parent's dropping through the scaffolding ends the memory. I focus on Flame, and she smiles the saddest smile I have ever seen. "They had to make an example of them."

"Enough."

It's like she doesn't hear me. "Harmless Silvers whose only crime was taking in orphans and loving books and they took them and they forced their heads—"

"Please, Flame, stop!"

She faces me suddenly. "So that's why, when you talk like we are the monsters"—her voice is rising—"like we are the ones to blame and not them, it takes everything I have, *everything*, to keep from hurting you."

I take a deep breath. Fighting with Flame will not make things better between us—or improve my odds at survival. "You mean hurting everyone," I amend carefully. "Because that's what you want, isn't it, Fienian? The whole world to burn?"

"Yes." Her eyes are dark pits of rage. "But I'll settle for you and your Gold boyfriend if I have to."

Caspian. Looking at Flame, the way her flesh nearly shivers with fury, I feel something surprising. Envy. How easy it would be to give in to my hatred and madness. To fill my hollow places with it, let it eat away anything I have left.

"Noted," I say, slipping under the covers. Flame's savage glare isn't enough to fight off the black tide of fatigue washing over me. "Big day tomorrow. Think I could get some rest without being murdered in my sleep?"

Flame blinks her sharp gray eyes at me. Then she pops up, stretching through a yawn—even Fienians have to rest, apparently—and turns her attention back to the mess of wires. Her fury seems to have vanished as fast as it came on. "Not making any promises."

I undo my hairpin, quietly slip it under my pillow—just in case—and make a paltry effort at sleep. But one thought keeps breaking through: Flame is wrong. I don't blame one side over the other anymore, and I have stopped seeing monsters in place of men.

Truly, I am beginning to suspect the entire world has simply gone mad. And I'm sleeping a few steps away from the maddest of them all.

CHAPTER THIRTY-ONE

Hands are shaking me. "You sleep like a corpse!" Flame's agitated voice accuses. "Get up!"

The Centurions burst in and lead me off before I can find my boots. Our hurried footsteps break the silence of the dark halls. Although I am pretty sure they are taking me to the Choosing Ceremony, they just as well could be leading me to the firing squad.

We pause by the door. A Centurion quickly drapes me in a satin, bell-shaped emerald-green cloak that swirls around my ankles. It is heavy, trimmed in black marten fur that descends down the front and borders the arm openings on each side, and extravagant beyond compare.

"He wanted you to have this," the Centurion says.

Thank goodness for whomever *he* is—Nicolai?—because the cool night air nips at my legs as soon as we exit.

It takes a moment to spot the other finalists, spread out in two parallel lines by order of status, facing each other. They shiver in their nightclothes, their milky breath fogging the air. A Centurion stands on either side of every finalist.

I am placed at the end of the line, next to Lady Laurel. My bare feet crunch on cool, dewy grass. Envious eyes roam my cloak, and I realize, once again, I am standing out from the others. I make a point to tell Nicolai no more special favors, however appreciated they are.

A torch sparks to life. One by one, the Centurions light their torches off the other until there are two glorious rows of crackling warmth. Then we are each handed an unlit torch.

I take this time to catalog the remaining finalists. Merida and Rhydian huddle together, their hands all but touching. Teagan, her tall form clad in a black men's silk tunic that barely covers the top of her grass-blade-thin thighs, stands two finalists down from Blaise, Merida, and Rhydian. Hugo and Lucy stand near the end. They are the only ones dressed for the chill, which means either they heard the Centurions coming—or more likely were prepared for it somehow.

In the silence, it's hard not to worry about which mentor will pick me. Will it be the mentor Nicolai has chosen for me or someone else? And what if it is someone I despise like Delphine or Roman?

From the distance comes the muffled whinny of horses. We all turn, focusing on the dark expanse where the sound originates. Slowly, two riders emerge, galloping to a sudden stop a few feet from where I stand. One of the horses, a huge white beast, rears, its hooves pawing the air.

When the rider gets the beast under control, he throws back his hood and I see it is Caspian, wearing his military jacket emblazoned with a golden phoenix. A Centurion hands him a burning torch. Spurring the horse to a high-kneed trot, he wheels in a circle around the finalists, his horse grunting milky clouds with every sharp turn. Caspian's eyes scour the two lines, searching. This is a different Caspian. Towering, imperial, a majestic figure cut from obsidian. I can picture him commanding armies and leading men into battle.

I realize there's a lot about Prince Caspian Laevus I don't know, and the thought puts me on edge.

When his horse gets to me, its chest is shiny with sweat and lips bubbly with froth. I freeze. My hair blows back with every loud, warm exhalation from the beast's velvety-gray nostrils. Made for galloping, the brute is cagy in one place and stamps its feet and throws its massive head about like a battering ram. Caspian doesn't budge.

Looking up, I squint to make out Caspian's face, but his expression is covered in shadow. There's a quiet, unsettling pause as the horse shifts nervously. Finally, Caspian leans down, firelight illuminating his face, and touches his flame to mine.

My torch erupts, kissing my nose and cheeks with radiant warmth. Before I understand what is happening, the Centurion to my right has me by the arm. Caspian halts him with an upraised palm. It takes a moment to understand he's asking me to choose the other finalist on my team.

I swallow. But there's only one person here I trust. My torch finds Merida's. Without a word, Caspian kicks his horse into a gallop and fades into the darkness.

Just as the dawn begins to break, Merida and I are put on separate horses and blindfolded. Even with my eyes covered, I can feel the resentful looks from the others. They must be wondering why us. Two exiled Golds from forgettable houses.

I'm wondering the same thing.

I don't know if this turn of events will work in my favor or not. The one thing I do know, however, is this was not in the plan, and Nicolai will not be pleased.

Sounds come to life. Hoof steps from a third rider. Merida's loud, nervous breathing. Someone takes the reins and begins to lead us across the lawn at a gallop. Although I have never ridden a horse before, Lady March has, and she holds a handful of mane and hugs the beast with her bare legs, her toes curling over the cold stirrups.

As we travel, I struggle to gather a rough outlay of our surroundings. We cross a wooden bridge. A stream. Long stretches of grass. At one point, tree branches scratch my face and I know we are in a forest.

A sudden stop. The sound of the third rider retreating on his horse. Something's about to happen, and I focus on gleaning whatever I can from our surroundings. Not much wind, so probably we are entrenched by woods or cliffs on at least two sides. I smell stagnant water and feel the horse sinking a bit in what has to be mud. There's the sound of someone walking lightly on stone and then I feel someone take my reins. We are moving.

I instinctively lean back in my saddle as I feel my horse begin to plunge down stairs, hooves clacking on stone. There are three winding sets of steep stairs and then, by the wet, hollow sound of it, a damp tunnel. After what seems like forever, we dismount, a keypad beeps, a door creaks open, and we are led inside.

The first thing I notice is the lack of sound. The second thing is my brain, which tingles and crawls, as if a tiny worm wiggles through its dense gray matter.

My blindfold slides off, and I gasp. Beside me, Merida inhales sharply. We are inside what has to be a Sim, suspended in infinite bluish-black space, surrounded on all sides by stars. And that's when I understand it is a perfect replica of our universe.

"Beautiful, isn't it?" I know who it is before I even look. Caspian is standing just behind me, smiling, starlight casting him in a diaphanous glow so his hair appears a rich, burnished gold.

"Amazing." As far as I can tell, there is no boundary, just an endless array of stars. I find the Orion Constellation. As I focus my eyes, it seems to get closer—or maybe that is my imagination. Orion's sword comes into view. Slowly, a pink and blue veil billows out like a net, wrapping us in its gaseous blanket.

We are inside the Orion Nebula.

Before I can speak, it changes again. I am inside a cluster of fat, shimmery stars, shining clear, bluish-white. I look around for the others but see only stars. I count six. That's when I realize I am formless, emanating with boundless energy and light.

I am one of the seven sisters inside the Pleiades star cluster. It doesn't take much to determine which one I am. The same one I was named after. The most beautiful, brightest one of them all.

Maia.

"Maia." My father's voice, a whisper across the void.

"Maia," he calls again. "Find the hall of the three-headed Sphinx caged in gold—" And then it's as if everything is sucked into a vacuum, the stars stretching out like taffy before a black rubber band of darkness snaps closed.

I come to on the floor inside a high-domed silver room, lying in a puddle of satin and fur. Something soft—Caspian's jacket—wedges beneath my head. I want to yell for my father, but Caspian is leaning over me.

Straightening my cumbersome cloak to better cover my bare thighs, I struggle to my feet, fighting off waves of dizziness. "What happened?"

"You disappeared," Merida says with a worried frown.

"Disappeared?"

"From the Simulation," Caspian clarifies. "I ejected immediately, and we found you unconscious."

Glancing around, I see the panel by the door. So this is an auto-Sim, an incredibly rare and expensive Simulator designed for use without an operator, which means Caspian had a remote ejector to push if something went wrong.

Which apparently, it did. That explains why I was ejected before my father could finish his message. My shoulders sag. Now I'll just have to find a way to steal the remote ejector, find my way back here, and guess the code to enter—all before the first trial starts.

Easy peezy.

"The last thing I remember is being with you and Merida," I lie. "How long was I out?"

Merida and Caspian look at each other.

"A long time," Caspian finally says.

"How long until Shadow Fall?"

Caspian pulls out a gold pocket watch, its chain jingling. "Two hours and fifty-two minutes."

Less than three hours until the first challenge. Not only will it be impossible to get back here before then, but we have wasted most of our time for preparation.

Merida toys with her nightgown as she looks to Caspian. "I wanted to get help, but he thought it best . . . ?"

"My father sees Rebels and Fienian Sympathizers in every corner," Caspian explains grimly. "What do you think he would do with you?"

String me up from the Tower, no doubt.

"It must have been an anomaly," I suggest.

Pausing, Caspian glances at Merida and gives a quick nod. "Lady Merida, you may leave now. An attendant will guide you to your apartment to await the trials."

The hasty curtsy Merida performs looks silly with her nightgown. As soon as the door shuts behind her, the formal stiffness melts from Caspian's body and he steps closer, pulling the cloak tighter around me. "You're okay?"

"Yes." I try to brush him away with my hand, but he persists.

"The cloak kept you warm?"

One hand absentmindedly slides down the silky-soft fur lining. "That was you?"

He allows a questioning smile. "Who else?"

"Oh. Thank you."

There is an awkward pause, and Caspian forces a laugh. "It's nothing. All the mentors present a gift to the finalists before the first trial, so . . ." He gives the cloak the once-over. "I just thought . . . Well, it's green and . . ."

"Ostentatious?" I am only half-teasing.

A frown settles on his face. I realize he's probably not used to such blatant honesty. "I was going to say it is the perfect shade for your eyes but"—he breaks into a slow grin—"it really is garish, isn't it? Fienian hell. O said get you something practical, but I tend not to listen very well."

For some reason, I feel myself smiling. "No, it's, uh, very warm." More awkward silence. I chew my lip, twisting on my toes. "So, this place . . . ?"

"Of course." Caspian exhales as he begins to make a slow circle around the walls. "My father had this built years ago. The man who designed it made it this beautiful metallic silver for reasons only he understood." He touches the slightly reflective wall. "It was the most comprehensive and advanced Simulator ever built, right up until the day it stopped working."

"But the stars—"

"Left by its creator." *My Father.* "A sort of default setting. And never once, not when it was working, not when it became what you saw, has it ever experienced an anomaly." An intense look darkens his face. "Until now."

My heart races. Just like the Sim before, my father was trying to tell me something before I was pulled.

Find the hall of the Three-Headed Sphinx caged in gold. It has to be a riddle of some sort.

I exit my thoughts to see Caspian watching me with sharp, unblinking eyes. I bite my lip. "Why are you looking at me like that?"

"Lady March, do you think I could have made it this far in my father's court without knowing how to spot when someone is hiding something?"

"Okay." I fiddle with my cape. "Why not alert the Gold Cloaks?"

Caspian exhales. "Honestly, I don't know."

We are close. I can feel his warm breath against my cheeks and see the interwoven stroma inside his warm honey irises. I want to trust him. If there's anyone I can trust, surely it's the prince I was matched with?

I rock on my heels. "Why did you bring me here?"

Caspian's eyes rake my face, as if poring over my features will give him the answer to some puzzle. "The day I found you by the telescope, it *responded* to you."

"And you wanted to see how the Sim would respond?"

"It's always seemed—I don't know—as if it was waiting for something . . . or *someone.*"

I bite my lip. "And now, what do you think?"

"There are even more questions."

My heart knocks against my ribcage. "For instance?"

"For instance, Lady March, who are you *really*?"

The question takes me aback. Even I don't know how to answer. I'm not Chosen, not anymore, but I'm not a Bronze, either. I'm not a courtier, nor am I the fallen Gold whose identity I inhabit. Parts of me are Lady March, yet parts of me are Maia Graystone.

And some dark part of me, the part I try to hide, the desperate, primal part, is the girl from the pit.

He is watching me, waiting for an answer. So I give him the only one I can. "I'm the girl who will be left standing at the end."

Hopefully.

"At least we know you're confident."

"Is that why you chose me?"

"Partly," he admits.

"The other part?"

His lips press together for a brief moment as he ponders my question. "Because you are different than the others. Count and Countess Bloodwood, they don't intimidate you."

"And," I say, finishing his thought, "if I make it all the way through, I wouldn't be afraid to ally with you against them."

"I think you misunderstand, Lady March. I don't want an ally against Countess Bloodwood. I want you to replace her."

I feel my heart give a wild kick. And maybe it's because we were matched, or because of all those nights spent memorizing his face and picturing our future together, but my mind goes there. "You want me to . . . *marry* you?"

A stupid grin transforms my face. It's like I am nine again. Looking at his picture. Imagining a happy, uncomplicated life. I want to go back there. I want to *feel* that way again.

But Caspian clears his throat, and my idiotic fantasy dies an awkward death. "Lady March," he says, "I think once again you have misunderstood. I was suggesting you replace Delphine's position in court. She offers the court brute strength and a sense of cruel leadership they understand. I need someone who can challenge her position, give my people something more, something *better*."

"Oh," is all I can think to say. *Stupid, Stupid.* "What about your wedding on Hyperion? I mean, if you feel that way about her—"

"How I feel, Lady March, has no bearing on my life or my obligations to the empire." Frowning, he runs a finger over his chin. "We were friends, once, the Countess and I. I used to be able to calm her unpredictable nature, but it's getting harder and harder to do."

"I suppose in a few short days you'll have a lifetime to try." I say this without thinking, a habit I'm learning Lady March suffers from.

Caspian chuckles darkly, his head tilted to the side as he peers at me.

"What?"

"It's just I can't remember the last time I actually enjoyed a conversation this much."

Funny, but I feel the same way. Talking to Caspian feels good, natural, like the easiest thing in the world.

Suddenly Caspian lifts his hands to the collar of my cloak, his knuckles warm against my throat as he pulls it tighter around me. His eyes hold mine. "Which is why, Lady Everly March, you have to survive the first trial. I need you"—he laughs softly—"I mean I need you as an ally . . . and I hope as a . . . a friend."

"Do you think I can win?" I want him to say yes, even if it is a lie. I *need* him to.

But Caspian blinks and pulls away from me, as if the fact that in a few hours I will probably be dead has finally registered. "It's late, Lady March. Best we use the remaining time to prepare you."

In the end, there's not much Caspian can tell me I don't already know about my mother and the Shadow Trials, but I pretend to be the doe-eyed student for his benefit. After we're done, Caspian holds out the blindfold.

I stretch my arms, talking through a yawn. "Is the . . . blindfold . . . necessary?"

Caspian's lips lift at the corners as he twirls his pointer finger by my head. I obey, turning my back to him so he can slide my blindfold back on. "This place and its location has remained a secret since inception, Lady March. I plan to keep it that way."

My mare is right outside the Sim door. Even blindfolded, I mount easily, gripping the saddle pommel, the pleasant smell of horse and leather intermingled with the dampness of the tunnel. I am just settling into the saddle when I feel a weight behind me. "Poseidon must have followed Merida's mare."

"Your horse?" I say, trying to find a comfortable way to sit without pressing into him.

Caspian casually pulls me against his chest so we fit on the saddle better. "Even on his good days," Caspian says, moving my hair to the side, out of his face, so his breath warms my neck, "Poseidon is more devil than horse."

I stiffen as his fingers graze my hip on the way to the reins.

"I can lead from the ground, if . . . uh, you prefer?" His voice makes me think he is smiling.

"No . . . This way will be faster."

I let myself sink into his warm chest. This is what it would have been like. If my father hadn't died. If I hadn't been sent to the pit. If my life had followed the path my mother had carved for me and I had been matched with Caspian. I force down a shiver. My body hums with electricity, and I feel light and heavy at the same time.

The feelings I feel—or *felt*—for Riser were sharp. Uncomfortable.

Splinters buried too deep to remove. But this is different. This is pleasant, safe. If I could choose, I would choose *this*.

Sunlight kisses my face. We are outside. As Caspian urges my mare up the stairs, gravity fitting my body to his like perfectly matched puzzle pieces, I shiver again and Caspian, thinking I'm cold, or perhaps scared, wraps his arms around me, sinking his chin into the curve of my neck.

"The answer is yes," he breathes. "I think you can win, all of it."

And I almost believe him.

CHAPTER THIRTY-TWO

Although Caspian thinks I'm headed to the recreational complex to practice, I find my room instead and keel onto the bed. My brain keeps going over the first line from my father's incomplete riddle. The only sphinx I've ever seen comes from the House Laevus Crest. But a three-headed sphinx? I rack my memories for stories from my book of gods and mythological creatures, but my eyes keep closing and the images blur . . .

Blackness. Mud. The smell of human excrement and decomposing flesh and fear. Howling sounds, like souls being ripped apart.

I am dying. Curled into myself.

Too exhausted to move after clawing over a hundred feet through the dirt and rocks and grime, I lie here thinking about Max and how I'm going to let him down. I tried, digging the tunnels so I could survive a little bit longer and somehow make it back to him, but there's no food or water here, and I'm too weak to go find any.

I can hear feet scuffing the dirt as they come for me. I hope they'll kill me first. I hope it is quick. But mostly I just hate the sense of gratitude I feel.

I wait, but nothing happens. Then I sense heat against my lips. Taste warm, salty richness. My body reacts, greedily sucking, making slurping-gasping-grunting-coughing noises.

As my lips feel the rim of the bowl and my tongue reaches out, my eyes flick open and I see Riser kneeling there. He smiles down at me with his one bruised eye and says, "Don't you dare give up, Digger Girl. Fight. Fight until your last dying breath."

I know as soon as my eyes flutter open it's time. I know before I walk to the window and spy the apricot-sized pit mere feet from the sun. Before I see Flame's intense, troubled look. Before I hear the knock on the door and the attendant summoning me.

Flame hands me a sporty onyx jumpsuit with Turkish legs and an open back and black patent leather boots—items once again delivered to our door by Merida. With all of the clothes she has loaned me, I am beginning to wonder just how well off they are.

Flame's contribution is a foxtail aigrette long and sharp enough to hold my complex system of braids into place on my head and, if necessary, pierce flesh and bone. Although I am sure I will hate it, it somehow finishes my look.

The wardrobe doors are closed, hiding whatever Flame is working on, but I glance pointedly at it and raise the question with my eyes: *Is it safe yet?*

Flame shakes her head.

No outside help from Nicolai or Flame. I am on my own.

At the door, she stops me. "Which eye is dominant?"

"I don't know. I guess my right—"

She pries my right eyelid open, her finger coming straight at my eyeball.

"There." She waits, as if I should thank her or something.

"Did you just . . . poke my eyeball?"

Rolling her eyes, she traipses to the open window and slides the thick mahogany drapes across, shutting out the light.

As soon as I register the darkness, I feel a slight twitch in my eye and the room resolves from the shadows. I watch her carefully cross the floor toward me. Her hands are out to feel for objects in her way . . . because it's dark, which means I shouldn't be able to see her.

I hold out my hands in front of me. "Remarkable."

With a swish of the drapes, my vision goes back to normal. "The night-vision lens I put in your eye can only be seen with a special light," Flame says. "If you need to get rid of it fast, close your eye and press for fifteen seconds to make it dissolve."

"Thanks, Fienian," I say. "I guess you have your uses."

She frowns. There's rustling as she pins something—the phoenix brooch—to my chest. "Wear this with honor." Clasping her fingers over mine, she slides her tiny hands down to cusp each of my elbows and bows her head. "Blood for freedom."

I bow my head. "Death for honor."

It's strange, speaking like a Fienian. But Flame is right; this is war, perhaps of a different kind, but war nonetheless.

And it's time to go to battle.

The carriage waiting for us, a regal, shiny black monstrosity requiring four massive black horses, flies two pennants. The Royalist Phoenix and the House Laevus Sphinx, a lion with a woman's head and large white wings against a black background. So this must be Caspian's personal carriage. Two sphinxes are engraved into the pristine white velvet upholstery, and I'm reminded that I'm not any closer to solving my father's riddle.

Merida and I sit quietly across from each other. Dressed in a baby-blue corselet satin jumper and white kimono-sleeved bodice, she almost looks angelic. Especially with her boots kicked off and her bare feet tucked beneath her like a child.

We spend the first few minutes gazing out the windows at the other carriages, trying to glimpse the other finalist pairings. Teagan enters a carriage with a thin boy I recognize from the Culling. Just before a wall of climbing roses blocks our view, Rhydian rounds a carriage, walking stiffly beside a girl I don't know in a bright-lavender riding frock.

I'm also searching for anything that might relate to the riddle. Now that I'm looking, though, sphinxes seem to be everywhere. On the carriage. In the gardens. Engraved in the stone archways and bridges. But none have three heads.

Merida breaks the silence. "That outfit looks as if I made it for you."

I pinch a square of silky fabric from my trousers. "You made this?"

"Of course. What else could I do surrounded by four sisters? I had to escape somehow!" She admires her own outfit. "They hated country life, so I started patching together gowns from the fabric leftover from my job. We would turn the living room into a ballroom and pretend we were still on the Island."

"You were Golds?"

"From the famous house Pope. But after our fall from court, we sold most of our High Colored gowns to pay our tithes and I became a seamstress." She laughs suddenly. "Maybe the first trial will involve sewing."

I feel myself smiling. "If that's the case, I'm done for."

"So, what skills *do* you possess, Lady March?"

Telling lies, I think bitterly. *Detecting weakness in others. Knowing where to slash the neck so the body will exsanguinate before the person can scream.*

Snuffing people. That's what I am good at.

"Stories," I say, remembering how I liked to entertain Max with the stories about gods and titans from my illicit book. "I used to be good at telling stories, I think."

"Perhaps you can regale me someday." Merida glances out the window. We are passing through the apple orchards, and the carriage bumps every so often as the wheels run over the rotten apples strewn on the dirt road. A thick cloying smell haunts the air.

I pause, knotting my fingers together. "Um . . . Thank you for, you know, staying with me in the Sim after I passed out. Most people would have left me."

Merida shakes her head, patches of sunlight dancing in her pale tresses. "I don't believe that, Everly. I think, given a chance, most people will surprise you."

Her naivety forms a cold pit in my stomach. Merida is not going to survive the first trial. I know this just like I know I can't do anything about it. Not if I want to come out alive. I clear my throat. "Well, thank you, anyway."

"I do wish you could have seen the Prince's face when he saw you lying there. Like he'd swallowed poison. He fell to his knees, shaking you and ordering you to wake up"—her voice goes masculine—"Open your eyes, Lady March, I command thee!"

Despite our nerves, we both burst into childlike giggles.

"And what about that goodbye with Lord Thornbrook?"

I shrug, wanting to slap my hands over my ears at the mention of Riser.

"You're lucky, even if they did send him away," she continues in a wistful voice. "I've never even been kissed."

"Well, there's always time for—" Realizing my mistake I shut up, but it's too late. Cold silence overtakes us.

"I know I'm going to die, Everly. Either I'll perish in the trials or I'll lose and die on the other side of the fence. I'm not as strong or brave as the others."

Even though Merida's quiet voice fades into the muffled sounds of the carriage, her words hang thick and heavy in the air. Her eyes glimmer as her gaze traces the sloping hills outside. In the painful silence, I almost tell her she's wrong a hundred times. But I don't want to lie to her. Somehow, that's important. After a while, she drags a hand over her cheek and fishes inside her pocket. The silver pillbox gleams as she opens it.

I know what the little round metallic pill is. Like most Centurions, my bodyguard, Gabriel, carried a similar pill in a secret compartment inside his pocket watch. It was an "in- case" pill. In case he was captured by Fienians and tortured. In case he failed to protect us. In case the world ended. In case death was the preferable option.

"In case I lose and am thrown back over the wall like Lord Thornbrook." She says this like she's telling me what she'll have for supper. "They say it's like going to sleep."

My eyes can't seem to leave the shiny pill. *Except you don't wake up, Merida.* But I don't say that either, because sometimes the truth is best left unspoken.

There's a sharp bump and she pockets the pill. Outside the window, I see we are crossing a stone bridge. On the other side, seeped in yellow sunlight and a dazzling array of wildflowers, a huge valley carves a swathe through the snow-capped mountains in the distance.

A single, stately Gold carriage waits in the center of the valley, its window dark, flanked by four Centurions. A little ways away stands a large pavilion, its crimson drapes flapping softly. It shades a long table of what looks to be food, and in the center, shimmering like a mirage, sits the hologram Emperor on his hologram throne. Beside him, Delphine's father, General Cornelius Bloodwood, rests on a real wooden throne almost as big as the Emperor's. Flags are positioned every sixty feet or so around it to create a huge circle.

Caspian and the other mentors wait for us on horses. Their House Sigils flash from their ceremonial robes, their hats and fascinators matching the colors of their House. Our carriage stops and is soon joined by the others.

We all pile out. No one speaks as the mentors, on horseback, lead us toward the pavilion and position us in front of each Chosen's House flag.

Caspian growls insults as he dismounts, Poseidon once again misbehaving, kicking and hopping in angry circles. It takes Caspian a minute to quiet him. Finally, he turns to face us. "Lady Pope, Lady March."

His eyes linger on mine, long enough for my breath to catch inside my chest. We both lower our heads and perform a quick bow.

Caspian circles around us, slow, methodical, as if he's sizing us up. "Finalists, your breathing tells me you are both scared. That's good. Fear helps you survive. Lose that and death is not far away." His voice is strong, commanding, and detached. *In case we don't make it.* "But I didn't choose you for your fear; I chose you because you have proven to be strong. Resourceful. Brave. You have proven yourselves under pressure." He pauses for a moment. "Today, you need to prove yourselves beyond that. You need to be warriors. Finalists, are you ready to do that?"

Merida slips her hand over mine. "Ready."

Caspian looks to me. "Lady March?"

I squeeze Merida's hand. "Ready."

"Good. I'll be waiting for you at the end."

From across the field, I hear the doors to the carriage open. My mother stands erect, taller than I remember, most of her silver wig covered by an elaborate royal blue fascinator and matching cape. As she slings one lithe leg over a steel-gray horse, sunlight plays off the two white doves on her cape. Four Centurions follow suit, their horses shadowing hers. She rides slowly, purposefully toward the first two finalists. A short conversation and she's on to the next.

The sun is hot on our faces as we wait our turn. Caspian's dark flag flails in the wind like an animal trying to escape a steel trap. There's the sound of my mother's horse galloping toward us. I blink and she is here, blocking the sun, her shadow cool on my cheeks. "Emperor's blessings, finalist," my mother says to Merida. "May your wits and courage see you to the other side."

It's weird. I didn't feel anything when I saw her exit the carriage. Nor when she was making her rounds. But now, as soon as I see her hazel eyes, the familiar crinkles around her thin lips and errant freckles over her neck and face, something primal inside me crumples. I am little again. Powerless to do anything but love her. I want her to fold me in her arms, press my cheek against hers. To whisper everything will be okay.

To love me.

With everything I possess, I want her to love me the way no one else ever will.

How could you, Mother?

Her eyes sweep over mine in a careless, Gold-you-are-nothing sort of way. I grind my teeth until my jaw muscles twitch, swallowing the tears burning the back of my throat.

"Emperor's blessings, finalist," my mother says, the way one talks to a stranger who doesn't have long to live.

How could you?

Something stirs inside her detached eyes—a sliver of emotion? The Centurions twitch on their horses as she suddenly dismounts in her quick, efficient way. She is breaking script.

And that never, ever happens.

CHAPTER THIRTY-THREE

"You are Lady Everly March?" she asks.

I nod. Her voice sounds as if it's coming from a far-away tunnel.

"You're the girl who defied the Lady Delphine and scored highest at the Culling? Yes, I have heard your name much since the trials began."

I study my bootlaces. "That was not my intention, Baroness."

Silence. I look up to see my mother staring at me, almost as if she's studying an old photo she recognizes but can't place. There, just below the glacial surface, something. A whisper of emotion. "Oh, but intentions are like jewels in a dagger, Lady March." She leans closer. "They don't particularly matter much in the end."

Her sharp tongue peels away at me, as if each word lashes pieces of my flesh from the bone to reveal Maia Graystone beneath. Weak, sad little Maia.

Don't you recognize me, Mother?

Addressing both of us now, she says, "Finalists, you have until the end of Shadow Fall to complete your first trial."

Then, without another word, she mounts her horse and digs into its flank, galloping to the next finalists.

"That went well," Merida jokes.

"Did it?" I reply, blinking away the panic. Now that she is gone I can relax, stretch my arms a bit. That's when I notice two groups down the Redgrave siblings stand alone next to a white flag. Inside the flag writhes Cerberus, the guardian of Hades, a three-headed black dog with a serpent's tail and long, curved fangs.

House Bloodwood. Which means their mentor could only be the Countess Delphine.

My ears prick at the distant sound of hoof beats. The riders round the bridge and set a furious pace toward us. Centurions, headed by a blond female rider, her hood covering most of her head, a ceremonial crimson cape flapping behind her. The Cerberus on the large flag held by the nearest Centurion seems to slither in the air above her, a ravenous monster eager for blood.

Before the riders can come to a complete stop, Delphine is off her horse. Caspian and my mother meet the Countess halfway, and my mother embraces her stiffly. Still, I swallow the bitterness forming at the back of my throat. If ever anyone could meet my mother's expectations, it would be Delphine.

After a few minutes, my mother and Caspian peer over their shoulders. I swear they are looking at me.

My heart skips a beat when Merida confirms my fear. "Are they talking about us?"

Caspian seems to deflate a bit, his shoulders slumping. Delphine nods to the Emperor and reaches into her waistband. As the image of her grandfather's revolver registers in my brain, adrenaline burns through me.

My only regret is I won't get to see my mother realize all the horrors she's caused. The thought makes me angry, and I turn to face Delphine. She is halfway to me now, walking with a purpose, the revolver swinging in her hand.

"What are you doing?" Merida whispers into my ear.

But at this point my heart is hammering so loudly I can barely hear her.

Deep down I know my choices are simple. I can let Delphine lodge a bullet into my brain, or I can fight back and maybe take her with me before I die.

A sudden gust of wind whips Delphine's cape out like a burst of blood, blowing back her deep-set hood to reveal her face. Her eyes are focused *behind* me. Once the implications of what I am seeing become clear, my muscles relax and I exhale. As she passes, she turns to me and grins, her caramel-blond eyebrows lifting.

As if to say, *don't worry, I haven't forgotten about you.*

After a few seconds, I hear a girl start to beg. The others turn to watch, but I stay still. I refuse to watch. Refuse to participate. I know it is not enough, not nearly, but it's *something.*

What happens next isn't a coincidence. Merida looks away, followed by Teagan and the frail boy beside her. Laurel and Blaise are next. A few others look around before joining us. And then, one by one, the other finalists in the circle turn their backs, until it is just the Redgrave siblings watching.

If I didn't know how futile our act of rebellion is, I would feel more pride. Hope, even. Instead I have given the illusion we have a choice. An illusion about to be smashed as soon as the trial begins.

From my position, I study my mother. She stands erect, stern, the wide brim of her fascinator lifted just enough from the wind to reveal her stoic expression. She seems to look beyond us, into the horizon. But I know better. She sees everything, my mother. The screaming girl's horror; Delphine's madness; our subtle, pointless rebellion.

The Emperor doesn't hide his annoyance, though, and even from here I can see his hands clenching the sides of his throne. But then his gaze travels behind me to the poor girl about to be executed, and his lips curl into a smile as he leans forward, drinking in the girl's fear the way a parched man would gulp water.

An abrupt scream pierces my thoughts, halted by a single gunshot. The sound reverberates through the valley for a moment and then all goes still. My mother nods once, as if an unwelcome task has been completed, and then commences her rounds giving the finalist speeches.

By the time I look, the body has already been dragged off. Rhydian now stands alone, which leads me to believe it was the purple-frocked girl who was executed. I don't have to wonder long why, because Caspian appears and explains. "They found someone inside the system and traced it back to Lady Kingston."

I cross my arms. "They could have simply let her outside the wall."

"Lady March," Caspian begins, in a curt voice not used to being challenged, "sometimes a *quick* death is the most merciful option." He pauses for that ugly realization to sink in. "I would have done the same for you."

I think it's meant to be an affectionate gesture. The thought forces a bitter smile to my face.

And then, for a cruel moment, the span of a heartbeat, I see Riser, surrounded, desperately fighting them off. *Could I have forced a dagger through his heart to spare him that torture?* I should have done that, at least.

It's what I'm good at.

Merida shifts on her feet. "I'm sad for her," she says amicably, trying to break the tension. "But now, at least, there's one less finalist to compete against."

A strange look comes over Caspian's face; he glances my way. "Not exactly."

I know what he means even before I notice the rider in my periphery. And suddenly it all makes sense. Flame framed someone else for our crime. Someone innocent. So we could live.

Or maybe it was all for one person.

Riser hits the ground like a cat, graceful and poised. His gaze furiously scans the circle. Then stops at me. Something passes between us—a sort of unspoken greeting that ripples through my body.

And then the rogue winks, and of course, I want to throttle him.

Caspian's eyes watch me below a furrowed brow, as if he's trying to gauge my reaction to Riser's second chance. But as Riser takes his place next to Rhydian, I realize I couldn't adequately express the complex jumble of emotions bombarding me if I tried.

We condemned another to die for us. I listened to her scream. I felt her fear. Probably even then I knew. Deep down I must have.

I should feel guilt.

I *should* hate myself.

Certainly I should feel *something*.

But the instant I saw Riser's face, the instant I understood, deep down, he was safe, it was like the feeling I had in the pit when the first tendrils of light broke through my black prison and an invisible weight I hadn't noticed around my neck was severed. As if I hadn't taken a single breath of air those entire seven years until that moment. That's how it feels now. Like I can *breathe* again.

On some hidden signal, the mentors move to the middle of the circle to join my mother. Caspian is the last to go. Before he does, he leans down, his hair tickling my cheek, and whispers, "I checked your Sim but, oddly, your experience was blank." Straightening back up, he smiles. "Perhaps when you come out the other side, you will finally trust me enough to tell me why."

I watch him lope across the field to the others. They stand in silence, waiting.

The shadow comes like a silent wave of brackish water crashing down from the mountains. The instant it touches the valley floor, there's a grating, rumbling noise all around us. At first I think it's the horizon moving, but then I realize the ground is trembling. I put out my arms for balance. It's happening—whatever they have planned for us. I exhale two forceful breaths and step back.

Rising from the earth, grating and graveling, is what looks to be a giant slab of curved stone that takes up the entire valley. Grass and dirt tumble from the top of the slab as it grows past my waist. Now I can see it's a giant circle, filled with intricate stone pathways that lead to the mentors in the middle. Directly in front of me looms an entrance.

Suddenly an enormous shadow of dread falls over me. I know what it is. A labyrinth.

Merida is breathing fast and loud, her lips tugged into a trembling frown. "I'm scared, Everly."

I know I shouldn't say it. Saying it only ties me to her, makes me weak. But some part of me is beginning to understand strength isn't measured by who's left standing at the end. That's what they want me to think. What keeps them strong and us weak.

I take Merida's hand between mine. "I'll get us through this, Merida. I promise."

It feels good, like a declaration of something. Merida squeezes my fingers. "I know, Everly. And I promise to try to be brave."

Just before the barricade blocks my vision, I meet eyes with Riser. His lips are pressed together in determination, his body tensed to run. He must know what it is as well.

Until my last dying breath. I think I say the words from my dream. Or maybe I only think them. It doesn't matter, because they reverberate inside my head, over and over, an angry, primal call to war.

Whatever happens in there, until my last dying breath I will fight to survive. Not just for myself or for Max, but for everyone left on Earth. Because if I don't make it out the other side, the thing my father hid dies with me—and so does any chance we have left of stopping Pandora.

Merida stands beside me, but I'm alone. The wall stops growing at three stories tall.

Silence.

"I'm ready!" I scream. I scream it to the wall. To the shadow murk. To my mother, and Delphine and the Emperor.

Sometimes, just like the truth needs to be unspoken, a lie needs to be shouted at the top of your lungs.

CHAPTER THIRTY-FOUR

The gate shuts behind us as soon as we enter. The smell of dank stone and torn earth fills the darkness. I pause to let my lens adjust and give myself a second to think. Undoubtedly the others will be running, thinking it a simple race.

I know better, though. My mother reveres violence for its ability to strip a man down to his essence, to who he really is. The only thing she loves more is riddles. Merida's heavy breathing fills the air, and I turn to see her feeling along the wall. Her eyes, now adjusted, find me. We begin walking side by side, Merida occasionally feeling along the walls for guidance.

It isn't long before another passageway opens up to our left. I hesitate, but both of us silently agree to keep going forward. We pass another a minute later on our right. A few more, grouped close together.

I feel the tiny lens in my eye adjust before I actually notice the light. It's around the curve, a torch in the wall about eye-level, shimmering bluish-white beneath my lens. My interest piques immediately— everything my mother does is by design, a puzzle piece to a larger picture. The lichen and moss covering the walls comes away easily under my fingers. Beneath I feel something, maybe random stone. Maybe something more. I wipe until a good section of the wall opposite the torch is clear, coughing as the crushed lichen enters my lungs, fingers wet and muddy from the moss.

Merida is the first to see it. "It's a . . . a horse?"

Standing back, I see she's right. I have uncovered most of the body up to the ears.

"What does it mean?"

"I have absolutely no idea." The air smells earthy, like the ground after a light rain. I rub away more of the wall, uncovering a woodland scene full of trees and flowers. Now that I know what to look for, I can make out more life-size horses beneath the thin lichen carpet, their muscular hindquarters and wild manes trapping shadow.

"It has to mean something." My voice teeters on desperation.

Merida shifts uncomfortably. "Or maybe it's just meant to slow us down."

She's right. With my mother, nothing is ever as it seems.

Both of us freeze. Muffled winding, clicking noises, like a gear shifting, emanate from deep within the stone. Something's happening. A noise on the other side of the tunnel. Voices, low and indecipherable. Someone cries out, followed by shouts.

The shouts become screams.

After the screams, we both have the silent understanding we need to keep going. But it's hard to leave the light. Even with my lens, which transforms the darkness into a grainy, greenish color, I recognize the shadows are where we are the weakest.

The second the screams stop, the wall makes a groaning noise. I steady my feet as the earth shakes. I think at first I'm walking sideways, but the wall is moving inward. It stops after a few seconds, leaving only an eerie silence, prickled by more far-away cries.

What was that? Why would the walls move? Perhaps my mother is having the labyrinth change shape, but if so, why? Merida turns to me, her elbow gouging my ribs. As I twist away from her and my back presses into hard stone, I understand.

It's not changing shape. Our passageway is getting smaller. Or, more likely, when the finalists on the other side of the wall died, their passageway became bigger. Only by a couple feet, I think. But two feet can be the difference between life and death if the walls are about to close in on us.

"These walls are interactive." My words come out breathy and fast. "We need to move. Now!" Panic and adrenaline course through me, intoxicating my mind.

Calm down. But the Doom has already taken over. A primordial part of me understands once these walls close in, I won't be able to handle it. Too much like the pit. I try to steady my breathing, pulling in fat drags of air, sucking them greedily through an invisible straw as the greenish darkness spins around me.

First my hands go numb, then my mouth. My mind goes blank and I'm on my knees, gasping, spinning out of control.

I'm hyperventilating.

It's Merida who goads me back to my senses. I awaken from my stupor to pain. She's slapping the shit out of me.

"Please!" Her voice sinks through my fear. "You promised. I cannot do this alone!"

But I don't just see her. I see Max. My father. The millions upon millions of people waiting to die.

Pull your shit together, Lady March.

Merida's terrified face comes into focus.

"I'm sorry." I feel as if I've let her down. "I've just . . . been here before. In another lifetime."

"Good." She pulls me to my feet. "If you survived it once, you can again."

I nod, embarrassed she witnessed Maia, the old me. Mud and grass cake my knees, and I wipe at them.

Suddenly I have an idea. "Give me your arm," I instruct, gathering more mud onto my fingertip.

Merida obliges without comment. I set to work, starting at her middle knuckle, pausing here and there to remember. When I'm through, I carefully drop her arm.

Merida peers at my work. "Tracing our steps?"

"Mapping the labyrinth. The dotted lines are the passageways we don't choose, and the full line is our path so far." I'm thankful she doesn't notice—or at least mention—I can see to do such a thing. There's a dull thump as I slap the stone. "The walls move inward, which means they also move outward, depending on what side you're on."

"But why would they give us more space when we die?"

"So when we're out of space, we'll start killing each other for more."

After that little pearl of insight, we travel in silence. I stick to the right when the passageway forks to make it easier to mark. There is no plan, which terrifies me.

There has to be a design to this, a riddle to solve. Something to guide us. A helpless feeling has crept over me, taken hold. Even with my lens, the walls are black, and my muddy, pixilated vision makes it seem like I'm dreaming. When we pass the torches, it's almost worse, having to go back into the shadows.

I don't know what alerts me to them. A muffled voice, perhaps. The sound of feet whispering over grass. Two feet farther and I pinpoint their position just inside the passageway on our right. It takes a few seconds to recognize them: Lady Hood and Lady Knowles. Unaware of our presence, they whisper to one another, nod, and take another step. When nothing happens, they walk a little faster, their silk trousers rustling in the silence.

Should we follow? Use them to ensure it's safe? I turn to Merida and then, without explanation, the hairs on my neck stick straight up. Peering back into the passageway, I see their silhouettes, small against the darkness. It takes a moment to actually hear what my body has already sensed. Barking, laughing noises trickle from the tunnel. It's a strange, unfamiliar noise, unlike dogs or any other animal I can think of. Some deep-rooted part of me screams for the girls to run.

Run!

Except I know my mother doesn't give second chances.

The ladies reappear. They are walking backward, slowly, their hands out. One of the girls kicks at something. Shapes part the shadows, waist high. More heckling growls and high-pitched yips.

The girls make it about twenty feet from us when I see what is making the sounds. Not dogs, exactly; they are larger. Wilder. With stout heads, short bat-like ears, and black snouts. Thick elongated necks lead to a curved back and crooked hind legs. Dark-brown spots speckle their long, grayish-red coats. A putrid, decaying smell creeps up my nose.

It's their movements that scare me. The way they circle the girls, studying them with their glittering eyes and cocked heads. The way they communicate with their bizarre staccato of noises that echo off the walls.

Hyena. The word lodges in the back of my throat, although I don't remember how I know it. Perhaps my father, then, or one of the Royalist museums I visited so long ago. The animals seem to be smiling as they stalk the girls, making excited grunting noises. The girls are pivoting, desperately kicking and waving their arms to ward off the predators, their eyes round white eggs inside their pale faces.

They don't think they're dogs, either.

One daring hyena darts forward. Lady Knowles yells, kicks out, and he jumps back with ease, a curious, almost intelligent look in his beady black eyes.

Lady Hood pulls something shiny out from her bodice and holds it in front of her. A dagger. She swings it back and forth, cursing.

But the hyenas don't even seem to notice it. Something has changed. They've stopped curiously prodding the girls, stopped their circling. The longer fur on their backs has ridged into a sort of mane.

The concerted attack is silent and efficient. Lady Knowles swings once, twice, and disappears with a surprised scream beneath a writhing mass of shaggy fur and guttural growls.

My stomach twists as the sounds of bones crunching echo off the walls, and their tunnel grates wider, while the one we occupy grows smaller.

Lady Hood has her arms out, stumbling wildly, her jumper in tatters. Somehow she has escaped. Just as her hopeful eyes lock on mine, a whooshing noise fills my ears and a roaring wall of orange flames block her exit, the heat blasting us backward.

Now our walls barely allow us to stand apart. I think Merida will protest leaving them, but she stays quiet. She pretends, just like I do, she cannot hear Lady Hood's screams for help, muffled behind the roar of the firewall and the horrible animalistic laughing noises.

My hands ball into knots at my sides as I struggle to fight off the panic. We have to think! There has to be a safe way out. Perhaps we can find another pair and follow them, using them the same way? No, too inefficient, and we cannot control our route. Even if we make it safely through, it's still a race against time.

My frustration only grows as we take a triangular path that leads us back to the same entrance. They're trying to confuse us. To confuse us and scare us and defeat us.

And so far it's working.

This time the tunnel opening is on the left. The mud has dried, so I use Brinley's phoenix brooch to poke my fingertip, using my blood to mark our progress. An X, nearly black in the light, marks where we saw the hyenas. As if to taunt us, the walls now depict muscly, ferocious canines drinking from a winding river.

Merida leans against the stone as I finish, disturbing a loose chunk that shifts in the wall. I wonder if this can help us in any way, feeling for any more weak spots, but there are none.

Merida puts one foot into the passageway. "Should I go first? Or maybe we could take turns?"

I don't answer. There has to be something that triggers it. Motion sensors? Without a second thought, I unlace my boot and hurl it into the darkness. It quietly thumps twenty feet away in the grass and comes to a rest against the barricade.

Nothing happens.

"Let me go," Merida insists. She has taken another step. She knows like I do every second we waste will cost us.

I am halfway ignoring her. If not motion sensors, what? If it were ground sensors triggered by weight, the shoe would have worked . . .

Unless it wasn't heavy enough.

"If we tried running in and back," I say, thinking aloud, "we wouldn't make it back out." So it needs to be something heavy that can be thrown and somehow retrieved.

From far away comes the sound of surprised yells. A moment later, our walls creep toward us. The loose stone Merida disturbed earlier tumbles out. It's bigger than I expected, about the size of a large watermelon, a crude rectangular chunk of gray.

Before I can think about what I'm doing, I dig my fingers into my corset and remove the wire, knotting it around the rock. Merida understands immediately and rips hers out too. We tie them securely together, affixing the loose end to my wrist, and lift the rock. It's heavier than I thought, which means it will probably only travel five feet at most. Hopefully that's far enough.

"On the count of three," I say, my mouth cottony with nerves.

"One."

"Two."

"Three!"

The rock tumbles through the air and lands with a heavy thud in the grass. As if on cue, the walls of our passageway rumble together. When it stops, there's only enough room for us to stand single file with Merida in the lead.

"The next one will crush us," Merida says, her voice breathless with panic.

"No, wait." I hold up my hand. The sound of something mechanical I can't place purrs from deep within the stone.

I don't see her move until it's too late. For a moment, as the metal against stone noise fills the air, like a large knife being sharpened, the word inside my mouth catches.

Then my breath bursts from my lungs. "*Duck!*"

Somehow over the screaming noise she hears me and falls, just as a flat sheet of sharpened waist-high metal shoots from a thread-thin crack in the stone.

The fire will be next. I drop, my hand slaps down on her ankle, and I pull, yanking her back into our little tunnel, where she flops down on top of me.

The heat inflicts instant, agonizing pain wherever it touches. Merida cries out and scrambles violently over the top of me in a desperate attempt at escaping the flames, her boots gouging my cheek.

By now the fire has turned the wire around the tender flesh of my wrist into a white-hot brand. I moan, dragging the rock and my body back through the tunnel until the air is cool enough to stop. I feel the ground, soft and pleasant against my back.

Merida's low groaning draws me to her. The smell of singed hair and flesh makes me want to gag. *Get up or you die.* But I seem to have no control over my body.

For a quiet, almost peaceful second, our panting mingles into a nice, lulling cadence. A small sliver of dark silvery-blue sky peers down at us from above. I could just close my eyes . . . just close them and go to sleep.

Then you will certainly die. I mull the words over in my mind, let them sink in. But the nice little bubble of apathy I have created keeps them from having much impact.

In the end, it's not the thought of death—certainly not as terrifying as what else undoubtedly awaits us in the labyrinth—but the promises I made.

Three, in fact. One to my father. One to Merida. And one to myself.

The hardest part is leaving my soft, safe spot on the ground. Once I'm on my feet, it's as if I snap out of a trance. Merida gapes up at me, exposing her face. All her beautiful hair from the crown down the left side of her skull is gone. Burned skin sloughs from her cheek, neck, and shoulder. Her tattered jumpsuit is melted to her body, pieces still smoldering.

She takes a deep, groaning lungful of air and struggles to her feet. "I'm sorry."

"Shh." I put my hand on her good shoulder, trying to keep my voice steady. "How is the pain?"

"I'm not sure. I don't . . . I don't feel *anything*." The whites of her eyes are huge, her skin bone-white. Her mouth is parted, slightly, panting. She is going into shock.

"Merida, we need to move. Can you do that?"

"Yes." She answers without hesitation as she begins to shuffle back the way we came. I drag the rock behind me, my wrist screaming where the wire cuts into the raw, blistered skin.

Walk. Stop. Breathe. Our progress is slow, painful. More torches. Merida cringes away from the flames, her eyes following them as we pass. Me dragging my arm, her wobbling on lifeless legs.

When we come upon the next entrance, I heft the rock, which barely makes it four feet, swallowing my scream as the wire gnaws through my flesh. We wait for two minutes and then enter. This tunnel is wide enough for me to move into the lead position, but now I'm stumbling, my legs seemingly disconnected from my body. It's a dead end, so we retrace our steps.

I hardly feel the brooch prick my finger. The blood smears into messy lines as I try to recall our progress so far. A circle marks the dead ends. Another toss of the rock. We wait longer than necessary, trying to gather our energy before entering.

It feels like forever until the next fork. I throw the rock to the left, biting the inside of my cheek to keep from crying out again. Blood trickles down my wrist into my palm, drips from my fingers. It takes two more times of pulling it back and throwing it again to make it far enough out. The pain in my wrist turns into a gnawing fire.

In our fatigue we must have miscalculated the time, because we make it four steps in when a sound pierces the fog wrapped around my brain.

Snuffling. Air being blown forcefully into the grass. No, something sniffing the ground. An animal. And there is only one reason an animal does that.

When it's tracking prey.

"Run—"

A furious, ungodly roar cuts off my warning. The sound reverberates off the stone and through my chest and wakes Merida from her stupor.

Not hyenas. Somehow, even with all our planning, we have stumbled onto something worse.

CHAPTER THIRTY-FIVE

Something enormous and black and *angry* erupts from the shadows, snorting and grunting, its talon-like claws gouging large chunks of earth in its wake.

An impossibly huge shaggy brown head, nearly as big as me, bobs up and down. I'm hit with a rangy, pungent, wet dog odor. Backpedaling, I slam into Merida. My foot gives out, the ground knocking the air from my chest. The ground vibrates my bones as the creature barrels closer, his body so large it seems to occlude the tunnel. The sound of my name being called registers dimly in the far recesses of my brain.

Digging my elbows into the grass, I kick with my feet, crab walking, my labored breath drowning out my pounding heartbeat. The thing lifts onto two legs, exposing an underside thick with tan fur, and lets out an earsplitting roar.

A word bubbles to the surface. Ursus Arctos. The grizzly bear. Max's favorite extinct animal from the museum.

The bear drops his full weight back down, rattling the ground, but we are past the entrance. Safe. Where is the fire?

An angry roar rocks the tunnels as it keeps coming. For its size, it's surprisingly fast. We need the fire. I know for certain there's no way we can outrun it.

Now it's six feet away. Five. Four.

All at once the bear stops as if hitting an invisible wall, his head tilted to the side, just as there's a crackling *whoosh* and the firewall leaps to the sky. The bear bellows and disappears behind it.

I'm not aware of moving, but somehow I make it two more feet before falling to my knees. I drop my head inside my hands. Swallow the vomit creeping up my throat. The smell of charred, gamey fur clings to my mouth. The bear calls out angrily a few times and then goes quiet.

I'm dizzy and nauseous with the after effects of adrenaline. Perhaps that's why it takes me a moment to realize what's happening. The tug is tentative. I watch my hand jump a few inches toward the fire. My eyes focus on the wire. It's taut. Realization hits as another harder tug jerks me closer.

"Merida!" I croak, craning my head back. She cowers near the wall, exhausted. "Help me get this—"

This time my head whips back with the force. I stumble, catching myself with my hands. My face smashes the ground. The bear grunts as he yanks the rock again. Straining the other way, I gouge my heels into the dirt and yell for Merida.

Merida flops down beside me, the flames turning her raw skin a bizarre orange color. Her breathing is shallow and rapid. With the protective layer of skin gone, it must be excruciating for her near the fire, but she doesn't make a sound as her fingernails dig uselessly into my wounded wrist. Another jerk. Something in my shoulder pops, and the pain ricochets from my arm into my lungs, where I force it out in a choking, desperate wail. Angry white stars of pain burst inside my eyelids. Next one will take off a hand. Or arm. It would be easier to just let him have me.

The thought is less disturbing than it should be. In desperation I imagine swallowing Merida's in-case pill. But no, I can't even do that because I made a stupid, naïve promise. And what would Pit Boy say?

I know the pain has really messed me up because now I can see him, Riser. His face, anyway, shimmering red with firelight. My body is contorted sideways away from the flames, my arm stretched out at a horrible, unnatural angle. I fantasize about my arm popping off. A sacrifice I would easily make to end the pain.

I watch my hallucination from my upside down world. His face pale, framed by stars, black locks of hair tumbling across his forehead. A knife twinkles by his side. In the strange, ethereal light of my lens and pain-induced haze, I think he looks like the Hades from my mother's paintings, the way he moves with the darkness, not a hint of doubt in his face, as if he owns the shadows, and death does not apply to him.

He bends down and begins sawing at the wire around my wrist. A moan escapes my lips. Shoulders pumping with effort, he catches my gaze. "Hold on, Everly. Keep fighting."

My lips peel into a wild grin. "Stop telling me what to do, Pit Boy."

All in the span of a second, the wire jerks hard, my arm springs free, my body rolls away from the heat, and the wire disappears into the flames.

My arm hangs dead and loose at my side. I stumble to Merida, huddled against the wall, leaning on someone, eyes half-closed. Whatever her body did earlier to protect her from the pain has run its course: She is shivering, eyes glazed with agony. Rhydian glances at me and nods before turning his attention back to Merida.

Her eyes flutter open. She focuses on me. "I tried, I did."

Using my good arm, I support her armpit, and Rhydian and I nudge her to a stand. "You've been so strong, Merida," I whisper, soothing her while fighting hot tears from my eyes. "Now you just have to be strong for a little longer."

A ripping sound turns my attention back to Riser. Without a word, he wraps a strip of his tunic around my wrist. I bite my lip to keep from crying out as his fingers explore my injured shoulder. "That hurt?"

"Only when I move it."

Riser nods. "Dislocated." Taking my arm, he presses it into my ribs. "Take a deep breath and count to five."

I get to two when he cracks it back in place. My vision goes black. I gasp, drawing in salving breaths. My throat is so dry I think it will crack open.

I open my mouth, half-groaning, "We need to move."

"I know." Riser places two fingertips just behind my jaw. They slide down to my chin, lifting it. He looks at me for a moment, silent, his eyes searching. "But you're okay?"

"Yes." I take my hand, the unhurt one, and rest my fingers over his. His hand is warm and sticky with what can only be blood. His, someone else's, mine—it's impossible to say. "You?"

"I'm fine *now*." He squeezes my hand, hard, and then drops a faded silver pocket watch into it. A sly smile transforms his face. "Picked it from one of the Dandies."

I examine it. Somewhere between the two and five is a thick obsidian line. Shadow Fall. According to the pocket watch, we have less than an hour. Riser leans in close. "If we leave Merida, I give our odds fifty-fifty."

I hand it back. "And if we don't?"

Riser glances at Merida. "Not a Fienian chance in hell."

There's a part of me that wants to run. Just run away from Merida and my stupid promise and my fear.

But I shake my head, Riser nods, and we both accept our fate. Riser checks on Merida and uses more shirt strips to bandage what he can, and we finally make our way down the path to our right.

The walls are nearly closed, so we walk single file. Riser first, then me, Rhydian, and Merida. I watch Riser, his careful gait, the way his body never touches the walls. Like me, he must hate the enclosed space, the claustrophobic feeling.

Either that or he's perfectly at home.

We pass two entrances. The first is still warm from the firewall. The second looks promising until, just around the curve, I notice a leather boot peeking out, the ground around it churning as if alive, and the low, faint hum of hissing. Something slithers over the boot and lifts its hooded head, a delicate forked tongue tasting the air.

We move on, and a new pathway emerges. Without the rock there's no way of testing it, so Rhydian goes first. After two minutes, we follow around a curve and down a long, narrow tunnel.

A torch flickers up ahead. When we are close enough to feel its heat, I spy a wide swath where someone has wiped away part of the moss from the stone.

A horse . . .

All the air evacuates my chest at once. *We are as good as dead.* An onslaught of anger and frustration well up inside me, and I slap furiously at the drawing, a hoarse cry erupting from my throat. "Circles! We're going in circles!"

I slump down the wall. The others have stopped to stare at me. I must look a sight, covered in green lichen-dust and blood. Massaging a palm into my forehead, I shake my head. "We passed this horse at the beginning. All of it was for nothing!"

A look of puzzlement flashes over Rhydian's face. "Horse? From here it looks like a unicorn."

I stand up and step back to look at it again. He's right: My desperate attack on the etching has revealed the rest of the horse's head, including a foot-long horn.

Riser comes up beside me. "When we started, there were men carved into the stone."

My heart skips a beat. "Describe them."

"One was leading a horse; the other carried a sword and shield. Otherwise, they appeared identical."

Identical. My brain is whirling so fast I can't complete a single thought.

"And," Riser continues, "the walls changed after a while to—"

"A dog?" I interrupt softly.

"Yes."

"Was it . . . um, I don't know, by a lake or an ocean, any type of water?"

His eyes narrow. "It was leaping out of a fountain. And then, toward the end, it burned in a funeral pyre."

"And it was small?"

"Yes."

"Canis Major and Canis Minor," I whisper. My breath comes out in excited puffs. Pushing past Riser, I fumble my way down the wall, counting the unicorns. Four. Depicting the four great stars, or canals, making up the constellation. Could it really be this simple?

"Merida!" I yell. I find her leaning on Rhydian, her eyes hooded and unfocused. I delicately lift her arm. Sweat and dirt burn my eyes, and I rub them, squinting at the crude map of sorts traced across her skin. Using my tongue, I wet my thumb and rub out the dangerous pathways and dead ends. I don't dare breathe as I follow the lines with my eyes. There, the tail, the legs. At the top, created with my blood, is the triangular path that doubled back on itself.

Not a triangle. The head. "Monoceros!"

Half of me thinks I'm mad with fear, conjuring fantasies from thin air.

The other half, though, the half that's kept me alive up until this point, that's whispered truths into my ear, is convinced I've finally figured out my mother's game.

CHAPTER THIRTY-SIX

The others are staring at me as if I've lost my mind. "Don't you see?" I shout, stabbing a finger at the sky. "It was right in front of us the entire time!" She has a cruel sense of humor, my mother. I lift Merida's arm. "Monoceros, the unicorn. And you," I point at Riser, "you started in the Gemini Constellation, the two brightest stars being Castor and Pollux. Right?" I can see by their confused expressions I'm not making sense. "They're twins, a horse trainer and a . . . a warrior."

"The dogs?" Riser asks, his brow furrowing.

"Between the Gemini Constellation and the Monoceros is Canis Minor. It's called Mera, I think, Icarus' water dog, who died to honor his master. And when Merida and I got lost, we ended up in Canis Major, dog of Orion." I inhale a deep breath. *I am talking too fast.* "That explains the river Merida and I saw. The ancient Egyptians used the Dog star to predict the Nile River's tides."

Silence. I look to Riser, begging him to believe me, but his lips are pressed into a thin, cryptic line.

"Can you get us out?"

"Do we have a choice?" Their wary faces tell me that was the wrong answer. "*Yes.*"

Rhydian squeezes Merida tighter. I can tell he wants to believe me but isn't convinced. He turns to Riser. "You trust her?"

Riser locks eyes with me, and I think of all the times he asked me to trust him and I failed. "With my life."

Rhydian nods, his shoulders slumping. "Okay, let's do it."

We need a new canvas for the map, so Riser strips off his coat and shirt. I begin tracing the Monoceros constellation on his back with my blood, starting at the base of his spine. His arms lift as my finger curves around his side, his muscles shivering beneath my fingertips. Satisfied with the unicorn, I mark the octagon-shaped center of the Orion Constellation in between his shoulder blades, working outward. The Bellatrix star, the star that begins Orion's arrow, goes at the base of Riser's neck. Then, lifting his hair, I continue the arrow to the dark hairline. Lastly, I run my bloody finger from just below one ear to the other for the curved bow.

"Orion and Monoceros," I say aloud, "should connect, I'm guessing . . . here." I smudge a bloody dotted line from the unicorn's second hoof to the M42 star, the Great Nebula of Orion, my finger slowly riding the hills of Riser's mid-spine.

Now that I'm done, I have a moment to step back and observe my plan. It's simple, daring, and a long shot. Judging by the fading stars and silvery light, we won't have time to correct it if I'm wrong.

Rhydian glares at my childish map. "So we just . . . follow the lines?"

"No," I say. "You follow me."

We walk fast, me in front and Riser and Rhydian on either side of Merida, helping her along. As soon as we pass the entrance with the bear, though, the walls close in so only two can fit at a time. On some unspoken command, we all begin to run, even Merida, who has somehow found enough energy to keep going.

Inside my head, I recreate the constellation. Up ahead will be the first test of my theory. If I'm correct, it will lead us to the second section of the maze, the Orion Constellation.

If I'm wrong, we die.

It doesn't take long to find out. Because of my lens, I notice the body before the others. I can tell he's dead by the way he lies: on his back, head tilted at an odd angle, foot resting against the wall. I must react somehow, because the others stop too.

"No!" I cry. I was so sure. This has to be the way. I scan Riser's back to double check, but I hardly look at it because I know I didn't make a mistake. This has to be it.

"Is that . . . a body?" Merida asks, trying hard to hide the disappointment in her voice.

"This is it." I jut out my chin. "I'm not wrong."

Rhydian's palm makes a dull *thwump* as it slaps the wall. "Because you couldn't possibly be wrong!"

"Not about this!"

Turning to Riser, I see he's staring into the tunnel. His eyes cut to me. "You say it's safe?"

"Yes."

"Okay."

Without another word, Riser enters the passage. My chest constricts as he bends over the body, examining something. After an eternity he straightens up.

"She's right!"

When we join him, I discover what he means. A circular, fingertip-sized hole gapes from the finalist's neck.

"The blade was small," Riser remarks. "A dirk or a stylet." *Or a push dagger hidden in a waistband.* He circles the body, touching the grass here and there. "He was taken by surprise by another finalist."

A chill runs through me. Only one name comes to mind. *Hugo Redgrave.*

Riser hops to his feet, I shoot Rhydian a defiant grin, and we resume our jogging pace. After a long, narrow tunnel, the passage forks. We stay left, passing what would be the Saiph star, Orion's foot. I run the plan through my head. Up, to the right, crossing Orion's belt. Left, straight up to the Bellatrix star. Out through Orion's arrow.

Out. It's finally a reality.

Out!

We are quiet. Buoyed on by the comforting concert of our feet striking the soft ground and our labored, hopeful breaths. After we pass a torch and the walls are illuminated, I see I was right. The form of a hunter, clad only in an armored battle skirt and golden centurion helmet, holds a bow and arrow, surrounded by hunting dogs. Seven doves fly away from the hunter, toward the sky, as if trying to escape him.

Orion and the Seven Pleiades.

Out! Everything is a daze now. Walls. Flickering flames. *Out!* Passageways strewn with bodies. *Out!* One of the entrances on the left harbors a body still sizzling with electricity, the smell indescribable.

Orion's belt turns out to be a long, convex tunnel. *Out!* I stop short at the next passageway, barely a crack wide enough for a child. "Turn sideways," I order. "And take off any extra clothing you can."

There's the sound of shedding clothes and then Riser's voice, calm in my ear. "Ready."

Rough stone rubs the skin from my cheeks, knuckles, and knees as I wedge myself in the tiny space. Merida goes next, her breath shallow and raspy with the effort.

"Almost there," I say, working to keep my excited voice calm.

As it turns out, I'm not lying. I don't see the passageway. Rather, I fall backward into it as the wall gives way. It's a bit wider than the previous tunnel, enough I can spread my arms a few inches from my thighs. Orion's Arrow. The shaft stretches straight out, thirty feet or so into what first appears to be darkness. I blink and the twinkling red fireflies come into view.

Torches.

Out!

Voices.

Out!

"Guys! We made it. Come look!"

Merida appears, a hesitant smile on her face. I laugh, relief trilling through me. *Out!*

Rhydian is next, and he too breaks into a smile. "Oh, thank the gods. Merida, look! We're safe. Do you see . . . ?"

Rhydian's smile dies.

Riser erupts behind Rhydian. "Go!" Riser is screaming. "Go! Go! *Run!*"

And then I hear it too.

The walls are closing.

CHAPTER THIRTY-SEVEN

I make it maybe two feet in when I realize our mistake. Facing forward we will be crushed. I pause to flatten sideways, parallel to the wall, and Merida slams into my shoulder, my head thudding against stone. When my eyes open, my world is suddenly dark and gray; my contact lens has come out.

It takes a moment for my eyes to again adjust. Once they do, though, there's enough light to make out the granules in the stone pressed into my face, which means Shadow Fall is almost over. The stone is wet, mossy. Slowly, so not to scrape my flesh, I turn my head back to check on the others.

It's worse than I imagined. Merida is wedged between the walls, facing forward, one arm caught above her head, the other trapped down by her side. The way her body is compacted and the angle of her arm tell me she has at least a few crushed bones. Her eyes gape wide, unblinking. Air whistles from her compressed lungs.

"Merida's stuck," I yell over Merida's head. "Can you move?"

"It's tight, but we can move," comes Riser's voice.

Okay, they can still move. Good. "Riser, I need you to put pressure on Merida's back. On the count of three."

With my left arm, I grab a fistful of Merida's jumper. "One! Two! Three!"

My shoulder screams as I yank uselessly, my arm threatening to pop out of socket again, Merida gurgling tiny, pitiful moans of pain.

Grunts escape my lungs as I jerk harder, rocking backward. She has to budge. We're so close. I promised!

She whimpers and I fall back, her charred blouse slipping from my fingers. I hear Riser, still pushing. Finally, his grunting stops and any hope I had left dissipates.

The wild, delirious look has faded from Merida's eyes. Now they are focused on me. I have to make myself look at her, because I want to look away, to hide the truth about her situation. But that would be cruel. "I'm sorry, Merida." My voice catches. "I don't know what else to do."

Her cracked, blackened lips part. "Tell Rhydian . . . I'm sorry."

"You tell him."

But we both know that won't happen. Groaning, Merida looks down. I understand immediately. The pill.

"No." But my gaze lingers on Merida's pocket where the pill hides as a little voice whispers, *we need the walls to open, and for that one of us has to die.*

A tear cuts a shiny path down her good cheek. She struggles to form a smile. "Like sleeping."

My choice is cruel but simple. Kill Merida and save the others, or let them all die. I want to refuse. To insist we keep trying. Merida is my friend, my sweet, kind, selfless friend. How can I execute her? I wrack my brain for another way, but there's no time. Maybe if Shadow Fall wasn't almost over, or if we weren't one death away from being crushed.

"I can't, Merida," I whisper. But even as I say these words, I know that I'll do it, I'll kill the only true friend I've ever had, and the relief I feel makes me sick to my stomach.

I give myself simple orders to make it through. *Get the pill, Everly. Put it in her mouth, Everly. Don't cry, Everly. Save the others, Everly. Kill your friend, Everly.*

I find the case, manage to get the poisoned pill out and into Merida's open mouth. Behind her, the muffled sound of Rhydian and Riser arguing grows louder.

"Merida!" Rhydian yells. "What's going on? Merida? Merida?" His voice cracks with desperation. "Merida, for Emperor's sake, talk to me!"

Tears drip from her chin as she ignores him. "I was brave, wasn't I, Everly?"

"Yes."

She swallows the pill and smiles. "Tell me . . . a . . . story."

My throat aches with unshed tears. I think of all the times I held Max and told him stories when he couldn't sleep. *It's just like that,* I tell myself. *You're helping her rest.*

"Have you heard the story of Iphigenia?" I clear the agony from my voice as I try to remember my favorite tale. "Iphigenia was the beloved daughter of Agamemnon, the King of Argos. This was during the Trojan War, and the entire Greek shipping fleet was stuck in the ocean without any winds. To move their ships, Artemis required Agamemnon to sacrifice Iphigenia. Although it broke his heart, Agamemnon called Iphigenia home under the pretense of marriage to Achilles—do you know who he is?"

Merida's breathing has slowed, but her eyelids flutter and I pretend it's a yes.

"Of course, she was overjoyed to be marrying Achilles, renowned for his courage and good-looks, so when she got to the altar and discovered her father's treachery, she was devastated"—I swallow down a sob—"but instead of . . . of pleading for her life, she did something very, very brave, just like you."

Merida's eyes are rolling erratically.

"You see, she sacrificed herself to help her people, and when Artemis saw her selflessness and courage, she spared her life and allowed her to go *free.*"

The sound of Rhydian screaming Merida's name fades beneath the noise of the gears inside the walls turning. Merida's eyes are half open, resting just behind me.

I guess in her own way she's free now too.

The walls growl open, releasing my torso enough so I can turn. Riser catches Merida's lifeless body before she can slump to the ground, and I slip an arm under her knees, walking backward toward the exit.

We carry my dead friend out to the sound of cheers.

The sun has broken through, and it warms my cheek. Over my shoulder I spot Caspian, his eyes unreadable as they trail my many injuries before landing on Merida. Finalists and mentors whoop and stomp their feet and call out our names from underneath the pavilion as the Emperor shoots us a bored glance. That's when I see the rift screens. They must have watched us scrambling for our lives.

We carry Merida past the vanguard of Centurions and Chosen, past the other lucky finalists. There is a nice spot in the grass we lay her on. Riser gently closes her eyelids while I arrange her ripped jumpsuit the best I can.

I wonder if, like me, Riser busies himself with Merida partially so he can gain control of his anger. One look at his tight jaw, the rage smoldering below his flat gaze, and I know I'm right. Perhaps he also saw the rift screens and it was too much. The idea of them watching us suffer and die gruesomely, clapping each other on the shoulders with hands greasy from the rich table of food spread in front of them. Did they applaud when I fed Merida the poison? When I killed the only person I'd ever come close to calling a friend?

A shadow falls over me. Caspian. His lips form a hollow smile as he limply holds out a thick wreath of black and white roses—his House colors. Some of the other surviving finalists wear their mentor's colors around their necks, so I assume I'm supposed to as well. But I'm not in the mood for flowers or hollow smiles and turn away from him.

Rhydian joins us. His arms hang by his sides, his cheeks shiny with tears. He's not crying now though. Like us, his emotions have become something else. Something dangerous. I move over so he can kneel, and he begins combing out what's left of her hair with his fingers.

Rhydian has just finished wiping the grime from her cheek when they come for us. My mother leads, flanked by Delphine. Caspian's tight frown tells me it's not simply a friendly, congratulatory visit. That I should probably play nice.

Unfortunately I'm incapable of that right now.

Stopping a few feet from us, my mother ignores Merida while we stand, flagrantly breaking protocol by not bowing.

"Your devotion is remarkable," my mother states, ignoring our disobedience. "One can never tell about these things. I just watched siblings and friends kill each other to live without a second thought. But not you three."

I struggle to determine what she's playing at. From the corner of my eye, I make out Riser's expression, a potent mix of contempt and disrespect. I hope for his sake he doesn't confuse my mother's calm, detached demeanor with weakness.

Riser's contempt grows only more obvious as she focuses her attention on him, ordering him to turn so she can examine his back. He hesitates, longer than he should, before complying. Her lips twitch at his insolence.

Slowly, my mother's sharp eyes trace the lines mapping his back.

"Clever, Lady March," she says without looking up.

"Dumb luck," I insist.

"Hmm." Her steely gaze casts my way. "I am beginning to think you are the luckiest girl in all the world."

Turning to Rhydian, she says, "Lord Pope, my condolences on the loss of Lady Pope. She was very brave and very selfless, and surely now the shadow of shame has fallen from House Pope once and for all." Again she looks to me. "Unfortunate, indeed, I am not Artemis to grant her a reprieve from such a fate."

Just like you left me to my fate, Mother? I swallow down the words I want to lob like daggers, and I smile coolly when I want to howl with rage.

Do you see what I am? What you made me?

The first hint something else is going on comes from Delphine. She fidgets, a gleeful, almost giddy expression twisting her face. It doesn't take long to discover why. Two Centurions arrive and box me in—in case, I suppose, I plan to fight, which is still undecided.

My mother nods to Delphine, who produces a small silver flashlight-looking instrument. I blink as the beam flicks over my eyes.

"Hold her eyes open," Delphine growls.

I instinctively flinch against the Centurions thick, brutish fingers.

Delphine releases a disappointed huff.

"Nothing, Countess Bloodwood," my mother says. It's impossible to determine if she's pleased or disappointed. Through a haze of starry red dots, I see my mother smile. "Once again, Lady March, the gods favor you."

As soon as my mother takes her leave, Delphine turns on me. "There's no way a worm like you survives the trials without cheating."

"Prove it!" I spit back.

Her pale eyes go cold. "One of these days you'll talk your head off your shoulders and onto a pike." Before I can react, one of Delphine's exquisite, steel-tipped boots rears back and brings its full force into Merida's torso. "The same goes for any worm stupid enough to befriend you."

"Delphine," Caspian says carefully, his fingers pressing into her arm, "you should take care not to seem rude, as I would hate for anyone to think ill of my betrothed."

Pushing off the tips of her boots, she nuzzles his ear. "And you should take care, my beloved, to remember they are little worms to be stomped beneath my boots if it so pleases me." Her eyes cut to me. "And right now it pleases me."

Before I know what I'm doing, my hand has hold of the foxtail Aigrette and is sliding it from my hair. *Between the fifth and the sixth intercostal . . .*

But for once in his life, Pit Boy isn't in a murdering mood, and his fingers lightly brush the nape of my neck, jolting me from my wild revenge fantasy. *Patience,* they seem to say. *We will have our day.*

Caspian narrows his eyes and looks at Riser's hand, lips tucked into a frown. "But then, my dear, you would remind Baroness Graystone why she banned you from the council . . . twice now, is it?" Turning his head, he presses his lips lightly onto Delphine's cheek. "I might find your impetuousness charming, but not everyone shares my taste."

There's a tense pause as we wait to see what will happen. "Whatever," Delphine finally says. "It's hot and I'm thirsty." She gestures to the Centurions waiting in the background. "Take this decaying worm and dump it over the wall with the other worms before it starts to reek."

That's twice now, I think, *Caspian has somehow reined her in with clever words.* But what happens when the day comes he can no longer control her? What sort of madness will she wreak?

Caspian holds up his hand and the Centurions halt, confusion in their eyes. "Give the finalists five minutes to mourn their dead, then you may take her."

"Thank you, my Liege." I keep my words impersonal lest they stir up another demon inside Delphine, but thankfully she prances off without a look back.

Before Caspian leaves, he kneels down and lays the wreath of flowers on Merida's chest. His gaze finds me. "I'm sorry she died, Everly. Truly."

Riser is the first to say goodbye. Staring down at Merida with his typical enigmatic gaze, he nods to her, somehow speaking in his silence more than I ever seem to say with my voice.

Rhydian is next. Hesitant, he kneels over her for a moment, seemingly lost, and then his lips form the words, "I forgive you," his forehead resting against hers for a brief second.

There's a murmur, and I turn in surprise to see the other finalists walking toward us. Some burned, others bloody and bruised, their faces haunted by the horrors my mother constructed. One by one, each finalist gets down on their knees and places a kiss on Merida's forehead. It's done without ceremony or speech, a seemingly impulsive and harmless act.

But we all know otherwise.

I am the last. Hard as I try, I cannot think of what to say. This isn't Merida; I know that. The real one, my *friend*, died in the labyrinth, seconds from safety. And it's not fair. She didn't get the chance I got, being made into someone stronger, smarter, braver. She was terrified from the beginning, and yet she still found a way to overcome it. All *I* did was cheat. Maybe Delphine's right. Someone like me, even with all my enhancements, could never win without rigging the game. I couldn't even save my friend, so how in the world am I supposed to make it to the end of this hell and find the Mercurian? I failed Merida, I failed Max, and I'm going to fail my father.

"I should have saved you," I say. I lean down and kiss the unburned side of her forehead, my lips dancing over cool, mottled flesh. "But I promise I'll make it right somehow."

As I glance over and see the Emperor watching me, a jeweled chalice in his hand and gloating smile on his face, I know this time I'll keep that promise—or die trying.

CHAPTER THIRTY-EIGHT

We make it to our apartments just before sunset. Flame, who watched the first trial with the other attendants and servants on a rift screen in the great hall, helps me wrestle out of my muddy, charred clothes. Too tired for a bath, I sit Indian-style on the bed, cradling Bramble, head bobbing, not asleep but not really awake as Flame wipes the grime and gore of the last four hours from my achy body.

I smell like fire. I smell like death. I want to die. Or sleep. I want to peel out of my skin, wipe the dirtiness from my soul, and stop seeing Merida pinned and broken.

I shiver, cold emanating from some deep, unreachable part of me, and let my mind go . . .

Flame is nudging me. It takes a few times for her sentence to get through. "Nicolai has something for you."

She is holding out her hand.

The Interceptor fits neatly in my palm. Shaped like a button, this tiny device is the portable version, easier to hide. I push it and watch the bluish hologram solidify into a four-dimensional shape above it. The adolescent boy blinks at me, gives an awkward grin, his large blue eyes crinkling. His shoulder-length strawberry-blond hair is pulled neatly back in the traditional Royalist style.

"Um . . . ?" He laughs nervously and looks at someone I cannot see. "Should I just, say anything?" He nods to the unseen person and looks back at me, his voice cracking with pubescence. "Okay, uh, here goes."

And I know, I just know. "They say you're my sister, Maia?"

The only sound I can hear, as his lips form what has to be more words, is my choking breath. Blood rushes inside my skull. Like water. Like angry, raging water.

Like drowning.

How can I talk to Max when the girl he thinks I am is dead? When I just killed my friend, and soon I'm going to have to murder the Emperor? If my brother knows what I am now, he'll hate me, and I can't lose him again.

Through my constricting vision, I see my hand reach out. See the hologram disrupt into a thousand tiny pixels as the Interceptor smashes against the wall.

Blackness. I'm in the hallway on my hands and knees. I'm no longer in the labyrinth, no longer in the tunnels in the pit, but the walls are crushing me just the same. If I could cry, scream out, if I could see the walls and bloody my fists against them, maybe I could get rid of this trapped, dying feeling. A different kind of Doom. The kind you can't reconstruct away. The kind you can't hide from.

I curl on my side and stare at the black roses on the carpet runner. My eyes ache to shed tears, but Lady March refuses. It comes to me I don't know who I am anymore. That I'm some faceless, shifting creature, a tangled cluster of programmed emotions and thoughts and actions, cobbled together by manipulators like my mother and Nicolai to serve their purposes.

If anything, Max needs to be protected from *me*, this creature of theirs.

Nervous beeping, as Bramble tentatively approaches. He's shivering. *He doesn't recognize me anymore.*

"Get away!" I scream, kicking at him. "Go, stupid machine! She's gone!" Covering my mouth with my arm, I wail, watching through blurry, unshed tears as Bramble scurries away. It's only when I stop I taste the blood and realize I have bitten through my flesh.

After a bit, I notice Flame watching me from the doorway. "Come inside, Princess."

I return to the apartment and sit back on the bed.

She holds up the Interceptor. "Want to try again?"

I shake my head.

"Good." Flame says this as if I've passed some test. She opens the wardrobe. "Let's get you dressed."

"For what?"

"The mandatory celebration."

My chin juts out. "I'm not going."

"Yes you are, Princess." She sits on the edge of the bed and pins me with her stern gaze. "You are going to get up, get dressed, and stop feeling sorry for yourself."

I snort. "And why in Fienian hell would I do that?"

"Because the Emperor has decided to join the court for the celebration tonight, and we're going to kill him."

The stars are out, the moon a big, beautiful ivory disc that carves the midnight sky. A light wind funnels through the portico I lean against. I wrap the cloak Caspian gave me tighter around my body, shivering against the heavy, aching cold gripping me. The gown I wear—to fit in with the revelers—offers little protection from the chill. Its glorious sunset-red color looks almost black under the stars, Brinley's brooch bright against it. According to Rhydian, it was the dress Merida planned to wear at the Final Feast, if she made it to the end.

Red, the color of uprising. It was her own gentle form of rebellion.

I tell myself she would've agreed with what we're doing now. But somewhere deep down, I know that's just another lie like all the others.

My gaze picks through the shadows. Riser is out there somewhere scouting the terrain while Cage gathers finalists he assures me are sympathetic to the cause. And Flame, well Flame and her two bulging black backpacks are out doing something rather Fienian-ish.

The bombs she's going to place in the fountain, to go off during the celebration, will be small, meant to distract the crowd just long enough for one of us to get to the Emperor. She assured me no one else would get hurt. Somehow I don't believe her, but I don't have much of a choice.

I should be focusing on how I'm going to be the one to kill the Emperor, but my mind keeps unhelpfully retrieving images of the nano-shredders. Surely Flame wouldn't use those tonight? Not when there are innocent people who can be hurt?

Focus on the plan. The Emperor will be surrounded by the Royal Guard. How will you get to him? And, more importantly, once you do kill him, how will you use the diversion to find the Mercurian?

Noises break my thoughts. I bend my head to listen, but it's only the sound of finalists talking loudly in one of the apartment windows above us as they prepare for the midnight celebration.

I shift impatiently and then force myself to sit on the steps. Where are the others? And Brogue, is he even up to this? The pungent, sweet almond smell from the Centurions' barracks where he stays still clings to my clothing. After I got dressed, I was sent to fetch him. I found him prostrate on the floor in a puddle of tarry vomit and worse, and even after I slapped his cheek, the bristle of his beard soggy with puke, his eyes were hardly more than slits.

I don't remember feeling any emotion, but all at once I had his limp head cradled in my lap, wiping his face. Moaning, his all-pupil eyes blinked open at me. My kneejerk reaction was to pummel his chest, yelling, "Stupid twitcher!" over and over until he rolled over, made a string of unintelligible rants, and hacked up bloody clots of sour-smelling bile.

I knew he was going to be okay when he began speaking real words.

"Forgith me," he muttered, gummy strings of saliva dancing from his lips.

"It's up for debate," I said, moving to help him up.

But I knew he was somewhere else when he said: "I didn't want to. By the gods, I looked . . . looked for another way."

"Okay, Merc," I said, struggling to pull him to a stand. My efforts were thwarted as he flopped to his knees and leaned over, dry heaving, his straining neck bright tomato red.

Done, he stretched, belched, and smashed his thumbs into his eyes. "It was Lil . . . Lillian," he said, swaying. "She said . . . only way . . ."

I froze, thinking I had misheard him say my mother's name, until he said, "Oh God, Lillian, what did we do?"

Filing that away for later, I busied myself with the plan. It took thirty more minutes for him to sober up enough so I could go over it with him. His task was to break into the armory and procure weapons. Flame had a long list on a scrap of paper he took.

For a man just learning of such an audacious plan mere minutes after being peeled off the floor, he seemed relatively calm. He cleaned up as best he could, slapped on his boots, and threw a sloppy wink in my direction. "I'll get you your weapons, girl, but I suspect all the weapons in the world won't help us now."

All in all, not very convincing.

Now, I'm still worrying over our plan and thinking about Brogue when Riser shows up. Resolving from the shadows, his eyes rest on me, drinking me in for a moment.

I can't help but do the same. Flame has him dressed for the ceremony, and starlight swims along his inky-blue hair pulled back by a midnight-blue ribbon to match the ribbons on his pale leather doublet. He wears a long sword and a piercing grin.

Something inside me stirs, an ache that fills my bones.

Inhaling deeply, he settles down next to me. "Centurions patrol the fountain every forty minutes."

Awkward silence. I know if I look at him now, with his breath tickling my face, his thigh warming mine, I won't be able to control my feelings, and the thought paralyzes me.

Two fingers hook my jaw, guiding my eyes to his.

"What?" I whisper, tactful as always.

He smiles again, softly, revealing the chipped tooth I noticed what seems like years ago. "Why won't you look at me?"

I blink under his unflinching gaze. How can I explain how I feel? How the deeper I fall for him, the more vulnerable I become? "Tell me this is real, Riser, because I can't stand one more lie."

He pauses for a moment, as if struggling to put his thoughts into words. "I'm not good at this, either. In the pit, you might be . . . attracted to someone, but you didn't care about them, and you didn't worry if they cared about you too; you simply took what you wanted."

I snort. "That's romantic."

"What I'm trying to say is"—he clears his throat—"it's not rational, but I care about you." The pad of his thumb carves the hollow of my collarbone. "And if you feel the same way, then it's real."

"But—"

His lips part mine. The kiss is quick, hungry. The way you kiss someone when you think you'll never see them again. Hot fingertips push into the base of my neck, press me deep into him, his hands slowly exploring a path down the exposed skin of my back.

"You can't say *this* isn't real," Riser murmurs, his breath hot on my lips.

I pull away, breathless, my lower lip tender and tingling. From my reconstructed memories, I remember the way the other boys kissed Lady March. Soft, sweet, hesitant kisses.

Riser's affections are nothing at all like that.

Looking at Riser's face, the emotions smoldering inside his eyes, there's still a part of me that's scared of him, the murderous boy from the pit. "I need to know if you're the one who tied me up in the pit."

He hesitates. "Yes."

"And you were going to . . . to let me die?"

Hurt flashes in his eyes. "Remember how you escaped?"

"Yes, of course. I slipped out of my bonds."

"Everly, do you really think I don't know how to tie a secure knot?"

The realization makes me gasp. "You helped me escape? But what about Ripper? Surely she would have known." I pause as he absentmindedly runs his finger over the brow bone above his new green eye. "Ripper took your eye . . . because of me?"

He grins. "And it was worth it."

"Why? Why help me?"

For the first time since we sat down, he looks away from me. "I was seven when they threw us in the pit. My mother didn't belong there; she was too bright, too good." He rakes a hand through his hair. "They attacked while we slept, and I"—his voice catches—"I fled while she fought them. I think by helping you, I thought I could somehow make up for abandoning her to die."

"Oh, Riser, I'm—"

"No." Two fingers press against my lips, halting my apology. "You were right to be wary of me. In the pit, something dark happened to me that a thousand Reconstructors couldn't erase." The backs of his fingers graze my cheek. "But I meant it when I said I would never hurt you. You're the only thing that makes me want to be better."

I shiver as his eyes anchor to mine: one light, one dark, a mirror of his conflicted soul.

"Which is why you must be careful tonight, because I cannot, I *will not* lose you like I did her."

"Okay." Dazed, I nod, lips still burning from our kiss, head swimming with questions Lady March won't dare let me ignore. What could the Fienians be up to? Who will get to the Emperor first? How will I find the Mercurian? And the most heartbreaking question of all: Could Riser be doing all of this just to catch me off guard so he can be the one to kill the Emperor? Would Riser go that far? Or are his emotions real?

Is this real?

I stand and gaze out at the shadows, working to pick through my emotions so I can understand what I'm feeling. "Brogue hasn't showed up."

Riser gets to his feet. "He will."

I swallow and force Riser, his words, and our kiss from my mind. I need to focus. I need . . . no, I *have* to find where the Mercurian's located and somehow manage to operate it. I wish I didn't have to find it alone, but Everly March refuses to trust anyone, even Riser.

Especially Riser.

The others arrive, and a quick head count checks off Rhydian, Laurel, Blaise, Cage, and Flame. Only Teagan and Brogue are missing. I frown, worried, but things are moving too fast to dwell on their absence.

We cut through the grass, skirting a wide path around the gardens to the backside of the lake. The sound of crickets and frogs echo off the shadowy forest behind us. Dirt escapes our feet and tumbles down the embankment, plopping into the water. The stars reflected in the water quiver, angry fairies disturbed from their rest.

My heart is racing. It feels good, as if every frantic beat of my heart is flushing out the poison from the last couple of days. We halt. The palace rises on the other side of the fountain. Warm light pours through the windows, and music and voices drift across the water. The balconies throng with Chosen couples dancing and laughing, their voices drunk and free.

Soon the celebration will move outside to the fountain as they await the winners' display. The bombs should be in place by then, and we can disappear into the crowd. My mouth goes dry as I imagine what will happen. How I will have to find a way to get close to the Emperor. And then . . . and then . . . My fingers slip around the cold handle of the knife sheathed inside my bodice. *No second thoughts, Everly. This is your only chance to get Max to safety.*

But part of me hesitates. This feels wrong. The bombing. The secretiveness. And what happens to the Mercurian if we fail? My father died for it. I have to find it. I have to.

"All right, Princess," Flame says, coming up beside me. "We're ready. Now where's the Merc?"

A twig snaps in the woods, and we turn to see a broad shape coming toward us. Brogue has regained his quick, stealthy gait, any evidence of his previous state gone. "Missed you too, little minx."

Flame eyes the giant duffel bag strapped to his back. "Any trouble getting them?"

He chuckles. "Depends on how you define the word. But they won't be missing them for a while, if that's your gist."

My eyes rivet to the bag weighing him down. Why would we need so many weapons? Brogue turns to me as if to say something, then he freezes. His hand goes for the revolver tucked into his belt just as I hear it: a startled neigh, followed by enraged nickering and branches breaking.

My eyes search out Riser as a sinking feeling comes over me, but he's nowhere to be found.

I know the beast is Poseidon the instant he emerges from the trees, jumpy and snorting, his muscles trembling beneath moon-shimmered flesh. Caspian sits atop him, his hands held in the air, face dark with the righteous anger of a prince not used to being detained. A second later, Riser follows, the sword he holds gleaming softly. Caspian's empty scabbard hangs from his belt.

"He was following us," Riser states, easily ducking an errant kick from Poseidon.

"Well," Caspian amends, glancing at me, "to be clear, I was following her."

The others exchange looks. This is obviously an unfortunate twist in the plan. The only one not upset by the turn in events is Flame. In fact, the wolfish grin she wears makes me think of the hyena from the maze right before it attacked.

"Evening, Prince," Flame purrs, taking Poseidon's reins while Riser moves to the front, his sword still trained on Caspian.

Riser nudges the air with the blade. "Dismount."

Ignoring Riser, Caspian casts his arrogant gaze on me. "No, I think I won't."

Coming up behind Caspian, Flame cuts off a piece of Poseidon's reins, and with the help of Riser, forces his arms back, binding his wrists.

"Do it, little prince," Flame commands.

Caspian, who does not look amused at her tone, narrows his eyes at me. "Is this who you are, Lady March? A Fienian terrorist?"

"Get down," I say, emotionless, but my heart is screaming.

"You know what they will do to me."

I blink away hot tears. Caspian, the boy who drew me. The boy who didn't care that I was different, that I was ugly. I know what we have to do, because there's no other way. He's seen our faces. If we let him go, we all die. And I can't let Max down. Not again. Not even for someone whose DNA says I'm supposed to love him.

Sighing, he swings one long leg over the saddle, his boots crunching the grass. His shoulders bulge as he strains against his binds, but Flame knows her stuff, and they refuse to budge. Poseidon, sensing his master's distress, wildly swings his huge head as his rear legs punch holes in the air. The others scatter, but Flame somehow manages to hold onto his reins.

While she works to get Poseidon under control, Rhydian searches Caspian.

At one point, Caspian says, "I'm sorry about your sister, Merida."

Rhydian ignores Caspian. After Rhydian is done searching, he leans down and spits at Caspian's feet. I want to say something, to comfort Caspian, but it's probably best if we don't talk at all. There's not much I could say now in the way of comfort, anyway, and by this point he probably hates me.

I gasp as static suddenly buzzes inside my skull. Words float in and out, too far away to hear at first. Then it becomes clearer. It's easy to decipher the voices as Nicolai and Flame.

Will she go through with it? Nicolai asks.

Yes, Flame replies. *I think she's ready.*

Good. He wasn't supposed to die until tonight, but now is even better.

It might break her. Flame's voice is unusually hesitant.

She's already broken.

And that's when I know they are talking about me. The voices fade. Whatever glitch allowed me to glean their conversation has been resolved.

I watch Flame whispering with Cage, a small knot forming in my stomach as things start to come together. The large cache of guns; the nano-shredders; the conversation I just heard.

What aren't they telling us?

But there's no way to stop this now, whatever they have planned. Not without jeopardizing Max's future and finding the Mercurian. So I take a deep breath and try to act normal as Cage approaches me.

"You have one final test." He nods to Caspian.

Riser hands me Caspian's sword. The same euphoric feeling I get every time I hold a blade settles in my bones as I glance over the ornate golden hilt, my fingers tracing the ruby-inlaid phoenix on the pommel.

Brogue leans into me; his thick fingers guide my hand around the grip. "Just like we practiced."

The rest hesitate for a moment and then separate, Flame and Rhydian making off to the boats while the others follow Brogue. Riser cuts his worried gaze at me before shadowing the others. Flame is whistling a Fienian tune.

Dandy Apples, Dandy Apples, smell like roses in the fall.

When they're swingin' and they're screamin',

Ain't they the dandiest sight of all?

"I thought you were different," Caspian says, the fight leaving his eyes. "I thought—"

"You could have saved them." My voice sounds robotic. "Brinley. Merida. The others."

He shakes his head. "And you think this, whatever you are doing, is what Merida would have wanted?"

"Don't talk like you knew her!" But his words wriggle under my skin as I remember my promise to her about making things right. Is that what I'm doing?

"It's true. I didn't know her well, but I would have liked to. Not everyone in court thinks as my father does." Defeat glimmers his eyes as they settle on me. "Just promise me you won't hurt my horse."

His concern for Poseidon cuts me to the bone. "I promise."

I startle as Caspian covers the few feet between us, my sweaty hand clenching the sword grip. "Then what are you waiting for, Lady March?"

In between the fifth and the sixth intercostal. It's hardwired into my brain now. All I have to do is think it and the message will instantaneously zip down my nerves, activating the right muscles that will plunge the blade into his heart.

I point the sword at his chest, the tip cutting into his leather jerkin. My fingers itch.

Do it.

I can't.

You must.

No.

Something inside me snaps, and I am circling around him. My hand touches his shoulder, and my breath spills out, and I bring the sword down.

CHAPTER THIRTY-NINE

The leather strap binding his wrists falls to the ground, and his arms spring free. Caspian lets out a trembling breath. "Why are you releasing me?"

"Oh, you mean other than the fact I'm apparently the queen of stupid decisions?" I smile sadly. "You're right, Merida wouldn't want this."

"You know I have to warn the Royal Guard—"

"No, you don't." I close the distance between us, until I'm close enough to feel his breath on my face. My heart pounds in my chest. By letting him live I'm risking everything—and I'm about to take an even bigger risk. Wetting my thumb with my tongue, I scrub my cheeks, revealing my freckles. "Do you remember me now, Prince Caspian?"

Caspian's breathing quickens as he looks from one cheek to the other. "But you're . . . *she's* . . . dead."

"Then I'm an apparition because it's me, Maia, the Bronze girl who wrote that silly poem and thought we would get married and life would be perfect."

It's true, I realize. That's who I've chosen to be. Maia.

"You're lying." His lips purse skeptically, but there's something there, in his eyes. He *wants* to believe me.

"What if I told you there's a way to stop the asteroid? That my father created a device that could knock it off course, that he hid that device here on the Island before your father murdered him because of it?"

Caspian's beautiful golden eyes widen, his lips parted in surprise. "But that would mean . . ."

"No one has to die. If I can find it—if you *help* me find it—we can save them, and no more finalists have to suffer."

"The others with you know about this? That's what they're doing?"

"No—it's complicated." I clear my throat. "But they're not here to hurt anyone." I'm astounded at how easily the lie pours from my lips. But I'm hoping somehow I can get to the Sim and find out the Mercurian's location before the bombs Flame planted go off.

Maybe, just maybe if I can convince the others there's a way to stop the asteroid, maybe no one has to get hurt. Maybe it's not a lie. *Maybe.* But everything hinges on Caspian.

As the sound of the revelers from the palace trickle across the lake, Caspian's eyes search my face. "You're asking me to trust you, a girl I barely knew years ago. To put the fate of the empire in your hands."

"It's already in my hands, Caspian, whether you're willing to admit it or not. I can be the change deep down in your heart you know the empire needs—but only if you help me."

Our eyes lock, and I will him to believe me. *Please, Caspian. We're running out of time.*

He swallows, massages the blond stubble curving his jaw, and lets out a breath. "Okay, what do I need to do?"

My body goes slack with relief. "Tell me where to find the Sim."

"I'll do better than that, Lady March. I'll take you there."

Terror. Excitement. Hope. All these conflicting emotions reverberate inside me as I mount Poseidon, Caspian right behind me, his body warm and tight and protective, Poseidon exploding beneath us.

We pierce the woods. Caspian must sense my urgency because Poseidon tears through the wispy, crooked path. With Caspian locked onto me, our bodies draped low to avoid the scraping branches, his chin cradling my neck, it feels as if we are one creature, rising and falling together, hearts in tandem. The smell of horse sweat and damp foliage fill my nostrils. A branch rips at my dress and I cry out, but Caspian clings to me, using his entire body to hold me steady, keep me safe.

Part of me hates how good this feels, Caspian and me, how right, because it stands in direct opposition to my feelings for Riser; but the other part knows this is how it was always supposed to be. Maia and Caspian.

It was fated in the stars, in our DNA.

Branches, leaves, bits of sky, they jumble together as my hope blossoms. Stars stretch the horizon, the green valley unfurling beneath Poseidon's hooves. Tears sting my eyes. This isn't some trick; Caspian is really taking me to the Sim. My father will tell me where to find the Mercurian, and there won't have to be any bombings, or trials. The Sleepers can wake up. No one has to execute the Emperor. No one else has to get hurt.

Everything my father wanted, everything he *died* for is finally coming to pass. And Max will be safe.

I'm coming, Daddy. My body aches from the maze, Poseidon's violent gate jostling my bones, but I feel so light, as if Caspian's embrace is the only thing keeping me from floating away.

Caspian's lips whisper right next to my ear, "Almost there."

The marshlands. Poseidon's hooves kick up sprays of water, and I close my eyes. *I'm coming, Daddy.* The lake shimmers in the distance. Caspian spurs Poseidon into a furious gallop, and we seem to be gliding over the water, reeds whipping my legs.

I'm coming, Daddy.

The shoreline. My boots hit the ground before Poseidon can make a full stop. Brackish water weighs down the hem of my skirt, and I lift it to my calves, my boots sinking in mud. There, just before the beginning of Penumbria Forest, the stairs that must lead down below, beneath the lake. That's where my father hid the Sim.

Poseidon rears, ears flattened as he knickers nervously.

"Wait—" Caspian orders, tugging the reins as he works to calm Poseidon.

But I only half hear him.

I'm coming.

My boots churn the sand. And it's like one of those horrible dreams where no matter how hard I try, I can hardly move.

"Wait, Everly!" I hear Caspian dismount behind me.

Daddy . . . Tears stream down my cheeks, melt my vision. The opening to the stairs yawns wide. *Daddy!*

And then, for some reason, I stop. Every nerve fiber in my body screams something is wrong.

Terribly, terribly wrong.

The shadow that stirs from the stairwell is tall and slender, like an arrow. I see my hand is holding the dagger from my bodice, the one meant for the Emperor, although I don't remember grabbing it.

"Move!" I shout, desperation cracking my voice.

The slender shadow laughs. A twang and the sand at my feet explodes. My eyes find the black-feathered arrow still twitching. The kind the Gold Cloaks use.

Caspian betrayed me.

But, no, he is unsheathing his sword, his eyes glinting with rage. Dark shadows spill from the trees, their gold cloaks swirling around them. They hold golden crossbows, the sabers at their waists glinting. They encircle Caspian, making hardly a sound.

Moonlight twinkles along Caspian's sword as he raises it, pivoting round and round to fix each one with an arrogant, murderous glare. The lifted corner of his mouth tells me some part of him actually enjoys this. "I take it you know who I am, so you know I mean what I say. Anyone that leaves now will be pardoned."

In answer, the Gold Cloaks trade their crossbows for sabers.

Caspian shrugs, running his fingertip over the razor-sharp edge of his sword. "Have it your way."

The shadow laughs again. "Disarm the Prince," she orders the Guard. "Remember, the Emperor doesn't want his firstborn son seriously injured, but a few cuts and bruises might do the royal brat some good."

I turn away, cringing at the metal-on-metal sound of swords clashing. Caspian may take out a few, but not enough to matter.

The shadow removes the hood of her cloak. Although I already know who it is, my knees hit the sand, the dagger slipping through my fingers. Every bit of hope I have bleeds from me, replaced by fear.

"Oh dear," says the Archduchess. "Someone's not happy to see me."

CHAPTER FORTY

The horse that carries me to my death shifts sideways, trying to dislodge me. My bound hands grip the saddle pommel, and I squeeze my thighs to stay mounted. I've heard somewhere animals can feel your fear.

Surely this horse feels mine.

The Archduchess sits tall and erect on the black horse in front of me. How proud she must be feeling. After all this time searching, she can finally present me to the Emperor, a gift with a shiny Bronze bow on top. At least they don't have Max. Not that it matters now. Because of my choice, he's going to perish on D-Day, knowing I failed him.

I crane my neck, searching for Caspian, but the Archduchess yanks the rope connected to my bonds and I fall forward, almost toppling from my horse. Caspian is the only hope I have now. Surely he won't just let them kill me.

Surely he'll do *something*.

The revelers already pack the lawn around the fountain, their happy, drunk voices stirring the air. No one notices me, a girl bound and hidden beneath a cloak, in the middle of ten Gold Cloaks. *They must be really drunk.*

We dismount. More Golds pack the castle. Torches line the hallways, and I count each one, thinking maybe if I concentrate on something, I can ease the fear that vices my chest and makes it impossible to breathe.

Massive marble doors part, and I'm led into the throne room. My breath catches at the sight of the Emperor. His silky purple-and-green damask robe slithers along the tile as he approaches. He is smiling.

"Hello, Maia." His voice is conversational, almost friendly. He waves the Royal Guard away. They retreat to the four corners of the room, their sharp eyes riveted to me. "I see you have been reconstructed into one of us." I flinch as he runs a finger over my cheek. "But we both know beneath that layer of perfect flesh, you're still a worm."

My spit makes a shiny splatter over his nose and left cheek, a glob hanging from his eyebrow. The floor squeaks as the Gold Cloaks move toward me in unison, but the Emperor holds up a hand.

At least he's no longer smiling.

The Archduchess makes a strange squeal of horror. Then she's flitting over the Emperor, wiping desperately at his face with the hem of her cloak, her breathing ragged. He tries to push her away, but she persists, rubbing the dark silk in tiny, sacrosanct circles over his flesh, as if she's polishing precious silver. The sight is so bizarre I can't look away, despite the revulsion their strange intimacy gives me.

"Enough," the Emperor growls.

As she backs away, her eyes fall on me and I know I'll pay for my insolence.

The Emperor clears his throat, holding out his white-gloved hand. "Shall we, Maia?"

When I hesitate, the Archduchess hits me in the back, and I stumble forward. His hand captures mine. The Archduchess takes his other arm, and he leads us out onto the huge balcony, the Royal Guard shadowing, to the sound of roaring cheers.

For the first time since Caspian helped me onto his horse, I think about the others. Have they already been captured? Is that how the Emperor knew where to find me? My eyes scour the fountain for any signs, but it's too far away, and Flame would have hid the bombs anyway. The crowd? But it's impossible to make out anyone in that dense mob.

Another punch to the back forces me to the railing. Why am I here and not in a cell? I find the stars, twinkling bits of glass, and suddenly, more than anything in the world, I want my mother. Is she here somewhere?

"Looking for someone, dear?" the Emperor asks.

I grit my teeth and stare at my hands.

The Archduchess's long fingernails gouge my chin as she forces me to look at the fountain. "Watch, worm. It's about to begin."

I wriggle my head from her claws. "You can't force me to watch the show."

The Archduchess and the Emperor both chuckle at the same time, as if they share some private joke.

They know. Somehow, *somehow* they know. My eyes fall over the tight mass of people circling the water, so close to the bomb. Too close. Why aren't they warning them?

"Order them back, away from the fountain," I say.

Folding his arms behind his back, the Emperor gazes out over the lawn. "Did you know I held pieces of my daughter in my palm? The most precious thing in my life reduced to jagged, oozing chunks of meat and bone." When he turns to me, his eyes are shiny and demented. "I can play that event over and over to the empire, but until the air shimmers with blood, until they feel it still warm on their cheeks and smell it in their clothes, they'll never truly understand why we have our rules. Why we have to be ruthless."

There's a scuffle, and the doors burst open. Caspian fights his way to me, throwing a Gold Cloak to the ground, sidestepping another. They've dressed him in his military finery, and his medals jangle off the sword strapped to his shoulder belt. Another sword glints at his waist.

Finally, two manage to capture him. Dried blood smears his chin, his right eye swollen nearly shut. His eyes search me out. Then they rest on the Emperor in unspoken challenge.

"Release her, Father." His voice carries an arrogant, commanding tone that would make anyone else tremble in fear.

Ignoring him, the Emperor motions and the guards force Caspian to the Emperor's side. "My son wasn't alive for the bombings that killed his mother and baby sister," he says, talking to me. "He's weak, full of naïve ideas, like that the daughter of a Bronze traitor could be trusted."

"She was trying to help us," Caspian spits, straining against his captors. "To help our people!"

The Emperor laughs at his son. "This worm was manipulating you to find the weapon the Fienian Rebels would use to wipe us out. And she preyed on you because you are soft, a sympathizing fool who almost gave our enemy the means to wipe us out."

"That's a lie." But his voice isn't as sure as before.

"Wait and see for yourself then."

Heart racing, I scan the crowd, searching for one of the others. My eyes blur with desperation as I realize there's no way they can get to the Emperor now. He'll have Centurions waiting for them after the bomb goes off.

They will all be killed.

I fling myself forward, nearly toppling over the railing. "It's a trap!"

But the din of the crowd swallows my words. Sharp pain lances my side. Crying out, I grip the railing to keep from falling to my knees and clutch the deep ache just above my hip where the Archduchess stabbed me.

"That's for defiling the Emperor," she purrs, wiping my blood from her hatpin in the same reverent manner she wiped down the Emperor.

I look to Caspian, but by now he has realized I'm not what I seem, perhaps I tricked him, and his eyes have gone cold. The muscles in his neck cord as he slowly looks away.

Suddenly a giant rift screen appears over the fountain. An image of the Emperor solidifies, sitting on his throne, his hands clasped. He opens his mouth to deliver a message to the revelers, but then something changes. Black eats away at his body. From the darkness bursts a flaming scorpion, burning brightly as it wraps around a shriveling phoenix. People scream as its fiery stinger pierces the phoenix, over and over. Each thrust a warning, a reminder.

The Emperor and all his Golds bleed too.

The crowd mutters with shock as another image appears. A crooked, hunched man appears wearing a red cloak that hoods his crudely carved red mask, the mouth twisted into a leer that stirs something in me close to fear. Even without seeing his ruined face, I know it's Nicolai.

What have we done?

But as I glance at the Emperor and see that same uneasy dread creeping over him, I feel a purl of satisfaction too. He wasn't expecting this.

Nicolai's bizarre, frightening voice erupts over the land, echoing off the valleys and trees. It rattles my teeth, my skull. "Emperor Laevus, King of murders and swine, this is a message from the nameless, the afflicted, the persecuted, and orphaned. You are no longer safe within your palace of greed. There is no place our tentacles cannot reach. We are everywhere, we are everyone, and we do not forgive." A raspy, rattling pause as Nicolai inhales. "Let the reckoning begin."

I crumple to the ground, the deep red folds of my dress masking the blood pouring from my wound. My throat chokes down a bizarre, horrified laugh. *Soon it will be a dress of blood.* I rest my head against the rough slats of the railing in defeat. The bombs will go off any second. I want to close my eyes, but I force them open, peering through the opening between two slats.

Watch what you have done, Maia. All the people who will die because of you. All for nothing.

My gaze falls upon a hooded figure just below. From my angle, I can see only his head, but it's obvious he is kneeling. Warning bells alarm inside my head. He should be watching the fountain like the others, curious to see what happens next. I trail the figure with my eyes as he quickly lopes away, into the crowd. Something so familiar about his gait . . .

I turn my head as the doors grate open to the balcony. O enters, looking radiant in a pale pink gossamer gown. Miniature white roses adorn her hair. She is beaming. She obviously didn't see the message on the rift screen.

Something about the hooded man calls back my attention. He's flickering through the crowd like a shadow now, nearly invisible.

Only one person I know moves like that.

Almost as if he can feel my stare, Riser turns around. Grunting with pain, I force myself to a stand, arms held high so he can see my binds. I can only hope if he sees I'm a prisoner of the Emperor, he'll know it's a trap.

I meant for him to see me and go the other way, toward safety, but now he's running toward me instead. Toward the danger I was trying to save him from. Smashing through Golds, his hood fallen back, screaming. Screaming like I never imagined Riser could, desperation and fear twisting his face.

My hands clench the railing.

And then I know what he was doing below and why he's screaming and why he's coming back.

I turn, to run, escape, but O stands in front of me. "Lady March, you're bleeding."

Oh God no. "You have to leave!" I beg her.

O's big, sweet eyes brim with concern. "You're hurt. Please, let me help you—"

"There's another bomb!" My voice cracks. "This entire balcony is going to—"

But the roar cuts me off.

CHAPTER FORTY-ONE

Time congeals into a silent, underwater scene of chaos. Stars churn above me; I am on my back. Sliding. My binds have been blown apart. Half of the balcony is now a gaping hole. O's face comes into view, haloed by black smoke. Her mouth splits in a silent scream. Somehow our hands lock together, and then the hole swallows us.

It seems like an eternity waiting to hit the ground. O's hand slips from mine. The miniature roses in her hair become floating stars . . .

I awaken to a sideways hell. Black fingers of smoke and debris and nanos reach up and tear off pieces of the sky. A staccato of bombs rattle the heap of rubble under my cheek. Stones as large as carriages become comets in the heavens. I watch in surreal fascination as a pale marble hand from the fountain bounces off the ground near my head.

A small moan escapes me. I feel strange, hollow, as if part of me has been spilled from my body. Screams haunt the air. The tang of smoke and blood and charred flesh floods my nose and conjures bile.

Riser. I search my sideways world for him, but all I see is death.

Mangled bodies.

Screaming bodies.

Dying bodies.

Get up, Maia. Pushing off my elbows, I use fragmented chunks of stone to leverage to my knees, but when I try to put weight on my right leg, I scream out. *Broken.* A few of my ribs ache when I try to breathe, so they're probably broken too. Others are getting up, the ones who can anyway. The shredders were more than efficient.

I catch sight of a mob of people running. Are they trying to get away from the bombs? But then I see they are dressed poorly, many emaciated and stumbling. They hold Royalist weapons. Swords. Sabers. Crossbows and pistols. A few shoot wildly into the crowd.

Nicolai and the Fienian Rebels have armed the people at the gate. This realization leads to another. This wasn't an assassination attempt.

This was a coup.

More yells, more screams, as the makeshift army swarms the injured, but they amble aimlessly, seemingly confused, their weapons awkward in their untrained hands. Who are they supposed to be fighting? Where are the Centurions? The Royal Guard?

A horn shreds the chaos, and I have my answer. Moonlight glances off the Centurions' golden shields. They are on horseback, spread out in two formations, each formation in neat rows of ten, thirty rows deep. General Bloodwood sits atop a horse at the front.

The Emperor was expecting this as well.

The people from the gate don't stand a chance. They try to run, but the two Centurion formations swoop down on them, the horses' hooves pounding the earth. I look away.

Find Riser. If I can find him and escape . . .

We see each other at the same time. A mountain of rubble separates us; shreds of my dress get caught on the jagged slabs as I claw and scrape my way toward him. My broken leg drags behind me, throbbing with pain.

Just a little more to Riser. To safety.

I notice the flowers first. Three perfect miniature roses, tinted red from the fiery sky. They sprout from strands of hair like roses on a pale vine. I follow the silky, silvery-blond tresses to the girl crumpled in the stone, her body contorted oddly. Like a doll, a beautiful, broken doll. "No," I whisper. "Please, no."

Ribbons of blood trickle from O's nose and mouth. Her eyes are half-slits gazing upon the sky.

We did this.

Riser tops the rubble. He does nothing for a moment. Just stares down at her, the innocent girl we murdered. The hell around us recedes as I focus on his face. *Tell me she's alive, Pit Boy. Make it all okay.*

He falls to his knees, cradling my chin with his palm. "We need to go," he murmurs, scooping the other hand beneath my knees as he works to lift me.

A chasm of anger splits open inside me. "Why?" Fighting from his arms, I slip a few feet down the rubble, screaming as something tears at my shattered shinbone. "Why did they do this?"

He holds out his hand. Behind him, the sound of fighting intensifies, and I recognize some of the others. Flame, a crossbow in each hand, five nano-shredders hooked to her shoulder belt. Rhydian and Blaise are fighting off Centurions with long swords. Farther off, Delphine discharges her pistol, grey smoke trickling from the muzzle as one of the fighters from the gate drops. The hulking form of Roman fights beside her.

I know Riser is right. We need to leave, but I can't move.

"Please, Everly," he breathes.

"We killed her. Don't you care?"

Part of his face is in shadow, but the visible part stiffens. "You think I don't?" His boots grate across the rubble as he closes the distance between us, his hand still out, still pleading with me. "I will never, never forgive myself for O's death. But if I let something happen to you too . . . Well, I'd rather die than feel that pain."

Tears blur my vision as I accept his hand, ignoring what has to be blood crusting his fingers. "Okay," I say, grinding my teeth against the pain, "let's go. I think I can walk but—"

The sound of a sword unsheathing draws our attention to O's body—and the shadow above it. Caspian. Except I hardly recognize this Caspian. With the blood darkening one side of his light hair, his cloak swirling behind him, he looks like one of the gods from my book—and not the benevolent kind. His eyes lock onto Riser, *murderous* eyes, brimming with silent, blistering fury.

Before I can scream, Caspian leaps to meet Riser, his cloak winging behind him, sword carving the air. Riser jumps back, somehow pushing me out of the way, and Caspian's sword clangs against the stone at our feet, shooting white sparks.

"Watch out!" I yell as Caspian's sword swings up and toward Riser's head.

Somehow Riser ducks, rolls sideways, and pops up, his sword glinting. His eyes promise retribution.

Caspian retrieves the second sword from his shoulder belt, twirling it in his left hand. Now he has two.

Two blades with which to kill Riser.

Two blades to exact revenge.

Something deep inside me knows this will end only when blood soaks the ground. But whose? The golden heir to the throne who genetics said was my perfect match, or the dark bastard prince who fed me and protected me in my darkest hour? Breathless with agony, my eyes follow every blade as it fights to pierce the other's flesh, my heart jumping with every near miss.

Which prince do I cheer for?

Which prince will I mourn?

Their swords clang together, over and over as they bite into each other, rattling my teeth, my heart. They thrust and counter and parry, grunting, each blow meant to take off the other's head.

"Murderer!" Caspian screams at Riser as his swords take turns slashing at Riser's head, his shoulders.

Even with his stealthy quickness, Riser barely manages to deflect the blows.

"Bastard!" Caspian roars, his swords unrelenting as they cut and stab and cleave in perfect tandem.

Riser scrabbles onto a higher slab right before Caspian's swords would have taken off his head. Caspian stalks Riser, unrelenting, tireless, merciless, a god awakened from his slumber. Riser's swordsmanship is exceptional, thanks to his lightning-quick reflexes and reconstruction, but Caspian is *better*.

I know what it is to hate someone, to wish them dead. To imagine killing them in a thousand ways. But this hatred, this blinding, murderous rage, is something I have never experienced before, and it fills me with terror.

As if a cold shadow passes over me, my body suddenly becomes weighted with suffocating dread.

"Worm." Caspian's sword just misses. "Killer." His second blade finds Riser's shoulder and Riser grunts, blood spurting from his arm. "Murderer!"

Caspian's sword comes down on Riser so hard I think it will cut right through him. There's a horrible clang as part of Riser's blade breaks away, leaving a short useless stub. Riser's foot trips over a small rock. And then he's falling. Grunting. Scrambling. Until a long stretch of railing traps him.

Screaming through the pain, I somehow make it closer, shards of debris scraping and cutting through my flesh. But I'm too late. Caspian's sword seems to cleave the moon from the sky as he hikes it above his head.

Then it comes down . . .

Riser's hand reaches out, plucks an apple-sized piece of stone from the rubble, and hurls it at Caspian's face.

The rock makes a sickly *thunk* over Caspian's left eye. Gasping, his sword slips from his hand, he drops to his knees, eyes glazed, and falls like a sack face first down the mangled rock.

"Riser!" I scream, pulling myself to the edge as Riser leaps after him, his boots crunching softly in the grass below. I say his name again, but he doesn't seem to hear me. His movements are smooth and predatory. This is the boy from the pit. The one who scares me.

Caspian rolls to his side, groaning, his arm outstretched toward his sword, but Riser pins Caspian's arm with his boot. Caspian's free arm delivers a volley of blows to Riser's leg, but Riser hardly seems to notice. His two hands grip his sword straight above him, shoulders trembling, sweat dripping down his temples.

Caspian pants beneath Riser, glaring up at the blade aimed for his heart, blood carving a path over his swollen eye. "Murderer." Caspian spits blood onto Riser's boot. "Filth. Worm."

Somehow I've made it down the rubble. "Don't do it, Riser," I plead. "Let him live."

Riser blinks at my voice; the sword lowers an inch. "Why? Because you were matched?" His voice catches on the last word, but he refuses to look at me. "Nicolai told me."

"We need to go. There's still time—but if you kill him, they will hunt you down. Us down."

"Do you still love him?" The pain in his voice cuts me.

"No." I try to swallow, but my mouth is full of cotton. "Maybe—I don't know. But I know how I feel about you. So, please, Riser, *please*, put the sword down."

"You know what he's done, what his father has done." The muscles in his jaw grind, his hands tightening on the sword grip. "Tell me one reason I should let him live."

My voice cracks with emotion and nerves and pain. "Because you told me I made you better. So prove it to me, Pit Boy."

Riser's shoulders soften as the rage leaves him. Slowly, so very, very slowly, his sword lowers. He exhales, turning to flash me a rare and glorious grin. "For you, Digger Girl—"

The bloodied tip of Caspian's sword sprouts from Riser's chest. Riser's eyes go wide with shock, and he staggers forward. Wobbling, Caspian props one boot on Riser's shoulder and yanks, the blade making a sick sound as it exits his body.

Riser crumples.

The scream lodged in my throat finally escapes. My eyes cling to Riser's body, searching for movement, willing him to rise. A black spot of blood rapidly spreads across the back of his leather doublet. *Is he breathing?*

"Protect the Prince!" I ignore the Gold Cloaks as they close ranks to form a wall around us.

The earth comes away beneath my fingers as I try to claw my way to Riser. "Riser! Hold on, I'm coming."

The soft ticking sound of thirty crossbows being cocked grabs my attention. I look up just in time to see Flame charging on horseback, two riders shadowing her. In the split second it would take the Gold Cloaks to release their arrows, the nano-shredder arcs through the air toward them.

I don't hear the explosion. I *feel* it. Like a million enraged hornets let loose their cage, thrumming the air, the vibrations wriggling through my marrow. Each shredder is about the size of a fly. They converge, a monstrous wave that blacks out the stars—lifting, lifting, lifting—and crash down onto the wall of Gold Cloaks.

Just like that, over half the Royal Guard is gone, a puddle of blood where they stood mirroring the sky.

"Grab Riser," I scream.

"Do it!" Flame commands her companion, red arrows whistling from the crossbow at her wrist. Two more guards succumb to her expert marksmanship. The horseman behind her goads his gray horse over the blood. Gripping the saddle's pommel, he leans down low, one long arm hooking Riser's belt, and slings Riser's limp body onto his lap, his horse wheeling and kicking as arrows whiz by.

An arrow sinks into the beast's exposed haunch, and the animal rears, knocking the horseman's hood back.

Horsewoman.

"Get some, you rotten Dandies!" Teagan's short sword carves the air, long legs kicking wildly at the circling guard, before spurring her horse into a furious gallop.

I sigh with relief as the melee swallows them. Now there's only Flame. Our eyes meet. *Please, Fienian,* I beg with my face, my whole being. *Don't leave me here to die.*

Impossibly long seconds tick by. *Will she save me? The girl she despises? I have the key. Will it be enough?*

The guards turn their weapons on Flame, but their actions seem to take forever. In slow motion she cracks her neck, dons a wicked smile, and comes for me. Tears of gratitude sting my eyes. Biting my lip, I fight through the pain to my knees. We have only one shot at this. Should I try to jump on the saddle behind her? Or will she stop long enough to help me?

I never find out.

The sharp cold metal that bites the back of my neck comes exactly as Flame jerks hard on her horse's reins, her face flashing with anger and surprise. In disbelief, I watch her flee. Some wild, desperate part of me thinks that as long as I can see her, she'll come back for me. My gaze trails her shrinking form. I watch her trample a cluster of guards, shadowed by a hail of arrows.

Then she is gone.

They are all gone.

And I am alone.

"Wipe that hope from your sniveling face."

Well, not quite.

The Archduchess's sword pushes deeper into the back of my skull, forcing me to my feet. There's a sick bone on bone feeling in my shin, the broken ends of my shinbone grinding together.

Overwhelmed with pain, I fall in a helpless heap. I try to curl in a fetal position to protect myself, but the Archduchess digs the point of her sword into my belly. A rancid smile cracks her face. "No one can help you now, maggot."

CHAPTER FORTY-TWO

Fight. Fight until your dying breath.

The whisper yanks me into lucidity. Cold darkness greets me. Pain nibbles my side and settles deep in my mangled leg. My fingers scrabble across the ground, searching for the familiar scrape of dirt. But there's only stone. Hard, wet, filthy stone. And the air, heavy, coated with the pungent aroma of old excrement and piss. My eyes pick out iron bars, a rusted lock. A slanted rectangle of bluish light spills over my torn dress and broken leg and onto the irregular stones of my cell. At least there is a window above me. At least there's that.

The Tower. My brain works to determine how long I've been here. Hours? Days? But my thoughts are slippery, impossible to grasp. I try to shift my hips to ease the ache in my side, and lighting roars up my leg. My dry throat cracks open, but all I can manage is a raspy groan.

"I don't advise moving too much," says a man in the corner. I look up to see the Emperor. He sits proudly on the end of the metal chair, the scabbard of his ceremonial long sword scraping the ground, his erect posture from someone used to uncomfortable, high-backed thrones.

Using my swollen tongue, I part my lips from my teeth, working to deposit moisture enough to talk. "My mother?"

The Emperor's smug chuckle echoes through the empty room. "Thinks you died years ago. Probably for the best, considering what you are now."

Terrorist. Murderer. Shame wells up in me. My body aches, my mind aches, but nothing hurts as bad as knowing what we did. What I did. "I'm sorry . . . They weren't supposed to die."

The ghost of a smile twitches his lips. He likes to see me like this. Broken, suffering, afraid. I hate that my fear and self-loathing give him pleasure. I hate the way he flushes with my every grimace, every groan. "I would have been disappointed if they didn't."

"They were your people," I snap, suddenly finding the strength to hate him too. "Your *daughter*."

His body stills so perfectly I think for a heartbeat time really has frozen, that he feels *something*, but then he blinks, as if he can blink Ophelia out of existence, and his eyes focus on me. "I had planned for Ophelia to die at the fountain, but no matter now."

Sure I have misheard him, I press further. "Why would you want your daughter to die?"

"She wasn't my daughter!" he seethes. "Not anymore. Not after she pledged her allegiance to the Fienians."

The mentor Nicolai said was working with him. It was Ophelia. My mind races to put it together. "But she was so . . . so innocent."

"We all have our weapons, Maia. Ophelia tried to use that innocence on me when I found her in the rubble. Begging, calling me daddy like she was a little girl again—"

"She was still alive?" And then realization hits me. "You . . . You killed her."

"No, Maia. You did. At least that's what the populace will think, and more importantly what Caspian will think."

He was two steps ahead of us the entire time. "You knew about me all along, didn't you?"

His eyes sparkle. "From the very moment you stepped onto the Island."

"Then why let it happen?" My voice breaks as I remember the explosions, the shredders. "Why not stop it?"

"Don't you question me, worm!" he spits, his chair scraping stone as he rises to pace between the cells. "The gods were afraid of their sons, did you know that?" One hand absentmindedly massages the flesh above his left eye. "The Titan Cronus ate his children, one by one, because he knew eventually one would betray him. But his last-born son, Zeus, survived to do exactly what his father feared. As soon as Zeus had a son, he suffered the same fears, so he swallowed his own firstborn just like the father he despised."

I blink, fighting the dizziness in my head. "I don't understand."

"My father poisoned my grandfather to ascend the throne. When my father fell ill, I forced him to name me Emperor in his stead and banished him to the very cell you sit in." He smiles, the shadows making his teeth look sharp and menacing. "It's a curse and blessing, to have a son. I thought my own son would be different, but he couldn't stomach my harsh policies and eventually he was going to split the court, perhaps even challenge me someday."

"You let all those people die . . . because you're paranoid?"

When he turns, his eyes shine brightly. "Fear, Maia, it's a powerful, tricky thing, and with every bomb you discharged, you reminded them there are things in this world I need to protect them from. Every single Sleeper felt it, every Silver and Gold and Bronze, the doubters and Fienian Sympathizers." His gloved fingers wrap around the bars to my cell. "But when Ophelia died, you gave my son something even stronger than fear. You gave him hatred, the same hatred Ezra gave to me when he murdered my wife and child. That rage will bind Caspian to my side, erasing our differences and any sympathies he might have held for your kind, forging my son into the Emperor who will continue my legacy long after I am gone and Hyperion is just a memory."

Angry thoughts cram my head. He used us. Allowed hundreds to suffer and die. Killed his daughter. All to secure his court and ensure his deranged ideology was embraced by his son. And I tumbled right into his trap. Just like Ezra, I betrayed the one person who could have helped me.

The one person I was meant to love.

The Fienians and the Royalists both used me for their own bloody ends, and I fell for it. Now Max will die, and the world will burn, and there's nothing I can do.

I rest my head against the wall, too tired to continue fighting the dizziness and pain, too sad to argue, too broken to move.

"What happened to my friends?" I whisper, wanting more than anything to know if Riser is alive. *Is he in pain? Worrying about me?*

"Most are dead," he says pleasantly. "A few are holed up fighting, but don't fret, they'll join you shortly." As if on cue, my ears pick up the sounds of gunshots and yelling far below. "As soon as Victoria finishes rounding them up, she will begin her work on you." A hollow pit forms in my belly as I realize he means the Archduchess. "After witnessing just how creative Victoria can be with your flesh, they will give up Max, we will find and destroy the Mercurian, and this whole mess will be over."

"No!" My fists pummel the floor until they are slippery with blood. "No! Please!" My words fall over and over like my fists, pounding the air until my voice frays. The voice in my head taunts me. *Stupid, Digger Girl. Stupid, cowardly Maia. You chose wrong. You should have chosen me.*

Sobs wrack my body. I hardly notice the Emperor leave. My father died trying to save me. Merida sacrificed herself to keep me alive. Riser saved me over and over and probably died because of me.

For what?

"Why?" I scream at the shadows. Bits of the slick, dank stone come away beneath my fingernails as I claw to the window, groaning with agony, ground shifting wildly beneath my feet.

Three-inch-thick bars stripe my rectangle of sky. Stars wink from their tapestry. *She* is up there somewhere with the gods, surveying Her kingdom, testing who is worthy and who should die, ready to cast Her shadow and watch us scramble for Her favor, killing each other like the beasts Orion promised to slay.

Voices ring out from below, and a strange warmth falls over me, despite the cool air. Muffled explosions vibrate my cell. My soul. They're fighting. Still fighting.

Fight.

Fight until your last breath, Digger Girl.

Maia of the stars.

Dead fallen Gold Girl.

Creature from the pit.

Whoever you are, fight until the very last breath trails from your lips and your flesh goes cold.

"I am going to get out of here," I whisper to Her, as if She is one of the goddesses from my book. Maybe She is. Maybe the gods of our past are only tales of men and things beyond our understanding. Maybe someday, after the dust has settled, someone will tell stories about Pandora, the angry goddess who tore the world apart, and the mortals who fought to save it.

"Somehow I'm going to escape and do what I should have done from the start," I promise Her, my heart thrumming to the sound of pistols and swords and the whisper of invisible gods. "I'm going to destroy you."

As if in answer to my challenge, a star streaks the sky and slowly, slowly flames out.

The End

She was carved from the rubble and forged with fire, the girl who clawed from the funeral pyre. Her eyes were diamonds and her hair was Gold, her lips sharp and lovely and bold. But a monster grew where her heart should be—
waiting for the day she would set it free.

Acknowledgements

This section was by far the hardest part for me to write. There are so many people who have helped me along the way and deserve thanks, and my words seem inadequate. However, I'm going to try.

First and foremost, my husband, Christopher, who taught me that life can be so much more. Not only did he give me two beautiful children and allow me to rescue four naughty dogs, he gives me unconditional love and a kick in the butt daily. To my children, Jack and Savannah, for enriching my life with love and laughter, and thinking I hung the moon. To my parents, Don and Kristin, for teaching me the importance of hard work and encouraging my persistence, or what some might call obstinacy, even when it made their life harder. Writing isn't always easy for me, and if not for their lessons, most of my stories would have gone unwritten. To my mother-in-law, Maxine, for watching my children as if they are her own, and being a wonderful traveling companion. Her unfailing support and advice is invaluable. To the Brown Girls, Debbie and Katy, for taking an interest in my writing and encouraging me. And to my brother, Wesley, for always being there for me.

There are two special people who were my first readers. Jill Tovar, my best friend, bonus sister, and cheerleader, who has accompanied me on this journey and always keeps my spirits up. And Angela Marlow, my twin sister and better half, who's read every book I've ever written and who fell in love with Maia and Riser immediately. She understood the importance of the pit to their history, and without her insistence that I finish their story, Shadow Fall wouldn't be here today.

A heartfelt thanks to the awesome team at Blaze Publishing, whose talents and hard work turned my manuscript into a novel: Mara Valderran, who guides me through the tricky waters of marketing and thinks my questions aren't dumb; Eliza Tilton, for rocking out SF's formatting and giving me her Pringles one night (because she's just that amazing); Kristen Troiani, who insisted the villains in SF need more page time (she was right), and whose snark and wit match the size of her big heart; Layla Cox, for keeping Mara sane, and cooking actual wild boar so she could write a foodie post using a dish from SF; honorary Blazer, Janelle Leonard Howard, my friend, fellow coffee addict, and sounding board for all things writerly; and, of course, our fearless leader, adverb slayer, editor-in-chief, and the reason Shadow Fall exists, Krystal Dehaba. She understood my voice and characters right away, and took a very complex world and made it accessible to the reader—all without making my cry. Somewhere in that process, we became friends, for which I'll always be grateful.

There are others to whom I'm appreciative. Jennifer Malone Wright for helping plan my online parties and grow my audience. Chelsea Starling, a beautiful soul who designed my author website and makes the world brighter. Kimberly Marsot, cover artist extraordinaire, who not only gave me an amazing cover for SF, but who patiently worked with me through horrible sketches and ideas to produce lovely character art. My fellow Blazers—authors Jacob Devlin, Tori Rigby, and Case Maynard. And to all the Utopians who became social media cheerleaders and continue to inspire me.

To those few friends who tolerate my expensive kombucha habit, daily uniform of yoga pants covered in dog hair, and inability to be normal—Lauren Guhl and Audrey Delay—your friendship and support mean the world to me, even if I never tell you that.

Lastly, thank you from the bottom of my heart to the bookworms, writers, and nerds that I interact with daily on social media. Feeling a sense of belonging is a rare thing indeed, and I've found that with you.

ABOUT THE AUTHOR

Audrey Grey lives in the charming state of Oklahoma, with her husband, two little people, and four mischievous dogs. You can usually find her hiding out in her office from said little people and dogs, surrounded by books and sipping kombucha while dreaming up wondrous worlds for her characters to live in.

You can find out more about Audrey on her website.
http://audreygrey.com/

THANK YOU FOR READING

Now that you've finished reading this book, we'd like to ask you to take a moment to leave a review. You never know how a few sentences might help other readers—and the author! And, as always, Blaze Publishing appreciates your time and support.

www.Blazepub.com

blaze
PUBLISHING

CHECK OUT OTHER BOOKS FROM BLAZE

"To cure fear, you must use fear."

Rose Briar claims no responsibility for the act that led to her imprisonment in an asylum. She wants to escape, until terrifying nightmares make her question her sanity and reach out to her doctor. He's understanding and caring in ways her parents never have been, but as her walls tumble down and Rose admits fault, a fellow patient warns her to stop the medications. Phillip believes the doctor is evil and they'll never make it out of the facility alive. Trusting him might be just the thing to save her. Or it might prove the asylum is exactly where she needs to be.

THE GIRL IN THE RED HOOD has been looking for her mother for six months, searching from the depths of New York's subways to the heights of its skyscrapers . . .

THE PRINCE looks like he's from another time entirely, or maybe he's just too good at his job at Ye Old Renaissance Faire . . .

THE ACTRESS is lighting up Hollywood Boulevard with her spellbinding and strikingly convincing portrayal of a famous fairy. Her name may be big, but her secrets barely fit in one world . . .

Fifteen-year-old Crescenzo never would have believed his father's carvings were anything more than "stupid toys." All he knows is a boring life in an ordinary Virginia suburb, from which his mother and his best friend have been missing for years. When his father disappears next, all Crescenzo has left is his goofy neighbor, Pietro, who believes he's really Peter Pan and that Crescenzo is the son of Pinocchio. What's more: Pietro insists that they can find their loved ones by looking to the strange collection of wooden figurines Crescenzo's father left behind.

With Pietro's help, Crescenzo sets off on an adventure to unite the real life counterparts to his figurines. It's enough of a shock that they're actually real, but the night he meets the Girl in the Red Hood, dark truths burst from the past. Suddenly, Crescenzo is tangled in a nightmare where magic mirrors and evil queens rule, and where everyone he loves is running out of time.

THE
SURRENDERED
CASE MAYNARD

After a financial collapse devastates the United States, the new government imposes a tax on the nation's most valuable resource—the children.

Surrendered at age ten—after her parents could no longer afford her exorbitant fees—Vee Delancourt has spent six hard years at the Mills, alongside her twin, Oliver. With just a year to freedom, they do what they can to stay off the Master's radar. But when Vee discovers unspeakable things happening to the younger girls in service, she has no choice but to take a stand—a decision that lands her on the run and outside the fence for the first time since the System robbed her of her liberty.

Vee knows the Master will stop at nothing to prove he holds ultimate authority over the Surrendered. But when he makes a threat that goes beyond what even she considers possible, she accepts the aid of an unlikely group of allies. Problem is, with opposing factions gunning for the one thing that might save them all, Vee must find a way to turn oppression and desperation into hope and determination—or risk failing all the children and the brother she left behind.

11-16

CPSIA information can be obtained
at www.ICGtesting.com
Printed in the USA
LVOW11s0332091116
512204LV00002B/2/P